THE INVISIBLE MAN
THE SECRET PLACES OF THE HEART

and

GOD THE INVISIBLE KING

by

H. G. WELLS

ODHAMS PRESS LIMITED
LONDON, W.C.2

Printed in Great Britain

THE INVISIBLE MAN

CONTENTS

CONTENTS

CHAPTER ONE

THE STRANGE MAN'S ARRIVAL

THE stranger came early in February one wintry day, through a biting wind and a driving snow, the last snowfall of the year, over the down, walking as it seemed from Bramblehurst railway station and carrying a little black portmanteau in his thickly gloved hand. He was wrapped up from head to foot, and the brim of his soft felt hat hid every inch of his face but the shiny tip of his nose ; the snow had piled itself against his shoulders and chest, and added a white crest to the burden he carried. He staggered into the Coach and Horses, more dead then alive as it seemed, and flung his portmanteau down. " A fire," he cried, " in the name of human charity ! A room and a fire ! " He stamped and shook the snow from off himself in the bar, and followed Mrs. Hall into her guest parlour to strike his bargain. And with that much introduction, that and a ready acquiescence to terms and a couple of sovereigns flung upon the table, he took up his quarters in the inn.

Mrs. Hall lit the fire and left him there while she went to prepare him a meal with her own hands. A guest to stop at Iping in the winter-time was an unheard-of piece of luck, let alone a guest who was no " haggler," and she was resolved to show herself worthy of her good fortune. As soon as the bacon was well under way, and Millie, her lymphatic aid, had been brisked up a bit by a few deftly chosen expressions of contempt, she carried the cloth, plates, and glasses into the parlour and began to lay them with the utmost *éclat.* Although the fire was burning up briskly, she was surprised to see that her visitor still wore his hat and coat, standing with his back to her and staring out of the window at the falling snow in the yard. His gloved hands were clasped behind him, and he seemed to be lost in thought. She noticed that the melted snow that still sprinkled his shoulders dripped upon her carpet. " Can I take your hat and coat, sir," she said, " and give them a good dry in the kitchen ? "

" No," he said without turning.

She was not sure she had heard him, and was about to repeat her question.

He turned his head and looked at her over his shoulder. " I prefer to keep them on," he said with emphasis, and she noticed that he wore big blue spectacles with side-lights and had a bushy side-whisker over his coat-collar that completely hid his face.

" Very well, sir," she said. " *As* you like. In a bit the room will be warmer."

He made no answer and had turned his face away from her

again ; and Mrs. Hall, feeling that her conversational advances
were ill-timed, laid the rest of the table things in a quick
staccato and whisked out of the room.   When she returned
he was still standing there like a man of stone, his back hunched,
his collar turned up, his dripping hat-brim turned down,
hiding his face and ears completely.   She put down the eggs
and bacon with considerable emphasis, and called rather than
said to him, " Your lunch is served, sir."

" Thank you," he said at the same time, and did not stir
until she was closing the door.   Then he swung round and
approached the table.

As she went behind the bar to the kitchen she heard a sound
repeated at regular intervals.   Chirk, chirk, chirk, it went, the
sound of a spoon being rapidly whisked round a basin.   " That
girl ! " she said.   " There !   I clean forgot it.   It's her being
so long ! "   And while she herself finished mixing the mustard,
she gave Millie a few verbal stabs for her excessive slowness.
She had cooked the ham and eggs, laid the table, and done
everything, while Millie (help indeed !) had only succeeded in
delaying the mustard.   And him a new guest and wanting to
stay !   Then she filled the mustard pot, and, putting it with
a certain stateliness upon a gold and black tea-tray, carried
it into the parlour.

She rapped and entered promptly.   As she did so her
visitor moved quickly, so that she got but a glimpse of a white
object disappearing behind the table.   It would seem he was
picking something from the floor.   She rapped down the
mustard pot on the table, and then she noticed the overcoat
and hat had been taken off and put over a chair in front of the
fire.   A pair of wet boots threatened rust to her steel fender.
She went to these things resolutely.   " I suppose I may have
them to dry now," she said in a voice that brooked no denial.

" Leave the hat," said her visitor in a muffled voice, and
turning she saw he had raised his head and was sitting looking
at her.

For a moment she stood gaping at him, too surprised to
speak.

He held a white cloth—it was a serviette he had brought
with him—over the lower part of his face, so that his mouth
and jaws were completely hidden, and that was the reason
of his muffled voice.   But it was not that which startled Mrs.
Hall.   It was the fact that all his forehead above his blue
glasses was covered by a white bandage, and that another
covered his ears, leaving not a scrap of his face exposed excepting only his pink, peaked nose.   It was bright pink, and shiny
just as it had been at first.   He wore a dark-brown velvet
jacket with a high black linen-lined collar turned up about his
neck.   The thick black hair, escaping as it could below and
between the cross bandages, projected in curious tails and
horns, giving him the strangest appearance conceivable.   This

muffled and bandaged head was so unlike what she had anticipated, that for a moment she was rigid.

He did not remove the serviette, but remained holding it, as she saw now, with a brown gloved hand, and regarding her with his inscrutable blue glasses. "Leave the hat," he said, speaking very distinctly through the white cloth.

Her nerves began to recover from the shock they had received. She placed the hat on the chair again by the fire. " I didn't know, sir," she began, " that——" and she stopped, embarrassed.

" Thank you," he said dryly, glancing from her to the door and then at her again.

" I'll have them nicely dried, sir, at once," she said, and carried his clothes out of the room. She glanced at his white-swathed head and blue goggles again as she was going out of the door ; but his napkin was still in front of his face. She shivered a little as she closed the door behind her, and her face was eloquent of her surprise and perplexity. "I *never*," she whispered. "There ! " She went quite softly to the kitchen, and was too preoccupied to ask Millie what she was messing about with *now*, when she got there.

The visitor sat and listened to her retreating feet. He glanced inquiringly at the window before he removed his serviette and resumed his meal. He took a mouthful, glanced suspiciously at the window, took another mouthful, then rose and, taking the serviette in his hand, walked across the room and pulled the blind down to the top of the white muslin that obscured the lower panes. This left the room in twilight. This done, he returned with an easier air to the table and his meal.

" The poor soul's had an accident or an opration or something," said Mrs. Hall. " What a turn them bandages did give me, to be sure ! "

She put on some more coal, unfolded the clothes-horse, and extended the traveller's coat upon this. " And they goggles ! Why, he looked more like a divin' helmet than a human man ! " She hung his muffler on a corner of the horse. " And holding that handkercher over his mouth all the time. Talkin' through it ! . . . Perhaps his mouth was hurt too—maybe."

She turned round, as one who suddenly remembers. " Bless my soul alive ! " she said, going off at a tangent ; "ain't you done them taters *yet*, Millie ? "

When Mrs. Hall went to clear away the stranger's lunch, her idea that his mouth must also have been cut or disfigured in the accident she supposed him to have suffered, was confirmed, for he was smoking a pipe, and all the time that she was in the room he never loosened the silk muffler he had wrapped round the lower part of his face to put the mouth-piece to his lips. Yet it was not forgetfulness, for she saw he glanced at it as it smouldered out. He sat in the corner with his back to the window-blind and spoke now, having eaten and drunk and being comfortably warmed through, with less aggressive brevity than before. The reflection of the fire lent a kind of red animation to his big spectacles they had lacked hitherto.

" I have some luggage," he said, " at Bramblehurst station," and he asked her how he could have it sent. He bowed his bandaged head quite politely in acknowledgment of her explanation. " To-morrow ! " he said. " There is no speedier delivery ? " and seemed quite disappointed when she answered, " No." Was she quite sure ? No man with a trap who would go over ?

Mrs. Hall, nothing loath, answered his questions and developed a conversation. " It's a steep road by the down, sir," she said in answer to the question about a trap ; and then, snatching at an opening, said, " It was there a carriage was upsettled, a year ago and more. A gentleman killed, besides his coachman. Accidents, sir, happen in a moment, don't they ? "

But the visitor was not to be drawn so easily. " They do," he said through his muffler, eyeing her quietly through his impenetrable glasses.

" But they take long enough to get well, sir, don't they ? . . . There was my sister's son, Tom, jest cut his arm with a scythe, tumbled on it in the 'ayfield, and, bless me ! he was three months tied up, sir. You'd hardly believe it. It's regular given me a dread of a scythe, sir."

" I can quite understand that," said the visitor.

" He was afraid, one time, that he'd have to have an opration—he was that bad, sir."

The visitor laughed abruptly, a bark of a laugh that he seemed to bite and kill in his mouth. " *Was* he ? " he said.

" He was, sir. And no laughing matter to them as had the doing for him, as I had—my sister being took up with her little ones so much. There was bandages to do, sir, and bandages to undo. So that if I may make so bold as to say it, sir——"

" Will you get me some matches ? " said the visitor, quite abruptly. " My pipe is out."

Mrs. Hall was pulled up suddenly. It was certainly rude of him, after telling him all she had done. She gasped at him for a moment, and remembered the two sovereigns. She went for the matches.

" Thanks," he said concisely, as she put them down, and turned his shoulder upon her and stared out of the window again. It was altogether too discouraging. Evidently he was sensitive on the topic of operations and bandages. She did not " make so bold as to say," however, after all. But his snubbing way had irritated her, and Millie had a hot time of it that afternoon.

The visitor remained in the parlour until four o'clock, without giving the ghost of an excuse for an intrusion. For the most part he was quite still during that time ; it would seem he sat in the growing darkness smoking in the firelight, perhaps dozing.

Once or twice a curious listener might have heard him at the coals, and for the space of five minutes he was audible pacing the room. He seemed to be talking to himself. Then the armchair creaked as he sat down again.

CHAPTER TWO

MR. TEDDY HENFREY'S FIRST IMPRESSIONS

At four o'clock, when it was fairly dark and Mrs. Hall was screwing up her courage to go in and ask her visitor if he would take some tea, Teddy Henfrey, the clock-jobber, came into the bar. "My sakes! Mrs. Hall," said he, "but this is terrible weather for thin boots!" The snow outside was falling faster.

Mrs. Hall agreed with him, and then noticed he had his bag and hit upon a brilliant idea. "Now you're here, Mr. Teddy," said she, "I'd be glad if you'd give th' old clock in the parlour a bit of a look. 'Tis going, and it strikes well and hearty; but the hour-hand won't do nuthin' but point at six."

And leading the way, she went across to the parlour door and rapped and entered.

Her visitor, she saw as she opened the door, was seated in the armchair before the fire, dozing it would seem, with his bandaged head drooping on one side. The only light in the room was the red glow from the fire—which lit his eyes like adverse railway signals, but left his downcast face in darkness—and the scanty vestiges of the day that came in through the open door. Everything was ruddy, shadowy, and indistinct to her, the more so since she had just been lighting the bar lamp, and her eyes were dazzled. But for a second it seemed to her that the man she looked at had an enormous mouth wide open—a vast and incredible mouth that swallowed the whole of the lower portion of his face. It was the sensation of a moment: the white-bound head, the monstrous goggle eyes, and this huge yawn below it. Then he stirred, started up in his chair, put up his hand. She opened the door wide, so that the room was lighter, and she saw him more clearly, with the muffler held to his face just as she had seen him hold the serviette before. The shadows, she fancied, had tricked her.

"Would you mind, sir, this man a-coming to look at the clock, sir?" she said, recovering from her momentary shock.

"Look at the clock?" he said, staring round in a drowsy manner and speaking over his hand, and then getting more fully awake, "certainly."

Mrs. Hall went away to get a lamp, and he rose and stretched himself. Then came the light, and Mr. Teddy Henfrey, entering, was confronted by this bandaged person. He was, he says, "taken aback."

"Good-afternoon," said the stranger, regarding him, as Mr. Henfrey says with a vivid sense of the dark spectacles, "like a lobster."

" I hope," said Mr. Henfrey, " that it's no intrusion."

" None whatever," said the stranger. " Though I under-stand," he said, turning to Mrs. Hall, " that this room is really to be mine for my own private use."

" I thought, sir," said Mrs. Hall, " you'd prefer the clock——" She was going to say " mended."

" Certainly," said the stranger, " certainly—but, as a rule, I like to be alone and undisturbed.

" But I'm really glad to have the clock seen to," he said, seeing a certain hesitation in Mr. Henfrey's manner. " Very glad." Mr. Henfrey had intended to apologise and withdraw, but this anticipation reassured him. The stranger stood round with his back to the fireplace and put his hands behind his back. " And presently," he said, " when the clock-mending is over, I think I should like to have some tea. But not till the clock-mending is over."

Mrs. Hall was about to leave the room—she made no con-versational advances this time, because she did not want to be snubbed in front of Mr. Henfrey—when her visitor asked her if she had made any arrangements about his boxes at Bramble-hurst. She told him she had mentioned the matter to the postman, and that the carrier could bring them over on the morrow. " You are certain that is the earliest ? " he said.

She was certain, with a marked coldness.

" I should explain," he added, " what I was really too cold and fatigued to do before, that I am an experimental in-vestigator."

" Indeed, sir," said Mrs. Hall, much impressed.

" And my baggage contains apparatus and appliances."

" Very useful things indeed they are, sir," said Mrs. Hall.

" And I'm naturally anxious to get on with my inquiries."

" Of course, sir."

" My reason for coming to Iping," he proceeded, with a certain deliberation of manner, " was—a desire for solitude. I do not wish to be disturbed in my work. In addition to my work, an accident——"

" I thought as much," said Mrs. Hall to herself.

" —necessitates a certain retirement. My eyes—are some-times so weak and painful that I have to shut myself up in the dark for hours together. Lock myself up. Sometimes—now and then. Not at present, certainly. At such times the slightest disturbance, the entry of a stranger into the room, is a source of excruciating annoyance to me—it is well these things should be understood."

" Certainly, sir," said Mrs. Hall. " And if I might make so bold as to ask——"

" That, I think, is all," said the stranger, with that quietly irresistible air of finality he could assume at will. Mrs. Hall reserved her question and sympathy for a better occasion.

After Mrs. Hall had left the room, he remained standing in

front of the fire, glaring, so Mr. Henfrey puts it, at the clock-mending. Mr. Henfrey not only took off the hands of the clock, and the face, but extracted the works ; and he tried to work in as slow and quiet and unassuming a manner as possible. He worked with the lamp close to him, and the green shade threw a brilliant light upon his hands, and upon the frame and wheels, and left the rest of the room shadowy. When he looked up, coloured patches swam in his eyes. Being con-stitutionally of a curious nature, he had removed the works—a quite unnecessary proceeding—with the idea of delaying his departure and perhaps falling into conversation with the stranger. But the stranger stood there, perfectly silent and still. So still, it got on Henfrey's nerves. He felt alone in the room and looked up, and there, grey and dim, was the bandaged head and huge blue lenses staring fixedly, with a mist of green spots drifting in front of them. It was so un-canny-looking to Henfrey that for a minute they remained staring blankly at one another. Then Henfrey looked down again. Very uncomfortable position ! One would like to say something. Should he remark that the weather was very cold for the time of year ?

He looked up as if to take aim with that introductory shot. " The weather "—he began.

" Why don't you finish and go ? " said the rigid figure, evidently in a state of painfully suppressed rage. " All you've got to do is to fix the hour-hand on its axle. You're simply humbugging——"

" Certainly, sir—one minute more, sir. I overlooked——" And Mr. Henfrey finished and went.

But he went off feeling excessively annoyed. " Damn it ! " said Mr. Henfrey to himself, trudging down the village through the thawing snow ; " a man must do a clock at times, sure-lie."

And again : " Can't a man look at you ?—Ugly ! "

And yet again : " Seemingly not. If the police was wanting you you couldn't be more wropped and bandaged."

At Gleeson's corner he saw Hall, who had recently married the stranger's hostess at the Coach and Horses, and who now drove the Iping conveyance, when occasional people required it, to Sidderbridge Junction, coming towards him on his return from that place. Hall had evidently been " stopping a bit " at Sidderbridge, to judge by his driving. " 'Ow do, Teddy ? " he said, passing.

" You got a rum un up home ! " said Teddy.

Hall very socially pulled up. " What's that ? " he asked.

" Rum-looking customer stopping at the Coach and Horses," said Teddy. " My sakes ! "

And he proceeded to give Hall a vivid description of his grotesque guest. " Looks a bit like a disguise, don't it ? I'd like to see a man's face if I had him stopping in *my* place," said Henfrey. " But women are that trustful—where strangers are concerned. He's took your rooms and he ain't even given a name, Hall."

" You don't say so ! " said Hall, who was a man of sluggish apprehension.

" Yes," said Teddy. " By the week. Whatever he is, you can't get rid of him under the week. And he's got a lot of luggage coming to-morrow, so he says. Let's hope it won't be stones in boxes, Hall."

He told Hall how his aunt at Hastings had been swindled by a stranger with empty portmanteaux. Altogether he left Hall vaguely suspicious. " Get up, old girl," said Hall. " I s'pose I must see 'bout this."

Teddy trudged on his way with his mind considerably relieved.

Instead of " seeing 'bout it," however, Hall on his return was severely rated by his wife on the length of time he had spent in Sidderbridge, and his mild inquiries were answered snappishly and in a manner not to the point. But the seed of suspicion Teddy had sown germinated in the mind of Mr. Hall in spite of these discouragements. " You wim' don't know everything," said Mr. Hall, resolved to ascertain more about the personality of his guest at the earliest possible oppor- tunity. And after the stranger had gone to bed, which he did about half-past nine, Mr. Hall went aggressively into the parlour and looked very hard at his wife's furniture, just to show that the stranger wasn't master there, and scrutinised closely and a little contemptuously a sheet of mathematical computation the stranger had left. When retiring for the night he instructed Mrs. Hall to look very closely at the stranger's luggage when it came next day.

" You mind your own business, Hall," said Mrs. Hall, " and I'll mind mine."

She was all the more inclined to snap at Hall because the stranger was undoubtedly an unusually strange sort of stranger, and she was by no means assured about him in her own mind. In the middle of the night she woke up dreaming of huge white heads like turnips, that came trailing after her at the end of interminable necks, and with vast black eyes. But being a sensible woman, she subdued her terrors and turned over and went to sleep again.

CHAPTER THREE

THE THOUSAND AND ONE BOTTLES

THUS it was that on the twenty-ninth day of February, at the beginning of the thaw, this singular person fell out of infinity into Iping Village. Next day his luggage arrived through the slush. And very remarkable luggage it was. There was a couple of trunks indeed, such as a rational man might need, but in addition there were a box of books—big, fat books, of which some were just in an incomprehensible handwriting—and a dozen or more crates, boxes, and cases, containing objects packed in straw, as it seemed to Hall, tugging with a casual curiosity at the straw—glass bottles. The stranger, muffled in hat, coat, gloves, and wrapper, came out impatiently to meet Fearenside's cart, while Hall was having a word or so of gossip preparatory to helping bring them in. Out he came, not noticing Fearenside's dog, who was sniffing in a *dilettante* spirit at Hall's legs. "Come along with those boxes," he said. "I've been waiting long enough."

And he came down the steps towards the tail of the cart as if to lay hands on the smaller crate.

No sooner had Fearenside's dog caught sight of him, however, than it began to bristle and growl savagely, and when he rushed down the steps it gave an undecided hop, and then sprang straight at his hand. "Whup!" cried Hall, jumping back, for he was no hero with dogs, and Fearenside howled, "Lie down!" and snatched his whip.

They saw the dog's teeth had slipped the hand, heard a kick, saw the dog execute a flanking jump and get home on the stranger's leg, and heard the rip of his trousering. Then the finer end of Fearenside's whip reached his property, and the dog, yelping with dismay, retreated under the wheels of the waggon. It was all the business of a half-minute. No one spoke, every one shouted. The stranger glanced swiftly at his torn glove and at his leg, made as if he would stoop to the latter, then turned and rushed up the steps into the inn. They heard him go headlong across the passage and up the uncarpeted stairs to his bedroom.

"You brute, you!" said Fearenside, climbing off the waggon with his whip in his hand, while the dog watched him through the wheel. "Come here!" said Fearenside—"You'd better."

Hall had stood gaping. "He wuz bit," said Hall. "I'd better go and see to en," and he trotted after the stranger. He met Mrs. Hall in the passage. "Carrier's darg," he said, "bit en."

He went straight upstairs, and the stranger's door being

ajar, he pushed it open and was entering without any ceremony, being of a naturally sympathetic turn of mind.

The blind was down and the room dim. He caught a
glimpse of a most singular thing, what seemed a handless arm
waving towards him, and a face of three huge indeterminate
spots on white, very like the face of a pale pansy. Then he
was struck violently in the chest, hurled back, and the door
slammed in his face and locked all so rapidly that he had no
time to observe. A waving of indecipherable shapes, a blow,
and a concussion. There he stood on the dark little landing,
wondering what it might be that he had seen.

After a couple of minutes he rejoined the little group that
had formed outside the Coach and Horses. There was
Fearenside telling about it all over again for the second time ;
there was Mrs. Hall saying his dog didn't have no business to
bite her guests ; there was Huxter, the general dealer from
over the road, interrogative ; and Sandy Wadgers from the
forge, judicial ; besides women and children—all of them
saying fatuities : "Wouldn't let en bite *me*, I knows " ;
"'Tasn't right *have* such dargs " ; "Whad 'e bite'n for then ? "
and so forth.

Mr. Hall, staring at them from the steps and listening, found
it incredible that he had seen anything very remarkable
happen upstairs. Besides, his vocabulary was altogether
too limited to express his impressions.

"He don't want no help, he says," he said in answer to his
wife's inquiry. "We'd better be a-takin' of his luggage in."

"He ought to have it cauterised at once," said Mr. Huxter ;
"especially if it's at all inflamed."

"I'd shoot en, that's what I'd do," said a lady in the group.

Suddenly the dog began growling again.

"Come along," cried an angry voice in the doorway, and
there stood the muffled stranger with his collar turned up, and
his hat-brim bent down. "The sooner you get those things
in the better I'll be pleased." It is stated by an anonymous
bystander that his trousers and gloves had been changed.

"Was you hurt, sir ? " said Fearenside. "I'm rare sorry
the darg——"

"Not a bit," said the stranger. "Never broke the skin.
Hurry up with those things."

He then swore to himself, so Mr. Hall asserts.

Directly the first crate was carried into the parlour, in
accordance with his directions, the stranger flung himself upon
it with extraordinary eagerness, and began to unpack it,
scattering the straw with an utter disregard of Mrs. Hall's
carpet. And from it he began to produce bottles—little fat
bottles containing powders, small and slender bottles containing coloured and white fluids, fluted blue bottles labelled
Poison, bottles with round bodies and slender necks,
large green-glass bottles, large white-glass bottles, bottles

with glass stoppers and frosted labels, bottles with fine corks, bottles with bungs, bottles with wooden caps, wine bottles, salad-oil bottles—putting them in rows on the chiffonnier, on the mantel, on the table under the window, round the floor, on the book-shelf—everywhere. The chemist's shop in Bramblehurst could not boast half so many. Quite a sight it was. Crate after crate yielded bottles, until all six were empty and the table high with straw ; the only things that came out of these crates besides the bottles were a number of test-tubes and a carefully packed balance.

And directly the crates were unpacked, the stranger went to the window and set to work, not troubling in the least about the litter of straw, the fire which had gone out, the box of books outside, nor for the trunks and other luggage that had gone upstairs.

When Mrs. Hall took his dinner in to him, he was already so absorbed in his work, pouring little drops out of the bottles into test-tubes, that he did not hear her until she had swept away the bulk of the straw and put the tray on the table, with some little emphasis perhaps, seeing the state that the floor was in. Then he half turned his head and immediately turned it away again. But she saw he had removed his glasses ; they were beside him on the table, and it seemed to her that his eye sockets were extraordinarily hollow. He put on his spectacles again, and then turned and faced her. She was about to complain of the straw on the floor when he anticipated her.

" I wish you wouldn't come in without knocking," he said in the tone of abnormal exasperation that seemed so characteristic of him.

" I knocked, but seemingly——"

" Perhaps you did. But in my investigations—my really very urgent and necessary investigations—the slightest disturbance, the jar of a door—I must ask you——"

" Certainly, sir. You can turn the lock if you're like that, you know—any time."

" A very good idea," said the stranger.

" This stror, sir, if I might make so bold as to remark——"

" Don't. If the straw makes trouble put it down in the bill." And he mumbled at her—words suspiciously like curses.

He was so odd, standing there, so aggressive and explosive, bottle in one hand and test-tube in the other, that Mrs. Hall was quite alarmed. But she was a resolute woman. " In which case, I should like to know, sir, what you consider——"

" A shilling. Put down a shilling. Surely a shilling's enough ? "

" So be it," said Mrs. Hall, taking up the tablecloth and beginning to spread it over the table. " If you're satisfied, of course——"

He turned and sat down, with his coat-collar towards her.

All the afternoon he worked with the door locked and, as Mrs. Hall testifies, for the most part in silence. But once there was a concussion and a sound of bottles ringing together as though the table had been hit, and the smash of a bottle flung violently down, and then a rapid pacing athwart the room. Fearing " something was the matter," she went to the door and listened, not caring to knock.

" I can't go on," he was raving. " I *can't* go on. Three hundred thousand, four hundred thousand ! The huge multitude ! Cheated ! All my life it may take me ! Patience ! Patience indeed ! Fool and liar ! "

There was a noise of hobnails on the bricks in the bar, and Mrs. Hall very reluctantly had to leave the rest of his soliloquy. When she returned the room was silent again, save for the faint crepitation of his chair and the occasional clink of a bottle. It was all over. The stranger had resumed work.

When she took in his tea she saw broken glass in the corner of the room under the concave mirror, and a golden stain that had been carelessly wiped. She called attention to it.

" Put it down in the bill," snapped the visitor. " For God's sake don't worry me. If there's damage done, put it down in the bill " ; and he went on ticking a list in the exercise-book before him.

" I'll tell you something," said Fearenside, mysteriously. It was late in the afternoon, and they were in the little beer-shop of Iping Hanger.

" Well ? " said Teddy Henfrey.

" This chap you're speaking of, what my dog bit. Well— he's black. Leastways, his legs are. I seed through the tear of his trousers and the tear of his glove. You'd have expected a sort of pinky to show, wouldn't you ? Well—there wasn't none. Just blackness. I tell you, he's as black as my hat."

" My sakes ! " said Henfrey. " It's a rummy case alto-gether. Why, his nose is as pink as paint ! "

" That's true," said Fearenside. " I knows that. And I tell 'ee what I'm thinking. That marn's a piebald, Teddy. Black here and white there—in patches. And he's ashamed of it. He's a kind of half-breed, and the colour's come off patchy instead of mixing. I've heard of such things before. And it's the common way with horses, as any one can see."

CHAPTER FOUR

MR. CUSS INTERVIEWS THE STRANGER

I HAVE told the circumstances of the stranger's arrival
in Iping with a certain fulness of detail, in order that
the curious impression he created may be understood by
the reader. But excepting two odd incidents, the circumstances of his stay until the extraordinary day of the Club
Festival may be passed over very cursorily. There were a
number of skirmishes with Mrs. Hall on matters of domestic
discipline, but in every case until late in April, when the first
signs of penury began, he over-rode her by the easy expedient
of an extra payment. Hall did not like him, and whenever he
dared he talked of the advisability of getting rid of him ; but
he showed his dislike chiefly by concealing it ostentatiously,
and avoiding his visitor as much as possible. " Wait till the
summer," said Mrs. Hall, sagely, " when the artisks are
beginning to come. Then we'll see. He may be a bit over-
bearing, but bills settled punctual is bills settled punctual,
whatever you like to say."

The stranger did not go to church, and indeed made no
difference between Sunday and the irreligious days, even in
costume. He worked, as Mrs. Hall thought, very fitfully.
Some days he would come down early and be continuously
busy. On others he would rise late, pace his room, fretting
audibly for hours together, smoke, sleep in the armchair by
the fire. Communication with the world beyond the village
he had none. His temper continued very uncertain ; for the
most part his manner was that of a man suffering under almost
unendurable provocation, and once or twice things were
snapped, torn, crushed, or broken in spasmodic gusts of
violence. He seemed under a chronic irritation of the greatest
intensity. His habit of talking to himself in a low voice
grew steadily upon him, but though Mrs. Hall listened con-
scientiously she could make neither head nor tail of what she
heard.

He rarely went abroad by daylight, but at twilight he would
go out muffled up enormously, whether the weather were cold
or not, and he chose the loneliest paths and those most over-
shadowed by trees and banks. His goggling spectacles and
ghastly bandaged face under the penthouse of his hat, came
with a disagreeable suddenness out of the darkness upon one
or two home-going labourers ; and Teddy Henfrey, tumbling
out of the Scarlet Coat one night at half-past nine, was scared
shamefully by the stranger's skull-like head (he was walking
hat in hand) lit by the sudden light of the opened inn door.
Such children as saw him at nightfall dreamt of bogies, and
it seemed doubtful whether he disliked boys more than they

disliked him, or the reverse—but there was certainly a vivid enough dislike on either side.

It was inevitable that a person of so remarkable an appearance and bearing should form a frequent topic in such a village as Iping. Opinion was greatly divided about his occupation. Mrs. Hall was sensitive on the point. When questioned, she explained very carefully that he was an "experimental investigator," going gingerly over the syllables as one who dreads pitfalls. When asked what an experimental investigator was, she would say with a touch of superiority that most educated people knew that, and would then explain that he "discovered things." Her visitor had had an accident, she said, which temporarily discoloured his face and hands; and being of a sensitive disposition, he was averse to any public notice of the fact.

Out of her hearing there was a view largely entertained that he was a criminal trying to escape from justice by wrapping himself up so as to conceal himself altogether from the eye of the police. This idea sprang from the brain of Mr. Teddy Henfrey. No crime of any magnitude dating from the middle or end of February was known to have occurred. Elaborated in the imagination of Mr. Gould, the probationary assistant in the National School, this theory took the form that the stranger was an Anarchist in disguise, preparing explosives, and he resolved to undertake such detective operations as his time permitted. These consisted for the most part in looking very hard at the stranger whenever they met, or in asking people who had never seen the stranger, leading questions about him. But he detected nothing.

Another school of opinion followed Mr. Fearenside, and either accepted the piebald view or some modification of it; as, for instance, Silas Durgan, who was heard to assert that "if he choses to show enself at fairs he'd make his fortune in no time," and being a bit of a theologian, compared the stranger to the man with the one talent. Yet another view explained the entire matter by regarding the stranger as a harmless lunatic. That had the advantage of accounting for everything straightaway.

Between these main groups there were waverers and compromisers. Sussex folk have few superstitions, and it was only after the events of early April that the thought of the supernatural was first whispered in the village. Even then it was only credited among the women-folks.

But whatever they thought of him, people in Iping on the whole agreed in disliking him. His irritability, though it might have been comprehensible to an urban brain-worker, was an amazing thing to these quiet Sussex villagers. The frantic gesticulations they surprised now and then, the headlong space after nightfall that swept him upon them round quiet corners, the inhuman bludgeoning of all the tentative advances of curiosity, the taste for twilight that led to the closing of doors, the pulling down of blinds, the extinction of candles and lamps—who could agree with such goings on ? They drew aside as he passed down the village, and when he had gone by, young humorists would up with coat-collars and down with hat-brims, and go pacing nervously after him in imitation of his occult bearing. There was a song popular at that time called the " Bogey Man " ; Miss Statchell sang it at the schoolroom concert (in aid of the church lamps), and thereafter whenever one or two of the villagers were gathered together and the stranger appeared, a bar or so of this tune, more or less sharp or flat, was whistled in the midst of them. Also belated little children would call " Bogey Man ! " after him, and make off tremulously elated.

Cuss, the general practitioner, was devoured by curiosity. The bandages excited his professional interest, the report of the thousand and one bottles aroused his jealous regard. All through April and May he coveted an opportunity of talking to the stranger ; and at last, towards Whitsuntide, he could stand it no longer, and hit upon the subscription-list for a village nurse as an excuse. He was surprised to find that Mr. Hall did not know his guest's name. " He gave a name," said Mrs. Hall—an assertion which was quite unfounded—" but I didn't rightly hear it." She thought it seemed so silly not to know the man's name.

Cuss rapped at the parlour door and entered. There was a fairly audible imprecation from within. " Pardon my intrusion," said Cuss, and then the door closed and cut Mrs. Hall off from the rest of the conversation.

She could hear the murmur of voices for the next ten minutes, then a cry of surprise, a stirring of feet, a chair flung aside, a bark of laughter, quick steps to the door, and Cuss appeared, his face white, his eyes staring over his shoulder. He left the door open behind him, and without looking at her strode across the hall and went down the steps, and she heard his feet hurrying along the road. He carried his hat in his hand. She stood behind the door, looking at the open door of the parlour. Then she heard the stranger laughing quietly, and then his footsteps came across the room. She could not see his face where she stood. The parlour door slammed, and the place was silent again.

Cuss went straight up the village to Bunting the vicar. " Am I mad ? " Cuss began abruptly, as he entered the shabby little study. " Do I look like an insane person ? "

" What's happened ? " said the vicar, putting the ammonite on the loose sheets of his forthcoming sermon.

" That chap at the inn——"

" Well ? "

" Give me something to drink," said Cuss, and he sat down.

When his nerves had been steadied by a glass of cheap sherry—the only drink the good vicar had available—he told him of the interview he had just had. " Went in," he gasped, " and began to demand a subscription for that Nurse Fund. He'd stuck his hands in his pockets as I came in, and he sat down lumpily in his chair. Sniffed. I told him I'd heard he took an interest in scientific things. He said yes. Sniffed again. Kept on sniffing all the time ; evidently recently caught an infernal cold. No wonder, wrapped up like that ! I developed the nurse idea, and all the while kept my eyes open. Bottles—chemicals—everywhere. Balance, test-tubes in stands, and a smell of—evening primrose. Would he subscribe ? Said he'd consider it. Asked him, point-blank, was he researching. Said he was. A long research ? Got quite cross. ' A damnable long research,' said he, blowing the cork out, so to speak. ' Oh,' said I. And out came the grievance. The man was just on the boil, and my question boiled him over. He had been given a prescription, most valuable prescription—what for he wouldn't say. Was it medical ? ' Damn you ! What are you fishing after ? ' I apologised. Dignified sniff and cough. He resumed. He'd read it. Five ingredients. Put it down ; turned his head. Draught of air from window lifted the paper. Swish, rustle. He was working in a room with an open fireplace, he said. Saw a flicker, and there was the prescription burning and lifting chimney-ward. Rushed towards it just as it whisked up chimney. So ! Just at that point, to illustrate his story, out came his arm."

" Well ? "

" No hand—just an empty sleeve. Lord ! I thought, *that's* a deformity ! Got a cork arm, I suppose, and has taken it off. Then, I thought, there's something odd in that. What the devil keeps that sleeve up and open, if there's nothing in it ? There was nothing in it, I tell you. Nothing down it, right down to the joint. I could see right down it to the elbow, and there was a glimmer of light shining through a tear of the cloth. ' Good God ! ' I said. Then he stopped. Stared at me with those black goggles of his, and then at his sleeve."

" Well ? "

" That's all. He never said a word ; just glared, and put his sleeve back in his pocket quickly. ' I was saying,' said he, ' that there was the prescription burning, wasn't I ? ' Inter-rogative cough. ' How the devil,' said I, ' can you move an empty sleeve like that ? ' ' Empty sleeve ? ' ' Yes,' said I, ' an empty sleeve.'

" ' It's an empty sleeve, is it ? You saw it was an empty sleeve ? ' He stood up right away. I stood up too. He came towards me in three very slow steps, and stood quite close. Sniffed venomously. I didn't flinch, though I'm nanged if that bandaged knob of his, and those blinkers, aren't enough to unnerve any one, coming quietly up to you.

" ' You said it was an empty sleeve ? ' he said. ' Certainly,' I said. At staring and saying nothing a barefaced man, unspectacled, starts scratch. Then very quietly he pulled his sleeve out of his pocket again, and raised his arm towards me as though he would show it to me again. He did it very, very slowly. I looked at it. Seemed an age. ' Well ? ' said I, clearing my throat, ' there's nothing in it.' Had to say something. I was beginning to feel frightened. I could see right down it. He extended it straight towards me, slowly, slowly— just like that—until the cuff was six inches from my face. Queer thing to see an empty sleeve come at you like that ! And then——"

" Well ? "

" Something—exactly like a finger and thumb it felt— nipped my nose."

Bunting began to laugh.

" There wasn't anything there ! " said Cuss, his voice running up into a shriek at the " there." " It's all very well for you to laugh, but I tell you I was so startled, I hit his cuff hard, and turned round and cut out of the room—I left him——"

Cuss stopped. There was no mistaking the sincerity of his panic. He turned round in a helpless way and took a second glass of the excellent vicar's very inferior sherry. " When I hit his cuff," said Cuss, " I tell you, it felt exactly like hitting an arm. And there wasn't an arm ! There wasn't the ghost of an arm ! "

Mr. Bunting thought it over. He looked suspiciously at Cuss. " It's a most remarkable story," he said. He looked very wise and grave indeed. " It's really," said Mr. Bunting with judicial emphasis, " a most remarkable story."

CHAPTER FIVE

THE BURGLARY AT THE VICARAGE

THE facts of the burglary at the vicarage came to us chiefly through the medium of the vicar and his wife. It occurred in the small hours of Whit-Monday—the day devoted in Iping to the Club festivities. Mrs. Bunting, it seems, woke up suddenly in the stillness that comes before the dawn, with the strong impression that the door of their bedroom had opened and closed. She did not arouse her husband at first, but sat up in bed listening. She then distinctly heard the pad, pad, pad of bare feet coming out of the adjoining dressing-room and walking along the passage towards the staircase. As soon as she felt assured of this, she aroused the Rev. Mr. Bunting as quietly as possible. He did not strike a light, but putting on his spectacles, her dressing-gown, and his bath slippers, he went out on the landing to listen. He heard quite distinctly a fumbling going on at his study desk downstairs, and then a violent sneeze.

At that he returned to his bedroom, armed himself with the most obvious weapon, the poker, and descended the staircase as noiselessly as possible. Mrs. Bunting came out on the landing.

The hour was about four, and the ultimate darkness of the night was past. There was a faint shimmer of light in the hall, but the study doorway yawned impenetrably black. Everything was still except the faint creaking of the stairs under Mr. Bunting's tread, and the slight movements in the study. Then something snapped, the drawer was opened, and there was a rustle of papers. Then came an imprecation, and a match was struck and the study was flooded with yellow light. Mr. Bunting was now in the hall, and through the crack of the door he could see the desk and the open drawer and a candle burning on the desk. But the robber he could not see. He stood there in the hall undecided what to do, and Mrs. Bunting, her face white and intent, crept slowly downstairs after him. One thing kept up Mr. Bunting's courage : the persuasion that this burglar was a resident in the village.

They heard the chink of money, and realised that the robber had found the housekeeping reserve of gold—two pounds ten in half-sovereigns altogether. At that sound Mr. Bunting was nerved to abrupt action. Gripping the poker firmly, he rushed into the room, closely followed by Mrs. Bunting. " Surrender ! " cried Mr. Bunting, fiercely, and then stopped amazed. Apparently the room was perfectly empty.

Yet their conviction that they had, that very moment, heard somebody moving in the room, had amounted to a certainty. For half a minute, perhaps, they stood gaping, then Mrs. Bunting went across the room and looked behind the screen, while Mr. Bunting, by a kindred impulse, peered under the desk. Then Mrs. Bunting turned back the window-curtains, and Mr. Bunting looked up the chimney and probed it with the poker. Then Mrs. Bunting scrutinised the waste-paper basket and Mr. Bunting opened the lid of the coal-scuttle. Then they came to a stop and stood with eyes inter-rogating each other.

" I could have sworn——" said Mr. Bunting.

" The candle ! " said Mr. Bunting. " Who lit the candle ? "

" The drawer ! " said Mrs. Bunting. " And the money's gone ! "

She went hastily to the doorway.

" Of all the extraordinary occurrences——"

There was a violent sneeze in the passage. They rushed out, and as they did so the kitchen door slammed. " Bring the candle," said Mr. Bunting, and led the way. They both heard a sound of bolts being hastily shot back.

As he opened the kitchen door he saw through the scullery that the back door was just opening, and the faint light of early dawn displayed the dark masses of the garden beyond. He is certain that nothing went out of the door. It opened, stood open for a moment, and then closed with a slam. As it did so, the candle Mrs. Bunting was carrying from the study flickered and flared. It was a minute or more before they entered the kitchen.

The place was empty. They refastened the back door, examined the kitchen, pantry, and scullery thoroughly, and at last went down into the cellar. There was not a soul to be found in the house, search as they would.

Daylight found the vicar and his wife, a quaintly-costumed little couple, still marvelling about on their own ground floor by the unnecessary light of a guttering candle.

CHAPTER SIX

THE FURNITURE THAT WENT MAD

Now it happened that in the early hours of Whit-Monday, before Millie was hunted out for the day, Mr. Hall and Mrs. Hall both rose and went noiselessly down into the cellar. Their business there was of a private nature, and had something to do with the specific gravity of their beer. They had hardly entered the cellar when Mrs. Hall found she had forgotten to bring down a bottle of sarsaparilla from their joint room. As she was the expert and principal operator in this affair, Hall very properly went upstairs for it.

On the landing he was surprised to see that the stranger's door was ajar. He went on into his own room and found the bottle as he had been directed.

But returning with the bottle, he noticed that the bolts of the front door had been shot back, that the door was in fact simply on the latch. And with a flash of inspiration he connected this with the stranger's room upstairs and the suggestions of Mr. Teddy Henfrey. He distinctly remembered holding the candle while Mrs. Hall shot these bolts overnight. At the sight he stopped, gaping, then with the bottle still in his hand went upstairs again. He rapped at the stranger's door. There was no answer. He rapped again ; then pushed the door wide open and entered.

It was as he expected. The bed, the room also, was empty. And what was stranger, even to his heavy intelligence, on the bedroom chair and along the rail of the bed were scattered the garments, the only garments so far as he knew, and the bandages of their guest. His big slouch-hat even was cocked jauntily over the bed-post.

As Hall stood there he heard his wife's voice coming out of the depth of the cellar, with that rapid telescoping of the syllables and interrogative cocking up of the final words to a high note, by which the West Sussex villager is wont to indicate a brisk impatience. " Gearge ! You gart what a wand ? "

At that he turned and hurried down to her. " Janny," he said, over the rail of the cellar steps, " 'tas the truth what Henfrey sez. 'E's not in uz room, 'e ent. And the front door's unbolted."

At first Mrs. Hall did not understand, and as soon as she did she resolved to see the empty room for herself. Hall still holding the bottle, went first. " If 'e ent there," he said, " his close are. And what's 'e doin' without his close, then ? 'Tas a most curious basness."

As they came up the cellar steps, they both, it was afterwards ascertained, fancied they heard the front door open and shut, but seeing it closed and nothing there, neither said a word to the other about it at the time. Mrs. Hall passed her husband in the passage and ran on first upstairs. Some one sneezed on the staircase. Hall, following six steps behind, thought that he heard her sneeze. She, going on first, was under the impression that Hall was sneezing. She flung open the door and stood regarding the room. " Of all the curious ! " she said.

She heard a sniff close behind her head as it seemed, and, turning, was surprised to see Hall a dozen feet off on the topmost stair. But in another moment he was beside her. She bent forward and put her hand on the pillow and then under the clothes.

" Cold," she said. " He's been up this hour or more."

As she did so, a most extraordinary thing happened—the bed-clothes gathered themselves together, leapt up suddenly into a sort of peak, and then jumped headlong over the bottom rail. It was exactly as if a hand had clutched them in the centre and flung them aside. Immediately after, the stranger's hat hopped off the bed-post, described a whirling flight in the air through the better part of a circle, and then dashed straight at Mrs. Hall's face. Then as swiftly came the sponge from the washstand ; and then the chair, flinging the stranger's coat and trousers carelessly aside, and laughing dryly in a voice singularly like the stranger's, turned itself up with its four legs at Mrs. Hall, seemed to take aim at her for a moment, and charged at her. She screamed and turned, and then the chair legs came gently but firmly against her back and impelled her and Hall out of the room. The door slammed violently and was locked. The chair and bed seemed to be executing a dance of triumph for a moment, and then abruptly everything was still.

Mrs. Hall was left almost in a fainting condition in Mr. Hall's arms on the landing. It was with the greatest difficulty that Mr. Hall and Millie, who had been roused by her scream of alarm, succeeded in getting her downstairs, and applying the restoratives customary in these cases.

" 'Tas sperrits," said Mrs. Hall. " I know 'tas sperrits. I've read in papers of en. Tables and chairs leaping and dancing !——"

" Take a drop more, Janny," said Hall. " 'Twill steady ye."

" Lock him out," said Mrs. Hall. " Don't let him come in again. I half guessed—I might ha' known. With them goggling eyes and bandaged head, and never going to church of a Sunday. And all they bottles—more'n it's right for any one to have. He's put the sperrits into the furniture. My good old furniture ! 'Twas in that very chair my poor dear mother used to sit when I was a little girl. To think it should rise up against me now ! "

" Just a drop more, Janny," said Hall. " Your nerves is all upset."

They sent Millie across the street through the golden five o'clock sunshine to rouse up Mr. Sandy Wadgers, the blacksmith. Mr. Hall's compliments and the furniture upstairs was behaving most extraordinary. Would Mr. Wadgers come round ? He was a knowing man, was Mr. Wadgers, and very resourceful. He took quite a grave view of the case. " Arm darmed ef thet ent witchcraft," was the view of Mr. Sandy Wadgers. " You warnt horseshoes for such gentry as he."

He came round greatly concerned. They wanted him to lead the way upstairs to the room, but he didn't seem to be in any hurry. He preferred to talk in the passage. Over the way Huxter's apprentice came out and began taking down the shutters of the tobacco window. He was called over to join the discussion. Mr. Huxter naturally followed in the course of a few minutes. The Anglo-Saxon genius for parliamentary government asserted itself ; there was a great deal of talk and no decisive action. " Let's have the facts first," insisted Mr. Sandy Wadgers. " Let's be sure we'd be acting perfectly right in bustin' that there door open. A door onbust is always open to bustin', but ye can't onbust a door once you've busted en."

And suddenly and most wonderfully the door of the room upstairs opened of its own accord, and as they looked up in amazement, they saw descending the stairs the muffled figure of the stranger staring more blackly and blankly than ever with those unreasonably large blue glass eyes of his. He came down stiffly and slowly, staring all the time ; he walked across the passage staring, then stopped.

" Look there ! " he said, and their eyes followed the direction of his gloved finger and saw a bottle of sarsaparilla hard by the cellar door. Then he entered the parlour, and suddenly, swiftly, viciously, slammed the door in their faces.

Not a word was spoken until the last echoes of the slam had died away. They stared at one another. " Well, if that don't lick everything ! " said Mr. Wadgers, and left the alternative unsaid.

" I'd go in and ask'n 'bout it," said Wadgers to Mr. Hall. " I'd d'mand an explanation."

It took some time to bring the landlady's husband up to that pitch. At last he rapped, opened the door, and got as far as, " Excuse me——"

" Go to the devil ! " said the stranger in a tremendous voice, and " Shut that door after you." So that brief interview terminated.

CHAPTER SEVEN

THE UNVEILING OF THE STRANGER

THE stranger went into the little parlour of the Coach and Horses about half-past five in the morning, and there he remained until near midday, the blinds down, the door shut, and none, after Hall's repulse, venturing near him.

All that time he must have fasted. Thrice he rang his bell, the third time furiously and continuously, but no one answered him. "Him and his ' go to the devil ' indeed ! " said Mrs. Hall. Presently came an imperfect rumour of the burglary at the vicarage, and two and two were put together. Hall, assisted by Wadgers, went off to find Mr. Shuckleforth, the magistrate, and take his advice. No one ventured upstairs. How the stranger occupied himself is unknown. Now and then he would stride violently up and down, and twice came an outburst of curses, a tearing of paper, and a violent smashing of bottles.

The little group of scared but curious people increased. Mrs. Huxter came over ; some gay young fellows resplendent in black ready-made jackets and *piqué* paper ties, for it was Whit-Monday, joined the group with confused interrogations. Young Archie Harker distinguished himself by going up the yard and trying to peep under the window-blinds. He could see nothing, but gave reason for supposing that he did, and others of the Iping youth presently joined him.

It was the finest of all possible Whit-Mondays, and down the village street stood a row of nearly a dozen booths and a shooting gallery, and on the grass by the forge were three yellow and chocolate waggons and some picturesque strangers of both sexes putting up a coco-nut shy. The gentlemen wore blue jerseys, the ladies white aprons and quite fashionable hats with heavy plumes. Wodger of the Purple Fawn and Mr. Jaggers the cobbler, who also sold second-hand ordinary bicycles, were stretching a string of union-jacks and royal ensigns (which had originally celebrated the Jubilee) across the road. . . .

And inside, in the artificial darkness of the parlour, into which only one thin jet of sunlight penetrated, the stranger, hungry we must suppose, and fearful, hidden in his uncomfortable hot wrappings, pored through his dark glasses upon his paper or chinked his dirty little bottles, and occasionally swore savagely at the boys, audible if invisible, outside the windows. In the corner by the fireplace lay the fragments of half a dozen smashed bottles, and a pungent tang of chlorine tainted the air. So much we know from what was heard at the time and from what was subsequently seen in the room.

About noon he suddenly opened his parlour door and stood

glaring fixedly at the three or four people in the bar. " Mrs Hall," he said. Somebody went sheepishly and called for Mrs' Hall.

Mrs. Hall appeared after an interval, a little short of breath, but all the fiercer for that. Hall was still out. She had deliberated over this scene, and she came holding a little tray with an unsettled bill upon it. " Is it your bill you're wanting, sir ? " she said.

" Why wasn't my breakfast laid ? Why haven't you prepared my meals and answered my bell ? Do you think I live without eating ? "

" Why isn't my bill paid ? " said Mrs. Hall. " That's what I want to know."

" I told you three days ago I was awaiting a remittance——"

" I told you two days ago I wasn't going to await no re-mittances. You can't grumble if your breakfast waits a bit, if my bill's been waiting these five days, can you ? "

The stranger swore briefly but vividly.

" Nar, nar ! " from the bar.

" And I'd thank you kindly, sir, if you'd keep your swearing to yourself, sir," said Mrs. Hall.

The stranger stood looking more like an angry diving-helmet than ever. It was universally felt in the bar that Mrs. Hall had the better of him. His next words showed as much.

" Look here, my good woman——" he began.

" Don't good woman *me*," said Mrs. Hall.

" I've told you my remittance hasn't come——"

" Remittance indeed ! " said Mrs. Hall.

" Still, I dare say in my pocket——"

" You told me two days ago that you hadn't anything but a sovereign's worth of silver upon you——"

" Well, I've found some more——"

" 'Ul-*lo* ! " from the bar.

" I wonder where you found it ! " said Mrs. Hall.

That seemed to annoy the stranger very much. He stamped his foot. " What do you mean ? " he said.

" That I wonder where you found it," said Mrs. Hall. " And before I take any bills or get any breakfasts, or do any such things whatsoever, you got to tell me one or two things I don't understand, and what nobody don't understand, and what everybody is very anxious to understand. I want know what you been doing t' my chair upstairs, and I want know how 'tis your room was empty, and how you got in again. Them as stops in this house comes in by the doors—— that's the rule of the house, and that you *didn't* do, and what I want know is how you *did* come in. And I want know——"

Suddenly the stranger raised his gloved hands clenched, stamped his foot, and said, " Stop ! " with such extraordinary violence that he silenced her instantly.

" You don't understand," he said, " who I am or what I

am. I'll show you. By Heaven ! I'll show you." Then he put his open palm over his face and withdrew it. The centre of his face became a black cavity. "Here," he said. He stepped forward and handed Mrs. Hall something which she, staring at his metamorphosed face, accepted automatically. Then, when she saw what it was, she screamed loudly, dropped it, and staggered back. The nose—it was the stranger's nose ! pink and shining—rolled on the floor.

Then he removed his spectacles, and every one in the bar gasped. He took off his hat, and with a violent gesture tore at his whiskers and bandages. For a moment they resisted him. A flash of horrible anticipation passed through the bar. " Oh, my Gard ! " said some one. Then off they came.

It was worse than anything. Mrs. Hall, standing open-mouthed and horror-struck, shrieked at what she saw, and made for the door of the house. Every one began to move. They were prepared for scars, disfigurements, tangible horrors, but *nothing !* The bandages and false hair flew across the passage into the bar, making a hobbledehoy jump to avoid them. Every one tumbled on every one else down the steps. For the man who stood there shouting some incoherent explanation, was a solid, gesticulating figure up to the coat-collar of him, and then—nothingness, no visible thing at all !

People down the village heard shouts and shrieks, and look-ing up the street saw the Coach and Horses violently firing out its humanity. They saw Mrs. Hall fall down and Mr. Teddy Henfrey jump to avoid tumbling over her, and then they heard the frightful screams of Millie, who, emerging suddenly from the kitchen at the noise of the tumult, had come upon the headless stranger from behind.

Forthwith every one all down the street, the sweetstuff seller, coco-nut-shy proprietor and his assistant, the swing man, little boys and girls, rustic dandies, smart wenches, smocked elders and aproned gipsies, began running towards the inn ; and in a miraculously short space of time a crowd of perhaps forty people, and rapidly increasing, swayed and hooted and inquired and exclaimed and suggested, in front of Mrs. Hall's establishment. Every one seemed eager to talk at once, and the result was babel. A small group supported Mrs. Hall, who was picked up in a state of collapse. There was a conference, and the incredible evidence of a vociferous eye-witness. " O' Bogey ! " " What's he been doin', then ? " " Ain't hurt the girl, 'as 'e ? " " Run at en with a knife, I believe." " No 'ed, I tell ye. I don't mean no manner of speaking, I mean *marn 'ithout a 'ed !* " " Narnsense ! 'tas some conjuring trick." " Fetched off 'is wrappin's, 'e did——"

In its struggles to see in through the open door, the crowd formed itself into a straggling wedge, with the more adven-turous apex nearest the inn. " He stood for a moment, I heerd the gal scream, and he turned. I saw her skirts whisk, and he went after her. Didn't take ten seconds. Back he comes with a knife in uz hand and a loaf ; stood just as if he was staring. Not a moment ago. Went in that there door. I tell 'e, 'e ain't gart no 'ed 't all. You just missed en——"

There was a disturbance behind, and the speaker stopped to step aside for a little procession that was marching very resolutely towards the house—first Mr. Hall, very red and determined, then Mr. Bobby Jaffers, the village constable, and then the wary Mr. Wadgers. They had come now armed with a warrant.

People shouted conflicting information of the recent circumstances. " 'Ed or no 'ed," said Jaffers, " I got to 'rest en, and 'rest en I *will*."

Mr. Hall marched up the steps, marched straight to the door of the parlour and flung it open. " Constable," he said, " do your duty."

Jaffers marched in, Hall next, Wadgers last. They saw in the dim light the headless figure facing them, with a gnawed crust of bread in one gloved hand and a chunk of cheese in the other.

" That's him ! " said Hall.

" What the devil's this ? " came in a tone of angry expostulation from above the collar of the figure.

" You're a damned rum customer, mister," said Mr. Jaffers. " But 'ed or no 'ed, the warrant says ' body,' and duty's duty——"

" Keep off ! " said the figure, starting back.

Abruptly he whipped down the bread and cheese, and Mr. Hall just grasped the knife on the table in time to save it. Off came the stranger's left glove and was slapped in Jaffers' face. In another moment Jaffers, cutting short some statement concerning a warrant, had gripped him by the handless wrist and caught his invisible throat. He got a sounding kick on the shin that made him shout, but he kept his grip. Hall sent the knife sliding along the table to Wadgers, who acted as goal-keeper for the offensive, so to speak, and then stepped forward as Jaffers and the stranger swayed and staggered towards him, clutching and hitting in. A chair stood in the way, and went aside with a crash as they came down together.

" Get the feet," said Jaffers between his teeth.

Mr. Hall, endeavouring to act on instructions, received a sounding kick in the ribs that disposed of him for a moment, and Mr. Wadgers, seeing the decapitated stranger had rolled over and got the upper side of Jaffers, retreated towards the door, knife in hand, and so collided with Mr. Huxter and the Siddermorton carter coming to the rescue of law and order. At the same moment down came three or four bottles from the chiffonnier and shot a web of pungency into the air of the room.

" I'll surrender," cried the stranger, though he had Jaffers down, and in another moment he stood up panting, a strange figure, headless and handless—for he had pulled off his right glove now as well as his left. " It's no good," he said, as if sobbing for breath.

It was the strangest thing in the world to hear that voice coming as if out of empty space, but the Sussex peasants are perhaps the most matter-of-fact people under the sun. Jaffers got up also and produced a pair of handcuffs. Then he started.

" I say ! " said Jaffers, brought up short by a dim realisation of the incongruity of the whole business, " Darm it ! Can't use 'em as I can see."

The stranger ran his arm down his waistcoat, and as if by a miracle the buttons to which his empty sleeve pointed became undone. Then he said something about his shin, and stooped down. He seemed to be fumbling with his shoes and socks.

" Why ! " said Huxter, suddenly, " that's not a man at all. It's just empty clothes. Look ! You can see down his collar and the linings of his clothes. I could put my arm——"

He extended his hand ; it seemed to meet something in mid-air, and he drew it back with a sharp exclamation. " I wish you'd keep your fingers out of my eye," said the aerial voice, in a tone of savage expostulation. " The fact is, I'm all here : head, hands, legs, and all the rest of it, but it happens I'm invisible. It's a confounded nuisance, but I am. That's no reason why I should be poked to pieces by every stupid bumpkin in Iping, is it ? "

The suit of clothes, now all unbuttoned and hanging loosely upon its unseen supports, stood up, arms akimbo.

Several other of the men-folks had now entered the room, so that it was closely crowded. " Invisible, eigh ? " said Huxter, ignoring the stranger's abuse. " Who ever heard the likes of that ? "

" It's strange, perhaps, but it's not a crime. Why am I assaulted by a policeman in this fashion ? "

" Ah ! that's a different matter," said Jaffers. " No doubt you are a bit difficult to see in this light, but I got a warrant and it's all correct. What I'm after ain't no invisibility—it's burglary. There's a house been broken into and money took."

" Well ? "

" And circumstances certainly point——"

" Stuff and nonsense ! " said the Invisible Man.

" I hope so, sir ; but I've got my instructions."

" Well," said the stranger, " I'll come. I'll *come*. But no handcuffs."

" It's the regular thing," said Jaffers.

" No handcuffs," stipulated the stranger.

" Pardon me," said Jaffers.

Abruptly the figure sat down, and before any one could realise what was being done, the slippers, socks, and trousers had been kicked off under the table. Then he sprang up again and flung off his coat.

"Here, stop that," said Jaffers, suddenly realising what was happening. He gripped the waistcoat ; it struggled, and the shirt slipped out of it and left it limp and empty in his hand. "Hold him ! " said Jaffers, loudly. "Once he gets they things off—— ! "

"Hold him ! " cried every one, and there was a rush at the fluttering white shirt which was now all that was visible of the stranger.

The shirt-sleeve planted a shrewd blow in Hall's face that stopped his open-armed advance, and sent him backward into old Toothsome the sexton, and in another moment the garment was lifted up and became convulsed and vacantly flapping about the arms, even as a shirt that is being thrust over a man's head. Jaffers clutched at it, and only helped to pull it off ; he was struck in the mouth out of the air, and incontinently drew his truncheon and smote Teddy Henfrey savagely upon the crown of his head.

"Look out ! " said everybody, fencing at random and hitting at nothing. "Hold him ! Shut the door ! Don't let him loose ! I got something ! Here he is ! " A perfect babel of noises they made. Everybody, it seemed, was being hit all at once, and Sandy Wadgers, knowing as ever and his wits sharpened by a frightful blow in the nose, reopened the door and led the rout. The others, following incontinently, were jammed for a moment in the corner by the doorway. The hitting continued. Phipps, the Unitarian, had a front tooth broken, and Henfrey was injured in the cartilage of his ear. Jaffers was struck under the jaw, and, turning, caught at something that intervened between him and Huxter in the *mêlée*, and prevented their coming together. He felt a muscular chest, and in another moment the whole mass of struggling, excited men shot out into the crowded hall.

"I got him ! " shouted Jaffers, choking and reeling through them all, and wrestling with purple face and swelling veins against his unseen enemy.

Men staggered right and left as the extraordinary conflict swayed swiftly towards the house door, and went spinning down the half-dozen steps of the inn. Jaffers cried in a strangled voice—holding tight, nevertheless, and making play with his knee—spun round, and fell heavily undermost with his head on the gravel. Only then did his fingers relax.

There were excited cries of "Hold him ! " "Invisible ! " and so forth, and a young fellow, a stranger in the place whose name did not come to light, rushed in at once, caught something, missed his hold, and fell over the constable's prostrate body. Half-way across the road a woman screamed as something pushed by her ; a dog, kicked apparently, yelped and ran howling into Huxter's yard, and with that the transit of the Invisible Man was accomplished. For a space people stood amazed and gesticulating, and then came Panic, and scattered them abroad through the village as a gust scatters dead leaves.

But Jaffers lay quite still, face upward and knees bent.

CHAPTER EIGHT

THE eighth chapter is exceedingly brief, and relates that Gibbins, the amateur naturalist of the district, while lying out on the spacious open downs without a soul within a couple of miles of him, as he thought, and almost dozing, heard close to him the sound as of a man coughing, sneezing, and then swearing savagely to himself ; and looking, beheld nothing. Yet the voice was indisputable. It continued to swear with that breadth and variety that distinguishes the swearing of a cultivated man. It grew to a climax, diminished again, and died away in the distance, going as it seemed to him in the direction of Adderdean. It lifted to a spasmodic sneeze and ended. Gibbins had heard nothing of the morning's occurrences, but the phenomenon was so striking and disturbing that his philosophical tranquillity vanished ; he got up hastily, and hurried down the steepness of the hill towards the village, as fast as he could go.

CHAPTER NINE

MR. THOMAS MARVEL

You must picture Mr. Thomas Marvel as a person of copious, flexible visage, a nose of cylindrical protrusion, a liquorish, ample, fluctuating mouth, and a beard of bristling eccentricity. His figure inclined to embonpoint; his short limbs accentuated this inclination. He wore a furry silk hat, and the frequent substitution of twine and shoe-laces for buttons, apparent at critical points of his costume, marked a man essentially bachelor.

Mr. Thomas Marvel was sitting with his feet in a ditch by the roadside over the down towards Adderdean, about a mile and a half out of Iping. His feet, save for socks of irregular open-work, were bare, his big toes were broad, and pricked like the ears of a watchful dog. In a leisurely manner—he did everything in a leisurely manner—he was contemplating trying on a pair of boots. They were the soundest boots he had come across for a long time, but too large for him; whereas the ones he had were, in dry weather, a very comfortable fit, but too thin-soled for damp. Mr. Thomas Marvel hated roomy boots, but then he hated damp. He had never properly thought out which he hated most, and it was a pleasant day, and there was nothing better to do. So he put the four boots in a graceful group on the turf and looked at them. And seeing them there among the grass and springing agrimony, it suddenly occurred to him that both pairs were exceedingly ugly to see. He was not at all startled by a voice behind him.

"They're boots, anyhow," said the voice.

"They are—charity boots," said Mr. Thomas Marvel, with his head on one side regarding them distastefully; "and which is the ugliest pair in the whole blessed universe, I'm darned if I know!"

"H'm," said the voice.

"I've worn worse—in fact, I've worn none. But none so owdacious ugly—if you'll allow the expression. I've been cadging boots—in particular—for days. Because I was sick of *them*. They're sound enough, of course. But a gentleman in tramp sees such a thundering lot of his boots. And if you'll believe me, I've raised nothing in the whole blessed county, try as I would, but THEM. Look at 'em! And a good county for boots, too, in a general way. But it's just my promiscuous luck. I've got my boots in this county ten years or more. And then they treat you like this."

"It's a beast of a county," said the voice. "And pigs for people."

"Ain't it?" said Mr. Thomas Marvel. "Lord! But them boots! It beats it."

He turned his head over his shoulder to the right, to look at the boots of his interlocutor with a view to comparisons, and lo! where the boots of his interlocutor should have been were neither legs nor boots. He turned his head over his shoulder to the left, and there also were neither legs nor boots. He was irradiated by the dawn of a great amazement. "Where *are* yer?" said Mr. Thomas Marvel over his shoulder and coming round on all-fours. He saw a stretch of empty downs with the wind swaying the remote green-pointed furze bushes.

"Am I drunk?" said Mr. Marvel. "Have I had visions? Was I talking to myself? What the——"

"Don't be alarmed," said a voice.

"None of your ventriloquising *me*," said Mr. Thomas Marvel, rising sharply to his feet. "Where *are* yer? Alarmed, indeed!"

"Don't be alarmed," repeated the voice.

"*You'll* be alarmed in a minute, you silly fool," said Mr Thomas Marvel. "Where *are* yer? Lemme get my mark on yer——

"Are you *buried*?" said Mr. Thomas Marvel, after an interval.

There was no answer. Mr. Thomas Marvel stood bootless and amazed, his jacket nearly thrown off.

"Peewit," said a peewit, very remote.

"Peewit, indeed!" said Mr. Thomas Marvel. "This ain't no time for foolery." The down was desolate, east and west, north and south; the road, with its shallow ditches and white bordering stakes, ran smooth and empty north and south, and, save for that peewit, the blue sky was empty too. "So help me," said Mr. Thomas Marvel, shuffling his coat on to his shoulders again "It's the drink! I might ha' known."

"It's not the drink," said the voice. "You keep your nerves steady."

"Ow!" said Mr. Marvel, and his face grew white amidst its patches. "It's the drink," his lips repeated noiselessly. He remained staring about him, rotating slowly backwards. "I could have *swore* I heard a voice," he whispered.

"Of course you did."

"It's there again," said Mr. Marvel, closing his eyes and clasping his hand on his brow with a tragic gesture. He was suddenly taken by the collar and shaken violently, and left more dazed than ever. "Don't be a fool," said the voice.

"I'm—off—my—blooming—chump," said Mr. Marvel. "It's no good. It's fretting about them blarsted boots. I'm off my blessed blooming chump. Or it's spirits."

"Neither one thing nor the other," said the voice. "Listen!"

"Chump," said Mr. Marvel.

"One minute," said the voice penetratingly—tremulous with self-control.

"Well?" said Mr. Thomas Marvel, with a strange feeling of having been dug in the chest by a finger.

"You think I'm just imagination? Just imagination?"

"What else *can* you be?" said Mr. Thomas Marvel, rubbing the back of his neck.

"Very well," said the voice, in a tone of relief. "Then I'm going to throw flints at you till you think differently."

"But where *are* yer?"

The voice made no answer. Whizz came a flint, apparently out of the air, and missed Mr. Marvel's shoulder by a hair's breadth. Mr. Marvel, turning, saw a flint jerk up into the air, trace a complicated path, hang for a moment, and then fling at his feet with almost invisible rapidity. He was too amazed to dodge. Whizz it came, and ricochetted from a bare toe into the ditch. Mr. Thomas Marvel jumped a foot and howled aloud. Then he started to run, tripped over an unseen obstacle, and came head over heels into a sitting position.

"*Now*," said the voice, as a third stone curved upward and hung in the air above the tramp. "Am I imagination?"

Mr. Marvel by way of reply struggled to his feet, and was immediately rolled over again. He lay quiet for a moment. "If you struggle any more," said the voice, "I shall throw the flint at your head."

"It's a fair do," said Mr. Thomas Marvel, sitting up, taking his wounded toe in hand and fixing his eye on the third missile. "I don't understand it. Stones flinging themselves. Stones talking. Put yourself down. Rot away. I'm done."

The third flint fell.

"It's very simple," said the voice. "I'm an invisible man."

"Tell us something I don't know," said Mr. Marvel, gasping with pain. "Where you've hid—how you do it—I *don't* know. I'm beat."

"That's all," said the voice. "I'm invisible. That's what I want you to understand."

"Any one could see that. There is no need for you to be so confounded impatient, mister. *Now* then. Give us a notion. How are you hid?"

"I'm invisible. That's the great point. And what I want you to understand is this——"

"But whereabouts?" interrupted Mr. Marvel.

"Here! Six yards in front of you."

"Oh, *come!* I ain't blind. You'll be telling me next you're just thin air. I'm not one of your ignorant tramps——"

"Yes, I am—thin air. You're looking through me."

"What! Ain't there any stuff to you? *Vox et*—what is it?—jabber. Is it that?"

"I am just a human being—solid, needing food and drink

needing covering too—— But I'm invisible. You see ? Invisible. Simple idea. Invisible."

" What, real like ? "

" Yes, real."

" Let's have a hand of you," said Marvel, " if you *are* real. It won't be so darn out-of-the-way like, then—— *Lord !* " he said, " how you made me jump !—gripping me like that ! "

He felt the hand that had closed round his wrist with his disengaged fingers, and his touch went timorously up the arm, patted a muscular chest, and explored a bearded face. Marvel's face was astonishment.

" I'm dashed ! " he said. " If this don't beat cock-fighting ! Most remarkable !—— And there I can see a rabbit clean through you, 'arf a mile away ! Not a bit of you visible —except——"

He scrutinised the apparently empty space keenly. " You 'aven't been eatin' bread and cheese ? " he asked, holding the invisible arm.

" You're quite right, and it's not quite assimilated into the system."

" Ah ! " said Mr. Marvel. " Sort of ghostly, though."

" Of course, all this isn't half so wonderful as you think."

" It's quite wonderful enough for *my* modest wants," said Mr. Thomas Marvel. " Howjer manage it ! How the dooce is it done ? "

" It's too long a story. And besides——"

" I tell you, the whole business fair beats me," said Mr. Marvel.

" What I want to say at present is this : I need help. I have come to that—I came upon you suddenly. I was wandering, mad with rage, naked, impotent. I could have murdered. And I saw you——"

" *Lord !* " said Mr. Marvel.

" I came up behind you—hesitated—went on——"

Mr. Marvel's expression was eloquent.

" — then stopped. ' Here,' I said, ' is an outcast like myself. This is the man for me.' So I turned back and came to you—you. And——"

" *Lord !* " said Mr. Marvel. " But I'm all in a dizzy. May I ask—How is it ? And what you may be requiring in the way of help ?— Invisible ! "

" I want you to help me get clothes—and shelter—and then, with other things. I've left them long enough. If you won't—well ! But you *will—must.*"

" Look here," said Mr. Marvel. " I'm too flabbergasted. Don't knock me about any more. And leave me go. I must get steady a bit. And you've pretty near broken my toe. It's all so unreasonable. Empty downs, empty sky. Nothing visible for miles except the bosom of Nature. And then comes

a voice.   A voice out of heaven !   And stones !   And a fist—
Lord ! "

" Pull yourself together," said the voice, " for you have to do
the job I've chosen for you."

Mr. Marvel blew out his cheeks, and his eyes were round.

" I've chosen you," said the voice.   " You are the only man
except some of those fools down there, who knows there is such
a thing as an invisible man.   You have to be my helper.
Help me—and I will do great things for you.   An invisible
man is a man of power."   He stopped for a moment to sneeze
violently.

" But if you betray me," he said, " if you fail to do as I
direct you——"

He paused and tapped Mr. Marvel's shoulder smartly.   Mr.
Marvel gave a yelp of terror at the touch.   " I don't want to
betray you," said Mr. Marvel, edging away from the direction
of the fingers.   " Don't you go a-thinking that, whatever
you do.   All I want to do is to help you—just tell me what I
got to do.   (Lord !)   Whatever you want done, that I'm most
willing to do."

CHAPTER TEN

AFTER the first gusty panic had spent itself, Iping became argumentative. Scepticism suddenly reared its
head—rather nervous scepticism, not at all assured of
its back, but scepticism nevertheless. It is so much easier not
to believe in an invisible man ; and those who had actually
seen him dissolve into air, or felt the strength of his arm, could
be counted on the fingers of two hands. And of these witnesses Mr. Wadgers was presently missing, having retired
impregnably behind the bolts and bars of his own house, and
Jaffers was lying stunned in the parlour of the Coach and
Horses. Great and strange ideas transcending experience
often have less effect upon men and women than smaller, more
tangible considerations. Iping was gay with bunting, and
everybody was in gala dress. Whit-Monday had been looked
forward to for a month or more. By the afternoon even those
who believed in the Unseen were beginning to resume their
little amusements in a tentative fashion, on the supposition
that he had quite gone away, and with the sceptics he was
already a jest. But people, sceptics and believers alike, were
remarkably sociable all that day.

Hayman's meadow was gay with a tent, in which Mrs.
Bunting and other ladies were preparing tea, while, without,
the Sunday-school children ran races and played games under
the noisy guidance of the curate and the Misses Cuss and Sack-
but. No doubt there was a slight uneasiness in the air, but
people for the most part had the sense to conceal whatever
imaginative qualms they experienced. On the village green
an inclined string, down which, clinging the while to a pulley-
swung handle, one could be hurled violently against a sack
at the other end, came in for considerable favour among the
adolescent. There were swings and coco-nut shies and
promenading, and the steam organ attached to the swings
filled the air with a pungent flavour of oil and with equally
pungent music. Members of the Club, who had attended
church in the morning, were splendid in badges of pink and
green, and some of the gayer-minded had also adorned their
bowler hats with brilliant-coloured favours of ribbon. Old
Fletcher, whose conceptions of holiday-making were severe,
was visible through the jasmine about his window or through
the open door (whichever way you chose to look), poised
delicately on a plank supported on two chairs, and white-
washing the ceiling of his front room.

About four o'clock a stranger entered the village from the
direction of the downs. He was a short, stout person in an
extraordinarily shabby top hat, and he appeared to be very

much out of breath. His cheeks were alternately limp and tightly puffed. His mottled face was apprehensive, and he moved with a sort of reluctant alacrity. He turned the corner by the church, and directed his way to the Coach and Horses. Among others old Fletcher remembers seeing him, and indeed the old gentleman was so struck by his peculiar agitation that he inadvertently allowed a quantity of white-wash to run down the brush into the sleeve of his coat while regarding him.

This stranger, to the perceptions of the proprietor of the coco-nut shy, appeared to be talking to himself, and Mr. Huxter remarked the same thing. He stopped at the foot of the Coach and Horses steps, and, according to Mr. Huxter, appeared to undergo a severe internal struggle before he could induce himself to enter the house. Finally he marched up the steps, and was seen by Mr. Huxter to turn to the left and open the door of the parlour. Mr. Huxter heard voices from within the room and from the bar apprising the man of his error. " That room's private ! " said Hall, and the stranger shut the door clumsily and went into the bar.

In the course of a few minutes he reappeared, wiping his lips with the back of his hand with an air of quiet satisfaction that somehow impressed Mr. Huxter as assumed. He stood looking about him for some moments, and then Mr. Huxter saw him walk in an oddly furtive manner towards the gates of the yard, upon which the parlour window opened. The stranger, after some hesitation, leant against one of the gate-posts, produced a short clay pipe, and prepared to fill it. His fingers trembled while doing so. He lit it clumsily, and fold-ing his arms began to smoke in a languid attitude, an attitude which his occasional quick glances up the yard altogether belied.

All this Mr. Huxter saw over the canisters of the tobacco window, and the singularity of the man's behaviour prompted him to maintain his observation.

Presently the stranger stood up abruptly and put his pipe in his pocket. Then he vanished into the yard. Forthwith Mr. Huxter, conceiving he was witness of some petty larceny, leapt round his counter and ran out into the road to intercept the thief. As he did so, Mr. Marvel reappeared, his hat askew, a big bundle in a blue table-cloth in one hand, and three books tied together—as it proved afterwards with the Vicar's braces —in the other. Directly he saw Huxter he gave a sort of gasp, and turning sharply to the left, began to run. " Stop thief ! " cried Huxter, and set off after him. Mr. Huxter's sensations were vivid but brief. He saw the man just before him and spurting briskly for the church corner and the hill road. He saw the village flags and festivities beyond, and a face or so turned towards him. He bawled, " Stop ! " again. He had hardly gone ten strides before his shin was caught in some mysterious fashion, and he was no longer running, but flying with inconceivable rapidity through the air. He saw the ground suddenly close to his face. The world seemed to splash into a million whirling specks of light, and subsequent proceedings interested him no more.

CHAPTER ELEVEN

Now in order clearly to understand what had happened in the inn, it is necessary to go back to the moment when Mr. Marvel first came into view of Mr. Huxter's window. At that precise moment Mr. Cuss and Mr. Bunting were in the parlour. They were seriously investigating the strange occurrences of the morning, and were, with Mr. Hall's permission, making a thorough examination of the Invisible Man's belongings. Jaffers had partially recovered from his fall and had gone home in the charge of his sympathetic friends. The stranger's scattered garments had been removed by Mrs. Hall and the room tidied up. And on the table under the window where the stranger had been wont to work, Cuss had hit almost at once on three big books in manuscript labelled " Diary."

" Diary ! " said Cuss, putting the three books on the table. " Now, at any rate, we shall learn something." The Vicar stood with his hands on the table.

" Diary," repeated Cuss, sitting down, putting two volumes to support the third, and opening it. " H'm —no name on the fly-leaf. Bother !—cypher. And figures."

The Vicar came round to look over his shoulder.

Cuss turned the pages over with a face suddenly disappointed. " I'm—dear me ! It's all cypher, Bunting."

" There are no diagrams ? " asked Mr. Bunting. " No illustrations throwing light——"

" See for yourself," said Mr. Cuss. " Some of it's mathematical and some of it's Russian or some such language (to judge by the letters), and some of it's Greek. Now the Greek I thought *you*——"

" Of course," said Mr. Bunting, taking out and wiping his spectacles and feeling suddenly very uncomfortable—for he had no Greek left in his mind worth talking about ; " yes— the Greek, of course, may furnish a clue."

" I'll find you a place."

" I'd rather glance through the volumes first," said Mr. Bunting, still wiping. " A general impression first, Cuss, and *then,* you know, we can go looking for clues."

He coughed, put on his glasses, arranged them fastidiously, coughed again, and wished something would happen to avert the seemingly inevitable exposure. Then he took the volume Cuss handed him in a leisurely manner. And then something did happen.

The door opened suddenly.

Both gentlemen started violently, looked round, and were relieved to see a sporadically rosy face beneath a furry silk hat. " Tap ? " asked the face, and stood staring.

"No," said both gentlemen at once.

"Over the other side, my man," said Mr. Bunting. And "Please shut that door," said Mr. Cuss, irritably.

"All right," said the intruder, as it seemed, in a low voice curiously different from the huskiness of its first inquiry. "Right you are," said the intruder in the former voice. "Stand clear!" and he vanished and closed the door.

"A sailor, I should judge," said Mr. Bunting. "Amusing fellows they are. Stand clear! indeed. A nautical term referring to his getting back out of the room, I suppose."

"I dare say so," said Cuss. "My nerves are all loose to-day. It quite made me jump—the door opening like that."

Mr. Bunting smiled as if he had not jumped. "And now," he said with a sigh, "these books."

"One minute," said Cuss, and went and locked the door. "Now I think we are safe from interruption."

Some one sniffed as he did so.

"One thing is indisputable," said Bunting, drawing up a chair next to that of Cuss. "There certainly have been very strange things happen in Iping during the last few days—very strange. I cannot of course believe in this absurd invisibility story——"

"It's incredible," said Cuss—"incredible. But the fact remains that I saw—I certainly saw right down his sleeve——"

"But did you—are you sure? Suppose a mirror, for instance—hallucinations are so easily produced. I don't know if you have ever seen a really good conjuror——"

"I won't argue again," said Cuss. "We've thrashed that out, Bunting. And just now there's these books—Ah! here's some of what I take to be Greek! Greek letters certainly."

He pointed to the middle of the page. Mr. Bunting flushed slightly and brought his face nearer, apparently finding some difficulty with his glasses. Suddenly he became aware of a strange feeling at the nape of his neck. He tried to raise his head, and encountered an immovable resistance. The feeling was a curious pressure, the grip of a heavy, firm hand, and it bore his chin irresistibly to the table. "*Don't move, little men,*" whispered a voice, "*or I'll brain you both!*" He looked into the face of Cuss, close to his own, and each saw a horrified reflection of his own sickly astonishment.

"I'm sorry to handle you roughly," said the Voice, "but it's unavoidable.

"Since when did you learn to pry into an investigator's private memoranda?" said the Voice; and two chins struck the table simultaneously, and two sets of teeth rattled.

"Since when did you learn to invade the private rooms of a man in misfortune?" and the concussion was repeated.

"Where have they put my clothes?

" Listen," said the Voice. " The windows are fastened and I've taken the key out of the door. I am a fairly strong man, and I have the poker handy—besides being invisible. There's not the slightest doubt that I could kill you both and get away quite easily if I wanted to—do you understand ? Very well. If I let you go will you promise not to try any nonsense and do what I tell you ? "

The Vicar and the Doctor looked at one another, and the Doctor pulled a face. " Yes," said Mr. Bunting, and the Doctor repeated it. Then the pressure on the necks relaxed, and the Doctor and the Vicar sat up, both very red in the face and wriggling their heads.

" Please keep sitting where you are," said the Invisible Man. " Here's the poker, you see.

" When I came into this room," continued the Invisible Man, after presenting the poker to the tip of the nose of each of his visitors, " I did not expect to find it occupied, and I expected to find, in addition to my books of memoranda, an outfit of clothing. Where is it ? No—don't rise. I can see it's gone. Now, just at present, though the days are quite warm enough for an invisible man to run about stark, the evenings are chilly. I want clothing—and other accommodation ; and I must also have those three books."

CHAPTER TWELVE

THE INVISIBLE MAN LOSES HIS TEMPER

IT is unavoidable that at this point the narrative should break off again, for a certain very painful reason that will presently be apparent. While these things were going on in the parlour, and while Mr. Huxter was watching Mr. Marvel smoking his pipe against the gate, not a dozen yards away were Mr. Hall and Teddy Henfrey discussing in a state of cloudy puzzlement the one Iping topic.

Suddenly there came a violent thud against the door of the parlour, a sharp cry, and then—silence.

" *Hul*—lo ! " said Teddy Henfrey.

" Hul—*lo !* " from the Tap.

Mr. Hall took things in slowly but surely. " That ain't right," he said, and came round from behind the bar towards the parlour door.

He and Teddy approached the door together, with intent faces. Their eyes considered. " Summat wrong," said Hall, and Henfrey nodded agreement. Whiffs of an unpleasant chemical odour met them, and there was a muffled sound of conversation, very rapid and subdued.

" You all raight thur ? " asked Hall, rapping.

The muttered conversation ceased abruptly, for a moment silence, then the conversation was resumed in hissing whispers, than a sharp cry of " No ! no, you don't ! " There came a sudden motion and the oversetting of a chair, a brief struggle. Silence again.

" What the dooce ? " exclaimed Henfrey, *sotto voce*.

" You—all—raight—thur ? " asked Mr. Hall sharply, again.

The Vicar's voice answered with a curious jerking intonation : " Quite ri—ight. Please don't—interrupt."

" Odd ! " said Mr. Henfrey.

" Odd ! " said Mr. Hall.

" Says, ' Don't interrupt,' " said Henfrey.

" I heerd 'n," said Hall.

" And a sniff," said Henfrey.

They remained listening. The conversation was rapid and subdued. " I *can't*," said Mr. Bunting, his voice rising ; " I tell you, sir, I *will* not."

" What was that ? " asked Henfrey.

" Says he wi' nart," said Hall. " Warn't speakin' to us, wuz he ? "

" Disgraceful ! " said Mr. Bunting, within.

" ' Disgraceful,' " said Mr. Henfrey. " I heard it —*distinct*.

" Who's that speaking now ? " asked Henfrey.

" Mr. Cuss, I s'pose," said Hall. " Can you hear—anything ? "

Silence. The sounds within indistinct and perplexing.

" Sounds like throwing the table-cloth about," said Hall.

Mrs. Hall appeared behind the bar. Hall made gestures of silence and invitation. This roused Mrs. Hall's wifely opposition. " What yer listenin' there for, Hall ? " she asked. " Ain't you nothin' better to do—busy day like this ? "

Hall tried to convey everything by grimaces and dumb show, but Mrs. Hall was obdurate. She raised her voice. So Hall and Henfrey, rather crestfallen, tiptoed back to the bar, gesticulating to explain to her.

At first she refused to see anything in what they had heard at all. Then she insisted on Hall keeping silence, while Henfrey told her his story. She was inclined to think the whole business nonsense—perhaps they were just moving the furniture about. " I heerd 'n say ' disgraceful ' ; *that* I did," said Hall.

" *I* heerd that, Mis' Hall," said Henfrey.

" Like as not——" began Mrs. Hall.

" Hsh ! " said Mr. Teddy Henfrey. " Didn't I hear the window ? "

" What window ? " asked Mrs. Hall.

" Parlour window," said Henfrey.

Every one stood listening intently. Mrs. Hall's eyes, directed straight before her, saw without seeing the brilliant oblong of the inn door, the road white and vivid, and Huxter's shop-front blistering in the June sun. Abruptly Huxter's door opened and Huxter appeared, eyes staring with excitement, arms gesticulating. " *Yap !* " cried Huxter. " Stop thief ! " and he ran obliquely across the oblong towards the yard gates, and vanished.

Simultaneously came a tumult from the parlour, and a sound of windows being closed.

Hall, Henfrey, and the human contents of the Tap rushed out at once pell-mell into the street. They saw some one whisk round the corner towards the down road, and Mr. Huxter executing a complicated leap in the air that ended on his face and shoulder. Down the street people were standing astonished or running towards them.

Mr. Huxter was stunned. Henfrey stopped to discover this, but Hall and the two labourers from the Tap rushed at once to the corner, shouting incoherent things, and saw Mr. Marvel vanishing by the corner of the church wall. They appear to have jumped to the impossible conclusion that this was the Invisible Man suddenly become visible, and set off at once along the lane in pursuit. But Hall had hardly run a dozen yards before he gave a loud shout of astonishment and went flying headlong sideways, clutching one of the labourers and bringing him to the ground. He had been charged just as one charges a man at football. The second labourer came round in a circle, stared, and conceiving that Hall had tumbled over of his own accord, turned to resume the pursuit, only to be tripped by the ankle just as Huxter had been. Then, as the first labourer struggled to his feet, he was kicked sideways by a blow that might have felled an ox.

As he went down, the rush from the direction of the village green came round the corner. The first to appear was the proprietor of the coco-nut shy, a burly man in a blue jersey. He was astonished to see the lane empty save for three men sprawling absurdly on the ground. And then something happened to his rearmost foot, and he went headlong and rolled sideways just in time to graze the feet of his brother and partner, following headlong. The two were then kicked, knelt on, fallen over, and cursed by quite a number of over-hasty people.

Now when Hall and Henfrey and the labourers ran out of the house, Mrs. Hall, who had been disciplined by years of experience, remained in the bar next the till. And suddenly the parlour door was opened, and Mr. Cuss appeared, and without glancing at her rushed at once down the steps towards the corner. "Hold him!" he cried. "Don't let him drop that parcel! You can see him so long as he holds the parcel." He knew nothing of the existence of Marvel. For the Invisible Man had handed over the books and bundle in the yard. The face of Mr. Cuss was angry and resolute, but his costume was defective, a sort of limp white kilt that could only have passed muster in Greece. "Hold him!" he bawled. "He's got my trousers! And every stitch of the Vicar's clothes!"

"'Tend to him in a minute!" he cried to Henfrey as he passed the prostrate Huxter, and coming round the corner to join the tumult, was promptly knocked off his feet into an indecorous sprawl. Somebody in full flight trod heavily on his finger. He yelled, struggled to regain his feet, was knocked against and thrown on all-fours again, and became aware that he was involved not in a capture, but a rout. Every one was running back to the village. He rose again and was hit severely behind the ear. He staggered and set off back to the Coach and Horses forthwith, leaping over the deserted Huxter, who was now sitting up, on his way.

Behind him as he was halfway up the inn steps he heard a sudden yell of rage rising sharply out of the confusion of cries, and a sounding smack in some one's face. He recognised the voice as that of the Invisible Man, and the note was that of a man suddenly infuriated by a painful blow.

In another moment Mr. Cuss was back in the parlour. "He's coming back, Bunting!" he said, rushing in. "Save yourself! He's gone mad!"

Mr. Bunting was standing in the window engaged in an attempt to clothe himself in the hearth-rug and a *West Surrey Gazette*. "Who's coming?" he said, so startled that his costume narrowly escaped disintegration.

" Invisible Man," said Cuss, and rushed to the window.
" We'd better clear out from here! He's fighting mad!
Mad!"

In another moment he was out in the yard.

" Good heavens!" said Mr. Bunting, hesitating between
two horrible alternatives. He heard a frightful struggle in
the passage of the inn, and his decision was made. He
clambered out of the window, adjusted his costume hastily,
and fled up the village as fast as his fat little legs would carry
him.

From the moment when the Invisible Man screamed with
rage and Mr. Bunting made his memorable flight up the
village, it became impossible to give a consecutive account of
affairs in Iping. Possibly the Invisible Man's original intention
was simply to cover Marvel's retreat with the clothes and
books. But his temper, at no time very good, seems to have
gone completely at some chance blow, and forthwith he set to
smiting and overthrowing, for the mere satisfaction of hurting.

You must figure the street full of running figures, of doors
slamming and fights for hiding-places. You must figure the
tumult suddenly striking on the unstable equilibrium of old
Fletcher's planks and two chairs—with cataclysmal results.
You must figure an appalled couple caught dismally in a
swing. And then the whole tumultuous rush has passed and
the Iping street with its gauds and flags is deserted save for
the still raging Unseen, and littered with coco-nuts, overthrown
canvas screens, and the scattered stock in trade of a sweetstuff
stall. Everywhere there is a sound of closing shutters and
shoving bolts, and the only visible humanity is an occasional
flitting eye under a raised eyebrow in the corner of a window
pane.

The Invisible Man amused himself for a little while by
breaking all the windows in the Coach and Horses, and then
he thrust a street lamp through the parlour window of Mrs.
Gribble. He it must have been who cut the telegraph wire
to Adderdean just beyond Higgins' cottage on the Adderdean
road. And after that, as his peculiar qualities allowed, he
passed out of human perceptions altogether, and he was
neither heard, seen, nor felt in Iping any more. He vanished
absolutely.

But it was the best part of two hours before any human
being ventured out again into the desolation of Iping street.

CHAPTER THIRTEEN

MR. MARVEL DISCUSSES HIS RESIGNATION

WHEN the dusk was gathering and Iping was just beginning to peep timorously forth again upon the shattered wreckage of its Bank Holiday, a short, thickset man in a shabby silk hat was marching painfully through the twilight behind the beechwoods on the road to Bramblehurst. He carried three books bound together by some sort of ornamental elastic ligature, and a bundle wrapped in a blue tablecloth. His rubicund face expressed consternation and fatigue ; he appeared to be in a spasmodic sort of hurry. He was accompanied by a Voice other than his own, and ever and again he winced under the touch of unseen hands.

" If you give me the slip again," said the Voice ; " if you attempt to give me the slip again——"

" Lord ! " said Mr. Marvel. " That shoulder's a mass of bruises as it is."

" —on my honour," said the Voice, " I will kill you."

" I didn't try to give you the slip," said Marvel in a voice that was not far remote from tears. " I swear I didn't. I didn't know the blessed turning, that was all ! How the devil was I to know the blessed turning ? As it is, I've been knocked about——"

" You'll get knocked about a great deal more if you don't mind," said the Voice, and Mr. Marvel abruptly became silent. He blew out his cheeks, and his eyes were eloquent of despair.

" It's bad enough to let these floundering yokels explode my little secret, without *your* cutting off with my books. It's lucky for some of them they cut and ran when they did ! Here am I—— No one knew I was invisible ! And now what am I to do ? "

" What am *I* to do ? " asked Marvel, *sotto voce*.

" It's all about. It will be in the papers ! Everybody will be looking for me ; every one on their guard——" The Voice broke off into vivid curses and ceased.

The despair of Mr. Marvel's face deepened, and his pace slacked.

" Go on ! " said the Voice.

Mr. Marvel's face assumed a greyish tint between the ruddier patches.

" Don't drop those books, stupid," said the Voice, sharply— overtaking him.

" The fact is," said the Voice, " I shall have to make use of you. You're a poor tool, but I must."

" I'm a *miserable* tool," said Marvel.

" You are," said the Voice.

" I'm the worst possible tool you could have," said Marvel.

" I'm not strong," he said after a discouraging silence.

" I'm not over strong," he repeated.

" No ? "

" And my heart's weak. That little business—I pulled it through, of course—but bless you ! I could have dropped."

" Well ? "

" I haven't the nerve and strength for the sort of thing you want."

" *I'll* stimulate you."

" I wish you wouldn't. I wouldn't like to mess up your plans, you know. But I might—out of sheer funk and misery."

" You'd better not," said the Voice, with quiet emphasis.

" I wish I was dead," said Marvel.

" It ain't justice," he said ; " you must admit—— It seems to me I've a perfect right——"

" *Get* on ! " said the Voice.

Mr. Marvel mended his pace, and for a time they went in silence again.

" It's devilish hard," said Mr. Marvel.

This was quite ineffectual. He tried another tack.

" What do I make by it ? " he began again in a tone of unendurable wrong.

" Oh ! *shut up !* " said the Voice, with sudden amazing vigour. " I'll see to you all right. You do what you're told. You'll do it all right. You're a fool and all that, but you'll do——"

" I tell you, sir, I'm not the man for it. Respectfully— but it is so——"

" If you don't shut up I shall twist your wrist again," said the Invisible Man. " I want to think."

Presently two oblongs of yellow light appeared through the trees, and the square tower of a church loomed through the gloaming. " I shall keep my hand on your shoulder," said the Voice, " all through the village. Go straight through and try no foolery. It will be the worse for you if you do."

" I know that," sighed Mr. Marvel, " I know all that."

The unhappy-looking figure in the obsolete silk hat passed up the street of the little village with his burdens, and vanished into the gathering darkness beyond the lights of the windows.

TEN o'clock the next morning found Mr. Marvel, un-shaven, dirty, and travel-stained, sitting with the books beside him and his hands deep in his pockets, looking very weary, nervous, and uncomfortable, and in-flating his cheeks at frequent intervals, on the bench outside a little inn on the outskirts of Port Stowe. Beside him were the books, but now they were tied with string. The bundle had been abandoned in the pine woods beyond Bramblehurst, in accordance with a change in the plans of the Invisible Man. Mr. Marvel sat on the bench, and although no one took the slightest notice of him, his agitation remained at fever heat. His hands would go ever and again to his various pockets with a curious nervous fumbling.

When he had been sitting for the best part of an hour however, an elderly mariner, carrying a newspaper, came out of the inn and sat down beside him. " Pleasant day," said the mariner.

Mr. Marvel glanced about him with something very like terror. " Very," he said.

" Just seasonable weather for the time of year," said the mariner, taking no denial.

" Quite," said Mr. Marvel.

The mariner produced a toothpick, and (saving his regard) was engrossed thereby for some minutes. His eyes meanwhile were at liberty to examine Mr. Marvel's dusty figure and the books beside him. As he had approached Mr. Marvel he had heard a sound like the dropping of coins into a pocket. He was struck by the contrast of Mr. Marvel's appearance with this suggestion of opulence. Thence his mind wandered back again to a topic that had taken a curiously firm hold of his imagination.

" Books ? " he said suddenly, noisily finishing with the toothpick.

Mr. Marvel started and looked at them. " Oh, yes," he said. " Yes, they're books."

" There's some extraordinary things in books," said the mariner.

" I believe you," said Mr. Marvel.

" And some extra-ordinary things out of 'em," said the mariner.

" True likewise," said Mr. Marvel. He eyed his interlocutor, and then glanced about him.

" There's some extraordinary things in newspapers, for example," said the mariner.

" There are."

" In *this* newspaper," said the mariner.

" Ah ! " said Mr. Marvel.

" There's a story," said the mariner, fixing Mr. Marvel with an eye that was firm and deliberate ; " there's a story about an Invisible Man, for instance."

Mr. Marvel pulled his mouth askew and scratched his cheek and felt his ears glowing. " What will they be writing next ? " he asked faintly. " Ostria, or America ? "

" Neither," said the mariner. " *Here !* "

" Lord ! " said Mr. Marvel, starting.

" When I say *here*," said the mariner, to Mr. Marvel's intense relief, " I don't of course mean here in this place, I mean hereabouts."

" An Invisible Man ! " said Mr. Marvel. " And what's *he* been up to ? "

" Everything," said the mariner, controlling Marvel with his eye, and then amplifying : " Every Blessed Thing."

" I ain't seen a paper these four days," said Marvel.

" Iping's the place he started at," said the mariner.

" In-*deed !* " said Mr. Marvel.

" He started there. And where he came from, nobody don't seem to know. Here it is : Pe Culiar Story from Iping. And it says in this paper that the evidence is extraordinary strong—extra-ordinary."

" Lord ! " said Mr. Marvel.

" But then, it's a extra-ordinary story. There is a clergyman and a medical gent witnesses—saw 'im all right and proper —or leastways, didn't see 'im. He was staying, it says, at the Coach an' Horses, and no one don't seem to have been aware of his misfortune, it says, aware of his misfortune, until in an Alteration in the inn, it says, his bandages on his head was torn off. It was then ob-served that his head was invisible. Attempts were At Once made to secure him, but casting off his garments, it says, he succeeded in escaping, but not until after a desperate struggle. In Which he had inflicted serious injuries, it says, on our worthy and able constable, Mr. J. A. Jaffers. Pretty straight story, eigh ? Names and everything."

" Lord ! " said Mr. Marvel, looking nervously about him, trying to count the money in his pockets by his unaided sense of touch, and full of a strange and novel idea. " It sounds most astonishing."

" Don't it ? Extra-ordinary, *I* call it. Never heard tell of Invisible Men before, I haven't, but nowadays one hears such a lot of extra-ordinary things—that——"

" That all he did ? " asked Marvel, trying to seem at his ease.

" It's enough, ain't it ? " said the mariner.

" Didn't go Back by any chance ? " asked Marvel. " Just escaped and that's all, eh ? "

" All ! " said the mariner. " Why !—ain't it enough ? "

" Quite enough," said Marvel.

" I should think it was enough," said the mariner. " I should think it was enough."

" He didn't have any pals—it don't say he had any pals, does it ? " asked Mr. Marvel, anxious.

" Ain't one of a sort enough for you ? " asked the mariner. " No, thank Heaven, as one might say, he didn't."

He nodded his head slowly. " It makes me regular uncomfortable, the bare thought of that chap running about the country ! He is at present At Large, and from certain evidence it is supposed that he has—taken—*took*, I suppose they mean—the road to Port Stowe. You see we're right *in* it ! None of your American wonders, this time. And just think of the things he might do ! Where'd you be, if he took a drop over and above, and had a fancy to go for you ? Suppose he wants to rob—who can prevent him ? He can trespass, he can burgle, he could walk through a cordon of policemen as easy as me or you could give the slip to a blind man ! Easier ! For these here blind chaps hear uncommon sharp, I'm told. And wherever there was liquor he fancied———"

" He's got a tremenjous advantage, certainly," said Mr. Marvel. " And—well."

" You're right," said the mariner. " He *has*."

All this time Mr. Marvel had been glancing about him intently, listening for faint footfalls, trying to detect imperceptible movements. He seemed on the point of some great resolution. He coughed behind his hand.

He looked about him again, listened, bent towards the mariner, and lowered his voice : " The fact of it is—I happen—to know just a thing or two about this Invisible Man. From private sources."

" Oh ! " said the mariner, interested. " *You ?* "

" Yes," said Mr. Marvel. " Me."

" Indeed ! " said the mariner. " And may I ask———"

" You'll be astonished," said Mr. Marvel behind his hand. " It's tremenjous."

" Indeed ! " said the mariner.

" The fact is," began Mr. Marvel eagerly in a confidential undertone. Suddenly his expression changed marvellously. " Ow ! " he said. He rose stiffly in his seat. His face was eloquent of physical suffering. " Wow ! " he said.

" What's up ? " said the mariner, concerned.

" Toothache," said Mr. Marvel, and put his hand to his ear. He caught hold of his books. " I must be getting on, I think," he said. He edged in a curious way along the seat away from his interlocutor. " But you was just agoing to tell me about this here Invisible Man ! " protested the mariner. Mr. Marvel seemed to consult with himself. " Hoax," said a voice. It's a hoax," said Mr. Marvel.

" But it's in the paper," said the mariner.

" Hoax all the same," said Marvel. " I know the chap that started the lie. There ain't no Invisible Man whatsoever —Blimey."

" But how 'bout this paper ? D'you mean to say—— ? "

" Not a word of it," said Marvel, stoutly.

The mariner stared, paper in hand. Mr. Marvel jerkily faced about. " Wait a bit," said the mariner, rising, and speaking slowly. " D'you mean to say—— ? "

" I do," said Mr. Marvel.

" Then why did you let me go on and tell you all this blarsted stuff, then ? What d'yer mean by letting a man make a fool of himself like that for ? Eigh ? "

Mr. Marvel blew out his cheeks. The mariner was suddenly very red indeed ; he clenched his hands. " I been talking here this ten minutes," he said ; " and you, you little pot-belied, leathery-faced son of an old boot, couldn't have the elementary manners——"

" Don't you come bandying words with *me*," said Mr. Marvel.

" Bandying words ! I'm a jolly good mind——"

" Come up," said a voice, and Mr. Marvel was suddenly whirled about and started marching off in a curious spasmodic manner. " You'd better move on," said the mariner. " *Who's* moving on ? " said Mr. Marvel. He was receding obliquely with a curious hurrying gait, with occasional violent jerks forward. Some way along the road he began a muttered monologue, protests and recriminations.

" Silly devil ! " said the mariner, legs wide apart, elbows akimbo, watching the receding figure. " I'll show you, you silly ass—hoaxing *me* ! It's here—on the paper ! "

Mr. Marvel retorted incoherently, and, receding, was hidden by a bend in the road, but the mariner still stood magnificent in the midst of the way, until the approach of a butcher's cart dislodged him. Then he turned himself towards Port Stowe. " Full of extra-ordinary asses," he said softly to himself. " Just to take me down a bit—that was his silly game—— It's on the paper ! "

And there was another extraordinary thing he was presently to hear, that had happened quite close to him. And that was a vision of a " fist full of money " (no less) travelling without visible agency, along by the wall at the corner of St. Michael's Lane. A brother mariner had seen this wonderful sight that very morning. He had snatched at the money forthwith and had been knocked headlong, and when he had got to his feet the butterfly money had vanished. Our mariner was in the mood to believe anything, he declared, but that was a bit *too* stiff. Afterwards, however, he began to think things over.

The story of the flying money was true. And all about that neighbourhood, even from the august London and Country Banking Company, from the tills of shops and inns—doors standing that sunny weather entirely open—money had been quietly and dexterously making off that day in handfuls and rouleaux, floating quietly along by walls and shady places, dodging quickly from the approaching eyes of men. And it had, though no man had traced it, invariably ended its mysterious flight in the pocket of that agitated gentleman in the obsolete silk hat, sitting outside the little inn on the outskirts of Port Stowe.

CHAPTER FIFTEEN

THE MAN WHO WAS RUNNING

IN the early evening time Doctor Kemp was sitting in his study in the belvedere on the hill overlooking Burdock. It was a pleasant little room, with three windows, north, west, and south, and bookshelves crowded with books and scientific publications, and a broad writing-table, and, under the north window, a microscope, glass slips, minute instruments, some cultures, and scattered bottles of reagents. Doctor Kemp's solar lamp was lit, albeit the sky was still bright with the sunset light, and his blinds were up because there was no offence of peering outsiders to require them pulled down. Doctor Kemp was a tall and slender young man, with flaxen hair and a moustache almost white, and the work he was upon would earn him, he hoped, the fellowship of the Royal Society, so highly did he think of it.

And his eye presently wandering from his work caught the sunset blazing at the back of the hill that is over against his own. For a minute perhaps he sat, pen in mouth, admiring the rich golden colour above the crest, and then his attention was attracted by the little figure of a man, inky black, running over the hill-brow towards him. He was a shortish little man, and he wore a high hat, and he was running so fast that his legs verily twinkled.

"Another of those fools," said Doctor Kemp. "Like that ass who ran into me this morning round a corner, with his ''Visible Man a-coming, sir!' I can't imagine what possesses people. One might think we were in the thirteenth century."

He got up, went to the window, and stared at the dusky hillside and the dark little figure tearing down it. "He seems in a confounded hurry," said Doctor Kemp, "but he doesn't seem to be getting on. If his pockets were full of lead, he couldn't run heavier.

"Spurted, sir," said Doctor Kemp.

In another moment the higher of the villas that had clambered up the hill from Burdock had occulted the running figure. He was visible again for a moment, and again, and then again, three times between the three detached houses that came next, and then the terrace hid him.

"Asses!" said Doctor Kemp, swinging round on his heel and walking back to his writing-table.

But those who saw the fugitive nearer, and perceived the abject teror on his perspiring face, being themselves in the open roadway, did not share in the doctor's contempt. By the man pounded, and as he ran he chinked like a well-filled purse that is tossed to and fro. He looked neither to the right nor the left, but his dilated eyes stared straight downhill to where the lamps were being lit, and the people were crowded in the street. And his ill-shaped mouth fell apart, and a glairy foam lay on his lips, and his breath came hoarse and noisy. All he passed stopped and began staring up the road and down, and interrogating one another with an inkling of discomfort for the reason of his haste.

And then presently, far up the hill, a dog playing in the road yelped and ran under a gate, and as they still wondered something—a wind—a pad, pad, pad—a sound like a panting breathing—rushed by.

People screamed. People sprang off the pavement. It passed in shouts, it passed by instinct down the hill. They were shouting in the street before Marvel was halfway there. They were bolting into houses and slamming the doors behind them, with the news. He heard it and made one last desperate spurt. Fear came striding by, rushed ahead of him, and in a moment had seized the town.

"The Invisible Man is coming ! *The Invisible Man !*"

CHAPTER SIXTEEN

IN THE JOLLY CRICKETERS

THE Jolly Cricketers is just at the bottom of the hill, where the tram-lines begin. The barman leant his fat red arms on the counter and talked of horses with an anæmic cabman, while a black-bearded man in grey snapped up biscuit and cheese, drank Burton, and conversed in America with a policeman off duty.

"What's the shouting about!" said the anæmic cabman going off at a tangent, trying to see up the hill over the dirty yellow blind in the low window of the inn. Somebody ran by outside. "Fire, perhaps," said the barman.

Footsteps approached, running heavily, the door was pushed open violently, and Marvel, weeping and dishevelled, his hat gone, the neck of his coat torn open, rushed in, made a convulsive turn, and attempted to shut the door. It was held half open by a strap.

"Coming!" he bawled, his voice shrieking with terror. "He's coming. The 'Visible Man! After me! For Gawd's sake! 'Elp! 'Elp! 'Elp!"

"Shut the doors," said the policeman. "Who's coming? What's the row?" He went to the door, released the strap, and it slammed. The American closed the other door.

"Lemme go inside," said Marvel, staggering and weeping, but still clutching the books. "Lemme go inside. Lock me in—somewhere. I tell you he's after me. I give him the slip. He said he'd kill me and he will."

"*You're* safe," said the man with the black beard. "The door's shut. What's it all about?"

"Lemme go inside," said Marvel, and shrieked aloud as a blow suddenly made the fastened door shiver and was followed by a hurried rapping and a shouting outside. "Hullo," cried the policeman, "who's there?" Mr. Marvel began to make frantic dives at panels that looked like doors. "He'll kill me—he's got a knife or something. For Gawd's sake!"

"Here you are," said the barman. "Come in here." And he held up the flap of the bar.

Mr. Marvel rushed behind the bar as the summons outside was repeated. "Don't open the door," he screamed. "*Please* don't open the door. *Where* shall I hide?"

"This, this Invisible Man, then?" asked the man with the black beard, with one hand behind him. "I guess it's about time we saw him."

The window of the inn was suddenly smashed in, and there was a screaming and running to and fro in the street. The policeman had been standing on the settee staring out, craning to see who was at the door. He got down with raised eyebrows. "It's that," he said. The barman stood in front of the bar-parlour door which was now locked on Mr. Marvel, stared at the smashed window, and came round to the two other men.

Everything was suddenly quiet. "I wish I had my truncheon," said the policeman, going irresolutely to the door. "Once we open, in he comes. There's no stopping him."

"Don't you be in too much hurry about that door," said the anæmic cabman, anxiously.

"Draw the bolts," said the man with the black beard, "and if he comes——" He showed a revolver in his hand.

"That won't do," said the policeman; "that's murder."

"I know what country I'm in," said the man with the beard. "I'm going to let off at his legs. Draw the bolts."

"Not with that thing going off behind me," said the barman, craning over the blind.

"Very well," said the man with the black beard, and stooping down, revolver ready, drew them himself. Barman, cabman, and policeman faced about.

"Come in," said the bearded man in an undertone, standing back and facing the unbolted doors with his pistol behind him. No one came in, the door remained closed. Five minutes afterwards when a second cabman pushed his head in cautiously, they were still waiting, and an anxious face peered out of the bar-parlour and supplied information. "Are all the doors of the house shut?" asked Marvel. "He's going round—prowling round. He's as artful as the devil."

"Good Lord!" said the burly barman. "There's the back! Just watch them doors! I say!——" He looked about him helplessly. The bar-parlour door slammed and they heard the key turn. "There's the yard door and the private door. The yard door——"

He rushed out of the bar.

In a minute he reappeared with a carving-knife in his hand. "The yard door was open!" he said, and his fat underlip dropped. "He may be in the house now!" said the first cabman.

"He's not in the kitchen," said the barman. "There's two women there, and I've stabbed every inch of it with this little beef slicer. And they don't think he's come in. They haven't noticed——"

"Have you fastened it?" asked the first cabman.

"I'm out of frocks," said the barman.

The man with the beard replaced his revolver. And even as he did so the flap of the bar was shut down and the bolt clicked, and then with a tremendous thud the catch of the door snapped and the bar-parlour door burst open. They heard Marvel squeal like a caught leveret, and forthwith they were clambering over the bar to his rescue. The bearded man's revolver cracked and the looking-glass at the back of the parlour was starred brightly and came smashing and tinkling down.

As the barman entered the room he saw Marvel, curiously crumpled up and struggling against the door that led to the yard and kitchen. The door flew open while the barman hesitated, and Marvel was dragged into the kitchen. There was a scream and a clatter of pans. Marvel, head down, and lugging back obstinately, was forced to the kitchen door, and the bolts were drawn.

Then the policeman, who had been trying to pass the barman, rushed in, followed by one of the cabmen, gripped the wrist of the invisible hand that collared Marvel, was hit in the face and went reeling back. The door opened, and Marvel made a frantic effort to obtain a lodgment behind it. Then the cabman clutched something. " I got him," said the cabman. The barman's red hands came clawing at the unseen. " Here he is ! " said the barman.

Mr. Marvel, released, suddenly dropped to the ground and made an attempt to crawl behind the legs of the fighting men. The struggle blundered round the edge of the door. The voice of the Invisible Man was heard for the first time, yelling out sharply, as the policeman trod on his foot. Then he cried out passionately and his fists flew round like flails. The cabman suddenly whooped and doubled up, kicked under the diaphragm. The door into the bar-parlour from the kitchen slammed and covered Mr. Marvel's retreat. The men in the kitchen found themselves clutching at and struggling with empty air.

" Where's he gone ? " cried the man with the beard. " Out ? "

" This way," said the policeman, stepping into the yard and stopping.

A piece of tile whizzed by his head and smashed among the crockery on the kitchen table.

" I'll show him," shouted the man with the black beard, and suddenly a steel barrel shone over the policeman's shoulder, and five bullets had followed one another into the twilight whence the missile had come. As he fired, the man with the beard moved his hand in a horizontal curve, so that his shots radiated out into the narrow yard like spokes from a wheel.

A silence followed. " Five cartridges," said the man with the black beard. " That's the best of all. Four aces and the joker. Get a lantern, some one, and come and feel about for his body."

CHAPTER SEVENTEEN

DOCTOR KEMP'S VISITOR

DOCTOR KEMP had continued writing in his study until the shots aroused him. Crack, crack, crack, they came one after the other.

"Hullo!" said Doctor Kemp, putting his pen into his mouth again and listening. "Who's letting off revolvers in Burdock? What are the asses at now?"

He went to the south window, threw it up, and leaning out stared down on the network of windows, beaded gas-lamps and shops with black interstices of roof and yard that made up the town at night. "Looks like a crowd down the hill," he said, "by the Cricketers," and remained watching. Thence his eyes wandered over the town to far away where the ships' lights shone, and the pier glowed, a little illuminated pavilion like a gem of yellow light. The moon in its first quarter hung over the western hill, and the stars were clear and almost tropically bright.

After five minutes, during which his mind had travelled into a remote speculation of social conditions of the future, and lost itself at last over the time dimension, Doctor Kemp roused himself with a sigh, pulled down the window again, and returned to his writing-desk.

It must have been about an hour after this that the front-door bell rang. He had been writing slackly and with intervals of abstraction, since the shots. He sat listening. He heard the servant answer the door, and waited for her feet on the staircase, but she did not come. "Wonder what that was," said Doctor Kemp.

He tried to resume his work, failed, got up, went downstairs from his study to the landing, rang, and called over the balustrade to the housemaid as she appeared in the hall below. "Was that a letter?" he asked.

"Only a runaway ring, sir," she answered.

"I'm restless to-night," he said to himself. He went back to his study, and this time attacked his work resolutely. In a little while he was hard at work again, and the only sounds in the room were the ticking of the clock and the subdued shrillness of his quill, hurrying in the very centre of the circle of light his lamp-shade threw on his table.

It was two o'clock before Doctor Kemp had finished his work for the night. He rose, yawned, and went downstairs to bed. He had already removed his coat and vest, when he noticed that he was thirsty. He took a candle and went down to the dining-room in search of a syphon and whisky.

Doctor Kemp's scientific pursuits had made him a very observant man, and as he recrossed the hall, he noticed a dark spot on the linoleum near the mat at the foot of the stairs. He went on upstairs, and then it suddenly occurred to him to ask himself what the spot on the linoleum might be. Apparently some sub-conscious element was at work. At any rate, he turned with his burden, went back to the hall, put down the syphon and whisky, and bending down touched the spot. Without any great surprise he found it had the stickiness and colour of drying blood.

He took up his burden again, and returned upstairs, looking about him and trying to account for the blood-spot. On the landing he saw something and stopped astonished. The door-handle of his own room was blood-stained.

He looked at his own hand. It was quite clean, and then he remembered that the door of his room had been open when he came down from his study, and that consequently he had not touched the handle at all. He went straight into his room, his face quite calm—perhaps a trifle more resolute than usual. His glance, wandering inquisitively, fell on the bed. On the counterpane was a mess of blood, and the sheet had been torn. He had not noticed this before because he had walked straight to the dressing-table. On the further side the bed-clothes were depressed as if some one had been recently sitting there.

Then he had an odd impression that he had heard a loud voice say, " Good Heavens !—*Kemp !* " But Doctor Kemp was no believer in Voices.

He stood staring at the tumbled sheets. Was that really a voice ? He looked about again, but noticed nothing further than the disordered and blood-stained bed. Then he distinctly heard a movement across the room, near the wash-hand stand. All men, however highly educated, retain some superstitious inklings. The feeling that is called " eerie " came upon him. He closed the door of the room, came forward to the dressing-table, and put down his burdens. Suddenly, with a start, he perceived a coiled and blood-stained bandage of linen rag hanging in mid-air, between him and the wash-hand stand.

He stared at this in amazement. It was an empty bandage, a bandage properly tied but quite empty. He would have advanced to grasp it, but a touch arrested him, and a voice speaking quite close to him.

" Kemp ! " said the Voice.

" Eigh ? " said Kemp, with his mouth open.

" Keep your nerve," said the Voice. " I'm an Invisible Man."

Kemp made no answer for a space, simply stared at the bandage. " Invisible Man," he said.

" I'm an Invisible Man," repeated the Voice.

The story he had been active to ridicule only that morning rushed through Kemp's brain. He does not appear to have been either very much frightened or very greatly surprised at the moment. Realisation came later.

"I thought it was all a lie," he said. The thought uppermost in his mind was the reiterated arguments of the morning. "Have you a bandage on ? " he asked.

"Yes," said the Invisible Man.

"Oh ! " said Kemp, and then roused himself. "I say ! " he said. "But this is nonsense. It's some trick." He stepped forward suddenly, and his hand, extended towards the bandage, met invisible fingers.

He recoiled at the touch and his colour changed.

"Keep steady, Kemp, for God's sake ! I want help badly. Stop ! "

The hand gripped his arm. He struck at it.

"Kemp ! " cried the Voice. "Kemp ! Keep steady ! " and the grip tightened.

A frantic desire to free himself took possession of Kemp. The hand of the bandaged arm gripped his shoulder, and he was suddenly tripped and flung backwards upon the bed. He opened his mouth to shout, and the corner of the sheet was thrust between his teeth. The Invisible Man had him down grimly, but his arms were free and he struck and tried to kick savagely.

"Listen to reason, will you ? " said the Invisible Man, sticking to him in spite of a pounding in the ribs. "By Heaven ! you'll madden me in a minute !

"Lie still, you fool ! " bawled the Invisible Man in Kemp's ear.

Kemp struggled for another moment and then lay still.

"If you shout I'll smash your face," said the Invisible Man, relieving his mouth.

"I'm an Invisible Man. It's no foolishness, and no magic. I really am an Invisible Man. And I want your help. I don't want to hurt you, but if you behave like a frantic rustic, I must. Don't you remember me, Kemp ?—Griffin, of University College ? "

"Let me get up," said Kemp. "I'll stop where I am. And let me sit quiet for a minute."

He sat up and felt his neck.

"I am Griffin, of University College, and I have made myself invisible. I am just an ordinary man—a man you have known—made invisible."

"Griffin ? " said Kemp.

"Griffin," answered the Voice—"a younger student, almost an albino, six feet high, and broad, with a pink and white face and red eyes—who won the medal for chemistry."

"I am confused," said Kemp. "My brain is rioting. What has this to do with Griffin ? "

"I *am* Griffin."

Kemp thought. " It's horrible," he said. " But what devilry must happen to make a man invisible ? "

" It's no devilry. It's a process, sane and intelligible enough——"

" It's horrible ! " said Kemp. " How on earth—— ? "

" It's horrible enough. But I'm wounded and in pain, and tired—— Great God ! Kemp, you are a man. Take it steady. Give me some food and drink, and let me sit down here."

Kemp stared at the bandage as it moved across the room, then saw a basket chair dragged across the floor and come to rest near the bed. It creaked, and the seat was depressed the quarter of an inch or so. He rubbed his eyes and felt his neck again. " This beats ghosts," he said, and laughed stupidly.

" That's better. Thank Heaven, you're getting sensible ! "

" Or silly," said Kemp, and knuckled his eyes.

" Give me some whisky. I'm near dead."

" It didn't feel so. Where are you ? If I get up shall I run into you ? *There !* All right. Whisky ? Here. Where shall I give it you ? "

The chair creaked and Kemp felt the glass drawn away from him. He let go by an effort ; his instinct was all against it. It came to rest poised twenty inches above the front edge of the seat of the chair. He stared at it in infinite perplexity. " This is—this *must* be—hypnotism. You must have suggested you are invisible."

" Nonsense," said the Voice.

" It's frantic."

" Listen to me."

" I demonstrated conclusively this morning," began Kemp, " that invisibility——"

" Never mind what you've demonstrated !—I'm starving," said the Voice, " and the night is—chilly to a man without clothes."

" Food ! " said Kemp.

The tumbler of whisky tilted itself. " Yes," said the Invisible Man rapping it down. " Have you got a dressing-gown ? "

Kemp made some exclamation in an undertone. He walked to a wardrobe and produced a robe of dingy scarlet. " This do ? " he asked. It was taken from him. It hung limp for a moment in mid-air, fluttered weirdly, stood full and decorous buttoning itself, and sat down in his chair. " Drawers, socks, slippers would be a comfort," said the Unseen, curtly. " And food."

" Anything. But this is the insanest thing I ever was in, in my life ! "

He turned out his drawers for the articles, and then went downstairs to ransack his larder. He came back with some cold cutlets and bread, pulled up a light table, and placed them before his guest. "Never mind knives," said his visitor, and a cutlet hung in mid-air, with a sound of gnawing.

"Invisible!" said Kemp, and sat down on a bedroom chair.

"I always like to get something about me before I eat," said the Invisible Man, with a full mouth, eating greedily. "Queer fancy!"

"I suppose that wrist is all right," said Kemp.

"Trust me," said the Invisible Man.

"Of *all* the strange and wonderful——"

"Exactly. But it's odd I should blunder into *your* house to get my bandaging. My first stroke of luck! Anyhow I meant to sleep in this house to-night. You must stand that! It's a filthy nuisance, my blood showing, isn't it? Quite a clot over there. Gets visible as it coagulates, I see. I've been in the house three hours."

"But how's it done?" began Kemp, in a tone of exasperation. "Confound it! The whole business—it's unreasonable from beginning to end."

"Quite reasonable," said the Invisible Man. "Perfectly reasonable."

He reached over and secured the whisky bottle. Kemp stared at the devouring dressing-gown. A ray of candlelight penetrating a torn patch in the right shoulder, made a triangle of light under the left ribs. "What were the shots?" he asked. "How did the shooting begin?"

"There was a fool of a man—a sort of confederate of mine—curse him!—who tried to steal my money. *Has* done so."

"Is *he* invisible too?"

"No."

"Well?"

"Can't I have some more to eat before I tell you all that? I'm hungry—in pain. And you want me to tell stories!"

Kemp got up. "*You* didn't do any shooting?" he asked.

"Not me," said his visitor. "Some fool I'd never seen fired at random. A lot of them got scared. They all got scared at me. Curse them!—— I say—I want more to eat than this, Kemp."

"I'll see what there is more to eat downstairs," said Kemp. "Not much, I'm afraid."

After he had done eating, and he made a heavy meal, the Invisible Man demanded a cigar. He bit the end savagely before Kemp could find a knife, and cursed when the outer leaf loosened. It was strange to see him smoking; his mouth and throat, pharynx and nares, became visible as a sort of whirling smoke cast.

"This blessed gift of smoking!" he said, and puffed vigorously. "I'm lucky to have fallen upon you, Kemp. You must help me. Fancy tumbling on you just now! I'm in a devilish scrape. I've been mad, I think. The things I have been through ! But we will do things yet. Let me tell you——"

He helped himself to more whisky and soda. Kemp got up, looked about him, and fetched himself a glass from his spare room. " It's wild—but I suppose I may drink."

" You haven't changed much, Kemp, these dozen years. You fair men don't. Cool and methodical—after the first collapse. I must tell you. We will work together ! "

" But how was it all done ? " said Kemp, " and how did you get like this ? "

" For God's sake, let me smoke in peace for a little while ! And then I will begin to tell you."

But the story was not told that night. The Invisible Man's wrist was growing painful, he was feverish, exhausted, and his mind came round to brood upon his chase down the hill and the struggle about the inn. He spoke in fragments of Marvel, he smoked faster, his voice grew angry. Kemp tried to gather what he could.

" He was afraid of me, I could see he was afraid of me," said the Invisible Man many times over. "He meant to give me the slip—he was always casting about ! What a fool I was !

" The cur !

" I should have killed him——"

" Where did you get the money ? " asked Kemp, abruptly.

The Invisible Man was silent for a space. " I can't tell you to-night," he said.

He groaned suddenly and leant forward, supporting his invisible head on invisible hands. " Kemp," he said, " I've had no sleep for near three days—except a couple of dozes of an hour or so. I must sleep soon."

" Well, have my room—have this room."

" But how can I sleep ? If I sleep—he will get away. Ugh ! What does it matter ? "

" What's the shot-wound ? " asked Kemp, abruptly.

" Nothing—scratch and blood. Oh, God ! How I want sleep ! "

" Why not ? "

The Invisible Man appeared to be regarding Kemp. " Because I've a particular objection to being caught by my fellow-men," he said slowly.

Kemp started.

" Fool that I am ! " said the Invisible Man, striking the table smartly. " I've put the idea into your head."

CHAPTER EIGHTEEN

THE INVISIBLE MAN SLEEPS

EXHAUSTED and wounded as the Invisible Man was, he refused to accept Kemp's word that his freedom should be respected. He examined the two windows of the bedroom, drew up the blinds, and opened the sashes, to confirm Kemp's statement that a retreat by them would be possible. Outside the night was very quiet and still, and the new moon was setting over the down. Then he examined the keys of the bedroom and the two dressing-room doors, to satisfy himself that these also could be made an assurance of freedom. Finally he expressed himself satisfied. He stood on the hearth-rug and Kemp heard the sound of a yawn.

"I'm sorry," said the Invisible Man, "if I cannot tell you all that I have done to-night. But I am worn out. It's grotesque, no doubt. It's horrible! But believe me, Kemp, it is quite a possible thing. I have made a discovery. I meant to keep it to myself. I can't. I must have a partner. And you—— We can do such things—— But to-morrow. Now, Kemp, I feel as though I must sleep or perish."

Kemp stood in the middle of the room staring at the headless garment. "I suppose I must leave you," he said. "It's —incredible. Three things happening like this, overturning all my preconceptions, would make me insane. But it's real! Is there anything more that I can get you?"

"Only bid me good-night," said Griffin.

"Good-night," said Kemp, and shook an invisible hand. He walked sideways to the door. Suddenly the dressing-gown walked quickly towards him. "Understand me!" said the dressing-gown. "No attempts to hamper me, or capture me! Or——"

Kemp's face changed a little. "I thought I gave you my word," he said.

Kemp closed the door softly behind him, and the key was turned upon him forthwith. Then, as he stood with an expression of passive amazement on his face, the rapid feet came to the door of the dressing-room and that too was locked. Kemp slapped his brow with his hand. "Am I dreaming? Has the world gone mad—or have I?"

He laughed, and put his hand to the locked door. "Barred out of my own bedroom, by a flagrant absurdity!" he said.

He walked to the head of the staircase, turned, and stared at the locked doors. "It's fact," he said. He put his fingers to his slightly bruised neck. "Undeniable fact!

"But——"

He shook his head hopelessly, turned, and went downstairs. He lit the dining-room lamp, got out a cigar, and began

pacing the room, ejaculating. Now and then he would argue
with himself.

"Invisible ! " he said.

"Is there such a thing as an invisible animal ? In the sea,
yes. Thousands ! millions ! All the larvæ, all the little
nauplii and tornarias, all the microscopic things, the jellyfish. In the sea there are more things invisible than visible !
I never thought of that before. And in the ponds too ! All
those little pond-life things—specks of colourless translucent
jelly ! But in air ? No !

"It can't be.

"But after all—why not ?

"If a man was made of glass he would still be visible."

His meditation became profound. The bulk of three cigars
had passed into the invisible or diffused as a white ash over
the carpet before he spoke again. Then it was merely an exclamation. He turned aside, walked out of the room, and
went into his little consulting-room and lit the gas there. It
was a little room, because Dr. Kemp did not live by practice,
and in it were the day's newspapers. The morning's paper
lay carelessly opened and thrown aside. He caught it up,
turned it over, and read the acount of a " Strange Story from
Iping " that the mariner at Port Stowe had spelt over so painfully to Mr. Marvel. Kemp read it swiftly.

"Wrapped up ! " said Kemp. " Disguised ! Hiding it !
' No one seems to have been aware of his misfortune.' What
the devil *is* his game ? "

He dropped the paper, and his eye went seeking. " Ah ! "
he said, and caught up the *St. James's Gazette*, lying folded up
as it arrived. " Now we shall get at the truth," said Dr.
Kemp. He rent the paper open ; a couple of columns confronted him. " An Entire Village in Sussex goes Mad " was
the heading.

"Good Heavens ! " said Kemp, reading eagerly an incredulous account of the events in Iping the previous afternoon, that have already been described. Over the leaf the
report in the morning paper had been reprinted.

He re-read it. " Ran through the streets striking right and
left. Jaffers insensible. Mr. Huxter in great pain—still
unable to describe what he saw. Painful humiliation—vicar.
Woman ill with terror ! Windows smashed. This extraordinary story probably a fabrication. Too good not to print
—*cum grano !* "

He dropped the paper and stared blankly in front of him.
"Probably a fabrication ! "

He caught up the paper again, and re-read the whole business. " But when does the Tramp come in ? Why the deuce
was he chasing a Tramp ? "

He sat down abruptly on the surgical couch. " He's not
only invisible," he said, " but he's mad ! Homicidal ! "

When dawn came to mingle its pallor with the lamp-light and cigar-smoke of the dining-room, Kemp was still pacing up and down, trying to grasp the incredible.

He was altogether too excited to sleep. His servants, descending sleepily, discovered him, and were inclined to think that over-study had worked this ill on him. He gave them extraordinary but quite explicit instructions to lay breakfast for two in the belvedere study—and then to confine themselves to the basement and ground-floor. Then he continued to pace the dining-room until the morning's paper came. That had much to say and little to tell, beyond the confirmation of the evening before and a very baldly written account of another remarkable tale from Port Burdock. This gave Kemp the essence of the happenings at the Jolly Cricketers, and the name of Marvel. "He has made me keep with him twenty-four hours," Marvel testified. Certain minor facts were added to the Iping story, notably the cutting of the village telegraph-wire. But there was nothing to throw light on the connection between the Invisible Man and the Tramp ; for Mr. Marvel had supplied no information about the three books, or the money with which he was lined. The incredulous tone had vanished and a shoal of reporters and inquirers were already at work elaborating the matter.

Kemp read every scrap of the report and sent his housemaid out to get every one of the morning papers she could. These also he devoured.

"He is invisible ! " he said. " And it reads like rage growing to mania ! The things he may do ! The things he may do ! And he's upstairs free as the air. What on earth ought I to do ?

"For instance, would it be a breach of faith if—— ? No."

He went to a little untidy desk in the corner, and began a note. He tore this up half written, and wrote another. He read it over and considered it. Then he took an envelope and addressed it to " Colonel Adye, Port Burdock."

The Invisible Man awoke even as Kemp was doing this. He awoke in an evil temper, and Kemp, alert for every sound, heard his pattering feet rush suddenly across the bedroom overhead. Then a chair was flung over and the wash-hand stand tumbler smashed. Kemp hurried upstairs and rapped eagerly.

CHAPTER NINETEEN

CERTAIN FIRST PRINCIPLES

"WHAT'S the matter ? " asked Kemp, when the Invisible Man admitted him.

"Nothing," was the answer.

"But, confound it ! The smash ? "

"Fit of temper," said the Invisible Man. "Forgot this arm ; and it's sore."

"You're rather liable to that sort of thing."

"I am."

Kemp walked across the room and picked up the fragments of broken glass. "All the facts are out about you," said Kemp, standing up with the glass in his hand ; "all that happened in Iping, and down the hill. The world has become aware of its invisible citizen. But no one knows you are here."

The Invisible Man swore.

"The secret's out. I gather it was a secret. I don't know what your plans are, but of course I'm anxious to help you."

The Invisible Man sat down on the bed.

"There's breakfast upstairs," said Kemp, speaking as easily as possible, and he was delighted to find his strange guest rose willingly. Kemp led the way up the narrow staircase to the belvedere.

"Before we can do anything else," said Kemp, "I must understand a little more about this invisibility of yours." He had sat down, after one nervous glance out of the window, with the air of a man who has talking to do. His doubts of the sanity of the entire business flashed and vanished again as he looked across to where Griffin sat at the breakfast-table—a headless, handless dressing-gown, wiping unseen lips on a miraculously held serviette.

"It's simple enough—and credible enough," said Griffin, putting the serviette aside and leaning the invisible head on an invisible hand.

"No doubt, to you, but——" Kemp laughed.

"Well, yes ; to me it seemed wonderful at first, no doubt. But now, great God !—— But we will do great things yet ! I came on the stuff first at Chesilstowe."

"Chesilstowe ? "

"I went there after I left London. You know I dropped medicine and took up physics ? No ?—well, I did. Light— fascinated me."

"Ah ! "

"Optical density ! The whole subject is a network of riddles—a network with solutions glimmering elusively

through. And being but two-and-twenty and full of enthusiasm, I said, ' I will devote my life to this. This is
worth while.' You know what fools we are at two-and-
twenty ? ''

" Fools then or fools now," said Kemp.

" As though Knowing could be any satisfaction to a
man !

" But I went to work—like a nigger. And I had hardly
worked and thought about the matter six months before light
came through one of the meshes suddenly—blindingly ! I
found a general principle of pigments and refraction—a
formula, a geometrical expression involving four dimensions.
Fools, common men, even common mathematicians, do not
know anything of what some general expression may mean
to the student of molecular physics. In the books—the books
that Tramp has hidden—there are marvels, miracles ! But
this was not a method, it was an idea that might lead to a
method by which it would be possible, without changing
any other property of matter—except, in some instances,
colours—to lower the refractive index of a substance, solid
or liquid, to that of air—so far as all practical purposes are
concerned.''

" Phew ! " said Kemp. " That's odd ! But still I don't
see quite—— I can understand that thereby you could
spoil a valuable stone, but personal invisibility is a far
cry."

" Precisely," said Griffin. " But consider : Visibility
depends on the action of the visible bodies on light. Either
a body absorbs light, or it reflects or refracts it, or does all
these things. If it neither reflects nor refracts nor absorbs
light, it cannot of itself be visible. You see an opaque red
box, for instance, because the colour absorbs some of the light
and reflects the rest, all the red part of the light, to you. If it
did not absorb any particular part of the light, but reflected it
all, then it would be a shining white box. Silver ! A diamond
box would neither absorb much of the light nor reflect much
from the general surface, but just here and there where the
surfaces were favourable the light would be reflected and
refracted so that you would get a brilliant appearance of
flashing reflections and translucencies—a sort of skeleton of
light. A glass box would not be so brilliant, not so clearly
visible, as a diamond box, because there would be less refraction and reflection. See that ? From certain points of view
you would see quite clearly through it. Some kinds of glass
would be more visible than others, a box of flint glass would
be brighter than a box of ordinary window glass. A box of
very thin common glass would be hard to see in a bad light,
because it would absorb hardly any light and refract and
reflect very little. And if you put a sheet of common white
glass in water, still more if you put it in some denser liquid

than water, it would vanish almost altogether, because light passing from water to glass is only slightly refracted or reflected or indeed affected in any way. It is almost as invisible as a jet of coal gas or hydrogen is in air. And for precisely the same reason ! "

" Yes," said Kemp, " that is pretty plain sailing."

" And here is another fact you will know to be true. If a sheet of glass is smashed, Kemp, and beaten into a powder, it becomes much more visible while it is in the air ; it becomes at last an opaque white powder. This is because the powdering multiplies the surfaces of the glass at which refraction and reflection occur. In the sheet of glass there are only two surfaces ; in the powder the light is reflected or refracted by each grain it passes through, and very little gets right through the powder. But if the white powdered glass is put into water, it forthwith vanishes. The powdered glass and water have much the same refractive index ; that is, the light undergoes very little refraction or reflection in passing from one to the other.

" You make the glass invisible by putting it into a liquid of nearly the same refractive index ; a transparent thing becomes invisible if it is put in any medium of almost the same refractive index. And if you will consider only a second, you will see also that the powder of glass might be made to vanish in air, if its refractive index could be made the same as that of air ; for then there would be no refraction or reflection as the light passed from glass to air."

" Yes, yes," said Kemp. " But a man's not powdered glass ! "

" No," said Griffin. " He's more transparent ! "

" Nonsense ! "

" That from a doctor ! How one forgets ! Have you already forgotten your physics, in ten years ? Just think of all the things that are transparent and seem not to be so. Paper, for instance, is made up of transparent fibres, and it is white and opaque only for the same reason that a powder of glass is white and opaque. Oil white paper, fill up the interstices between the particles with oil so that there is no longer refraction or reflection except at the surfaces, and it becomes as transparent as glass. And not only paper, but cotton fibre, linen fibre, wool fibre, woody fibre, and *bone*, Kemp, *flesh*, Kemp, *hair*, Kemp, *nails* and *nerves*, Kemp, in fact the whole fabric of a man except the red of his blood and the black pigment of hair, are all made up of transparent, colourless tissue. So little suffices to make us visible one to the other. For the most part the fibres of a living creature are no more opaque than water."

" Great Heavens ! " cried Kemp. " Of course, of course ! I was thinking only last night of the sea larvæ and all jellyfish ! "

" *Now* you have me ! And all that I knew and had in mind a year after I left London—six years ago. But I kept it to myself. I had to do my work under frightful disadvantages. Oliver, my professor, was a scientific bounder, a journalist by instinct, a thief of ideas—he was always prying ! And you know the knavish system of the scientific world. I simply would not publish, and let him share my credit. I went on working, I got nearer and nearer making my formula into an experiment, a reality. I told no living soul, because I meant to flash my work upon the world with crushing effect—to become famous at a blow. I took up the question of pigments to fill up certain gaps. And suddenly, not by design but by accident, I made a discovery in physiology."

" Yes ? "

" You know the red colouring matter of blood ; it can be made white—colourless—and remain with all the functions it has now ! "

Kemp gave a cry of incredulous amazement.

The Invisible Man rose and began pacing the little study. " You may well exclaim. I remember that night. It was late at night—in the daytime one was bothered with the gaping, silly students—and I worked then sometimes till dawn. It came suddenly, splendid and complete into my mind. I was alone ; the laboratory was still, with the tall lights burning brightly and silently. In all my great moments I have been alone. 'One could make an animal—a tissue— transparent ! One could make it invisible ! All except the pigments. I could be invisible ! ' I said, suddenly realising what it meant to be an albino with such knowledge. It was overwhelming. I left the filtering I was doing, and went and stared out of the great window at the stars. ' I could be invisible ! ' I repeated.

" To do such a thing would be to transcend magic. And I beheld, unclouded by doubt, a magnificent vision of all that invisibility might mean to a man—the mystery, the power, the freedom. Drawbacks I saw none. You have only to think ! And I, a shabby, poverty-struck, hemmed-in demonstrator, teaching fools in a provincial college, might suddenly become—this. I ask you, Kemp, if *you*—— Any one, I tell you, would have flung himself upon that research. And I worked three years, and every mountain of difficulty I toiled over showed another from its summit. The infinite details ! And the exasperation—a professor, a provincial professor, always prying. ' When are you going to publish this work of yours ? ' was his everlasting question. And the students, the cramped means ! Three years I had of it——

" And after three years of secrecy and exasperation, I found that to complete it was impossible—impossible."

" How ? " asked Kemp.

" Money," said the Invisible Man, and went again to stare out of the window.

He turned round abruptly. " I robbed the old man—robbed my father.

" The money was not his, and he shot himself."

CHAPTER TWENTY

FOR a moment Kemp sat in silence, staring at the back of the headless figure at the window. Then he started, struck by a thought, rose, took the Invisible Man's arm, and turned him away from the outlook.

"You are tired," he said, "and while I sit, you walk about. Have my chair."

He placed himself between Griffin and the nearest window.

For a space Griffin sat silent, and then he resumed abruptly :

"I had left the Chesilstowe cottage already," he said, "when that happened. It was last December. I had taken a room in London, a large unfurnished room in a big ill-managed lodging-house in a slum near Great Portland Street. The room was soon full of the appliances I had bought with his money ; the work was going on steadily, successfully, drawing near an end. I was like a man emerging from a thicket, and suddenly coming on some unmeaning tragedy. I went to bury him. My mind was still on this research, and I did not lift a finger to save his character I remember the funeral, the cheap hearse, the scant ceremony, the windy frost-bitten hillside, and the old college friend of his who read the service over him—a shabby, black, bent old man with a snivelling cold.

"I remember walking back to the empty home, through the place that had once been a village and was now patched and tinkered by the jerry builders into the ugly likeness of a town. Every way the roads ran out at last into the desecrated fields and ended in rubble heaps and rank wet weeds. I remember myself as a gaunt black figure, going along the slippery, shiny pavement, and the strange sense of detachment I felt from the squalid respectability, the sordid commercialism of the place.

"I did not feel a bit sorry for my father. He seemed to me to be the victim of his own foolish sentimentality. The current cant required my attendance at his funeral, but it was really not my affair.

"But going along the High Street, my old life came back to me for a space, for I met the girl I had known ten years since. Our eyes met.

"Something moved me to turn back and talk to her. She was a very ordinary person.

"It was all like a dream, that visit to the old places. I did not feel then that I was lonely, that I had come out from the world into a desolate place. I appreciated my loss of sympathy, but I put it down to the general inanity of things. Re-entering my room seemed like the recovery of reality.

There were the things I knew and loved. There stood the apparatus, the experiments arranged and waiting. And now there was scarcely a difficulty left, beyond the planning of details.

" I will tell you, Kemp, sooner or later, all the complicated processes. We need not go into that now. For the most part, saving certain gaps I chose to remember, they are written in cypher in those books that Tramp has hidden. We must hunt him down. We must get those books again. But the essential phase was to place the transparent object whose refractive index was to be lowered between two radiating centres of a sort of ethereal vibration, of which I will tell you more fully later. No, not these Röntgen vibrations—I don't know that these others of mine have been described. Yet they are obvious enough. I needed two little dynamos, and these I worked with a cheap gas engine. My first experiment was with a bit of white wool fabric. It was the strangest thing in the world to see it in the flicker of the flashes soft and white, and then to watch it fade like a wreath of smoke and vanish.

" I could scarcely believe I had done it. I put my hand into the emptiness, and there was the thing as solid as ever. I felt it awkwardly, and threw it on the floor. I had a little trouble finding it again.

" And then came a curious experience. I heard a miaow behind me, and turning, saw a lean white cat, very dirty, on the cistern cover outside the window. A thought came into my head. ' Everything ready for you,' I said, and went to the window, opened it, and called softly. She came in, purring—the poor beast was starving—and I gave her some milk. All my food was in a cupboard in the corner of the room. After that she went smelling round the room—evidently with the idea of making herself at home. The invisible rag upset her a bit ; you should have seen her spit at it ! But I made her comfortable on the pillow of my truckle-bed. And I gave her butter to get her to wash."

" And you processed her ? "

" I processed her. But giving drugs to a cat is no joke, Kemp ! And the process failed."

" Failed ! "

" In two particulars. These were the claws and the pigment stuff—what is it ?—at the back of the eye in a cat. You know ? "

" Tapetum."

" Yes, the tapetum. It didn't go. After I'd given the stuff to bleach the blood and done certain other things to her, I gave the beast opium, and put her and the pillow she was sleeping on, on the apparatus. And after all the rest had faded and vanished, there remained two little ghosts of her eyes."

" Odd ! "

" I can't explain it. She was bandaged and clamped, of course—so I had her safe ; but she woke while she was still misty, and miaowled dismally, and some one came knocking. It was an old woman from downstairs, who suspected me of vivisecting—a drink-sodden old creature, with only a white cat to care for in all the world. I whipped out some chloroform, and applied it, and answered the door. ' Did I hear a cat ? ' she asked. ' My cat ? ' ' Not here,' said I, very politely. She was a little doubtful and tried to peer past me into the room ; strange enough to her no doubt—bare walls, uncurtained windows, truckle-bed, with the gas engine vibrating, and the seethe of the radiant points, and that faint ghastly stinging of chloroform in the air. She had to be satisfied at last and went away again."

" How long did it take ? " asked Kemp.

" Three or four hours—the cat. The bones and sinews and the fat were the last to go, and the tips of the coloured hairs. And, as I say, the back part of the eye, tough iridescent stuff it is, wouldn't go at all.

" It was night outside long before the business was over, and nothing was to be seen but the dim eyes and the claws. I stopped the gas engine, felt for and stroked the beast, which was still insensible, and then, being tired, left it sleeping on the invisible pillow and went to bed. I found it hard to sleep. I lay awake thinking weak aimless stuff, going over the experiment over and over again, or dreaming feverishly of things growing misty and vanishing about me, until everything, the ground I stood on, vanished, and so I came to that sickly falling nightmare one gets. About two, the cat began miaowling about the room. I tried to hush it by talking to it, and then I decided to turn it out. I remember the shock I had when striking a light—there were just the round eyes shining green—and nothing round them. I would have given it milk, but I hadn't any. It wouldn't be quiet, it just sat down and miaowled at the door. I tried to catch it, with an idea of putting it out of the window, but it wouldn't be caught, it vanished. Then it began miaowling in different parts of the room. At last I opened the window and made a bustle. I suppose it went out at last. I never saw any more of it.

" Then—Heaven knows why—I fell thinking of my father's funeral again, and the dismal windy hillside, until the day had come. I found sleeping was hopeless, and, locking my door after me, wandered out into the morning streets."

" You don't mean to say there's an invisible cat at large ! " said Kemp.

" If it hasn't been killed," said the Invisible Man. " Why not ? "

" Why not ? " said Kemp. " I didn't mean to interrupt."

" It's very probably been killed," said the Invisible Man.
" It was alive four days after, I know, and down a grating in
Great Titchfield Street ; because I saw a crowd round the
place, trying to see whence the miaowling came."

He was silent for the best part of a minute. Then he
resumed abruptly :—

" I remember that morning before the change very vividly.
I must have gone up Great Portland Street. I remember the
barracks in Albany Street, and the horse soldiers coming out,
and at last I found myself sitting in the sunshine and feeling
very ill and strange, on the summit of Primrose Hill. It was a
sunny day in January—one of those sunny, frosty days that
came before the snow this year. My weary brain tried to
formulate the position, to plot out a plan of action.

" I was surprised to find, now that my prize was within my
grasp, how inconclusive its attainment seemed. As a matter
of fact I was worked out ; the intense stress of nearly four
years' continuous work left me incapable of any strength of
feeling. I was apathetic, and I tried in vain to recover the
enthusiasm of my first inquiries, the passion of discovery that
had enabled me to compass even the downfall of my father's
grey hairs. Nothing seemed to matter. I saw pretty clearly
this was a transient mood, due to overwork and want of sleep,
and that either by drugs or rest it would be possible to recover
my energies.

" All I could think clearly was that the thing had to be
carried through ; the fixed idea still ruled me. And soon, for
the money I had was almost exhausted. I looked about me
at the hillside, with children playing and girls watching them,
and tried to think of all the fantastic advantages an invisible
man would have in the world. After a time I crawled home,
took some food and a strong dose of strychnine, and went to
sleep in my clothes on my unmade bed. Strychnine is a grand
tonic, Kemp, to take the flabbiness out of a man."

" It's the devil," said Kemp. " It's the palæolithic in a
bottle."

" I awoke vastly invigorated and rather irritable. You
know ? "

" I know the stuff."

" And there was some one rapping at the door. It was my
landlord with threats and inquiries, an old Polish Jew in a
long grey coat and greasy slippers. I had been tormenting a
cat in the night, he was sure—the old woman's tongue had
been busy. He insisted on knowing all about it. The laws
of this country against vivisection were very severe—he might
be liable. I denied the cat. Then the vibration of the little
gas engine could be felt all over the house, he said. That was
true, certainly. He edged round me into the room, peering
about over his German-silver spectacles, and a sudden dread
came into my mind that he might carry away something of my

secret. I tried to keep between him and the concentrating apparatus I had arranged, and that only made him more curious. What was I doing ? Why was I always alone and secretive ? Was it legal ? Was it dangerous ? I paid nothing but the usual rent. His had always been a most respectable house—in a disreputable neighbourhood. Suddenly my temper gave way. I told him to get out. He began to protest, to jabber of his right of entry. In a moment I had him by the collar ; something ripped, and he went spinning out into his own passage. I slammed and locked the door and sat down quivering.

" He made a fuss outside, which I disregarded, and after a time he went away.

" But this brought matters to a crisis. I did not know what he would do, nor even what he had power to do. To move to fresh apartments would have meant delay ; all together I had barely twenty pounds left in the world—for the most part in a bank—and I could not afford that. Vanish ! It was irresistible. Then there would be an inquiry, the sacking of my room——

" At the thought of the possibility of my work being exposed or interrupted at its very climax, I became angry and active. I hurried out with my three books of notes, my cheque-book— the Tramp has them now—and directed them from the nearest Post Office to a house of call for letters and parcels in Great Portland Street. I tried to go out noiselessly. Coming in, I found my landlord going quietly upstairs ; he had heard the door close, I suppose. You would have laughed to see him jump aside on the landing as I came tearing after him. He glared at me as I went by him, and I made the house quiver with the slamming of my door. I heard him come shuffling up to my floor, hesitate, and go down. I set to work upon my preparations forthwith.

" It was all done that evening and night. While I was still sitting under the sickly, drowsy influence of the drugs that decolourise blood, there came a repeated knocking at the door. It ceased, footsteps went away and returned, and the knocking was resumed. There was an attempt to push something under the door—a blue paper. Then in a fit of irritation I rose and went and flung the door wide open. ' Now then ? ' said I.

" It was my landlord, with a notice of ejectment or something. He held it out to me, saw something odd about my hands, I expect, and lifted his eyes to my face.

" For a moment he gaped. Then he gave a sort of inarticulate cry, dropped candle and writ together, and went blundering down the dark passage to the stairs. I shut the door, locked it, and went to the looking-glass. Then I understood his terror. My face was white—like white stone.

" But it was all horrible. I had not expected the suffering. A night of racking anguish, sickness and fainting. I set my teeth, though my skin was presently afire, all my body afire ; but I lay there like grim death. I understood now how it was the cat had howled until I chloroformed it. Lucky it was I lived alone and untended in my room. There were times when I sobbed and groaned and talked. But I stuck to it. I became insensible and woke languid in the darkness.

" The pain had passed. I thought I was killing myself and I did not care. I shall never forget that dawn, and the strange horror of seeing that my hands had become as clouded glass, and watching them grow clearer and thinner as the day went by, until at last I could see the sickly disorder of my room through them, though I closed my transparent eyelids. My limbs became glassy, the bones and arteries faded, vanished, and the little white nerves went last. I ground my teeth and stayed there to the end. At last only the dead tips of the finger-nails remained, pallid and white, and the brown stain of some acid upon my fingers.

" I struggled up. At first I was as incapable as a swathed infant—stepping with limbs I could not see. I was weak and very hungry. I went and stared at nothing in my shaving-glass, at nothing save where an attenuated pigment still remained behind the retina of my eyes, fainter than mist. I had to hang on to the table and press my forehead to the glass.

" It was only by a frantic effort of will that I dragged myself back to the apparatus and completed the process.

" I slept during the forenoon, pulling the sheet over my eyes to shut out the light, and about midday I was awakened again by a knocking. My strength had returned. I sat up and listened and heard a whispering. I sprang to my feet and as noiselessly as possible began to detach the connections of my apparatus, and to distribute it about the room, so as to destroy the suggestions of its arrangement. Presently the knocking was renewed and voices called, first my landlord's, and then two others. To gain time I answered them. The invisible rag and pillow came to hand and I opened the window and pitched them out on to the cistern cover. As the window opened, a heavy crash came at the door. Some one had charged it with the idea of smashing the lock. But the stout bolts I had screwed up some days before stopped him. That startled me, made me angry. I began to tremble and do things hurriedly.

" I tossed together some loose paper, straw, packing paper and so forth, in the middle of the room, and turned on the gas. Heavy blows began to rain upon the door. I could not find the matches. I beat my hands on the wall with rage. I turned down the gas again, stepped out of the window on the cistern cover, very softly lowered the sash, and sat down, secure and invisible, but quivering with anger, to watch events. They split a panel, I saw, and in another moment they had broken away the staples of the bolts and stood in the open doorway. It was the landlord and his two step-sons, sturdy young men of three- or four-and-twenty. Behind them fluttered the old hag of a woman from downstairs.

" You may imagine their astonishment on finding the room empty. One of the younger men rushed to the window at once, flung it up and stared out. His staring eyes and thick-lipped bearded face came a foot from my face. I was half minded to hit his silly countenance, but I arrested my doubled fist. He stared right through me. So did the others as they joined him. The old man went and peered under the bed, and then they all made a rush for the cupboard. They had to argue about it at length in Yiddish and Cockney English. They concluded I had not answered them, that their imagination had deceived them. A feeling of extraordinary elation took the place of my anger as I sat outside the window and watched these four people—for the old lady came in, glancing suspiciously about her like a cat, trying to understand the riddle of my behaviour.

" The old man, so far as I could understand his *patois*, agreed with the old lady that I was a vivisectionist. The sons protested in garbled English that I was an electrician, and appealed to the dynamos and radiators. They were all nervous against my arrival, although I found subsequently, that they had bolted the front door. The old lady peered into the cupboard and under the bed, and one of the young men pushed up the register and stared up the chimney. One of my fellow lodgers, a costermonger who shared the opposite room with a butcher, appeared on the landing, and he was called in and told incoherent things.

" It occurred to me that the radiators, if they fell into the hands of some acute well-educated person, would give me away too much, and watching my opportunity, I came into the room and tilted one of the little dynamos off its fellow on which it was standing, and smashed both apparatus. Then, while they were trying to explain the smash, I dodged out of the room and went softly downstairs.

" I went into one of the sitting-rooms and waited until they came down, still speculating and argumentative, all a little disappointed at finding no ' horrors,' and all a little puzzled how they stood with regard to me. Then I slipped up again with a box of matches, fired my heap of paper and rubbish, put the chairs and bedding thereby, led the gas to the affair, by means of an india-rubber tube, and waving a farewell to the room left it for the last time."

" You fired the house ! " exclaimed Kemp .

" Fired the house. It was the only way to cover my trail—and no doubt it was insured. I slipped the bolts of the front door quietly and went out into the street. I was invisible, and I was only just beginning to realise the extraordinary advantage my invisibility gave me. My head was already teeming with plans of all the wild and wonderful things I had now impunity to do.

CHAPTER TWENTY-ONE

IN OXFORD STREET

"IN going downstairs the first time I found an unexpected difficulty because I could not see my feet ; indeed I stumbled twice, and there was an unaccustomed clumsiness in gripping the bolt. By not looking down, however, I managed to walk on the level passably well.

"My mood, I say, was one of exaltation. I felt as a seeing man might do, with padded feet and noiseless clothes, in a city of the blind. I experienced a wild impulse to jest, to startle people, to clap men on the back, fling people's hats astray, and generally revel in my extraordinary advantage.

"But hardly had I emerged upon Great Portland Street, however (my lodging was close to the big draper's shop there), when I heard a clashing concussion and was hit violently behind, and turning saw a man carrying a basket of soda-water syphons, and looking in amazement at his burden. Although the blow had really hurt me, I found something so irresistible in his astonishment that I laughed aloud. 'The devil's in the basket,' I said, and suddenly twisted it out of his hand. He let go incontinently, and I swung the whole weight into the air.

"But a fool of a cabman, standing outside a public house, made a sudden rush for this, and his extending fingers took me with excruciating violence under the ear. I let the whole down with a smash on the cabman, and then, with shouts and the clatter of feet about me, people coming out of shops, vehicles pulling up, I realised what I had done for myself, and cursing my folly, backed against a shop window and prepared to dodge out of the confusion. In a moment I should be wedged into a crowd and inevitably discovered. I pushed by a butcher boy, who luckily did not turn to see the nothingness that shoved him aside, and dodged behind the cabman's four-wheeler. I do not know how they settled the business. I hurried straight across the road, which was happily clear, and hardly heeding which way I went, in the fright of detection the incident had given me, plunged into the afternoon throng of Oxford Street.

"I tried to get into the stream of people, but they were too thick for me, and in a moment my heels were being trodden upon. I took to the gutter, the roughness of which I found painful to my feet, and forthwith the shaft of a crawling hansom dug me forcibly under the shoulder blade, reminding me that I was already bruised severely. I staggered out of the way of the cab, avoided a perambulator by a convulsive movement, and found myself behind the hansom. A happy thought saved me, and as this drove slowly along I followed in

its immediate wake, trembling and astonished at the turn of
my adventure. And not only trembling, but shivering. It
was a bright day in January and I was stark naked and the
thin slime of mud that covered the road was freezing. Foolish
as it seems to me now, I had not reckoned that, transparent
or not, I was still amenable to the weather and all its consequences.

" Then suddenly a bright idea came into my head. I ran
round and got into the cab. And so, shivering, scared, and
sniffing with the first intimations of a cold, and with the
bruises in the small of my back growing upon my attention,
I drove slowly along Oxford Street and past Tottenham Court
Road. My mood was as different from that in which I had
sallied forth ten minutes ago as it is possible to imagine. *This*
invisibility indeed ! The one thought that possessed me
was—how was I to get out of the scrape I was in ?

" We crawled past Mudie's, and there a tall woman with five
or six yellow-labelled books hailed my cab, and I sprang out
just in time to escape her, shaving a railway van narrowly in
my flight. I made off up the roadway to Bloomsbury Square,
intending to strike north past the Museum and so get into the
quiet district. I was now cruelly chilled, and the strangeness
of my situation so unnerved me that I whimpered as I ran.
At the northward corner of the Square a little white dog ran
out of the Pharmaceutical Society's offices, and incontinently
made for me, nose down.

" I had never realised it before, but the nose is to the mind
of a dog what the eye is to the mind of a seeing man. Dogs
perceive the scent of a man moving as men perceive his vision.
This brute began barking and leaping, showing, as it seemed to
me, only too plainly that he was aware of me. I crossed
Great Russell Street, glancing over my shoulder as I did so,
and went some way along Montagu Street before I realised
what I was running towards.

" Then I became aware of a blare of music, and looking
along the street saw a number of people advancing out of
Russell Square, red shirts, and the banner of the Salvation
Army to the fore. Such a crowd, chanting in the roadway
and scoffing on the pavement, I could not hope to penetrate,
and dreading to go back and farther from home again, and
deciding on the spur of the moment, I ran up the white steps
of a house facing the Museum railings, and stood there until the
crowd should have passed. Happily the dog stopped at the
noise of the band too, hesitated, and turned tail, running back
to Bloomsbury Square again.

" On came the band, bawling with unconscious irony some
hymn about ' When shall we see His Face ? ' and it seemed an
interminable time to me before the tide of the crowd washed
along the pavement by me. Thud, thud, thud, came the
drum with a vibrating resonance, and for the moment I did

not notice two urchins stopping at the railings by me. ' See 'em,' said one. ' See what ? ' said the other, ' Why—them footmarks—*bare*. Like what you makes in mud.'

" I looked down and saw the youngsters had stopped and were gaping at the muddy footmarks I had left behind me up the newly whitened steps. The passing people elbowed and jostled them, but their confounded intelligence was arrested. ' Thud, thud, thud, When, thud, shall we see, thud, His Face, thud, thud.' ' There's a barefoot man gone up them steps, or I don't know nothing,' said one. ' And he ain't never come down again. And his foot was a-bleeding.'

" The thick of the crowd had already passed. ' Looky there, Ted,' quoth the younger of the detectives, with the sharpness of surprise in his voice, and pointed straight to my feet. I looked down and saw at once the dim suggestion of their outline sketched in splashes of mud. For a moment I was paralysed.

" ' Why, that's rum,' said the elder. ' Dashed rum ! It's just like the ghost of a foot, ain't it ? ' He hesitated and advanced with outstretched hand. A man pulled up short to see what he was catching, and then a girl. In another moment he would have touched me. Then I saw what to do. I made a step, the boy started back with an exclamation, and with a rapid movement I swung myself over into the portico of the next house. But the smaller boy was sharp-eyed enough to follow the movement, and before I was well down the steps and upon the pavement, he had recovered from his momentary astonishment and was shouting out that the feet had gone over the wall.

" They rushed round and saw my new footmarks flash into being on the lower step and upon the pavement. ' What's up ? ' asked some one. ' Feet ! Look ! Feet running ! ' Everybody in the road, except my three pursuers, was pouring along after the Salvation Army, and this not only impeded me but them. There was an eddy of surprise and interrogation. At the cost of bowling over one young fellow I got through, and in another moment I was rushing headlong round the circuit of Russell Square, with six or seven astonished people following my footmarks. There was no time for explanation, or else the whole host would have been after me.

" Twice I doubled round corners, thrice I crossed the road and came back on my tracks, and then, as my feet grew hot and dry, the damp impressions began to fade. At last I had a breathing space and rubbed my feet clean with my hands, and so got away altogether. The last I saw of the chase was a little group of a dozen people perhaps, studying with infinite perplexity a slowly drying footprint that had resulted from a puddle in Tavistock Square—a footprint as isolated and incomprehensible to them as Crusoe's solitary discovery.

" This running warmed me to a certain extent, and I went

on with a better courage through the maze of less frequented
roads that runs hereabouts. My back had now become very
stiff and sore, my tonsils were painful from the cabman's
fingers, and the skin of my neck had been scratched by his
nails ; my feet hurt exceedingly and I was lame from a little
cut on one foot. I saw in time a blind man approaching me,
and fled limping, for I feared his subtle intuitions. Once or
twice accidental collisions occurred and I left people amazed,
with unaccountable curses ringing in their ears. Then came
something silent and quiet against my face, and across the
Square fell a thin veil of slowly falling flakes of snow. I had
caught a cold, and do as I would I could not avoid an occasional
sneeze. And every dog that came in sight, with its pointing
nose and curious sniffing, was a terror to me.

" Then came men and boys running, first one and then
others, and shouting as they ran. It was a fire. They ran
in the direction of my lodging, and looking back down a street
I saw a mass of black smoke streaming up above the roofs and
telephone wires. It was my lodging burning ; my clothes, my
apparatus, all my resources indeed, except my cheque-book
and the three volumes of memoranda that awaited me in
Great Portland Street, were there. Burning ! I had burnt
my boats—if ever a man did ! The place was blazing."

The Invisible Man paused and thought. Kemp glanced
nervously out of the window. " Yes ? " he said. " Go on."

CHAPTER TWENTY-TWO

" So last January, with the beginnings of a snow-storm in the air about me—and if it settled on me it would betray me!—weary, cold, painful, inexpressibly wretched, and still but half convinced of my invisible quality, I began this new life to which I am committed. I had no refuge, no appliances, no human being in the world in whom I could confide. To have told my secret would have given me away—made a mere show and rarity of me. Nevertheless, I was half minded to accost some passer-by and throw myself upon his mercy. But I knew too clearly the terror and brutal cruelty my advances would evoke. I made no plans in the street. My sole object was to get shelter from the snow, to get myself covered and warm ; then I might hope to plan. But even to me, an Invisible Man, the rows of London houses stood latched, barred, and bolted impregnably.

" Only one thing could I see clearly before me, the cold exposure and misery of the snowstorm and the night.

" And then I had a brilliant idea. I turned down one of the roads leading from Gower Street to Tottenham Court Road, and found myself outside Omniums, the big establishment where everything is to be bought—you know the place— meat, grocery, linen, furniture, clothing, oil paintings even— a huge meandering collection of shops rather than a shop. I had thought I should find the doors open, but they were closed, and as I stood in the wide entrance a carriage stopped outside, and a man in uniform—you know the kind of personage with ' Omnium ' on his cap—flung open the door. I contrived to enter, and walking down the shop—it was a department where they were selling ribbons and gloves and stockings and that kind of thing—came to a more spacious region devoted to picnic baskets and wicker furniture.

" I did not feel safe there, however ; people were going to and fro, and I prowled restlessly about until I came upon a huge section in an upper floor containing scores and hundreds of bedsteads, and beyond these I found a resting-place at last among a huge pile of folded flock mattresses. The place was already lit up and agreeably warm ,and I decided to remain where I was, keeping a cautious eye on the two or three sets of shopmen and customers who were meandering through the place until closing time came. Then I should be able, I thought, to rob the place for food and clothing, and disguised, prowl through it and examine its resources, perhaps sleep on some of the bedding. That seemed an acceptable plan. My idea was to procure clothing to make myself a muffled but acceptable figure, to get money, and then to recover my books and parcels where they awaited me, take a lodging somewhere and elaborate plans for the complete realisation of the advantages my invisibility gave me (as I still imagined) over my fellow-men.

"Closing time arrived quickly enough ; it could not have been more than an hour after I took up my position on the mattresses before I noticed the blinds of the windows being drawn, and customers being marched doorward. And then a number of brisk young men began with remarkable alacrity to tidy up the goods that remained disturbed. I left my lair as the crowds diminished, and prowled cautiously out into the less desolate parts of the shop. I was really surprised to observe how rapidly the young men and women whipped away the goods displayed for sale during the day. All the boxes of goods, the hanging fabrics, the festoons of lace, the boxes of sweets in the grocery section, the displays of this and that, were being whipped down, folded up, slapped into tidy receptacles, and everything that could not be taken down and put away had sheets of some coarse stuff like sacking flung over it. Finally all the chairs were turned up on to the counters, leaving the floor clear. Directly each of these young people had done, he or she made promptly for the door with such an expression of animation as I have rarely observed in a shop assistant before. Then came a lot of youngsters scattering sawdust and carrying pails and brooms. I had to dodge to get out of the way, and as it was, my ankle got stung with the sawdust. For some time, wandering through the swathed and darkened departments, I could hear the brooms at work. And at last a good hour or more after the shop had been closed, came a noise of locking doors. Silence came upon the place, and I found myself wandering through the vast and intricate shops, galleries and showrooms of the place, alone. It was very still ; in one place I remember passing near one of the Tottenham Court Road entrances and listening to the tapping of boot-heels of the passers-by.

"My first visit was to the place where I had seen stockings and gloves for sale. It was dark, and I had the devil of a hunt after matches, which I found at last in the drawer of the little cash desk. Then I had to get a candle. I had to tear down wrappings and ransack a number of boxes and drawers, but at last I managed to turn out what I sought ; the box label called them lambswool pants, and lambswool vests. Then socks, a thick comforter, and then I went to the clothing place and got trousers, a lounge jacket, an overcoat and a slouch hat—a clerical sort of hat with the brim turned down. I began to feel a human being again, and my next thought was food.

"Upstairs was a refreshment department, and there I got cold meat. There was coffee still in the urn, and I lit the gas and warmed it up again, and altogether I did not do badly.

Afterwards, prowling through the place in search of blankets—
I had to put up at last with a heap of down quilts—I came
upon a grocery section with a lot of chocolate and candied
fruits, more than was good for me indeed—and some white
burgundy. And near that was a toy department, and I had
a brilliant idea. I found some artificial noses—dummy noses,
you know, and I thought of dark spectacles. But Omniums
had no optical department. My nose had been a difficulty
indeed—I had thought of paint. But the discovery set my
mind running on wigs and masks and the like. Finally I went
to sleep in a heap of down quilts, very warm and comfortable.

" My last thoughts before sleeping were the most agreeable
I had had since the change. I was in a state of physical
serenity, and that was reflected in my mind. I thought that I
should be able to slip out unobserved in the morning with my
clothes upon me, muffling my face with a white wrapper I
had taken, purchase, with the money I had taken, spectacles
and so forth, and so complete my disguise. I lapsed into
disorderly dreams of all the fantastic things that had happened during the last few days. I saw the ugly little Jew of a
landlord vociferating in his rooms ; I saw his two sons marvelling, and the wrinkled old woman's gnarled face as she
asked for her cat. I experienced again the strange sensation
of seeing the cloth disappear, and so I came round to the
windy hillside and the sniffing old clergyman mumbling ' Dust
to dust, earth to earth,' and my father's open grave.

" ' You also,' said a voice, and suddenly I was being forced
towards the grave. I struggled, shouted, appealed to the
mourners, but they continued stonily following the service ;
the old clergyman, too, never faltered droning and sniffing
through the ritual. I realised I was invisible and inaudible,
that overwhelming forces had their grip on me. I struggled
in vain, I was forced over the brink, the coffin rang hollow
as I fell upon it, and the gravel came flying after me in spade-
fuls. Nobody heeded me, nobody was aware of me. I made
convulsive struggles and awoke.

" The pale London dawn had come, the place was full of a
chilly grey light that filtered round the edges of the window
blinds. I sat up, and for a time I could not think where this
ample apartment, with its counters, its piles of rolled stuff,
its heap of quilts and cushions, its iron pillars, might be. Then,
as recollection came back to me, I heard voices in conversation.

" Then far down the place, in the brighter light of some
department which had already raised its blinds, I saw two
men approaching. I scrambled to my feet, looking about me
for some way of escape, and even as I did so the sound of my
movement made them aware of me. I suppose they saw
merely a figure moving quietly and quickly away. ' Who's
that ? ' cried one, and ' Stop there ! ' shouted the other. I
dashed round a corner and came full tilt—a faceless figure,

mind you !—on a lanky lad of fifteen. He yelled and I bowled him over, rushed past him, turned another corner, and by a happy inspiration threw myself flat behind a counter. In another moment feet went running past and I heard voices shouting, ' All hands to the doors ! ' asking what was ' up,' and giving one another advice how to catch me.

" Lying on the ground, I felt scared out of my wits. But— odd as it may seem—it did not occur to me at the moment to take off my clothes as I should have done. I had made up my mind, I suppose, to get away in them, and that ruled me. And then down the vista of the counters came a bawling of ' Here he is ! '

" I sprang to my feet, whipped a chair off the counter, and sent it whirling at the fool who had shouted, turned, came into another round a corner, sent him spinning, and rushed up the stairs. He kept his footing, gave a view-hallo ! and came up the staircase hot after me. Up the staircase were piled a multitude of those bright-coloured pot things—what are they ? "

" Art pots," suggested Kemp.

" That's it ! Art pots. Well, I turned at the top step and swung round, plucked one out of a pile and smashed it on his silly head as he came at me. The whole pile of pots went headlong, and I heard shouting and footsteps running from all parts. I made a mad rush for the refreshment place, and there was a man in white like a man cook, who took up the chase. I made one last desperate turn and found myself among lamps and ironmongery. I went behind the counter of this, and waited for my cook, and as he bolted in at the head of the chase, I doubled him up with a lamp. Down he went, and I crouched behind the counter and began whipping off my clothes as fast as I could. Coat, jacket, trousers, shoes were all right, but a lambswool vest fits a man like a skin. I heard more men coming, my cook was lying quiet on the other side of the counter, stunned or scared speechless, and I had to make another dash for it, like a rabbit hunted out of a wood-pile.

" ' This way, policeman ! ' I heard some one shouting. I found myself in my bedstead store-room again, and at the end a wilderness of wardrobes. I rushed among them, went flat, got rid of my vest after infinite wriggling, and stood a free man again, panting and scared, as the policeman and three of the shopmen came round the corner. They made a rush for the vest and pants, and collared the trousers. ' He's dropping his plunder,' said one of the young men. ' He *must* be some- where here.'

" But they did not find me all the same.

" I stood watching them hunt for me for a time, and cursing my ill-luck in losing the clothes. Then I went into the refresh- ment-room, drank a little milk I found there, and sat down by the fire to consider my position.

" In a little while two assistants came in and began to talk over the business very excitedly and like the fools they were. I heard a magnified account of my depredations, and other speculations as to my whereabouts. Then I fell to scheming again. The insurmountable difficulty of the place, especially now it was alarmed, was to get any plunder out of it.   I went down into the warehouse to see if there was any chance of packing and addressing a parcel, but I could not understand the system of checking. About eleven o'clock, the snow having thawed as it fell, and the day being finer and a little warmer than the previous one, I decided that the Emporium was hopeless, and went out again, exasperated at my want of success, with only the vaguest plans of action in my mind."

CHAPTER TWENTY-THREE

IN DRURY LANE

" B UT you begin to realise now," said the Invisible Man, "the full disadvantage of my condition. I had no shelter, no covering. To get clothing was to forego all my advantage, to make of myself a strange and terrible thing. I was fasting ; for to eat, to fill myself with unassimilated matter, would be to become grotesquely visible again."

" I never thought of that," said Kemp.

" Nor had I. And the snow had warned me of other dangers. I could not go abroad in snow—it would settle on me and expose me. Rain, too, would make me a watery outline, a glistening surface of a man—a bubble. And fog—I should be like a fainter bubble in a fog, a surface, a greasy glimmer of humanity. Moreover, as I went abroad—in the London air—I gathered dirt about my ankles, floating smuts and dust upon my skin. I did not know how long it would be before I should become visible from that cause also. But I saw clearly it could not be for long.

" Not in London at any rate.

" I went into the slums towards Great Portland Street, and found myself at the end of the street in which I had lodged. I did not go that way, because of the crowd halfway down it opposite to the still smoking ruins of the house I had fired. My most immediate problem was to get clothing. What to do with my face puzzled me. Then I saw in one of those little miscellaneous shops—news, sweets, toys, stationery, belated Christmas tomfoolery, and so forth—an array of masks and noses. I realised that problem was solved. In a flash I saw my course. I turned about, no longer aimless, and went—circuitously in order to avoid the busy ways, towards the back streets north of the Strand ; for I remembered, though not very distinctly where, that some theatrical costumiers had shops in that district.

" The day was cold, with a nipping wind down the north-ward running streets. I walked fast to avoid being overtaken. Every crossing was a danger, every passenger a thing to watch alertly. One man as I was about to pass him at the top of Bedford Street, turned upon me abruptly and came into me, sending me into the road and almost under the wheel of a passing hansom. The verdict of the cab-rank was that he had had some sort of stroke. I was so unnerved by this encounter that I went into Covent Garden Market and sat down for some time in a quiet corner by a stall of violets, panting and trembling. I found I had caught a fresh cold, and had to turn out after a time lest my sneezes should attract attention.

" At last I reached the object of my quest, a dirty fly-blown little shop in a byway near Drury Lane, with a window full of tinsel robes, sham jewels, wigs, slippers, dominoes and theatrical photographs. The shop was old-fashioned and low and dark, and the house rose above it for four storeys, dark and dismal. I peered through the window and, seeing no one within, entered. The opening of the door set a clanking bell ringing. I left it open, and walked round a bare costume stand, into a corner behind a cheval glass. For a minute or so no one came. Then I heard heavy feet striding across a room, and a man appeared down the shop.

" My plans were now perfectly definite. I proposed to make my way into the house, secrete myself upstairs, watch my opportunity, and when everything was quiet, rummage out a wig, mask, spectacles, and costume, and go into the world, perhaps a grotesque but still a credible figure. And incidentally of course I could rob the house of any available money.

" The man who had entered the shop was a short, slight, hunched, beetle-browed man, with long arms and very short bandy legs. Apparently I had interrupted a meal. He stared about the shop with an expression of expectation. This gave way to surprise, and then anger, as he saw the shop empty. ' Damn the boys ! ' he said. He went to stare up and down the street. He came in again in a minute, kicked the door to with his foot spitefully, and went muttering back to the house door.

" I came forward to follow him, and at the noise of my movement he stopped dead. I did so too, startled by his quickness of ear. He slammed the house door in my face.

" I stood hesitating. Suddenly I heard his quick footsteps returning, and the door reopened. He stood looking about the shop like one who was still not satisfied. Then, murmuring to himself, he examined the back of the counter and peered behind some fixtures. Then he stood doubtful. He had left the house door open and I slipped into the inner room.

" It was a queer little room, poorly furnished and with a number of big masks in the corner. On the table was his belated breakfast, and it was a confoundedly exasperating thing for me, Kemp, to have to sniff his coffee and stand watching while he came in and resumed his meal. And his table manners were irritating. Three doors opened into the little room, one going upstairs and one down, but they were all shut. I could not get out of the room while he was there, I could scarcely move because of his alertness, and there was a draught down my back. Twice I strangled a sneeze just in time.

" The spectacular quality of my sensations was curious and novel, but for all that I was heartily tired and angry long before he had done his eating. But at last he made an end, and putting his beggarly crockery on the black tin tray upon which he had had his teapot, and gathering all the crumbs up on the mustard-stained cloth, he took the whole lot of things after him. His burden prevented his shutting the door behind him—as he would have done ; I never saw such a man for shutting doors—and I followed him into a very dirty underground kitchen and scullery. I had the pleasure of seeing him begin to wash up, and then, finding no good in keeping down there, and the brick floor being cold to my feet, I returned upstairs and sat in his chair by the fire. It was burning low, and scarcely thinking, I put on a little coal. The noise of this brought him up at once, and he stood aglare. He peered about the room and was within an ace of touching me. Even after that examination, he scarcely seemed satisfied. He stopped in the doorway and took a final inspection before he went down.

"I waited in the little parlour for an age, and at last he came up and opened the upstairs door. I just managed to get by him.

"On the staircase he stopped suddenly, so that I very nearly blundered into him. He stood looking back right into my face and listening. ' I could have sworn,' he said. His long hairy hand pulled at his lower lip. His eye went up and down the staircase. Then he grunted and went on up again.

"His hand was on the handle of a door, and then he stopped again with the same puzzled anger on his face. He was becoming aware of the faint sounds of my movements about him. The man must have had diabolically acute hearing. He suddenly flashed into rage. ' If there's any one in this house,' he cried with an oath, and left the threat unfinished. He put his hand in his pocket, failed to find what he wanted, and rushing past me went blundering noisily and pugnaciously downstairs. But I did not follow him. I sat on the head of the staircase until his return.

"Presently he came up again, still muttering. He opened the door of the room, and before I could enter, slammed it in my face.

"I resolved to explore the house, and spent some time in doing so as noiselessly as possible. The house was very old and tumble-down, damp so that the paper in the attics was peeling from the walls, and rat-infested. Some of the door handles were stiff and I was afraid to turn them. Several rooms I did inspect were unfurnished, and others were littered with theatrical lumber, bought second-hand, I judged, from its appearance. In one room next to his I found a lot of old clothes. I began routing among these, and in my eagerness forgot again the evident sharpness of his ears. I heard a stealthy footstep and, looking up just in time, saw him peering in at the tumbled heap and holding an old-fashioned revolver in his hand. I stood perfectly still while he stared about openmouthed and suspicious. ' It must have been her,' he said slowly. ' Damn her ! '

"He shut the door quietly, and immediately I heard the key turn in the lock. Then his footsteps retreated. I realised abruptly that I was locked in. For a minute I did not know what to do. I walked from door to window and back, and stood perplexed. A gust of anger came upon me. But I decided to inspect the clothes before I did anything further, and my first attempt brought down a pile from an upper shelf. This brought him back, more sinister than ever. That time he actually touched me, jumped back with amazement and stood astonished in the middle of the room.

"Presently he calmed a little. 'Rats,' he said in an undertone, fingers on lip. He was evidently a little scared. I edged quietly out of the room, but a plank creaked. Then the infernal little brute started going all over the house, revolver in hand and locking door after door and pocketing the keys. When I realised what he was up to I had a fit of rage—I could hardly control myself sufficiently to watch my opportunity. By this time I knew he was alone in the house, and so I made no more ado, but knocked him on the head."

"Knocked him on the head!" exclaimed Kemp.

"Yes—stunned him—as he was going downstairs. Hit him from behind with a stool that stood on the landing. He went downstairs like a bag of old boots."

"But——! I say! The common conventions of humanity——"

"Are all very well for common people. But the point was, Kemp, that I had to get out of that house in a disguise without his seeing me. I couldn't think of any other way of doing it. And then I gagged him with a Louis Quatorze vest and tied him up in a sheet."

"Tied him up in a sheet!"

"Made a sort of bag of it. It was rather a good idea to keep the idiot scared and quiet, and a devilish hard thing to get out of—head away from the string. My dear Kemp, it's no good your sitting and glaring as though I was a murderer. It had to be done. He had his revolver. If once he saw me he would be able to describe me——"

"But still," said Kemp, "in England—to-day. And the man was in his own house, and you were—well, robbing."

"Robbing! Confound it! You'll call me a thief next! Surely, Kemp, you're not fool enough to dance on the old strings. Can't you see my position?"

"And his too," said Kemp.

The Invisible Man stood up sharply. "What do you mean to say?"

Kemp's face grew a trifle hard. He was about to speak and checked himself. "I suppose, after all," he said with a sudden change of manner, "the thing had to be done. You were in a fix. But still——"

"Of course I was in a fix—an infernal fix. And he made

me wild too—hunting me about the house, fooling about with his revolver, locking and unlocking doors. He was simply exasperating. You don't blame me, do you ? You don't blame me ? "

" I never blame any one," said Kemp. " It's quite out of fashion. What did you do next ? "

" I was hungry. Downstairs I found a loaf and some rank cheese—more than sufficient to satisfy my hunger. I took some brandy and water, and then went up past my impromptu bag—he was lying quite still—to the room containing the old clothes. This looked out upon the street, two lace curtains brown with dirt guarding the window. I went and peered out through their interstices. Outside the day was bright—by contrast with the brown shadows of the dismal house in which I found myself, dazzlingly bright. A brisk traffic was going by, fruit carts, a hansom, a four-wheeler with a pile of boxes, a fishmonger's cart. I turned with spots of colour swimming before my eyes to the shadowy fixtures behind me. My excitement was giving place to a clear apprehension of my position again. The room was full of a faint scent of benzoline, used, I suppose, in cleaning the garments.

" I began a systematic search of the place. I should judge the hunchback had been alone in the house for some time. He was a curious person. Everything that could possibly be of service to me I collected in the clothes store-room, and then I made a deliberate selection. I found a handbag I thought a suitable possession, and some powder, rouge, and sticking-plaster.

" I had thought of painting and powdering my face and all that there was to show of me, in order to render myself visible, but the disadvantage of this lay in the fact that I should require turpentine and other appliances and a considerable amount of time before I could vanish again. Finally I chose a mask of the better type, slightly grotesque but not more so than many human beings, dark glasses, greyish whiskers, and a wig. I could find no underclothing, but that I could buy subsequently, and for the time I swathed myself in calico dominoes and some white cashmere scarfs. I could find no socks, but the hunchback's boots were rather a loose fit and sufficed. In a desk in the shop were three sovereigns and about thirty shillings' worth of silver, and in a locked cupboard I burst in the inner room were eight pounds in gold. I could go forth into the world again, equipped.

" Then came a curious hesitation. Was my appearance really—credible ? I tried myself with a little bedroom looking-glass, inspecting myself from every point of view to discover any forgotten chink, but it all seemed sound. I was grotesque to the theatrical pitch, a stage miser, but I was certainly not a physical impossibility. Gathering confidence, I took my looking-glass down into the shop, pulled down the shop blinds, and surveyed myself from every point of view with the help of the cheval glass in the corner.

"I spent some minutes screwing up my courage and then unlocked the shop door and marched out into the street, leaving the little man to get out of his sheet again when he liked. In five minutes a dozen turnings intervened between me and the costumier's shop. No one appeared to notice me very pointedly. My last difficulty seemed overcome."

He stopped again.

"And you troubled no more about the hunchback?" said Kemp

"No," said the Invisible Man. "Nor have I heard what became of him. I suppose he untied himself or kicked himself out. The knots were pretty tight."

He became silent, and went to the window and stared out.

"What happened when you went out into the Strand?"

"Oh!—disillusionment again. I thought my troubles were over. Practically I thought I had impunity to do whatever I chose, everything—save to give away my secret. So I thought. Whatever I did, whatever the consequences might be, was nothing to me. I had merely to fling aside my garments and vanish. No person could hold me. I could take my money where I found it. I decided to treat myself to a sumptuous feast, and then put up at a good hotel, and accumulate a new outfit of property. I felt amazingly confident—it's not particularly pleasant recalling that I was an ass. I went into a place and was already ordering a lunch, when it occurred to me that I could not eat unless I exposed my invisible face. I finished ordering the lunch, told the man I should be back in ten minutes, and went out exasperated. I don't know if you have ever been disappointed in your appetite."

"Not quite so badly," said Kemp, "but I can imagine it."

"I could have smashed the silly devils. At last, faint with the desire for tasteful food, I went into another place and demanded a private room. 'I am disfigured,' I said. 'Badly.' They looked at me curiously, but of course it was not their affair—and so at last I got my lunch. It was not particularly well served, but it sufficed; and when I had had it, I sat over a cigar, trying to plan my line of action. And outside a snowstorm was beginning.

"The more I thought it over, Kemp, the more I realised what a helpless absurdity an Invisible Man was—in a cold and dirty climate and a crowded civilised city. Before I made this mad experiment I had dreamt of a thousand advantages. That afternoon it seemed all disappointment. I went over the heads of the things a man reckons desirable. No doubt invisibility made it possible to get them, but it made it impossible to enjoy them when they are got. Ambition—what is the good of pride of place when you cannot appear there?

What is the good of the love of woman when her name must needs be Delilah ? I have no taste for politics, for the black-guardisms of fame, for philanthropy, for sport. What was I to do ? And for this I had become a wrapped-up mystery, a swathed and bandaged caricature of a man ! "

He paused, and his attitude suggested a roving glance at the window.

" But how did you get to Iping ? " said Kemp, anxious to keep his guest busy talking.

" I went there to work. I had one hope. It was a half idea ! I have it still. It is a full-blown idea now. A way of getting back ! Of restoring what I have done. When I choose. When I have done all I mean to do invisibly. And that is what I chiefly want to talk to you about now."

" You went straight to Iping ? "

" Yes. I had simply to get my three volumes of memor-anda and my cheque-book, my luggage and underclothing, order a quantity of chemicals to work out this idea of mine—I will show you the calculations as soon as I get my books—and then I started. Jove ! I remember the snowstorm now, and the accursed bother it was to keep the snow from damping my pasteboard nose."

" At the end," said Kemp, " the day before yesterday, when they found you out, you rather—to judge by the papers——"

" I did. Rather. Did I kill that fool of a constable ? "

" No," said Kemp. " He's expected to recover."

" That's his luck, then. I clean lost my temper, the fools ! Why couldn't they leave me alone ? And that grocer lout ? "

" There are no deaths expected," said Kemp.

" I don't know about that Tramp of mine," said the Invisible Man, with an unpleasant laugh.

" By Heaven, Kemp, you don't know what rage *is* ! To have worked for years, to have planned and plotted, and then to get some fumbling purblind idiot messing across your course ! Every conceivable sort of silly creature that has ever been created has been sent to cross me.

" If I have much more of it, I shall go wild—I shall start mowing 'em.

" As it is, they've made things a thousand times more difficult."

" No doubt it's exasperating," said Kemp, dryly.

CHAPTER TWENTY-FOUR

THE PLAN THAT FAILED

"BUT now," said Kemp, with a side glance out of the window, "what are we to do?"

He moved nearer his guest as he spoke in such a manner as to prevent the possibility of a glimpse of the three men who were advancing up the hill road—with an intolerable slowness, as it seemed to Kemp.

"What were you planning to do when you were heading for Port Burdock? *Had* you any plan?"

"I was going to clear out of the country. But I have altered that plan rather since seeing you. I thought it would be wise, now the weather is hot and invisibility possible, to make for the South. Especially as my secret was known, and every one would be on the lookout for a masked and muffled man. You have a line of steamers from here to France. My idea was to get aboard one and run the risks of the passage. Thence I could go by train into Spain, or else get to Algiers. It would not be difficult. There a man might always be invisible—and yet live. And do things. I was using that Tramp as a money box and luggage carrier, until I decided how to get my books and things sent over to meet me."

"That's clear."

"And then the filthy brute must needs try and rob me! He has hidden my books, Kemp. Hidden my books! If I can lay my hands on him!"

"Best plan to get the books out of him first."

"But where is he? Do you know?"

"He's in the town police station, locked up, by his own request, in the strongest cell in the place."

"Cur!" said the Invisible Man.

"But that hangs up your plans a little."

"We must get those books; those books are vital."

"Certainly," said Kemp, a little nervously, wondering if he heard footsteps outside. "Certainly we must get those books. But that won't be difficult, if he doesn't know they're for you."

"No," said the Invisible Man, and thought.

Kemp tried to think of something to keep the talk going, but the Invisible Man resumed of his own accord.

"Blundering into your house, Kemp," he said, "changes all my plans. For you are a man that can understand. In spite of all that has happened, in spite of this publicity, of the loss of my books, of what I have suffered, there still remain great possibilities, huge possibilities——"

"You have told no one I am here?" he asked abruptly.

Kemp hesitated. "That was implied," he said.

" No one ? " insisted Griffin.

" Not a soul."

" Ah ! Now——" The Invisible Man stood up, and sticking his arms akimbo began to pace the study.

" I made a mistake, Kemp, a huge mistake, in carrying this thing through alone. I have wasted strength, time, opportunities. Alone—it is wonderful how little a man can do alone ! To rob a little, to hurt a little, and there is the end.

" What I want, Kemp, is a goal-keeper, a helper, and a hiding-place, an arrangement whereby I can sleep and eat and rest in peace, and unsuspected. I must have a confederate. With a confederate, with food and rest—a thousand things are possible.

" Hitherto I have gone on vague lines. We have to consider all that invisibility means, all that it does not mean. It means little advantage for eavesdropping and so forth—one makes sounds. It's of little help, a little help perhaps—in housebreaking and so forth. Once you've caught me you could easily imprison me. But on the other hand I am hard to catch. This invisibility, in fact, is only good in two cases : It's useful in getting away, it's useful in approaching. It's particularly useful, therefore, in killing. I can walk round a man, whatever weapon he has, choose my point, strike as I like. Dodge as I like. Escape as I like."

Kemp's hand went to his moustache. Was that a movement downstairs ?

" And it is killing we must do, Kemp."

" It is killing we must do," repeated Kemp. " I'm listening to your plan, Griffin, but I'm not agreeing, mind. *Why* killing ? "

" Not wanton killing, but a judicious slaying. The point is, they know there is an Invisible Man—as well as we know there is an Invisible Man. And that Invisible Man, Kemp, must now establish a Reign of Terror. Yes—no doubt it's startling. But I mean it. A Reign of Terror. He must take some town like your Burdock and terrify and dominate it. He must issue his orders. He can do that in a thousand ways—scraps of paper thrust under doors would suffice. And all who disobey his orders he must kill, and kill all who would defend the disobedient."

" Humph ! " said Kemp, no longer listening to Griffin but to the sound of his front door opening and closing.

" It seems to me, Griffin," he said, to cover his wandering attention, " that your confederate would be in a difficult position."

" No one would know he was a confederate," said the Invisible Man, eagerly. And then suddenly, " *Hush !* What's that downstairs ? "

" Nothing," said Kemp, and suddenly began to speak loud

and fast. " I don't agree to this, Griffin," he said. " Understand me, I don't agree to this. Why dream of playing a game against the race ? How can you hope to gain happiness ? Don't be a lone wolf. Publish your results ; take the world— take the nation at least—into your confidence. Think what you might do with a million helpers——"

The Invisible Man interrupted Kemp. " There are footsteps coming upstairs," he said in a low voice.

" Nonsense," said Kemp.

" Let me see," said the Invisible Man, and advanced, arm extended, to the door.

Kemp hesitated for a second and then moved to intercept him. The Invisible Man started and stood still. " Traitor !" cried the Voice, and suddenly the dressing-gown opened, and sitting down the Unseen began to disrobe. Kemp made three swift steps to the door, and forthwith the Invisible Man—his legs had vanished—sprang to his feet with a shout. Kemp flung the door open.

As it opened, there came a sound of hurrying feet downstairs and voices.

With a quick movement Kemp thrust the Invisible Man back, sprang aside, and slammed the door. The key was outside and ready. In another moment Griffin would have been alone in the belvedere study, a prisoner. Save for one little thing. The key had been slipped in hastily that morning. As Kemp slammed the door it fell noisily upon the carpet.

Kemp's face became white. He tried to grip the door handle with both hands. For a moment he stood lugging. Then the door gave six inches. But he got it closed again. The second time it was jerked a foot wide, and the dressing-gown came wedging itself into the opening. His throat was gripped by invisible fingers, and he left his hold on the handle to defend himself. He was forced back, tripped and pitched heavily into the corner of the landing. The empty dressing-gown was flung on the top of him.

Halfway up the staircase was Colonel Adye, the recipient of Kemp's letter, the chief of the Burdock police. He was staring aghast at the sudden appearance of Kemp, followed by the extraordinary sight of clothing tossing empty in the air. He saw Kemp felled, and struggling to his feet. He saw him rush forward, and go down again, felled like an ox.

Then suddenly he was struck violently. By nothing ! A vast weight, it seemed, leapt upon him, and he was hurled headlong down the staircase, with the grip at his throat and a knee in his groin. An invisible foot trod on his back, a ghostly patter passed downstairs, he heard the two police officers in the hall shout and run, and the front door of the house slammed violently.

He rolled over and sat up staring. He saw, staggering down the staircase, Kemp, dusty and dishevelled, one side of his face white from a blow, his lip bleeding, holding a pink dressing-gown and some underclothing in his arms.

" My God ! " cried Kemp, " the game's up ! He's gone ! "

CHAPTER TWENTY-FIVE

THE HUNTING OF THE INVISIBLE MAN

FOR a space Kemp was too inarticulate to make Adye understand the swift things that had just happened. The two men stood on the landing, Kemp speaking swiftly, the grotesque swathings of Griffin still on his arm. But presently Adye began to grasp something of the situation.

"He is mad," said Kemp ; "inhuman. He is pure selfishness. He thinks of nothing but his own advantage, his own safety. I have listened to such a story this morning of brutal self-seeking ! He has wounded men. He will kill them unless we can prevent him. He will create a panic. Nothing can stop him. He is going out now—furious ! "

"He must be caught," said Adye. "That is certain."

"But how ? " cried Kemp, and suddenly became full of ideas. "You must begin at once. You must set every available man to work. You must prevent his leaving this district. Once he gets away, he may go through the country-side as he wills, killing and maiming. He dreams of a reign of terror ! A reign of terror, I tell you. You must set a watch on trains and roads and shipping. The garrison must help. You must wire for help. The only thing that may keep him here is the thought of recovering some books of notes he counts of value. I will tell you of that ! There is a man in your police station—Marvel."

"I know," said Adye, "I know. Those books—yes."

"And you must prevent him from eating or sleeping ; day and night the country must be astir for him. Food must be locked up and secured, all food, so that he will have to break his way to it. The houses everywhere must be barred against him. Heaven send us cold nights and rain ! The whole country-side must begin hunting and keep hunting. I tell you, Adye, he is a danger, a disaster ; unless he is pinned and secured, it is frightful to think of the things that may happen."

"What else can we do ? " said Adye. "I must go down at once and begin organising. But why not come ? Yes—you come too ! Come, and we must hold a sort of council of war—get Hopps to help—and the railway managers. By Jove ! it's urgent. Come along—tell me as we go. What else is there we can do ? Put that stuff down."

In another moment Adye was leading the way downstairs. They found the front door open and the policemen standing outside staring at empty air. "He's got away, sir," said one.

"We must go to the central station at once," said Adye. "One of you go on down and get a cab to come up and meet us —quickly. And now, Kemp, what else ? "

" Dogs," said Kemp. " Get dogs. They don't see him, but they wind him. Get dogs."

" Good," said Adye. " It's not generally known, but the prison officials over at Halstead know a man with bloodhounds. Dogs. What else ? "

" Bear in mind," said Kemp, " his food shows. After eating, his food shows until it is assimilated. So that he has to hide after eating. You must keep on beating—every thicket, every quiet corner. And put all weapons, all implements that might be weapons, away. He can't carry such things for long. And what he can snatch up and strike men with must be hidden away."

" Good again," said Adye. " We shall have him yet ! "

" And on the roads," said Kemp, and hesitated.

" Yes ? " said Adye.

" Powdered glass," said Kemp. " It's cruel, I know. But think of what he may do ! "

Adye drew the air in between his teeth sharply. " It's unsportsmanlike. I don't know. But I'll have powdered glass got ready. If he goes too far——"

" The man's become inhuman, I tell you," said Kemp. " I am as sure he will establish a reign of terror—so soon as he has got over the emotions of this escape—as I am sure I am talking to you. Our only chance is to be ahead. He has cut himself off from his kind. His blood be upon his own head."

CHAPTER TWENTY-SIX

THE WICKSTEED MURDER

THE Invisible Man seems to have rushed out of Kemp's house in a state of blind fury. A little child playing near Kemp's gateway was violently caught up and thrown aside, so that its ankle was broken, and thereafter for some hours the Invisible Man passed out of human perceptions. No one knows where he went nor what he did. But one can imagine him hurrying through the hot June forenoon, up the hill and on to the open downland behind Port Burdock, raging and despairing at his intolerable fate, and sheltering at last, heated and weary, amid the thickets of Hintondean, to piece together again his shattered schemes against his species. That seems the most probable refuge for him, for there it was he reasserted himself in a grimly tragical manner about two in the afternoon.

One wonders what his state of mind may have been during that time, and what plans he devised. No doubt he was almost ecstatically exasperated by Kemp's treachery, and though we may be able to understand the motives that led to that deceit, we may still imagine and even sympathise a little with the fury the attempted surprise must have occasioned. Perhaps something of the stunned astonishment of his Oxford Street experiences may have returned to him, for evidently he had counted on Kemp's co-operation in his brutal dream of a terrorised world. At any rate he vanished from human ken about midday, and no living witness can tell what he did until about half-past two. It was a fortunate thing, perhaps, for humanity, but for him it was a fatal inaction.

During that time a growing multitude of men scattered over the countryside were busy. In the morning he had still been simply a legend, a terror ; in the afternoon, by virtue chiefly of Kemp's dryly worded proclamation, he was presented as a tangible antagonist, to be wounded, captured, or overcome, and the countryside began organising itself with inconceivable rapidity. By two o'clock even he might still have removed himself out of the district by getting aboard a train, but after two that became impossible. Every passenger train along the lines on a great parallelogram between Southampton, Manchester, Brighton, and Horsham, travelled with locked doors, and the goods traffic was almost entirely suspended. And in a great circle of twenty miles round Port Burdock, men armed with guns and bludgeons were presently setting out in groups of three and four, with dogs, to beat the roads and fields.

Mounted policemen rode along the country lanes, stopping at every cottage and warning the people to lock up their houses, and keep indoors unless they were armed, and all the elementary schools had broken up by three o'clock, and the children, scared and keeping together in groups, were hurrying home. Kemp's proclamation—signed indeed by Adye—was posted over almost the whole district by four or five o'clock in the afternoon. It gave briefly but clearly all the conditions of the struggle, the necessity of keeping the Invisible Man from food and sleep, the necessity for incessant watchfulness and for a prompt attention to any evidence of his movements. And so swift and decided was the action of the authorities, so prompt and universal was the belief in this strange being, that before nightfall an area of several hundred square miles was in a stringent state of siege. And before nightfall, too, a thrill of horror went through the whole watching nervous country-side. Going from whispering mouth to mouth, swift and certain over the length and breadth of the county, passed the story of the murder of Mr. Wicksteed.

If our supposition that the Invisible Man's refuge was the Hintondean thickets, then we must suppose that in the early afternoon he sallied out again bent upon some project that involved the use of a weapon. We cannot know what the project was, but the evidence that he had the iron rod in hand before he met Wicksteed is to me at least overwhelming.

We can know nothing of the details of the encounter. It occurred on the edge of a gravel pit, not two hundred yards from Lord Burdock's lodge gate. Everything points to a desperate struggle—the trampled ground, the numerous wounds Mr. Wicksteed received, his splintered walking-stick ; but why the attack was made—save in a murderous frenzy— it is impossible to imagine. Indeed the theory of madness is almost unavoidable. Mr. Wicksteed was a man of forty-five or forty-six, steward to Lord Burdock, of inoffensive habits and appearance, the very last person in the world to provoke such a terrible antagonist. Against him it would seem the Invisible Man used an iron rod dragged from a broken piece of fence. He stopped this quiet man, going quietly home to his midday meal, attacked him, beat down his feeble defences, broke his arm, felled him, and smashed his head to a jelly.

He must have dragged this rod out of the fencing before he met his victim ; he must have been carrying it ready in his hand. Only two details beyond what has already been stated seem to bear on the matter. One is the circumstance that the gravel pit was not in Mr. Wicksteed's direct path home, but nearly a couple of hundred yards out of his way. The other is the assertion of a little girl to the effect that, going to her afternoon school, she saw the murdered man " *trotting* " in a peculiar manner across a field towards the gravel pit. Her pantomime of his action suggests a man pursuing something on the ground before him and striking at it ever and again with his walking-stick. She was the last person to see him alive. He passed out of her sight to his death, the struggle being hidden from her only by a clump of beech trees and a slight depression in the ground.

Now this, to the present writer's mind at least, lifts the murder out of the realm of the absolutely wanton. We may imagine that Griffin had taken the rod as a weapon indeed, but without any deliberate intention of using it in murder. Wicksteed may then have come by and noticed this rod inexplicably moving through the air. Without any thought of the Invisible Man—for Port Burdock is ten miles away—he may have pursued it. It is quite conceivable that he may not even have heard of the Invisible Man. One can then imagine the Invisible Man making off—quietly in order to avoid discovering his presence in the neighbourhood, and Wicksteed, excited and curious, pursuing this unaccountably locomotive object—finally striking at it.

No doubt the Invisible Man could easily have distanced his middle-aged pursuer under ordinary circumstances, but the position in which Wicksteed's body was found suggests that he had the ill luck to drive his quarry into a corner between a drift of stinging nettles and the gravel pit. To those who appreciate the extraordinary irascibility of the Invisible Man, the rest of the encounter will be easy to imagine.

But this is pure hypothesis. The only undeniable facts—for stories of children are often unreliable—are the discovery of Wicksteed's body, done to death, and of the blood-stained iron rod flung among the nettles. The abandonment of the rod by Griffin, suggests that in the emotional excitement of the affair, the purpose for which he took it—if he had a purpose—was abandoned. He was certainly an intensely egotistical and unfeeling man, but the sight of his victim, his first victim, bloody and pitiful at his feet, may have released some long pent fountain of remorse to flood for a time whatever scheme of action he had contrived.

After the murder of Mr. Wicksteed, he would seem to have struck across the country towards the downland. There is a story of a voice heard about sunset by a couple of men in a field near Fern Bottom. It was wailing and laughing, sobbing and groaning, and ever and again it shouted. It must have been queer hearing. It drove up across the middle of a clover field and died away towards the hills.

That afternoon the Invisible Man must have learnt something of the rapid use Kemp had made of his confidences. He must have found houses locked and secured ; he may have loitered about railway stations and prowled about inns, and no doubt he read the proclamations and realised something of the nature of the campaign against him. And as the evening advanced, the fields became dotted here and there with groups of three or four men, and noisy with the yelping of dogs. These men-hunters had particular instructions as to the way they should support one another in the case of an encounter. He avoided them all. We may understand something of his exasperation, and it could have been none the less because he himself had supplied the information that was being used so remorselessly against him. For that day at least he lost heart ; for nearly twenty-four hours, save when he turned on Wicksteed, he was a hunted man. In the night, he must have eaten and slept ; for in the morning he was himself again, active, powerful, angry, and malignant, prepared for his last great struggle against the world.

CHAPTER TWENTY-SEVEN

THE SIEGE OF KEMP'S HOUSE

KEMP read a strange missive, written in pencil on a greasy sheet of paper.

"You have been amazingly energetic and clever," this letter ran, "though what you stand to gain by it I cannot imagine. You are against me. For a whole day you have chased me ; you have tried to rob me of a night's rest. But I have had food in spite of you, I have slept in spite of you, and the game is only beginning. The game is only beginning. There is nothing for it, but to start the Terror. This announces the first day of the Terror. Port Burdock is no longer under the Queen, tell your Colonel of Police, and the rest of them ; it is under me—the Terror ! This is day one of year one of the new epoch—the Epoch of the Invisible Man. I am Invisible Man the First. To begin with the rule will be easy. The first day there will be one execution for the sake of example —a man named Kemp. Death starts for him to-day. He may lock himself away, hide himself away, get guards about him, put on armour if he likes ; Death, the unseen Death, is coming. Let him take precautions ; it will impress my people. Death starts from the pillar box by midday. The letter will fall in as the postman comes along, then off ! The game begins. Death starts. Help him not, my people, lest Death fall upon you also. To-day Kemp is to die."

Kemp read this letter twice. "It's no hoax," he said. "That's his voice ! And he means it."

He turned the folded sheet over and saw on the addressed side of it the postmark Hintondean, and the prosaic detail, "2d. to pay."

He got up, leaving his lunch unfinished—the letter had come by the one o'clock post—and went into his study. He rang for his housekeeper, and told her to go round the house at once, examine all the fastenings of the windows, and close all the shutters. He closed the shutters of his study himself. From a locked drawer in his bedroom he took a little revolver, examined it carefully, and put it into the pocket of his lounge jacket. He wrote a number of brief notes, one to Colonel Adye, gave them to his servant to take, with explicit instructions as to her way of leaving the house. "There is no danger," he said, and added a mental reservation, "to you." He remained meditative for a space after doing this, and then returned to his cooling lunch.

He ate with gaps of thought. Finally he struck the table sharply. "We will have him ! " he said ; "and I am the bait. He will come too far."

He went up to the belvedere, carefully shutting every door

after him. "It's a game," he said, "an odd game—but the chances are all for me, Mr. Griffin, in spite of your invisibility. Griffin *contra mundum*—with a vengeance ! "

He stood at the window staring at the hot hillside. "He must get food every day—and I don't envy him. Did he really sleep last night ? Out in the open somewhere—secure from collisions. I wish we could get some good cold wet weather instead of the heat.

"He may be watching me now."

He went close to the window. Something rapped smartly against the brickwork over the frame, and made him start violently.

"I'm getting nervous," said Kemp. But it was five minutes before he went to the window again. "It must have been a sparrow," he said.

Presently he heard the front-door bell ringing, and hurried downstairs. He unbolted and unlocked the door, examined the chain, put it up, and opened cautiously without showing himself. A familiar voice hailed him. It was Adye.

"Your servant's been assaulted, Kemp," he said round the door.

"What ! " exclaimed Kemp.

"Had that note of yours taken away from her. He's close about here. Let me in."

Kemp released the chain, and Adye entered through as narrow an opening as possible. He stood in the hall, looking with infinite relief at Kemp refastening the door. "Note was snatched out of her hand. Scared her horribly. She's down at the station. Hysterics. He's close here. What was it about ? "

Kemp swore.

"What a fool I was," said Kemp. "I might have known. It's not an hour's walk from Hintondean. Already ! "

"What's up ? " said Adye.

"Look here ! " said Kemp, and led the way into his study. He handed Adye the Invisible Man's letter. Adye read it and whistled softly. "And you—— ? " said Adye.

"Proposed a trap—like a fool," said Kemp, "and sent my proposal out by a maid-servant. To him."

Adye followed Kemp's profanity.

"He'll clear out," said Adye.

"Not he," said Kemp.

A resounding smash of glass came from upstairs. Adye had a silvery glimpse of a little revolver half out of Kemp's pocket. "It's a window, upstairs ! " said Kemp, and led the way up. There came a second smash while they were still on the staircase. When they reached the study they found two of the three windows smashed, half the room littered with splintered glass, and one big flint lying on the writing-table. The two men stopped in the doorway, contemplating the wreckage. Kemp swore again, and as he did so the third window went with a snap like a pistol, hung starred for a moment, and collapsed in jagged, shivering triangles into the room.

" What's this for ? " said Adye.

" It's a beginning," said Kemp.

" There's no way of climbing up here ? "

" Not for a cat," said Kemp.

" No shutters ? "

" Not here. All the downstairs rooms—— Hullo ! "

Smash, and then whack of boards hit hard came from downstairs. " Confound him ! " said Kemp. " That must be—yes—it's one of the bedrooms. He's going to do all the house. But he's a fool. The shutters are up, and the glass will fall outside. He'll cut his feet."

Another window proclaimed its destruction. The two men stood on the landing perplexed. " I have it ! " said Adye. " Let me have a stick or something, and I'll go down to the station and get the bloodhounds put on. That ought to settle him ! They're hard by—not ten minutes——"

Another window went the way of its fellows.

" You haven't a revolver ? " asked Adye.

Kemp's hand went to his pocket. Then he hesitated. " I haven't one—at least to spare."

" I'll bring it back," said Adye, " you'll be safe here."

Kemp handed him the weapon.

" Now for the door," said Adye.

As they stood hesitating in the hall, they heard one of the first-floor bedroom windows crack and clash. Kemp went to the door and began to slip the bolts as silently as possible. His face was a little paler than usual. " You must step straight out," said Kemp. In another moment Adye was on the doorstep and the bolts were dropping back into the staples. He hesitated for a moment, feeling more comfortable with his back against the door. Then he marched, upright and square, down the steps. He crossed the lawn and approached the gate. A little breeze seemed to ripple over the grass. Something moved near him. " Stop a bit," said a Voice, and Adye stopped dead and his hand tightened on the revolver.

" Well ? " said Adye, white and grim, and every nerve tense.

" Oblige me by going back to the house," said the Voice, as tense and grim as Adye's.

" Sorry," said Adye a little hoarsely, and moistened his lips with his tongue. The Voice was on his left front, he thought. Suppose he were to take his luck with a shot ?

" What are you going for ? " said the Voice, and there was a quick movement of the two, and a flash of sunlight from the open lip of Adye's pocket.

Adye desisted and thought. " Where I go," he said slowly,

" is my own business." The words were still on his lips, when an arm came round his neck, his back felt a knee, and he was sprawling backward. He drew clumsily and fired absurdly, and in another moment he was struck in the mouth and the revolver wrested from his grip. He made a vain clutch at a slippery limb, tried to struggle up and fell back. " Damn ! " said Adye. The Voice laughed. " I'd kill you now if it wasn't the waste of a bullet," it said. He saw the revolver in mid-air, six feet off, covering him.

" Well ? " said Adye, sitting up.

" Get up," said the Voice.

Adye stood up.

" Attention," said the Voice, and then fiercely, " Don't try any games. Remember I can see your face if you can't see mine. You've got to go back to the house."

" He won't let me in," said Adye.

" That's a pity," said the Invisible Man. " I've got no quarrel with you."

Adye moistened his lips again. He glanced away from the barrel of the revolver and saw the sea far off very blue and dark under the midday sun, the smooth green down, the white cliff of the Head, and the multitudinous town, and suddenly he knew that life was very sweet. His eyes came back to this little metal thing hanging between heaven and earth, six yards away. " What am I to do ? " he said sullenly.

" What am *I* to do ? " asked the Invisible Man. " You will get help. The only thing is for you to go back."

" I will try. If he lets me in will you promise not to rush the door ? "

" I've got no quarrel with you," said the Voice.

Kemp had hurried upstairs after letting Adye out, and now crouching among the broken glass and peering cautiously over the edge of the study window-sill, he saw Adye stand parleying with the Unseen. " Why doesn't he fire ? " whispered Kemp to himself. Then the revolver moved a little and the glint of the sunlight flashed in Kemp's eyes. He shaded his eyes and tried to see the source of the blinding beam.

" Surely ! " he said, " Adye has given up the revolver."

" Promise not to rush the door," Adye was saying. " Don't push a winning game too far. Give a man a chance."

" You go back to the house. I tell you flatly I will not promise anything."

Adye's decision seemed suddenly made. He turned towards the house, walking slowly with his hands behind him. Kemp watched him — puzzled. The revolver vanished, flashed again into sight, vanished again, and became evident on a closer scrutiny as a little dark object following Adye. Then things happened very quickly. Adye leapt backwards, swung round, clutched at this little object, missed it, threw up his hands and fell forward on his face, leaving a little puff of blue in the air.   Kemp did not hear the sound of the shot. Adye writhed, raised himself on one arm, fell forward, and lay still.

For a space Kemp remained staring at the quiet carelessness of Adye's attitude.   The afternoon was very hot and still, nothing seemed stirring in all the world save a couple of yellow butterflies chasing each other through the shrubbery between the house and the road gate.   Adye lay on the lawn near the gate.   The blinds of all the villas down the hill-road were drawn, but in one little green summer-house was a white figure, apparently an old man asleep.   Kemp scrutinised the surroundings of the house for a glimpse of the revolver, but it had vanished.   His eyes came back to Adye.   The game was opening well.

Then came a ringing and knocking at the front door, that grew at last tumultuous, but pursuant to Kemp's instructions the servants had locked themselves into their rooms.   This was followed by a silence.   Kemp sat listening and then began peering cautiously out of the three windows, one after another.   He went to the staircase head and stood listening uneasily.   He armed himself with his bedroom poker, and went to examine the interior fastenings of the ground-floor windows again.   Everything was safe and quiet.   He returned to the belvedere.   Adye lay motionless over the edge of the gravel just as he had fallen.   Coming along the road by the villas were the housemaid and two policemen.

Everything was deadly still.   The three people seemed very slow in approaching.   He wondered what his antagonist was doing.

He started.   There was a smash from below.   He hesitated and went downstairs again.   Suddenly the house resounded with heavy blows and the splintering of wood.   He heard a smash and the destructive clang of the iron fastenings of the shutters.   He turned the key and opened the kitchen door. As he did so, the shutters, split and splintering, came flying inward.   He stood aghast.   The window-frame, save for one cross bar, was still intact, but only little teeth of glass remained in the frame.   The shutters had been driven in with an axe, and now the axe was descending in sweeping blows upon the window-frame and the iron bars defending it.   Then suddenly it leapt aside and vanished.   He saw the revolver lying on the path outside, and then the little weapon sprang into the air. He dodged back.   The revolver cracked just too late, and a splinter from the edge of the closing door flashed over his head. He slammed and locked the door, and as he stood outside he heard Griffin shouting and laughing.   Then the blows of the axe with their splitting and smashing accompaniments were resumed.

Kemp stood in the passage trying to think.   In a moment

the Invisible Man would be in the kitchen. This door would not keep him a moment, and then——"

A ringing came at the front door again. It would be the policemen. He ran into the hall, put up the chain, and drew the bolts. He made the girl speak before he dropped the chain, and the three people blundered into the house in a heap, and Kemp slammed the door again.

"The Invisible Man!" said Kemp. "He has a revolver, with two shots—left. He's killed Adye. Shot him anyhow. Didn't you see him on the lawn? He's lying there."

"Who?" said one of the policemen.

"Adye," said Kemp.

"We came round the back way," said the girl.

"What's that smashing?" asked one of the policemen.

"He's in the kitchen—or will be. He has found an axe——"

Suddenly the house was full of the Invisible Man's resounding blows on the kitchen door. The girl stared towards the kitchen, shuddered, and retreated into the dining-room. Kemp tried to explain in broken sentences. They heard the kitchen door give.

"This way," cried Kemp, starting into activity, and bundled the policemen into the dining-room doorway.

"Poker," said Kemp, and rushed to the fender. He handed a poker to each policeman. He suddenly flung himself backward.

"Whup!" said one policeman, ducked, and caught the axe on his poker. The pistol snapped its penultimate shot and ripped a valuable Sidney Cooper. The second policeman brought his poker down on the little weapon, as one might knock down a wasp, and sent it rattling to the floor.

At the first clash the girl screamed, stood screaming for a moment by the fireplace, and then ran to open the shutters—possibly with an idea of escaping by the shattered window.

The axe receded into the passage, and fell to a position about two feet from the ground. They could hear the Invisible Man breathing. "Stand away, you two," he said. "I want that man Kemp."

"We want you," said the first policeman, making a quick step forward and wiping with his poker at the Voice. The Invisible Man must have started back. He blundered into the umbrella stand. Then, as the policeman staggered with the swing of the blow he had aimed, the Invisible Man countered with the axe, the helmet crumpled like paper, and the blow sent the man spinning to the floor at the head of the kitchen stairs. But the second policeman, aiming behind the axe with his poker, hit something soft that snapped. There was a sharp exclamation of pain and then the axe fell to the ground. The policeman wiped again at vacancy and hit nothing; he put his foot on the axe, and struck again. Then he stood, poker clubbed, listening intent for the slightest movement.

He heard the dining-room window open, and a quick rush of feet within. His companion rolled over and sat up, with the blood running down between his eye and ear. "Where is he ?" asked the man on the floor.

"Don't know. I've hit him. He's standing somewhere in the hall. Unless he's slipped past you. Doctor Kemp—sir."

Pause.

"Doctor Kemp," cried the policeman again.

The second policeman struggled to his feet. He stood up. Suddenly the faint pad of bare feet on the kitchen stairs could be heard. "Yap !" cried the first policeman, and incontinently flung his poker. It smashed a little gas bracket.

He made as if he would pursue the Invisible Man downstairs. Then he thought better of it and stepped into the dining-room.

"Doctor Kemp," he began, and stopped short——

"Doctor Kemp's in here," he said, as his companion looked over his shoulder.

The dining-room window was wide open, and neither housemaid nor Kemp was to be seen.

The second policeman's opinion of Kemp was terse and vivid.

CHAPTER TWENTY-EIGHT

THE HUNTER HUNTED

M R. HEELAS, Mr. Kemp's nearest neighbour among the villa holders, was asleep in his summer-house when the siege of Kemp's house began. Mr. Heelas was one of the sturdy minority who refused to believe "in all this nonsense" about an Invisible Man. His wife, however, as he was to be reminded subsequently, did. He insisted upon walking about his garden just as if nothing was the matter, and he went to sleep in the afternoon in accordance with the custom of years. He slept through the smashing of the windows, and then woke up suddenly with a curious persuasion of something wrong. He looked across at Kemp's house, rubbed his eyes and looked again. Then he put his feet to the ground, and sat listening. He said he was damned, and still the strange thing was visible. The house looked as though it had been deserted for weeks—after a violent riot. Every window was broken, and every window, save those of the belvedere study, was blinded by the internal shutters.

"I could have sworn it was all right"—he looked at his watch—"twenty minutes ago."

He became aware of a measured concussion and the clash of glass, far away in the distance. And then, as he sat open-mouthed, came a still more wonderful thing. The shutters of the drawing-room window were flung open violently, and the housemaid in her outdoor hat and garments, appeared struggling in a frantic manner to throw up the sash. Suddenly a man appeared beside her, helping her—Dr. Kemp! In another moment the window was open, and the housemaid was struggling out ; she was pitched forward and vanished among the shrubs. Mr. Heelas stood up, exclaiming vaguely and vehemently at all these wonderful things He saw Kemp stand on the sill, spring from the window, and reappear almost instantaneously running along a path in the shrubbery and stooping as he ran, like a man who evades observation. He vanished behind a laburnum, and appeared again clambering a fence that abutted on the open down. In a second he had tumbled over and was running at a tremendous pace down the slope towards Mr. Heelas.

"Lord !" cried Mr. Heelas, struck with an idea ; "it's that Invisible Man brute ! It's right, after all ! "

With Mr. Heelas to think things like that was to act, and his cook watching him from the top window was amazed to see him come pelting towards the house at a good nine miles an hour. "Thought he wasn't afraid," said the cook. "Mary, just come here ! " There was a slamming of doors, a ringing of bells, and the voice of Mr. Heelas bellowing like

a bull. "Shut the doors, shut the windows, shut everything! the Invisible Man is coming!" Instantly the house
was full of screams and directions and scurrying feet. He ran
to shut the French windows himself that opened on the
veranda; as he did so Kemp's head and shoulders and knee
appeared over the edge of the garden fence. In another
moment Kemp had ploughed through the asparagus, and was
running across the tennis lawn to the house.

"You can't come in," said Mr. Heelas, shutting the bolts.
"I'm very sorry if he's after you, but you can't come in!"

Kemp appeared with a face of terror close to the glass,
rapping and then shaking frantically at the French windows.
Then, seeing his efforts were useless, he ran along the veranda,
vaulted the end, and went to hammer at the side door. Then
he ran round by the side gate to the front of the house, and so
into the hill-road. And Mr. Heelas staring from his window—
a face of horror—had scarcely witnessed Kemp vanish, ere
the asparagus was being trampled this way and that by feet
unseen. At that Mr. Heelas fled precipitately upstairs, and
the rest of the chase is beyond his purview. But as he passed
the staircase window, he heard the side gate slam.

Emerging into the hill-road, Kemp naturally took the down-
ward direction, and so it was he came to run in his own person
the very race he had watched with such a critical eye from the
belvedere study only four days ago. He ran it well for a man
out of training; and though his face was white and wet, his
wits were cool to the last. He ran with wide strides, and
wherever a patch of rough ground intervened, wherever there
came a patch of raw flints, or a bit of broken glass shone
dazzling, he crossed it and left the bare invisible feet that
followed to take what line they would.

For the first time in his life Kemp discovered that the
hill-road was indescribably vast and desolate, and that the
beginnings of the town far below at the hill foot were strangely
remote. Never had there been a slower or more painful
method of progression than running. All the gaunt villas,
sleeping in the afternoon sun, looked locked and barred; no
doubt they were locked and barred—by his own orders. But
at any rate they might have kept a lookout for an eventuality
like this! The town was rising up now, the sea had dropped
out of sight behind it, and people down below were stirring.
A tram was just arriving at the hill foot. Beyond that was
the police station. Was that footsteps he heard behind him?
Spurt.

The people below were staring at him, one or two were
running, and his breath was beginning to saw in his throat.
The tram was quite near now, and the Jolly Cricketers was
noisily barring its doors. Beyond the tram were posts and
heaps of gravel—the drainage works. He had a transitory
idea of jumping into the tram and slamming the doors, and

then he resolved to go for the police station. In another moment he had passed the door of the Jolly Cricketers, and was in the blistering fag end of the street, with human beings about him. The tram driver and his helper—arrested by the sight of his furious haste—stood staring with the tram horses unhitched. Further on the astonished features of navvies appeared above the mounds of gravel.

His pace broke a little, and then he heard the swift pad of his pursuer, and leapt forward again. " The Invisible Man ! " he cried to the navvies, with a vague indicative gesture, and by an inspiration leapt the excavation and placed a burly group between him and the chase. Then abandoning the idea of the police station he turned into a little side street, rushed by a greengrocer's cart, hesitated for the tenth of a second at the door of a sweetstuff shop, and then made for the mouth of an alley that ran back into the main Hill Street again. Two or three little children were playing here, and shrieked and scattered running at his apparition, and forthwith doors and windows opened and excited mothers revealed their hearts. Out he shot into Hill Street again, three hundred yards from the tram-line end, and immediately he became aware of a tumultuous vociferation and running people.

He glanced up the street towards the hill. Hardly a dozen yards off ran a huge navvy, cursing in fragments and slashing viciously with a spade, and hard behind him came the tram conductor with his fists clenched. Up the street others followed these two, striking and shouting. Down towards the town, men and women were running, and he noticed clearly one man coming out of a shop-door with a stick in his hand. " Spread out ! Spread out ! " cried some one. Kemp suddenly grasped the altered condition of the chase. He stopped, and looked round, panting. " He's close here ! " he cried. " Form a line across——"

" Aha ! " shouted a voice.

He was hit hard under the ear, and went reeling, trying to face round towards his unseen antagonist. He just managed to keep his feet, and he struck a vain counter in the air. Then he was hit again under the jaw, and sprawled headlong on the ground. In another moment a knee compressed his diaphragm and a couple of eager hands gripped his throat, but the grip of one was weaker than the other ; he grasped the wrists, heard a cry of pain from his assailant, and then the spade of the navvy came whirling through the air above him, and struck something with a dull thud. He felt a drop of moisture on his face. The grip at his throat suddenly relaxed, and with a convulsive effort Kemp loosed himself, grasped a limp shoulder, and rolled uppermost. He gripped the unseen elbows near the ground. " I've got him ! " screamed Kemp. " Help ! Help hold ! He's down ! Hold his feet ! "

In another second there was a simultaneous rush upon the

struggle, and a stranger coming into the road suddenly might have thought an exceptionally savage game of Rugby football was in progress. And there was no shouting after Kemp's cry—only a sound of blows and feet and a heavy breathing.

Then came a mighty effort, and the Invisible Man threw off a couple of his antagonists and rose to his knees. Kemp clung to him in front like a hound to a stag, and a dozen hands gripped, clutched, and tore at the Unseen. The tram conductor suddenly got the neck and shoulders and lugged him back.

Down went the heap of struggling men again and rolled over. There was, I am afraid, some savage kicking. Then suddenly a wild scream of " Mercy ! Mercy ! " that died down swiftly to a sound like choking.

" Get back, you fools ! " cried the muffled voice of Kemp, and there was a vigorous shoving back of stalwart forms. " He's hurt, I tell you. Stand back ! "

There was a brief struggle to clear a space, and then the circle of eager eyes saw the doctor kneeling, as it seemed, fifteen inches in the air, and holding invisible arms to the ground. Behind him a constable gripped invisible ankles.

" Don't you leave go of en," cried the big navvy, holding a bloodstained spade ; " he's shamming."

" He's not shamming," said the doctor, cautiously raising his knee ; " and I'll hold him." His face was bruised and already going red ; he spoke thickly because of a bleeding lip. He released one hand and seemed to be feeling at the face. " The mouth's all wet," he said. And then, " Good God ! "

He stood up abruptly and then knelt down on the ground by the side of the thing unseen. There was a pushing and shuffling, a sound of heavy feet as fresh people turned up to increase the pressure of the crowd. People now were coming out of the houses. The doors of the Jolly Cricketers were suddenly wide open. Very little was said.

Kemp felt about, his hand seeming to pass through empty air. " He's not breathing," he said, and then, " I can't feel his heart. His side—ugh ! "

Suddenly an old woman, peering under the arm of the big navvy, screamed sharply. " Looky there ! " she said, and thrust out a wrinkled finger.

And looking where she pointed, every one saw, faint and transparent as though it was made of glass, so that veins and arteries and bones and nerves could be distinguished, the outline of a hand, a hand limp and prone. It grew clouded and opaque even as they stared.

" Hullo ! " cried the constable. " Here's his feet a-showing ! "

And so, slowly, beginning at his hands and feet and creeping along his limbs to the vital centres of his body, that strange change continued. It was like the slow spreading of a poison.

First came the little white nerves, a hazy grey stretch of a limb, then the glassy bones and intricate arteries, then the flesh and skin, first a faint fogginess and then growing rapidly dense and opaque. Presently they could see his crushed chest and his shoulders, and the dim outline of his drawn and battered features.

When at last the crowd made way for Kemp to stand erect, there lay, naked and pitiful on the ground, the bruised and broken body of a young man about thirty. His hair and beard were white—not grey with age but white with the whiteness of albinism, and his eyes were like garnets. His hands were clenched, his eyes wide open, and his expression was one of anger and dismay.

" Cover his face ! " said a man. " For Gawd's sake, cover that face ! " and three little children, pushing forward through the crowd, were suddenly twisted round and sent packing off again.

Some one brought a sheet from the Jolly Cricketers ; and having covered him, they carried him into that house.

THE EPILOGUE

So ends the story of the strange and evil experiment of the Invisible Man. And if you would learn more of him you must go to a little inn near Port Stowe and talk to the landlord. The sign of the inn is an empty board save for a hat and boots, and the name is the title of this story. The landlord is a short and corpulent little man with a nose of cylindrical protrusion, wiry hair, and a sporadic rosiness of visage. Drink generously, and he will tell you generously of all the things that happened to him after that time, and of how the lawyers tried to do him out of the treasure found upon him.

"When they found they couldn't prove who's money was which, I'm blessed," he says, "if they didn't try to make me out a blooming treasure trove ! Do I *look* like a Treasure Trove ? And then a gentleman gave me a guinea a night to tell the story at the Empire Music 'all—just tell 'em in my own words—barring one."

And if you want to cut off the flow of his reminiscences abruptly, you can always do so by asking if there weren't three manuscript books in the story. He admits there were and proceeds to explain, with asseverations that everybody thinks *he* has 'em ! But bless you ! he hasn't. "The Invisible Man it was took 'em off to hide 'em when I cut and ran for Port Stowe. It's that Mr. Kemp put people on with the idea of *my* having 'em."

And then he subsides into a pensive state, watches you furtively, bustles nervously with glasses, and presently leaves the bar.

He is a bachelor man—his tastes were ever bachelor, and there are no women-folk in the house. Outwardly he buttons —it is expected of him—but in his more vital privacies, in the matter of braces for example, he still turns to string. He conducts his house without enterprise, but with eminent decorum. His movements are slow, and he is a great thinker. But he has a reputation for wisdom and for a respectable parsimony in the village, and his knowledge of the roads of the South of England would beat Cobbett.

And on Sunday mornings, every Sunday morning all the year round, while he is closed to the outer world, and every night after ten, he goes into his bar parlour bearing a glass of gin faintly tinged with water ; and having placed this down, he locks the door and examines the blinds, and even looks under the table. And then, being satisfied of his solitude, he unlocks the cupboard and a box in the cupboard and a drawer in that box, and produces three volumes bound in brown leather, and places them solemnly in the middle of the table. The covers are weather-worn and tinged with an algal green—for once they sojourned in a ditch and some of the pages have been washed blank by dirty water. The landlord sits down in an armchair, fills a long clay pipe slowly—gloating over the books the while. Then he pulls one towards him and opens it, and begins to study it—turning over the leaves backwards and forwards.

His brows are knit and his lips move painfully. "Hex, little two up in the air, cross and a fiddle-de-dee. Lord! what a one he was for intellect!"

Presently he relaxes and leans back, and blinks through his smoke across the room at things invisible to other eyes. "Full of secrets," he says. "Wonderful secrets!

"Once I get the haul of them—— *Lord!*

"I wouldn't do what *he* did ; I'd just—well!" He pulls at his pipe.

So he lapses into a dream, the undying wonderful dream of his life. And though Kemp has fished unceasingly, and Adye has questioned closely, no human being save the landlord knows those books are there, with the subtle secret of invisibility and a dozen other strange secrets written therein. And none other will know of them until he dies.

THE END

THE SECRET PLACES OF
THE HEART

CONTENTS

CHAPTER ONE

THE CONSULTATION

§ 1

THE maid was a young woman of great natural calmness ; she was accustomed to let in visitors who had this air of being annoyed and finding one umbrella too numerous for them. It mattered nothing to her that the gentleman was asking for Dr. Martineau as if he was asking for something with an unpleasant taste. Almost imperceptibly she relieved him of his umbrella and juggled his hat and coat on to a massive mahogany stand. " What name, sir ? " she asked, holding open the door of the consulting room.

" Hardy," said the gentleman, and then yielding it reluctantly with its distasteful three-year-old honour, " Sir Richmond Hardy."

The door closed softly behind him and he found himself in undivided possession of the large indifferent apartment in which the nervous and mental troubles of the outer world eddied for a time on their way to the distinguished specialist. A bowl of daffodils, a handsome bookcase containing bound Victorian magazines and antiquated medical works, some paintings of Scotch scenery, three big armchairs, a buhl clock, and a bronze Dancing Faun, by their want of any collective idea enhanced rather than mitigated the promiscuous disregard of the room. He drifted to the midmost of the three windows and stared out despondently at Harley Street.

For a minute or so he remained as still and limp as an empty jacket on its peg, and then a gust of irritation stirred him.

" Damned fool I was to come here," he said. . . . " *Damned fool* !

" Rush out of the place ? . . .

" I've given my name. . . ."

He heard the door behind him open and for a moment pretended not to hear. Then he turned round. " I don't see what you can do for me," he said.

" I'm sure *I* don't," said the doctor. " People come here and talk."

There was something reassuringly inaggressive about the figure that confronted Sir Richmond. Dr. Martineau's heigh' wanted at least three inches of Sir Richmond's five feet eleven ; he was humanly plump, his face was round and pink and cheerfully wistful, a little suggestive of the full moon, of what the full moon might be if it could get fresh air and exercise. Either his tailor had made his trousers too short or he had braced them too high so that he seemed to have grown out of them quite recently. Sir Richmond had been dreading an encounter with some dominating and mesmeric personality ; this amiable presence dispelled his preconceived resistances.

Dr. Martineau, a little out of breath as though he had been running upstairs, with his hands in his trouser pockets, seemed intent only on disavowals. " People come here and talk. It does them good and sometimes I am able to offer a suggestion.

" Talking to some one who understands a little," he expanded the idea.

" I'm jangling damnably . . . over-work. . . ."

" Not overwork," Dr. Martineau corrected. " Not overwork. Overwork never hurt any one. Fatigue stops that. A man can work—good straightforward work, without internal resistance, until he drops—and never hurt himself. You must be working against friction."

" Friction ! I'm like a machine without oil. I'm grinding to death. . . . And it's so *damned* important I *shouldn't* break down. It's *vitally* important."

He stressed his words and reinforced them with a quivering gesture of his upraised clenched hand. " My temper's in rags. I explode at any little thing. I'm *raw*. I can't work steadily for ten minutes and I can't leave off working."

" Your name," said the doctor, " is familiar. Sir Richmond Hardy ? In the papers. What is it ? "

" Fuel."

" Of course ! The Fuel Commission. Stupid of me ! We certainly can't afford to have you ill."

" I *am* ill. But you can't afford to have me absent from that Commission."

" Your technical knowledge——"

" Technical knowledge be damned ! Those men mean to corner the national fuel supply. And waste it ! For their profits. That's what I'm up against. You don't know the job I have to do. You don't know what a Commission of that sort is. The moral tangle of it. You don't know how its possibilities and limitations are canvassed and schemed about, long before a single member is appointed. Old Cassidy worked the whole thing with the Prime Minister. I can see that now as plain as daylight. I might have seen it at first. . . . Three experts who'd been got at ; they thought I'd been got at ; two Labour men who'd do anything you wanted them to do provided you called them ' level-headed,' Wagstaffe the socialist art critic who could be trusted to play the fool and make nationalisation look silly, and the rest mine owners, railway managers, oil profiteers, financial adventurers. . . ."

He was fairly launched. " It's the blind folly of it ! In the days before the war it was different. Then there was abundance. A little grabbing or cornering was all to the good. All to the good. It prevented things being used up too fast. And the world was running by habit; the inertia was tremendous. You could take all sorts of liberties. But all this is altered. We're living in a different world. The public won't stand things it used to stand. It's a new public. It's—wild. It'll smash up the show if they go too far. Everything short and running shorter—food, fuel, material. But these people go on. They go on as though nothing had changed. . . . Strikes, Russia, nothing will warn them. There are men on that Commission who would steal the brakes off a mountain railway just before they went down in it. . . . It's a struggle with suicidal imbeciles. It's——! But I'm talking ! I didn't come here to talk Fuel."

" You think there may be a smash-up ? "

" I lie awake at nights, thinking of it."

" A social smash-up."

" Economic. Social. Yes. Don't you ? "

" A social smash-up seems to me altogether a possibility. All sorts of people I find think that," said the doctor. " All sorts of people lie awake thinking of it."

" I wish some of my damned Committee would ! "

The doctor turned his eyes to the window. " I lie awake too," he said and seemed to reflect. But he was observing his patient acutely—with his ears.

" But you see how important it is," said Sir Richmond, and left his sentence unfinished.

" I'll do what I can for you," said the doctor, and considered swiftly what line of talk he had best follow.

§ 2

" This sense of a coming smash is epidemic," said the doctor. " It's at the back of all sorts of mental trouble. It is a new state of mind. Before the war it was abnormal— a phase of neurasthenia. Now it is almost the normal state with whole classes of intelligent people. Intelligent, I say. The others always have been casual and adventurous and always will be. A loss of confidence in the general background of life. So that we seem to float over abysses."

" We do," said Sir Richmond.

" And we have nothing but the old habits and ideas acquired in the days of our assurance. There is a discord, a jarring."

The doctor pursued his train of thought. " A new, raw and dreadful sense of responsibility for the universe. Accompanied by a realisation that the job is overwhelmingly too big for us."

" We've got to stand up to the job," said Sir Richmond. " Anyhow, what else is there to do ? We *may* keep things together. . . . I've got to do my bit. And if only I could hold myself at it, I could beat those fellows. But that's where the devil of it comes in. Never have I been so desirous

to work well in my life. And never have I been so slack
and weak-willed and inaccurate. . . . Sloppy. . . . Indolent.
. . . *Vicious !* . . ."

The doctor was about to speak but Sir Richmond interrupted him. " What's got hold of me ? What's got hold of
me ? I used to work well enough. It's as if my will had
come untwisted and was ravelling out into separate strands.
I've lost my unity. I'm not a man but a mob. I've got to
recover my vigour. At any cost."

Again as the doctor was about to speak the word was
taken out of his mouth. " And what I think of it, Dr.
Martineau, is this : it's fatigue. It's mental and moral
fatigue. Too much effort. On too high a level. And too—
austere. One strains and fags. *Flags !* ' Flags,' I meant
to say. One strains and flags, and then the lower stuff in
one, the subconscious stuff, takes control."

There was a flavour of popularised psycho-analysis about
this, and the doctor drew in the corners of his mouth, and
gave his head a critical slant. " M'm." But this only made
Sir Richmond raise his voice and quicken his speech. " I
want," he said, " a good tonic. A pick-me-up, a stimulating
harmless drug of some sort. That's indicated anyhow. To
begin with. Something to pull me together, as people say.
Bring me up to the scratch again."

" I don't like the use of drugs," said the doctor.

The expectation of Sir Richmond's expression changed to
disappointment. " But that's not reasonable," he cried.
" That's not reasonable. That's superstition. Call a thing
a drug and condemn it ! Everything is a drug. Everything
that affects you. Food stimulates or tranquillises. Drink.
Noise is a stimulant and quiet an opiate. What is life but
response to stimulants ? Or reaction after them ? When
I'm exhausted I want food. When I'm over-active and sleepless I want tranquillising. When I'm dispersed I want pulling
together."

" But we don't know how to use drugs," the doctor objected.

" But you ought to know."

Dr. Martineau fixed his eye on a first floor window-sill on
the opposite side of Harley Street. His manner suggested a
lecturer holding on to his theme.

" A day will come when we shall be able to manipulate
drugs—all sorts of drugs—and work them in to our general
way of living. I have no prejudice against them at all. A
time will come when we shall correct our moods, get down
to our reserves of energy by their help, suspend fatigue, put
off sleep during long spells of exertion. At some sudden
crisis for example. When we shall know enough to know
just how far to go with this, that or the other stuff. And how
to wash out its after effects. . . . I quite agree with you—
in principle. . . . But that time hasn't come yet. . . .

Decades of research yet. . . . If we tried that sort of thing now, we should be like children playing with poisons and explosives. . . . It's out of the question."

" I've been taking a few little things already. Easton Syrup, for example."

" Strychnine. It carries you for a time and drops you by the way. Has it done you any good—any *nett* good ? It has—I can see—broken your sleep."

The doctor turned round again to his patient and looked up into his troubled face.

" Given physiological trouble I don't mind resorting to a drug. Given structural injury I don't mind surgery. But except for any little mischief your amateur drugging may have done, you do not seem to me to be either sick or injured. You've no trouble either of structure or material. You're—worried—ill in your mind, and otherwise perfectly sound. It's the current of your thoughts, fermenting. If the trouble is in the mental sphere, why go out of the mental sphere for a treatment ? Talk and thought ; these are your remedies. Cool deliberate thought. You're unravelled. You say it yourself. Drugs will only make this or that unravelled strand behave disproportionately. You don't want that. You want to take stock of yourself as a whole—find out where you stand."

" But the Fuel Commission ? "

" Is it sitting now ? "

" Adjourned till after Whitsuntide. But there's heaps of work to be done.

" Still," he added, " this is my one chance of any treatment."

The doctor made a little calculation. " Three weeks. . . . It's scarcely time enough to begin."

" You're certain that no regimen of carefully planned and chosen tonics——? "

" Dismiss the idea. Dismiss it." He decided to take a plunge. " I've just been thinking of a little holiday for myself. But I'd like to see you through this. And if I am to see you through, there ought to be some sort of beginning now. In this three weeks. Suppose . . ."

Sir Richmond leapt to his thought. " I'm free to go any-where."

" Golf would drive a man of your composition mad ? "

" It would."

" That's that. Still—— . . . The country must be getting beautiful again now—after all the rain we have had. I have a little two-seater. I don't know—— The repair people promise to release it before Friday."

" But *I* have a choice of two very comfortable little cars. Why not be my guest ? "

" That might be more convenient."

" I'd prefer my own car."

" Then what do you say ? "

" I agree. Peripatetic treatment."

" South and west. We could talk on the road. In the evenings. By the wayside. We might make the beginnings of a treatment. . . . A simple tour. Nothing elaborate. You wouldn't bring a man ? "

" I always drive myself."

§ 3

" There's something very pleasant," said the doctor envisaging his own rash proposal, " in travelling along roads you don't know and seeing houses and parks and villages and towns for which you do not feel in the slightest degree responsible. They hide all their troubles from the road. Their backyards are tucked away out of sight, they show a brave face ; there's none of the nasty self-betrayals of the railway approach. And everything will be fresh still. There will still be a lot of apple-blossom—and bluebells. . . . And all the while we can be getting on with your affair."

He was back at the window now. " I want the holiday myself," he said.

He addressed Sir Richmond over his shoulder. " Have you noted how fagged and unstable *everybody* is getting ? Everybody intelligent, I mean."

" It's an infernally worrying time."

" Exactly. Everybody suffers."

" It's no *good* going on in the old ways——"

" It isn't. And it's a frightful strain to get into any new ways. So here we are."

" A man," the doctor expanded, " isn't a creature *in vacuo*. He's himself and his world. He's a surface of contact, a system of adaptations, between his essential self and his surroundings. Well, our surroundings have become—how shall I put it ?— a landslide. The war which seemed such a definable catastrophe in 1914 was, after all, only the first loud crack and smash of the collapse. The war is over and—nothing is over. This peace is a farce, reconstruction an exploded phrase. The slide goes on—it goes, if anything, faster, without a sign of stopping. And all our poor little adaptations ! Which we have been elaborating and trusting all our lives ! . . . One after another they fail us. We are stripped. . . . We have to begin all over again. . . . I'm fifty-seven and I feel at times nowadays like a chicken new hatched in a thunderstorm."

The doctor walked towards the bookcase and turned.

" Everybody is like that. . . . It isn't—what are you going to do ? It isn't—what am I going to do ? It's—what are we all going to do ? . . . Lord ! How safe and established everything was in 1910, say. We talked of this great war that was coming, but nobody thought it would come. We had been born in peace, comparatively speaking ; we had been brought up in peace. There was talk of wars. There were wars—little wars—that altered nothing material. . . . Consols used to be at 112 and you fed your household on ten shillings a head a week. You could run over all Europe, barring Turkey and Russia, without even a passport. You could get to Italy in a day. Never were life and comfort so safe— for respectable people. And we *were* respectable people. . . . That was the world that made us what we are. That was the sheltering and friendly greenhouse in which we grew. We fitted our minds to that. . . . And here we are with the greenhouse falling in upon us lump by lump, smash and clatter, the wild winds of heaven tearing in through the gaps."

Upstairs on Doctor Martineau's desk lay the typescript of the opening chapters of a book that was intended to make a great splash in the world, his *Psychology of a New Age*. He had his metaphors ready.

" We said : ' This system will always go on. We needn't bother about it.' We just planned our lives accordingly. It was like a bird building its nest of frozen snakes. My father left me a decent independence. I developed my position ; I have lived between here and the hospital, doing good work, enormously interested, prosperous, mildly distinguished. I had been born and brought up on the good ship Civilization. I assumed that some one else was steering the ship all right. I never knew ; I never inquired."

" Nor did I," said Sir Richard, " but——"

" And nobody was steering the ship," the doctor went on. " Nobody had ever steered the ship. It was adrift."

" I realised that. I——"

" It is a new realisation. Always hitherto men have lived by faith—as children do, as the animals do. At the back of the healthy mind, human or animal, has been this persuasion—' This is all right. This will go on. If I keep the rules, if I do so-and-so, all will be well. I need not trouble further ; things are cared for.' "

" If we could go on like that ! " said Sir Richmond.

" We can't. That faith is dead. The war—and the peace —have killed it."

The doctor's round face became speculative. His resemblance to the full moon increased. He seemed to gaze at remote things. " It may very well be that man is no more capable of living out of that atmosphere of assurance than a tadpole is of living out of water. His mental existence may be conditional on that. Deprived of it he may become incapable of sustained social life. He may become frantically self-seeking—incoherent . . . a stampede. . . . Human sanity may—*disperse*.

" That's our trouble," the doctor completed. "Our fundamental trouble. All our confidences and our accustomed
adaptations are destroyed. We fit together no longer. We
are—loose. We don't know where we are nor what to do.
The psychology of the former time fails to give safe responses,
and the psychology of the New Age has still to develop."

§ 4

" That is all very well," said Sir Richmond in the resolute
voice of one who will be pent no longer.

" That is all very well as far as it goes. But it does not
cover my case. I am not suffering from inadaptation. I
have adapted. I have thought things out. I think—much
as you do. Much as you do. So it's not that. But—— . . .
Mind you, I am perfectly clear where I am. Where we are.
What is happening to us all is the break-up of the entire
system. Agreed ! We have to make another system or
perish amidst the wreckage. I see that clearly. Science and
plan have to replace custom and tradition in human affairs.
Soon. Very soon. Granted. Granted. We used to say all
that. Even before the war. Now we mean it. We've
muddled about in the old ways over-long. Some new sort of
world, planned and scientific, has to be got going. Civilisation
renewed. Rebuilding civilisation—while the premises are
still occupied and busy. It's an immense enterprise, but it
is the only thing to be done. In some ways it's an enormously attractive enterprise. Inspiring. It grips my imagination. I think of the other men who must be at work.
Working as I do rather in the dark as yet. With whom I
shall presently join up. . . . The attempt may fail ; all
things human may fail ; but on the other hand it may succeed.
I never had such faith in anything as I have in the rightness
of the work I am doing now. I begin at that. But here is
where my difficulty comes in. The top of my brain, my
innermost self says all that I have been saying, but——
The rest of me won't follow. The rest of me refuses to attend,
forgets, straggles, misbehaves."

" Exactly."

The word irritated Sir Richmond. " Not ' exactly ' at all.
' Amazingly,' if you like. . . . I have this unlimited faith in
our present tremendous necessity—for work—for devotion—
I believe my share—the work I am doing, is essential—to
the whole thing—and I work sluggishly. I work reluctantly.
I work damnably."

" Exact——" The doctor checked himself. " All that is
explicable. Indeed it is. Listen for a moment to me !
Consider what you are. Consider what we are. Consider
what a man is before you marvel at his ineptitudes of will.
Face the accepted facts. Here is a creature not ten thousand

generations from the ape his ancestor. Not ten thousand And that ape again, not a score of thousands from the monkey his forebear. A man's body, his bodily powers, are just the body and powers of an ape, a little improved, a little adapted to novel needs. That brings me to my point. *Can his mind and will be anything better?* For a few generations, a few hundreds at most, knowledge and wide thought have flared out on the darknesses of life. . . . But the substance of man is ape still. He may carry a light in his brain, but his instincts move in the darkness. Out of that darkness he draws his motives."

" Or fails to draw them," said Sir Richmond.

" Or fails. . . . And that is where these new methods of treatment come in. We explore that failure. Together. What the psycho-analyst does—and I will confess that I owe much to the psycho-analyst—what he does is to direct thwarted, disappointed and perplexed people to the realities of their own nature. Which they have been accustomed to ignore and forget. They come to us with high ambitions or lovely illusions about themselves, torn, shredded, spoilt. They are morally denuded. Dreams they hate pursue them ; abhorrent desires draw them ; they are the prey of irresistible yet uncongenial impulses ; they succumb to black despairs. The first thing we ask them is this : ' What else could you expect ? ' "

" What else could I expect ? " Sir Richmond repeated, looking down on him. " H'm ! "

" The wonder is not that you are sluggish, reluctantly unselfish, inattentive, spasmodic. The wonder is that you are ever anything else. . . . Do you realise that a few million generations ago, everything that stirs in us, everything that exalts human life, self-devotions, heroisms, the utmost triumphs of art, the love—for love it is—that makes you and me care indeed for the fate and welfare of all this round world, was latent in the body of some little lurking beast that crawled and hid among the branches of vanished and forgotten Mesozoic trees ? A petty egg-laying, bristle-covered beast it was, with no more of the rudiments of a soul than bare hunger, weak lust and fear. . . . People always seem to regard that as a curious fact of no practical importance. It isn't : it's a vital fact of the utmost practical importance. That is what you are made of. Why should you expect—because a war and a revolution have shocked you—that you should suddenly be able to reach up and touch the sky ? "

" H'm ! " said Sir Richmond. " Have I been touching the sky ? "

" You are trying to play the part of an honest rich man."

" I don't care to see the whole system go smash."

" Exactly," said the doctor, before he could prevent himself.

" But is it any good to tell a man that the job he is attempting is above him—that he is just a hairy reptile twice removed—and all that sort of thing ? "

" Well, it saves him from hoping too much and being too greatly disappointed. It recalls him to the proportions of the job. He gets something done by not attempting everything. . . . And it clears him up. We get him to look into himself, to see directly and in measurable terms what it is that puts him wrong and holds him back. He's no longer vaguely incapacitated. He knows."

" That's diagnosis. That's not treatment."

" Treatment by diagnosis. To analyse a mental knot is to untie it."

" You propose that I shall spend my time, until the Commission meets, in thinking about myself. . . . I wanted to forget myself."

" Like a man who tries to forget that his petrol is running short and a cylinder missing fire. . . . No. Come back to the question of what you are," said the doctor. " A creature of the darkness with new lights. Lit and half-blinded by science and the possibilities of controlling the world that it opens out. In that light your will is all for service ; you care more for mankind than for yourself. You begin to understand something of the self beyond your self. But it is a partial and a shaded light as yet ; a little area about you it makes clear, the rest is still the old darkness—of millions of intense and narrow animal generations. . . . You are like some one who awakens out of an immemorial sleep to find himself in a vast chamber, in a great and ancient house, a great and ancient house high amidst frozen and lifeless mountains—in a sunless universe. You are not alone in it. You are not lord of all you survey. Your leadership is disputed. The darkness even of the room you are in is full of ancient and discarded but quite unsubjugated powers and purposes. . . . They thrust ambiguous limbs and claws suddenly out of the darkness into the light of your attention. They snatch things out of your hand, they trip your feet and jog your elbow. They crowd and cluster behind you. Wherever your shadow falls, they creep right up to you, creep upon you and struggle to take possession of you. The souls of apes, monkeys, reptiles and creeping things haunt the passages and attics and cellars of this living house in which your consciousness has awakened. . . ."

The doctor gave this quotation from his unpublished book the advantages of an abrupt break and a pause.

Sir Richmond shrugged his shoulders and smiled. " And you propose a vermin hunt in the old tenement ? "

" The modern man has to be master in his own house. He has to take stock and know what is there."

" Three weeks of self vivisection."

" To begin with. Three weeks of perfect honesty with yourself. As an opening. . . . It will take longer than that if we are to go through with the job."

" It's a considerable—process."

" It is."

" Yet you shrink from simple things like drugs ! "

" Self knowledge—without anæsthetics."

" Has this sort of thing ever done any one any good at all ? "

" It has turned hundreds back to sanity and steady work."

" How frank are we going to be ? How full are we going to be ? Anyhow—we can break off at any time——. . . . We'll try it. We'll try it. . . . And so for this journey into the west of England. . . . And—if we can get there—I'm not sure that we can get there—into the secret places of my heart."

CHAPTER TWO

LADY HARDY

THE patient left the house with much more self-possession than he had shown when entering it. Doctor Martineau had thrust him back from his intenser prepossessions to a more generalised view of himself, had made his troubles objective and detached him from them. He could even find something amusing now in his situation. He liked the immense scope of the theoretical duet in which they had indulged. He felt that most of it was entirely true—and, in some untraceable manner, absurd. There were entertaining possibilities in the prospect of the doctor drawing him out— he himself partly assisting and partly resisting.

He was a man of extensive reservations. His private life was in some respects exceptionally private.

" I don't confide. . . . Do I even confide in myself ? I imagine I do. . . . Is there anything in myself that I haven't looked squarely in the face ? . . . How much are we going into ? Even as regards facts ?

" Does it really help a man—to see himself ? " . . .

Such thoughts engaged him until he found himself in his study. His desk and his writing-table were piled high with a heavy burthen of work. Still a little preoccupied with Doctor Martineau's exposition, he began to handle this confusion. . . .

At half-past nine he found himself with three hours of good work behind him. It had seemed like two. He had not worked like this for many weeks. " This is very cheering," he said. " And unexpected. Can old Moon-face have hypnotised me ? Anyhow—— . . . Perhaps I've only imagined I was ill. . . . Dinner ? " He looked at his watch and was amazed at the time. " Good Lord ! I've been at it three hours. What can have happened ? Funny I didn't hear the gong."

He went downstairs and found Lady Hardy reading a magazine in a dining-room armchair and finely poised between devotion and martyrdom. A shadow of vexation fell athwart his mind at the sight of her.

" I'd no idea it was so late," he said. " I heard no gong."

" After you swore so at poor Bradley I ordered that there should be no gongs when we were alone. I did come up to your door about half-past eight. I crept up. But I was afraid I might upset you if I come in."

" But you've not waited——"

" I've had a mouthful of soup." Lady Hardy rang the bell.

" I've done some work at last," said Sir Richmond, astride on the hearthrug.

"I'm glad," said Lady Hardy, without gladness. "I waited for three hours."

Lady Hardy was a frail little blue-eyed woman with uneven shoulders and a delicate sweet profile. Hers was that type of face that under even the most pleasant and luxurious circumstances still looks bravely and patiently enduring. Her refinement threw a tinge of coarseness over his eager consumption of his excellent clear soup.

"What's this fish, Bradley?" he asked.

"Turbot, Sir Richmond."

"Don't you have any?" he asked his wife.

"I've had a little fish," said Lady Hardy.

When Bradley was out of the room, Sir Richmond remarked : "I saw that nerves man, Dr. Martineau, to-day. He wants me to take a holiday."

The quiet patience of the lady's manner intensified. She said nothing. A flash of resentment lit Sir Richmond's eyes. When he spoke again, he seemed to answer unspoken accusations. "Dr. Martineau's idea is that he should come with me."

The lady adjusted herself to a new point of view.

"But won't that be reminding you of your illness and worries?"

"He seems a good sort of fellow. . . . I'm inclined to like him. He'll be as good company as any one. . . . This *tournedos* looks excellent. Have some."

"I had a little bird," said Lady Hardy, "when I found you weren't coming."

"But I say—don't wait here if you've dined. Bradley can see to me."

She smiled and shook her head with the quiet conviction of one who knew her duty better. "Perhaps I'll have a little ice pudding when it comes," she said.

Sir Richmond detested eating alone in an atmosphere of observant criticism. And he did not like talking with his mouth full to an unembarrassed interlocutor who made no conversational leads of her own. After a few mouthfuls he pushed his plate away from him. "Then let's have up the ice pudding," he said with a faint note of bitterness.

"But have you finished——?"

"The ice pudding !" he exploded wrathfully. "The ice pudding !"

Lady Hardy sat for a moment a picture of meek distress. Then, her delicate eyebrows raised, and the corners of her mouth drooping, she touched the button of the silver table-bell.

CHAPTER THREE

THE DEPARTURE

§ 1

No wise man goes out upon a novel expedition without misgivings. And between their first meeting and the appointed morning both Sir Richmond Hardy and Dr. Martineau were the prey of quite disagreeable doubts about each other, themselves, and the excursion before them. At the time of their meeting each had been convinced that he gauged the other sufficiently for the purposes of the proposed tour. Afterwards each found himself trying to recall the other with greater distinctness and able to recall nothing but queer, ominous and minatory traits. The doctor's impression of the great fuel specialist grew ever darker, leaner, taller and more impatient. Sir Richmond took on the likeness of a monster obdurate and hostile, he spread upwards until like the Djinn out of the bottle, he darkened the heavens. And he talked too much. He talked ever so much too much. . . .

Sir Richmond also thought that the doctor talked too much. In addition, he read into his imperfect memory of the doctor's face, an expression of protruded curiosity. What was all this problem of motives and inclinations that they were " going into " so gaily ? He had merely consulted the doctor on a simple, straightforward need for a nervous tonic —that was what he had needed—a tonic. Instead he had engaged himself for—he scarcely knew what—an indiscreet, indelicate and altogether undesirable experiment in confidences.

Both men were considerably reassured when at last they set eyes on each other again. Indeed each was surprised to find something almost agreeable in the appearance of the other. Dr. Martineau at once perceived that the fierceness of Sir Richmond was nothing more than the fierceness of an overwrought man, and Sir Richmond realised at a glance that the curiosity of Dr. Martineau's bearing had in it nothing personal or base ; it was just the fine alertness of the scientific mind.

Sir Richmond had arrived nearly forty minutes late, and it would have been evident to a much less highly trained observer than Dr. Martineau that some dissension had arisen between the little, ladylike, cream and black Charmeuse car and its owner. There was a faint air of resentment and protest between them. As if Sir Richmond had been in some way rude to it.

The cap of the radiator was adorned with a little brass figure of a flying Mercury. Frozen in a sprightly attitude, its

146

stiff-bound and its fixed heavenward stare was highly suggestive
of a forced and tactful disregard of current unpleasantness.

Nothing was said, however, to confirm or dispel this suspicion
of a disagreement between the man and the car. Sir Richmond directed and assisted Dr. Martineau's man to adjust
the luggage at the back, and Dr. Martineau watched proceedings from his dignified front door. He was wearing a suit
of fawn tweeds, a fawn Homburg hat and a light Burberry,
with just that effect of special preparation for a holiday which
betrays the habitually busy man. Sir Richmond's brown
gauntness was, he noted, greatly set off by his suit of grey.
There had certainly been some sort of quarrel. Sir Richmond
was explaining the straps to Dr. Martineau's butler with the
coldness a man betrays when he explains the uncongenial
habits of some unloved intimate. And when the moment
came to start and the little engine did not immediately respond
to the electric starter, he said : " Oh ! *Come* up you—— ! "

His voice sank at the last word as though it was an entirely
confidential communication to the little car. And it was
an extremely low and disagreeable word. So Dr. Martineau
decided that it was not his business to hear it. . . .

It was speedily apparent that Sir Richmond was an experienced and excellent driver. He took the Charmeuse out
into the traffic of Baker Street and westward through brisk
and busy streets and roads to Brentford and Hounslow
smoothly and swiftly, making a score of unhesitating and
accurate decisions without apparent thought. There was
very little conversation until they were through Brentford.
Near Shepherd's Bush Sir Richmond had explained, "This is
not my own particular car. That was butted into at the
garage this morning, and its radiator cracked. So I had to
fall back on this. It's quite a good little car. In its way.
My wife drives it at times. It has one or two constitutional
weaknesses—incidental to the make—gear-box over the
back-axle for example—gets all the vibration. Whole machine
rather on the flimsy side. Still——"

He left the topic at that.

Dr. Martineau said something of no consequence about its
being a very comfortable little car.

Somewhere between Brentford and Hounslow, Sir Richmond
plunged into the matter between them. "I don't know how
deep we are going into these psychological probings of yours,"
he said. "But I doubt very much if we shall get anything
out of them."

"Probably not," said Dr. Martineau.

"After all, what I want is a tonic. I don't see that there
is anything positively wrong with me. A certain lack of
energy——"

"Lack of balance," corrected the doctor. "You are
wasting energy upon internal friction."

" But isn't that inevitable ? No machine is perfectly efficient. No man either. There is always a waste. Waste of the type ; waste of the individual idosyncrasy. This little car, for instance, isn't pulling as she ought to pull—she never does. She's low in her class. So with myself ; there is a natural and necessary high rate of energy waste. Moods of apathy and indolence are natural to me. (Damn that omnibus ! All over the road !) "

" We don't deny the imperfection——" began the doctor.

" One has to fit oneself to one's circumstances," said Sir Richmond, opening up another line of thought.

" We don't deny the imperfection," the doctor stuck to it. " These new methods of treatment are based on the idea of imperfection. We begin with that. I began with that last Tuesday. . . ."

Sir Richmond, too, was sticking to his argument. " A man, and for that matter the world he lives in, is a tangle of accumulations. Your psycho-analyst starts, it seems to me, with a notion of stripping down to something fundamental. The ape before us was a tangle of accumulations, just as we are. So it was with his forebears. So it has always been. All life is an endless tangle of accumulations."

" Recognise it," said the doctor.

" And then ? " said Sir Richmond controversially.

" Recognise in particular your own tangle."

" Is my particular tangle very different from the general tangle ? (Oh ! Damn this feeble little engine !) I am a creature of undecided will, urged on by my tangled heredity to do a score of entirely incompatible things. Mankind, all life, is that."

" But our concern is the particular score of incompatible things you are urged to do. We examine and weigh—— We weigh——"

The doctor was still saying these words when a violent and ultimately diastrous struggle began between Sir Richmond and the little Charmeuse car. The doctor stopped in mid-sentence.

It was near Taplow station that the mutual exasperation of man and machine was brought to a crisis by the clumsy emergence of a laundry cart from a side road. Sir Richmond was obliged to pull up smartly and stopped his engine. It refused an immediate obedience to the electric starter. Then it picked up, raced noisily, disengaged great volumes of bluish smoke, and displayed an unaccountable indisposition to run on any gear but the lowest. Sir Richmond thought aloud, unpleasing thoughts. He addressed the little car as a person ; he referred to ancient disputes and temperamental incompatibilities. His anger betrayed him a coarse, ill-bred man. The little car quickened under his reproaches. There were some moments of hope, dashed by the necessity of going dead slow behind an interloping van. Sir Richmond did not notice the outstretched arm of the driver of the van, and stalled his engine for a second time. The electric starter refused its office altogether.

For some moments Sir Richmond sat like a man of stone.

" I must wind it up," he said at last in a profound and awful voice. " I must wind it up."

" I get out, don't I ? " asked the doctor, unanswered, and did so. Sir Richmond, after a grim search and the displacement and replacement of the luggage, produced a handle from the locker at the back of the car and prepared to wind.

There was a little difficulty. " Come *up* ! " he said, and the small engine roared out like a stage lion.

The two gentlemen resumed their seats. The car started, and then by an unfortunate inadvertency Sir Richmond pulled the gear lever over from the first speed to the reverse. There was a metallic clangour beneath the two gentlemen, and the car slowed down and stopped, although the engine was still throbbing wildly, and the dainty veil of blue smoke still streamed forward from the back of the car before a gentle breeze. The doctor got out almost precipitately, followed by a gaunt madman, mouthing vileness, who had only a minute or so before been a decent British citizen. He made some blind lunges at the tremulous but obdurate car, but rather as if he looked for offences and accusations than for displacements to adjust. Quivering and refusing, the little car was extraordinarily like some recalcitrant little old aristocratic lady in the hands of revolutionaries, and this made the behaviour of Sir Richmond seem even more outrageous than it would otherwise have done. He stopped the engine, he went down on his hands and knees in the road to peer up at the gear-box, then without restoring the spark, he tried to wind up the engine again. He spun the little handle with an insane violence, faster and faster for—as it seemed to the doctor—the better part of a minute. Beads of perspiration appeared upon his brow and ran together ; he bared his teeth in a snarl ; his hat slipped over one eye. He groaned with rage. Then, using the starting handle as a club, he assailed the car. He smote the brazen Mercury from its foothold and sent it and a part of the radiator cap with it flying across the road. He beat at the wings of the bonnet, until they bent in under his blows. Finally, he hurled the starting-handle at the wind-screen and smashed it. The starting-handle rattled over the bonnet and fell to the ground. . . .

The paroxysm was over. Ten seconds later this cataclysmal lunatic had reverted to sanity—a rather sheepish sanity.

He thrust his hands into his trouser pockets and turned his back on the car. He remarked in a voice of melancholy detachment : " It was a mistake to bring that Coupé."

Dr. Martineau had assumed an attitude of trained observation on the side path. His hands rested on his hips and his hat was a little on one side. He was inclined to agree with Sir Richmond. "I don't know," he considered. "You wanted some such blow-off as this."

"Did I?"

"The energy you have! That car must be somebody's whipping boy."

"The devil it is!" said Sir Richmond, turning round sharply and staring at it as if he expected it to display some surprising and yet familiar features. Then he looked questioningly and suspiciously at his companion.

"These outbreaks do nothing to amend the originating grievance," said the doctor. "No. And at times they are even costly. But they certainly lift a burthen from the nervous system. . . . And now I suppose we have to get that little ruin to Maidenhead."

"Little ruin!" repeated Sir Richmond. "No. There's lots of life in the little beast yet."

He reflected. "She'll have to be towed." He felt in his breast pocket. "Somewhere I have the R.A.C. order paper, the Badge that will Get You Home. We shall have to hail some passing car to take it into Maidenhead."

Dr. Martineau offered and Sir Richmond took and lit a cigarette.

For a little while conversation hung fire. Then for the first time Dr. Martineau heard his patient laugh.

"Amazing savage!" said Sir Richmond. "Amazing savage!"

He pointed to his handiwork. "The little car looks ruffled. Well it may."

He became grave again. "I suppose I ought to apologise."

Dr. Martineau weighed the situation. "As between doctor and patient," he said. "No."

"Oh!" said Sir Richmond, turned to a new point of view. "But where the patient ends and the host begins. . . . I'm really very sorry."

He reverted to his original train of thought which had not concerned Dr. Martineau at all. "After all, the little car was only doing what she was made to do."

§ 2

The affair of the car effectively unsealed Sir Richmond's mind. Hitherto Dr. Martineau had perceived the possibility and danger of a defensive silence or of a still more defensive irony; but now that Sir Richmond had once given himself away, he seemed prepared to give himself away to an unlimited extent. He embarked upon an apologetic discussion of the choleric temperament.

He began as they stood waiting for the relief car from the Maidenhead garage. " You were talking of the ghosts of apes and monkeys that suddenly come out from the darkness of the subconscious. . . ."

" You mean—when we first met at Harley Street ? "

" That last apparition of mine seems to have been a gorilla at least."

The doctor became precise. " Gorillaesque. We are not descended from gorillas."

" Queer thing a fit of rage is ! "

" It's one of nature's cruder expedients. Crude, but I doubt if it is fundamental. There doesn't seem to be rage in the vegetable world, and even among the animals——— ? No, it is not universal." He ran his mind over classes and orders. " Wasps and bees certainly seem to rage, but if one comes to think, most of the invertebrata show very few signs of it."

" I'm not so sure," said Sir Richmond. " I've never seen a snail in a towering passion or an oyster slamming its shell behind it. But these are sluggish things. Oysters sulk, which is after all a smouldering sort of rage. And take any more active invertebrate. Take a spider. Not a smashing and swearing sort of rage perhaps, but a disciplined, cold-blooded malignity. . . . Crabs fight. . . . A conger eel in a boat will rage—dangerously."

" A vertebrate. Yes. But even among the vertebrata ; who has ever seen a furious rabbit ? "

" Don't the bucks fight ? " questioned Sir Richmond.

Dr. Martineau admitted the point.

" I've always had these fits of passion. As far back as I can remember. I was a kicking, screaming child. I threw things. I once threw a fork at my elder brother and it stuck in his forehead, doing no serious damage—happily. There were whole days of wrath—days, as I remember them. Perhaps they were only hours. . . . I've never thought before what a peculiar thing all this raging is in the world. *Why* do we rage ? They used to say it was the devil. If it isn't the devil, then what the devil is it ?

" After all," he went on as the doctor was about to answer his question, " as you pointed out, it isn't the lowlier things that rage. It's the *higher* things and *us*."

" The devil nowadays," the doctor reflected after a pause, " so far as man is concerned, is understood to be the ancestral ape. And more particularly the old male ape."

But Sir Richmond was away on another line of thought. " Life itself, flaring out. Brooking no contradiction." He came round suddenly to the doctor's qualification. " Why male ? Don't little girls smash things just as much ? "

" They don't," said Dr. Martineau. " Not nearly as much."

Sir Richmond went off at a tangent again. " I suppose you have watched any number of babies ? "

" Not nearly as many as a general practitioner would do. There's a lot of rage about most of them at first, male or female."

" Queer little eddies of fury. . . . Recently—it happens—I've been seeing one. A spit of red wrath, clenching its fists and squalling threats at a damned disobedient universe."

The doctor was struck by an idea, and glanced quickly and questioningly at his companion's profile.

" Blind driving force," said Sir Richmond, musing.

" Isn't that after all what we really are ? " he asked the doctor. " Essentially—Rage. A rage in dead matter, making it alive."

" Schopenhauer," footnoted the doctor. " Boehme."

" Plain fact," said Sir Richmond. " No Rage—no Go."

" But rage without discipline ? "

" Discipline afterwards. The rage first."

" But rage against what ? And *for* what ? "

" Against the Universe. And for—— ? That's more difficult. What *is* the little beast squalling itself crimson for ? Ultimately ? . . . What is it clutching after ? In the long run, what will it get ? "

(" Yours the car in distress what sent this ? " asked an unheeded voice.)

" Of course, if you were to say ' desire,' " said Dr. Martineau, " then you would be in line with the psycho-analysts. They talk of *libido*, meaning a sort of fundamental desire. Jung speaks of it at times almost as if it were the universal driving force."

" No," said Sir Richmond, in love with his new idea. " Not desire. Desire would have a definite direction, and that is just what this driving force hasn't. It's rage."

" Yours the car in distress what sent this ? " the voice repeated. It was the voice of a mechanic in an Overland car. He was holding up the blue request for assistance that Sir Richmond had recently filled in.

The two philosphers returned to practical matters.

§ 3

For half an hour after the departure of the little Charmeuse car with Sir Richmond and Dr. Martineau, the brass Mercury lay unheeded in the dusty roadside grass. Then it caught the eye of a passing child.

He was a bright little boy of five. From the moment when he caught the gleam of brass he knew that he had made the find of his life. But his nurse was a timorous, foolish thing. " You did ought to of left it there Masterrarry," she said.

" Findings ain't keeping nowadays, not by no manner of means Masterrarry.

" *Yew*'d look silly if a policeman come along arsting people if they seen a goldennimage.

" Arst yer 'ow you come by it and look pretty straight at you."

All of which grumblings Master Harry treated with an experienced disregard. He knew definitely that he would never relinquish this bright and lovely possession again. It was the first beautiful thing he had ever possessed. He was the darling of fond and indulgent parents, and his nursery was crowded with hideous rag and sawdust dolls, golliwogs, comic penguins, comic lions, comic elephants and comic policemen, and every variety of suchlike humorous idiocy and visual beastliness. This figure, solid, delicate and gracious, was a thing of a different order.

There was to be much conflict and distress, tears and wrath, before the affinity of that clean-limbed, shining figure and his small soul was recognised. But he carried his point at last. The Mercury became his inseparable darling, his symbol, his private god, the one dignified and serious thing in a little life much congested by the quaint, the burlesque, and all the smiling, dull condescensions of adult love.

CHAPTER FOUR

AT MAIDENHEAD

§ 1

THE little Charmeuse was towed to hospital and the two psychiatrists took up their quarters at the Radiant Hotel, with its pleasant lawns and graceful landing-stage at the bend towards the bridge. Sir Richmond, after some trying work at the telephone, got into touch with his own proper car. A man would bring that down in two days' time at latest and afterwards the detested coupé could go back to London. The day was still young, and after lunch and coffee upon a sunny lawn a boat seemed indicated. Sir Richmond astonished the doctor by going to his room, re-appearing dressed in tennis flannels and looking very well in them. It occurred to the doctor as a thing hitherto unnoted that Sir Richmond was not indifferent to his personal appearance. The doctor had no flannels, but he had brought a brown holland umbrella lined with green that he had acquired long ago in Algiers, and this served to give him something of the riverside quality.

The day was full of sunshine and the river had a Maytime animation. Pink geraniums, vivid green lawns, gay awnings, bright glass, white paint and shining metal set the tone of Maidenhead life. At lunch there had been five or six small tables with quietly affectionate couples who talked in under-tones, a tableful of bright-coloured Jews who talked in over-tones, and a family party from the Midlands, badly smitten with shyness, who did not talk at all. "A resort of honey-moon couples," said the doctor, and then rather knowingly: "Temporary honeymoons, I fancy, in one or two of the cases."

"Decidedly temporary," said Sir Richmond, considering the company—"in most of the cases anyhow. The two in the corner might be married. You never know nowadays."

He became reflective. . . .

After lunch and coffee he rowed the doctor up the river towards Cliveden.

"The last time I was here," he said, returning to the subject, "I was here on a temporary honeymoon."

The doctor tried to look as though he had not thought that could be possible.

"I know my Maidenhead fairly well," said Sir Richmond. "Acquatic activities, such as rowing, punting, messing about with a boat-hook, tying-up, buzzing about in motor launches, fouling other people's boats, are merely the stage business of the drama. The ruling interests of this place are love—largely illicit—and persistent drinking. . . . Don't you think the bridge charming from here ?"

" I shouldn't have thought—*drinking*," said Dr. Martineau, after he had done justice to the bridge over his shoulder.

" Yes, the place has a floating population of quiet industrious soakers. The incurable river man and the river girl end at that."

Dr. Martineau encouraged Sir Richmond by an appreciative silence.

" If we are to explore the secret places of the heart," Sir Richmond went on, " we shall have to give some attention to this Maidenhead side of life. It is very material to my case. I have—as I have said—*been here*. This place has beauty and charm ; these piled-up woods behind which my Lords Astor and Desborough keep their state, this shining mirror of the water, brown and green and sky blue, this fringe of reeds and scented rushes and forget-me-not and lilies, and these perpetually posing white swans : they make a picture. A little artificial it is true ; one feels the presence of a Conservancy Board, planting the rushes and industriously nicking the swans ; but none the less delightful. And this setting has appealed to a number of people as an invitation, as, in a way, a promise. They come here, responsive to that promise of beauty and happiness. They conceive of themselves here, rowing swiftly and gracefully, punting beautifully, brandishing boat-hooks with ease and charm. They look to meet, under pleasant or romantic circumstances, other possessors and worshippers of grace and beauty here. There will be glowing evenings, warm moonlight, distant voices singing. . . . There is your desire, doctor, the desire you say is the driving force of life. But reality mocks it. Boats bump and lead to coarse ungracious quarrels ; rowing can be curiously fatiguing ; punting involves dreadful indignities. The romance here tarnishes very quickly. Romantic encounters fail to occur ; in our impatience we resort to—accosting. Chilly mists arise from the water and the magic of distant singing is provided, even excessively, by boatloads of cads—with collecting dishes. When the weather keeps warm there presently arises an extraordinary multitude of gnats—and when it does not there is a need for stimulants. That is why the dreamers who come here first for a light delicious brush with love, come down at last to the Thames-side barmaid with her array of spirits and cordials as the quintessence of all desire."

" I say," said the doctor. " You tear the place to pieces."

" The desires of the place," said Sir Richmond. " I'm using the place as a symbol."

He held his sculls awash, rippling in the water.

" The real force of life, the rage of life, isn't here," he said. " It's down underneath, sulking and smouldering. Every now and then it strains and cracks the surface. This stretch of the Thames, this pleasure stretch, has in fact a curiously quarrelsome atmosphere. People scold and insult one another for the most trivial things, for passing too close, for taking the wrong side, for tying up or floating loose. Most of these notice-boards on the bank show a thoroughly nasty spirit. People on the banks jeer at any one in the boats. You hear people quarrelling in boats, in the hotels, as they walk along the towing path. There is remarkably little happy laughter here. The *rage*, you see, is hostile to this place, the *rage* breaks through. . . . The people who drift from one pub to another, drinking, the people who fuddle in the riverside hotels, are the last fugitives of pleasure, trying to forget the rage. . . ."

"Isn't it that there is some greater desire at the back of the human mind ? " the doctor suggested. " Which refuses to be content with pleasure as an end ? "

"What greater desire ? " asked Sir Richmond, disconcertingly.

"Oh ! . . ." The doctor cast about.

"There is no such greater desire," said Sir Richmond. " You cannot name it. It is just blind drive. I admit its discontent with pleasure as an end—but has it any end of its own ? At the most you can say that the rage in life is seeking its desire and hasn't found it."

"Let us help in the search," said the doctor, with an afternoon smile under his green umbrella. " Go on."

§ 2

"Since our first talk in Harley Street," said Sir Richmond, " I have been trying myself over in my mind. (We can drift down this backwater.)"

"Big trees these are," said the doctor with infinite approval.

"I am astonished to discover what a bundle of discordant motives I am. I do not seem to deserve to be called a personality. I cannot discover even a general direction. Much more am I like a taxi-cab in which all sorts of aims and desires have travelled to their destination and got out. Are we all like that ? "

"A bundle held together by a name and address and a certain thread of memory ? " said the doctor, and considered. " More than that. More than that. We have leading ideas, associations, possessions, liabilities."

"We build ourselves a prison of circumstances that keeps us from complete dispersal."

"Exactly," said the doctor. " And there is also something, a consistency, that we call character."

"It changes."

"Consistently with itself."

"I have been trying to recall my sexual history," said Sir

Richmond, going off at a tangent. "My sentimental education. I wonder if it differs very widely from yours or most
men's."

"Some men are more eventful in these matters than others,"
said the doctor—it sounded—wistfully.

"They have the same jumble of motives and traditions, I
suspect, whether they are eventful or not. The brakes may
be strong or weak but the drive is the same. I can't remember
much of the beginnings of curiosity and knowledge in these
matters. Can you ? "

"Not much," said the doctor. "No."

"Your psycho-analysts tell a story of fears, suppressions,
monstrous imaginations, symbolic replacements. I don't
remember much of that sort of thing in my own case. It may
have faded out of my mind. There were probably some
uneasy curiosities, a grotesque dream or so perhaps ; I can't
recall anything of that sort distinctly now. I had a very
lively interest in women, even when I was still quite a little
boy, and a certain—what shall I call it ?—imaginative slavishness—not towards actual women but towards something
magnificently feminine. My first love——"

Sir Richmond smiled at some secret memory. "My first
love was Britannia—as depicted by Tenniel in the cartoons in
Punch. I must have been a very little chap at the time of
the Britannia affair. I just clung to her in my imagination
and did devoted things for her. Then I recall, a little later,
a secret abject adoration for the white goddesses of the
Crystal Palace. Not for any particular one of them that I can
remember—for all of them. But I don't remember anything
very monstrous or incestuous in my childish imaginations—
such things as Freud, I understand, lays stress upon. If
there is an Œdipus complex or anything of that sort in my
case it has been very completely washed out again. Perhaps
a child which is brought up in a proper mursery of its own
and sees a lot of pictures of the nude human body, and so
on, gets its mind shifted off any possible concentration upon
—the domestic aspect of sex. I got to definite knowledge
pretty early. By the time I was eleven or twelve."

"Normally ? "

"What is normally ? Decently, anyhow. Here again I
may be forgetting much secret and shameful curiosity. I got
my ideas into definite form out of a little straightforward
physiological teaching and some dissecting of rats and mice.
My schoolmaster was a capable sane man in advance of his
times, and my people believed in him. I think much of this
distorted perverse stuff that grows up in people's minds about
sex and develops into evil vices and still more evil habits, is
due to the mystery we make about these things."

"Not entirely," said the doctor.

"Largely. What child under a modern upbringing ever

goes through the stuffy horrors described in James Joyce's *Portrait of the Author as a Young Man ? "*

" I've not read it."

" A picture of the Catholic atmosphere ; a young soul shut up in darkness and ignorance to accumulate filth. In the name of purity and decency and under threats of hell fire."

" Horrible ! "

" Quite. A study of intolerable tensions, the tensions that make young people write unclean words in secret places."

" Yes, we certainly ventilate and sanitate in those matters nowadays. Where nothing is concealed, nothing can explode."

" On the whole I came up to adolescence pretty straight and clean," said Sir Richmond. " What stands out in my memory now is this idea of a sort of woman goddess who was very lovely and kind and powerful and wonderful. That ruled my secret imaginations as a boy, but it was very much in my mind as I grew up."

" The mother complex," said Dr. Martineau as a passing botanist might recognise and name a flower.

Sir Richmond stared at him for a moment.

" It had not the slightest connection with my mother or any mother or any particular woman at all. Far better to call it the goddess complex."

" The connection is not perhaps immediately visible," said the doctor.

" There was no connection," said Sir Richmond. "The women of my adolescent dreams were stripped and strong and lovely. They were great creatures. They came, it was clearly traceable, from pictures, sculpture—and from a definite response in myself to their beauty. My mother had nothing whatever to do with that. The women and girls about me were fussy bunches of clothes that I am sure I never even linked with that dream-world of love and worship."

" Were you co-educated ? "

" No. But I had a couple of sisters, one older, one younger than myself, and there were plenty of girls in my circle. I thought some of them pretty—but that was a different affair. I know that I didn't connect them with the idea of the loved and worshipped goddesses at all, because I remember when I first saw the goddess in a real human being and how amazed I was at the discovery. . . . I was a boy of twelve or thirteen. My people took me one summer to Dymchurch in Romney Marsh ; in those days before the automobile had made the Marsh accessible to the Hythe and Folkestone crowds, it was a little old forgotten silent wind-bitten village crouching under the lee of the great sea wall. At low water there were miles of sand as smooth and shining as the skin of a savage brown woman. Shining and with a texture—the very same. And one day as I was mucking about by myself on the beach, boy fashion—there were some ribs of a wrecked boat buried in the sand near a groin and I was busy with them—a girl ran out from a tent high up on the beach and across the sands to the water. She was dressed in a tight bathing dress and not in the clumsy skirts and frills that it was the custom to inflict on women in those days. Her hair was tied up in a blue handkerchief. She ran swiftly and gracefully, intent upon the white line of foam ahead. I can still remember how the sunlight touched her round neck and cheek as she went past me. She was the loveliest, most shapely thing I have ever seen—to this day. She lifted up her arms and thrust through the dazzling white and green breakers and plunged into the water and swam ; she swam straight out for a long way as it seemed to me, and presently came in and passed me again on her way back to her tent, light and swift and sure. The very prints of her feet on the sand were beautiful. Suddenly I realised that there could be living people in the world as lovely as any goddess. . . . She wasn't in the least out of breath.

"That was my first human love. And I love that girl still. I doubt sometimes whether I have ever loved any one else. I kept the thing so very secret. I wonder now why I have kept the thing so secret. Until now I have never told a soul about it. I resorted to all sorts of tortuous devices and excuses to get a chance of seeing her again without betraying what it was I was after."

Dr. Martineau retained a simple fondness for a story.

"And did you meet her again ? "

"Never. Of course I may have seen her as a dressed-up person and not recognised her. A day or so later I was stabbed to the heart by the discovery that the tent she came out of had been taken away."

"She had gone ? "

"For ever."

Sir Richmond smiled brightly at the doctor's disappointment.

§ 3

"I was never wholehearted and simple about sexual things," Sir Richmond resumed presently. "Never. I do not think any man is. We are too much plastered-up things, too much the creatures of a tortuous and complicated evolution."

Dr. Martineau, under his green umbrella, nodded his conceded agreement.

"This—what shall I call it ?—this Dream of Women, grew up in my mind as I grew up—as something independent of and much more important than the reality of Women. It came only very slowly into relation with that. That girl on the Dymchurch beach was one of the first links, but she ceased very speedily to be real—she joined the women of dreamland at last altogether. She became a sort of legendary incarnation. I thought of these dream-women not only as something beautiful but as something exceedingly kind and helpful. The girls and women I met belonged to a different creation. . . ."

Sir Richmond stopped abruptly and rowed a few long strokes.

Dr. Martineau sought information.

" I suppose," he said, " there was a sensuous element in these dreamings ? "

" Certainly. A very strong one. It didn't dominate but it was a very powerful undertow."

" Was there any tendency in all this imaginative stuff to concentrate ? To group itself about a single figure, the sort of thing that Victorians would have called an ideal ? "

" Not a bit of it," said Sir Richmond with conviction. " There was always a tremendous lot of variety in my mind. In fact the thing I liked least in the real world was the way it was obsessed by the idea of pairing off with one particular set and final person. I liked to dream of a blonde goddess in her own Venusberg one day, and the next I would be off over the mountains with an armed Brunhild."

" You had little thought of children ? "

" As a young man ? "

" Yes."

" None at all. I cannot recall a single philoprogenitive moment. These dream-women were all conceived of, and I was conceived of, as being concerned in some tremendous enterprise—something quite beyond domesticity. It kept us related—gave us dignity. . . . Certainly it wasn't babies."

" All this is very interesting, very interesting, from the scientific point of view. *A priori* it is not what one might have expected. Reasoning from the idea that all instincts and natural imaginations are adapted to a biological end and seeing that sex is essentially a method of procreation, one might reasonably expect a convergence, if not a complete concentration, upon the idea of offspring. It is almost as if there were other ends to be served. It is clear that Nature has not worked this impulse out to any sight of its end. Has not perhaps troubled to do so. The instinct of the male for the female isn't primarily for offspring—not even in the most intelligent and far-seeing types. The desire just points to glowing satisfactions and illusions. Quite equally I think the desire of the female for the male ignores its end. Nature has set about this business in a *cheap* sort of way. She is like some pushful advertising tradesman. She isn't frank with us ; she just humbugs us into what she wants with us. All very well in the early Stone Age—when the poor dear things never realised that their mutual endearments meant all the troubles and responsibilities of parentage. But *now*—— ! "

He shook his head sideways and twirled the green umbrella like an animated halo around his large broad-minded face.

Sir Richmond considered. " Desire has never been the chief incentive of my relations with women. Never. So far as I can analyse the thing, it has been a craving for a particular sort of life-giving companionship."

" That I take it is Nature's device to keep the lovers to-gether in the interest of the more or less unpremeditated offspring."

" A poor device, if that is its end. It doesn't keep parents together ; more often it tears them apart. The wife or the mistress, so soon as she is encumbered with children, becomes all too manifestly *not* the companion goddess. . . ."

Sir Richmond brooded over his sculls and thought.

" Throughout my life I have been an exceedingly busy man. I have done a lot of scientific work and some of it has been very good work. And very laborious work. I've travelled much. I've organised great business developments. You might think that my time has been fairly well filled without much philandering. And all the time, all the time, I've been —about women—like a thirsty beast looking for water. . . . Always. Always. All through my life."

Dr. Martineau waited through another silence.

" I was very grave about it at first. I married young. I married very simply and purely. I was not one of those young men who sow a large crop of wild oats. I was a fairly decent youth. It suddenly appeared to me that a certain smiling dainty girl could make herself into all the goddesses of my dreams. I had but to win her and this miracle would occur. Of course I forget now the exact things I thought and felt then, but surely I had some such persuasion. Or why should I have married her ? My wife was seven years younger than myself, a girl of twenty. She was charming. She *is* charming. She is a wonderfully intelligent and understanding woman. She has made a home for me—a delightful home. I am one of those men who have no instinct for home making. I owe my home and all the comfort and dignity of my life to her ability. I have no excuse for any misbehaviour—so far as she is concerned. None at all. By all the rules I should have been completely happy. But instead of my marriage satisfying me, it presently released a storm of long controlled desires and imprisoned cravings. A voice within me became more and more urgent. ' This will not do. This is not love. Where are your goddesses ? This is not love.' . . . And I was unfaithful to my wife within four years of my marriage. It was a sudden overpowering impulse. But I suppose the ground had been preparing for a long time. I forget now all the emotions of that adventure. I suppose at the time it seemed beautiful and wonderful. . . . I do not excuse myself.

Still less do I condemn myself. I put the facts before you. So it was."

" There were no children by your marriage ? "

" Your line of thought, doctor, is too philoprogenitive. We have had three. My daughter was married two years ago. She is in America. One little boy died when he was three. The other is in India ; taking up the Mardipore power scheme again now that he is out of the army. . . . No, it is simply that I was hopelessly disappointed with everything that a good woman and a decent marriage had to give me. Pure disappointment and vexation. The anti-climax to an immense expectation built up throughout an imaginative boyhood and youth and early manhood. I was shocked and ashamed at my own disappointment. I thought it mean and base. Nevertheless this orderly household into which I had placed my life, these almost methodical connubialities . . ."

He broke off in mid-sentence.

Dr. Martineau shook his head disapprovingly.

" No," he said, " it wasn't fair to your wife."

" It was shockingly unfair. I have always realised that. I've done what I could to make things up to her. . . . Heaven knows what counter disappointments she has concealed. . . . But it is no good arguing about rights and wrongs now. This is not an apology for my life. I am telling you what happened."

" Not for me to judge," said Dr. Martineau.   " Go on."

" By marrying I had got nothing that my soul craved for, I had satisfied none but the most transitory desires, and I had incurred a tremendous obligation. That obligation didn't restrain me from making desperate lunges at something vaguely beautiful that I felt was necessary to me ; but it did cramp and limit these lunges. So my story flops down into the comedy of the lying, cramped intrigues of a respectable married man. I was still driven by my dream of some extravagantly beautiful inspiration called love, and I sought it like an area sneak. Gods ! What a story it is when one brings it altogether ! I couldn't believe that the glow and sweetness I dreamt of were not in the world—somewhere. Hidden away from me. I seemed to catch glimpses of the dear lost thing, now in the corners of a smiling mouth, now in dark eyes beneath a black smoke of hair, now in a slim form seen against the sky. Often I cared nothing for the woman I made love to. I cared for the thing she seemed to be hiding from me. . . ."

Sir Richmond's voice altered.

" I don't see what possible good it can do to talk over these things." He began to row and rowed perhaps a score of strokes. Then he stopped, and the boat drove on with a whisper of water at the bow and over the outstretched oar blades.

" What a muddle and mockery the whole thing is ! " he cried. " What a fumbling old fool old Mother Nature has been ! She drives us into indignity and dishonour : and she doesn't even get the children which are her only excuse for her mischief. See what a fantastic thing I am when you take the machine to pieces ! I have been a busy and responsible man throughout my life. I have handled complicated public and industrial affairs not unsuccessfully and discharged quite big obligations fully and faithfully. And all the time, hidden away from the public eye, my life has been laced by the thread of these—what can one call them ?—love adventures. How many ? you ask. I don't know. Never have I been a whole-hearted lover ; never have I been able to leave love alone. . . . Never has love left me alone.

" And as I am made," said Sir Richmond with sudden insistence, " *as I am made*—I do not believe that I can go on without these affairs. I know that you will be disposed to dispute that."

Dr. Martineau made a reassuring noise.

" These affairs are at once unsatisfying and vitally necessary. It is only latterly that I have begun to perceive this. Women *make* life for me. Whatever they touch or see or desire becomes worth while and otherwise it is not worth while. Whatever is lovely in my world, whatever is delightful, has been so conveyed to me by some woman. Without the vision they give me, I should be a hard dry industry in the world, a worker ant, a soulless rage, making much, valuing nothing."

He paused.

" You are, I think, abnormal," considered the doctor.

" Not abnormal. Excessive, if you like. Without women I am a wasting fever of distressful toil. Without them there is no kindness in existence, no rest, no sort of satisfaction. The world is a battlefield, trenches, barbed wire, rain, mud, logical necessity and utter desolation—with nothing what-ever worth fighting for. Whatever justifies effort, whatever restores energy is hidden in women. . . ."

" An access of sex," said Dr. Martineau. " This is a phase. . . ."

" It is how I am made," said Sir Richmond.

A brief silence fell upon that. Dr. Martineau persisted. " It isn't how you are made. We are getting to something in all this. It is, I insist, a *mood* of how you are made. A distinctive and indicative mood."

Sir Richmond went on, almost as if he soliloquised.

" I would go through it all again. . . . There are times when the love of women seems the only real thing in the world to me. And always it remains the most real thing. I do not know how far I may be a normal man or how far I may not be, so to speak, abnormally male, but to me life has very little personal significance, and no value or power until it has a woman as intermediary. Before life can talk to me and say anything that matters a woman must be present as a medium. I don't mean that it has no significance mentally and logically ; I mean that irrationally and emotionally it has no significance. Works of art, for example, bore me, literature bores me, scenery bores me, even the beauty of a woman bores me, unless I find in it some association with a woman's feeling. It isn't that I can't tell for myself that a picture is fine or a mountain valley lovely, but that it doesn't matter a rap to me whether it is or whether it isn't until there is a feminine response, a sexual motif, if you like to call it that, coming in. Whatever there is of loveliness or pride in life doesn't *live* for me until somehow a woman comes in and breathes upon it the breath of life. I cannot even rest until a woman makes holiday for me. Only one thing can I do without women and that is work, joylessly but effectively, and latterly for some reason that it is up to you to discover, doctor, even the power of work has gone from me.

§ 4

" This afternoon brings back to me very vividly my previous visit here. It was perhaps a dozen or fifteen years ago. We rowed down this same backwater. I can see my companion's hand, she had very pretty hands with rosy palms, trailing in the water, and her shadowed face smiling quietly under her sunshade, with little faint streaks of sunlight, reflected from the ripples, dancing and quivering across it. She was one of those people who seem always to be happy and to radiate happiness.

" By ordinary standards," said Sir Richmond, " she was a thoroughly bad lot. She had about as much morality in the narrower sense of the word, as a monkey. And yet she stands out in my mind as one of the most honest women I have ever met. She was certainly one of the kindest. Part of that effect of honesty may have been due to her open brow, her candid blue eyes, the smiling frankness of her manner. . . . But—no ! She was really honest.

" We drifted here as we are doing now. She pulled at the sweet rushes and crushed them in her hand. She adds a remembered brightness to this afternoon.

" Honest. Friendly. Of all the women I have known, this woman who was here with me came nearer to being my friend. You know, what we call virtue in a woman is a tremendous handicap to any real friendliness with a man. Until she gets to an age when virtue and fidelity are no longer urgent practical concerns, a good woman, by the very definition of feminine goodness, isn't truly herself. Over a vast extent of her being she is *reserved*. She suppresses a vast amount of her being, holds back, denies, hides. On the other hand, there is a frankness and honesty in openly bad women arising out of the admitted fact that they are bad, that they hide no treasure from you, they have no peculiarly precious and delicious secrets to keep, and no poverty to conceal. Intellectually they seem to be more manly and vigorous because they are, as people say, unsexed. Many old women, thoroughly respectable old women, have the same quality. Because they have gone out of the personal sex business. Haven't you found that ? "

" I have never," said the doctor, " known what you call an openly bad woman—at least, at all intimately. . . ."

Sir Richmond looked with quick curiosity at his companion. " You have avoided them ? "

" They don't attract me."

" They repel you ? "

" For me," said the doctor, " for any friendliness, a woman must be modest. . . . My habits of thought are old-fashioned, I suppose, but the mere suggestion about a woman that there were no barriers, no reservation, that in any fashion she might more than meet me half-way . . ."

His facial expression completed his sentence.

" Now I wonder," whispered Sir Richmond, and hesitated for a moment before he carried the great research into the explorer's country. " You are afraid of women ? " he said, with a smile to mitigate the impertinence.

" I respect them."

" An element of fear."

" Well, I am afraid of them then. Put it that way if you like. Anyhow, I do not let myself go with them. I have never let myself go."

" You lose something. You lose a reality of insight."

There was a thoughtful interval.

" Having found so excellent a friend," said the doctor, " why did you ever part from her ? "

Sir Richmond seemed indisposed to answer, but Dr. Martineau's face remained slantingly interrogative. He had found the effective counter attack and he meant to press it.

" I was jealous of her," Sir Richmond admitted. " I couldn't stand that side of it."

§ 5

After a meditative silence the doctor became briskly professional again.

" You care for your wife," he said. " You care very much for your wife. She is, as you say, your great obligation and you are a man to respect obligations. I grasp that. Then you tell me of these women who have come and gone. . . . About them too you are perfectly frank. . . . There remains some one else."

Sir Richmond stared at his physician.

" Well," he said and laughed.   " I didn't pretend to have made my autobiography anything more than a sketch."

" No, but there is a special person, the current person."

" I haven't dilated on my present situation, I admit."

" From some little things that have dropped from you, I should say there is a child."

" That," said Sir Richmond after a brief pause, " is a good guess."

" Not older than three."

" Two years and a half."

" You and this lady who is, I guess, young, are separated. At any rate, you can't go to her.   That leaves you at loose ends, because for some time, for two or three years at least, you have ceased to be—how shall I put it ?—an emotional wanderer."

" I begin to respect your psycho-analysis."

" Hence your overwhelming sense of the necessity of feminine companionship for weary men.   I guess she is a very jolly companion to be with, amusing, restful—interesting."

" H'm," said Sir Richmond.   " I think that is a fair description.   When she cares, that is.   When she is in good form."

" Which she isn't at present," hazarded the doctor.

He exploded a mine of long pent exasperation.

" She is the clumsiest hand at keeping well that I have ever known.   Health is a woman's primary duty.   But she is incapable of the most elementary precautions.   She is maddeningly receptive to every infection.   At the present moment, when I am ill, when I am in urgent need of help and happiness, she has let that wretched child get measles and she herself won't let me go near her because she has got something disfiguring, something nobody else could ever have or think of having, called *carbuncle*.   Carbuncle ! "

" It is very painful," said Dr. Martineau.

" No doubt it is," said Sir Richmond.   " No doubt it is." His voice grew bitter.   He spoke with deliberation.   " A perfectly aimless, useless illness—and as painful as it *can* be."

He spoke as if he slammed a door viciously.   And indeed he had slammed a door.   The doctor realised that for the present there was no more self-dissection to be got from Sir Richmond.

For some time Sir Richmond had been keeping the boat close up to the foaming weir to the left of the lock by an occasional stroke.   Now with a general air of departure he swung the boat round and began to row down stream towards the bridge and the Radiant Hotel.

" Time we had tea," he said.

§ 6

After tea Dr. Martineau left Sir Richmond in a chair upon
the lawn, brooding darkly—apparently over the crime of the
carbuncle. The doctor went to his room, ostensibly to write
a couple of letters and put on a dinner jacket, but really to
make a few notes of the afternoon's conversation and meditate
over his impressions while they were fresh.

His room proffered a comfortable armchair and into this
he sank. . . . A number of very discrepant things were busy
in his mind. He had experienced a disconcerting personal
attack. There was a whirl of active resentment in the
confusion.

" Apologetics of a rake," he tried presently.

" A common type, stripped of his intellectual dressing.
Every third manufacturer from the midlands or the north has
some such undertow of 'affairs.' A physiological uneasiness,
an imaginative laxity, the temptations of the trip to London
—weakness masquerading as a psychological necessity. The
Lady of the Carbuncle seems to have got rather a hold
upon him. She has kept him in order for three or four
years."

The doctor scrutinised his own remarks with a judicious
expression.

" I am not being fair. He ruffled me. Even if it is true,
as I said, that every third manufacturer from the midlands is
in much the same case as he is, that does not dismiss the case.
It makes it a more important one, much more important : it
makes it a type case with the exceptional quality of being self-
expressive. . . . Almost too self-expressive.

" Sir Richmond does, after all, make out a sort of case for
himself. . . .

" A valid case ? "

The doctor sat deep in his chair, frowning judicially with
the fingers of one hand apposed to the fingers of the other.
" He makes me bristle because all his life and ideas challenge
my way of living. . . . But if I eliminate the personal
element ? "

He pulled a sheet of note-paper towards him and began
to jot down notes with a silver-cased pencil. Soon he dis-
continued writing and sat tapping his pencil-case on the
table.

" The amazing selfishness of his attitude ! I do not think
that once—not once—has he judged any woman except as a
contributor to his energy and peace of mind. . . . Except in
the case of his wife. . . .

" For her his habit of respect was formed before his ideas
developed. . . .

" That I think explains *her*. . . .

" What was his phrase about the unfortunate young woman with the carbuncle ? . . . ' Totally useless and unnecessary illness,' was it ? . . .

" Now has a man any right by any standards to use women as this man has used them ?

" By any standards ? "

The doctor frowned and nodded his head slowly with the corners of his mouth drawn in.

For some years now an intellectual reverie had been playing an increasing part in the good doctor's life. He was writing this book of his, writing it very deliberately and laboriously, *The Psychology of a New Age,* but much more was he dreaming and thinking about this book. Its publication was to mark an epoch in human thought and human affairs generally, and create a considerable flutter of astonishment in the doctor's own little world. It was to bring home to people some various aspects of one very startling proposition : that human society had arrived at a phase when the complete re-statement of its fundamental ideas had become urgently necessary, a phase when the slow inadequate partial adjustments to two centuries of changing conditions had to give place to a rapid reconstruction of new fundamental ideas. And it was a fact of great value in the drama of these secret dreams that the directive force towards this fundamentally reconstructed world should be the pen of an unassuming Harley Street physician, hitherto not suspected of any great excesses of enterprise.

The written portions of this book were already in a highly polished state. They combined a limitless freedom of proposal with a smooth urbanity of manner, a tacit denial that the thoughts of one intelligent being could possibly be shocking to another. Upon this the doctor was very insistent. Conduct, he held, could never be sufficiently discreet, thought could never be sufficiently free. As a citizen one had to treat a law or an institution as a thing as rigidly right as natural law. That the social well-being demands. But as a scientific man, in one's stated thoughts and in public discussion, the case was altogether different. There was no offence in any possible hypothesis or in the contemplation of any possibility. Just as when one played a game one was bound to play in unquestioning obedience to the laws and spirit of the game, but if one was not playing that game then there was no reason why one should not contemplate the completest reversal of all its methods and the alteration and abandonment of every rule. Correctness of conduct, the doctor held, was an imperative concomitant of all really free thinking. Revolutionary speculation is one of those things that must be divorced absolutely from revolutionary conduct. It was to the neglect of these obvious principals, as the doctor considered them, that the general muddle in contemporary marital affairs was very largely due. We left divorce-law revision to exposed adulterers and marriage reform to hot adolescents and craving spinsters driven by the furies within them to assertions that established nothing and to practical demonstrations that only left everybody thoroughly uncomfortable. Far better to leave all these matters to calm, patient men in easy-chairs, weighing typical cases impartially, ready to condone, indisposed to envy.

In return for which restraint on the part of the eager and adventurous, the calm patient man was prepared in his thoughts to fly high and go far. Without giving any guarantee, of course, that he might not ultimately return to the comfort-able point of inaction from which he started.

In Sir Richmond, Dr. Martineau found the most interesting and encouraging confirmation of the fundamental idea of *The Psychology of a New Age*, the immediate need of new criteria of conduct altogether. Here was a man whose life was evidently ruled by standards that were at once very high and very generous. He was overworking himself to the pitch of extreme distress, and apparently he was doing this for ends that were essentially unselfish. Manifestly there were many things that an ordinary industrial or political magnate would do that Sir Richmond would not dream of doing, and a number of things that such a man would not feel called upon to do that he would regard as imperative duties. And mixed up with so much fine intention and fine conduct was this dis-reputable streak of intrigue and this extraordinary claim that such misconduct was necessary to continued vigour of action.

"To energy of thought it is *not* necessary," said Dr. Mar-tineau, and considered for a time.

"Yet—certainly—I am not a man of action. I admit it. I make few decisions."

The chapters of *The Psychology of a New Age* dealing with women were still undrafted, but they had already greatly exercised the doctor's mind. He found now that the case of Sir Richmond had stirred his imagination. He sat with his hands apposed, his head on one side, and an expression of great intellectual contentment on his face while these emancipated ideas gave a sort of gala performance in his mind.

The good doctor did not dislike women, he had always guarded himself very carefully against misogyny, but he was very strongly disposed to regard them as much less necessary in the existing scheme of things than was generally assumed. Women, he conceded, had laid the foundations of social life ; through their contrivances and sacrifices and patience the fierce and lonely patriarchal family-herd of a male and his women and offspring had grown into the clan and tribe ; the woven tissue of related families that constitute the human comity had been woven by the subtle, persistent protection of sons and daughters by their mothers against the intolerant, jealous, possessive Old Man. But that was a thing of the remote past. Little was left of those ancient struggles now but a few infantile dreams and nightmares. The greater human community, human society, was made for good. And being made, it had taken over the ancient tasks of the woman, one by one, until now in its modern forms it cherished more sedulously than she did, it educated, it housed and comforted, it clothed and served and nursed, leaving the wife privileged, honoured, protected, for the sake of tasks she no longer did and of a burthen she no longer bore. " Progress has *trivialised* women," said the doctor and made a note of the word for later consideration.

" And woman has trivialised civilisation," the doctor tried.

" She has retained her effect of being central, she still makes the social atmosphere, she raises men's instinctive hopes of help and direction. Except," the doctor stipulated, " for a few highly developed modern types, most men found the sense of achieving her a necessary condition for sustained exertion. And there is no direction in her any more.

" She spends," said the doctor, " she just spends. She spends excitingly and competitively for her own pride and glory, she drives all the energy of men over the weirs of gain. . . .

" What are we to do with the creature ? " whispered the doctor.

Apart from the procreative necessity, was woman an unavoidable evil ? The doctor's untrammelled thoughts began to climb high, spin, nose dive and loop the loop. Nowadays we took a proper care of the young, we had no need for high birth rates, quite a small proportion of women with a gift in that direction could supply all the offspring that the world wanted. Given the power of determining sex that science was slowly winning to-day, and why should we have so many women about ? A drastic elimination of the creatures would be quite practicable. A fantastic world to a vulgar imagination, no doubt, but to a calmly reasonable mind by no means fantastic. But this was where the case of Sir Richmond became so interesting. Was it really true that the companionship of women was necessary to these energetic creative types ? Was it the fact that the drive of life towards action, as distinguished from contemplation, arose out of sex and needed to be refreshed by the reiteration of that motive ? It was a plausible proposition ; it marched with all the doctor's ideas of natural selection and of the conditions of a survival that have made us what we are. It was in tune with the Freudian analyses.

" *Sex not only a renewal of life in the species*," noted the doctor's silver pencil ; " *sex may be also a renewal of energy in the individual.*"

After some musing he crossed out " sex " and wrote it
" sexual love."

" That is practically what he claims," Dr. Martineau said.
" In which case we want the completest revision of all our
standards of sexual obligation. We want a new system of
restrictions and imperatives altogether."

It was a fixed idea of the doctor's that women were quite
incapable of producing ideas in the same way that men do,
but he believed that with suitable encouragement they could
be induced to respond quite generously to such ideas. Suppose
therefore we really educated the imaginations of women ;
suppose we turned their indubitable capacity for service
towards social and political creativeness, not in order to make
them the rivals of men in these fields, but their moral and
actual helpers.

" A man of this sort wants a mistress-mother," said the
doctor. " He wants a sort of woman who cares more for
him and his work and honour than she does for child or home
or clothes or personal pride.

" But are there such women ?

" Can there be such a woman ?

" His work needs to be very fine to deserve her help. But
admitting its fineness ? . . .

" The alternative seems to be to teach the sexes to get along
without each other.

" A neutralised world. A separated world. How we
should jostle in the streets ! But the early Christians have
tried it already. The thing is impossible.

" Very well, then, we have to make women more responsible
again. In a new capacity. We have to educate them far
more seriously as sources of energy—as guardians and helpers
of men. And we have to suppress them far more rigorously
as tempters and dissipators. Instead of mothering babies
they have to mother the race. . . ."

A vision of women made responsible floated before his eyes.

" Is that man working better since you got hold of him ?
If not, why not ?

" Or again—Jane Smith was charged with neglecting her
lover to the common danger. . . . The inspector said the
man was in a pitiful state, morally quite uncombed and
infested with vulgar, showy ideas. . . ."

The doctor laughed, telescoped his pencil and stood up.

§ 7

It became evident after dinner that Sir Richmond also had
been thinking over the afternoon's conversation.

He and Dr. Martineau sat in wide-armed cane chairs on the
lawn with a wickerwork table bearing coffee-cups and little
glasses between them. A few other diners chatted and

whispered about similar tables but not too close to our talkers to disturb them ; the dining-room behind them had cleared its tables and depressed its illumination.   The moon, in its first quarter, hung above the sunset, sank after twilight, shone brighter and brighter among the western trees, and presently had gone, leaving the sky to an increasing multitude of stars. The Maidenhead river wearing its dusky blue draperies and its jewels of light had recovered all the magic Sir Richmond had stripped from it in the afternoon.   The grave arches of the bridge, made complete circles by the reflection of the water, sustained, as if by some unifying and justifying reason, the erratic flat flashes and streaks and glares of traffic that fretted to and fro overhead.   A voice sang intermittently and a banjo tinkled, but remotely enough to be indistinct and agreeable.

" After all," Sir Richmond began abruptly, " the search for some sort of sexual *modus vivendi* is only a means to an end. One does not want to live for sex but only through sex.   The main thing in my life has always been my work.   This after-noon, under the Maidenhead influence, I talked too much of sex.   I babbled.   Of things one doesn't usually—— . . ."

" It was very illuminating," said the doctor.

" No doubt.   But a temporary phase.   It is the defec-tive bearing talks. . . . Just now—— I happen to be irritated."

The darkness concealed a faint smile on the doctor's face.

" The work is the thing," said Sir Richmond.   " So long as one can keep one's grip on it."

" What," said the doctor after a pause, leaning back and sending wreaths of smoke up towards the star-dusted zenith, " what is your idea of your work ?   I mean, how do you see it in relation to yourself—and things generally ? "

" Put in the most general terms ? "

" Put in the most general terms."

" I wonder if I can put it in general terms for you at all. It is hard to put something one is always thinking about in general terms or to think of it as a whole. . . . Now. . . . Fuel ? . . .

" I suppose it was my father's business interests that pushed me towards specialisation in fuel.   He wanted me to have a thoroughly scientific training in days when a scientific training was less easy to get for a boy than it is to-day.   And much more inspiring when you got it.   My mind was framed, so to speak, in geology and astronomical physics.   I grew up to think on that scale.   Just as a man who has been trained in history and law grows to think on the scale of the Roman empire.   I don't know what your pocket map of the universe is—the map, I mean, by which you judge all sorts of other general ideas.   To me this planet is a little ball of oxides and

nickel steel ; life a sort of tarnish on its surface. And we—
the minutest particles in that tarnish. Who can nevertheless, in some unaccountable way, take in the idea of this
universe as one whole—who begin to dream of taking control
of it."

" That is not a bad statement of the scientific point of view.
I suppose I have much the same general idea of the world.
On rather more psychological lines."

" We think, I suppose," said Sir Richmond, " of life as
something that is only just beginning to be aware of what it is
—and what it might be."

" Exactly," said the doctor. " Good."

He went on eagerly. " That is precisely how I see it. You
and I are just particles in the tarnish, as you call it, who are
becoming dimly awake to what we are, to what we have in
common. Only a very few of us have got as far even as this.
. . . These others here, for example. . . ."

He indicated the rest of Maidenhead by a movement.

" Desire, mutual flattery, egotistical dreams, greedy
solicitudes fill them up. They haven't begun to get out of
themselves."

" We, I suppose, have," doubted Sir Richmond.

" We have."

The doctor had no doubt. He lay back in his chair, with
his hands behind his head and his smoke ascending vertically
to heaven. With the greatest contentment he began quoting
himself. " This getting out of one's individuality—this
conscious getting out of one's individuality—is one of the
most important and interesting aspects of the psychology of
the new age that is now dawning. As compared with any
previous age. Unconsciously, of course, every true artist,
every philosopher, every scientific investigator, so far as his
art or thought went, has always got out of himself—has forgotten his personal interests and become Man thinking for
the whole race. And intimations of the same thing have been
at the heart of most religions. But now people are beginning
to get this detachment without any distinctively religious
feeling or any distinctive æsthetic or intellectual impulse, as if
it were a plain matter of fact. Plain matter of fact—that we
are only incidentally ourselves. That really each one of us
is also the whole species, is really indeed all life."

" A part of it."

" An integral part—as sight is part of a man . . . with no
absolute separation from all the rest—no more than a separation of the imagination. The whole so far as his distinctive
quality goes. I do not know how this takes shape in your
mind, Sir Richmond, but to me this idea of actually being life
itself upon the world, a special phase of it dependent upon
and connected with all other phases, and of being one of a
small but growing number of people who apprehend that, and

want to live in the spirit of that, is quite central. It is my fundamental idea. We—this small but growing minority—constitute that part of life which knows and wills and tries to rule its destiny. This new realisation, the new psychology arising out of it, is a fact of supreme importance in the history of life. It is like the appearance of self-consciousness in some creature that has not hitherto had self-consciousness. And so far as we are concerned—— We are the true kingship of the world. Necessarily. We who know, are the true king. . . . I wonder how this appeals to you. It is stuff I have thought out very slowly and carefully and written and approved. It is the very core of my life. . . . And yet when one comes to say these things to some one else, face to face. . . . It is much more difficult to say than to write."

Sir Richmond noted how the doctor's chair creaked as he rolled to and fro with the uneasiness of these intimate utterances.

" I agree," said Sir Richmond presently. " One *does* think in this fashion. Something in this fashion. What one calls one's work does belong to something much bigger than ourselves.

" Something much bigger," he expanded.

" Which something we become," the doctor urged, " in so far as our work takes hold of us."

Sir Richmond made no answer to this for a little while. " Of course we trail a certain egotism into our work," he said.

" Could we do otherwise ? But it has ceased to be purely egotism. It is no longer, ' I am I ' but ' I am part.' . . . One wants to be an honourable part."

" You think of man upon his planet," the doctor pursued. " I think of life rather as a mind that tries itself over in millions and millions of trials. But it works out to the same thing."

" I think in terms of fuel," said Sir Richmond.

He was still debating the doctor's generalisation. " I suppose it would be true to say that I think of myself as mankind on his planet, with very considerable possibilities and with only a limited amount of fuel at his disposal to achieve them. Yes. . . . I agree that I think in that way. . . . I have not thought much before of the way in which I think about things—but I agree that it is in that way. Whatever enterprises mankind attempts are limited by the sum total of that store of fuel upon the planet. That is very much in my mind. Besides that he has nothing but his annual allowance of energy from the sun."

" I thought that presently we were to get unlimited energy from atoms," said the doctor.

" I don't believe in that as a thing immediately practicable. No doubt getting a supply of energy from atoms is a theoretical possibility—just as flying was in the time of Dædalus ; probably there were actual attempts at some sort of glider in ancient Crete. But before we get to the actual utilisation of atomic energy there will be ten thousand difficult corners to turn ; we may have to wait three or four thousand years for it. We cannot count on it. We haven't it in hand. There may be some impasse. All we have surely is coal and oil— there is no surplus of wood now—only an annual growth. And water-power is income also, doled out day by day. We cannot anticipate it. Coal and oil are our only capital. They are all we have for great important efforts. They are a gift to mankind to use to some supreme end or to waste in trivialities. Coal is the key to metallurgy and oil to transit. When they are done we shall either have built up such a fabric of apparatus, knowledge and social organisation that we shall be able to manage without them—or we shall have travelled a long way down the slopes of waste towards extinction. . . . To-day, in getting, in distribution, in use we waste enormously. . . . As we sit here all the world is wasting fuel—fantastically."

"Just as mentally—educationally we waste," the doctor interjected.

"And my job is to stop what I can of that waste, to do what I can to organise, first of all sane fuel getting and then sane fuel using. And that second proposition carries us far. Into the whole use we are making of life.

"First things first," said Sir Richmond. "If we set about getting fuel sanely, if we do it as the deliberate, co-operative act of the whole species, then it follows that we shall look very closely into the use that is being made of it. When all the fuel getting is brought into one view as a common interest, then it follows that all the fuel burning will be brought into one view. At present we are getting fuel in a kind of scramble with no general aim. We waste and lose almost as much as we get. And of what we get, the waste is idiotic.

"I won't trouble you," said Sir Richmond, "with any long discourse on the ways of getting fuel in this country. But land as you know is owned in patches and stretches that were determined in the first place chiefly by agricultural necessities. When it was divided up among its present owners nobody was thinking about the minerals beneath. But the lawyers settled long ago that the landowner owned his land right down to the centre of the earth. So we have the superficial landlord as coal owner trying to work his coal according to the superficial divisions, quite irrespective of the lie of the coal underneath. Each man goes for the coal under his own land in his own fashion. You get three shafts where one would suffice and none of them in the best possible place. You get the coal coming out at this point when it would be far more convenient to bring it out at that—miles away. You get boundary walls of coal between the estates, abandoned, left in the ground for ever. And each coal owner sells his coal in his own pettifogging manner. . . . But you know of these things. You know too how we trail the coal all over the country, spoiling it as we trail it, until at last we get it into the silly coal scuttles beside the silly, wasteful, air-poisoning, fog-creating fireplace.

" And this stuff," said Sir Richmond, bringing his hand down so smartly on the table that the startled coffee-cups cried out upon the tray, " was given to men to give them power over metals, to get knowledge with, to get more power with. . . ."

" The oil story, I suppose is as bad."

" The oil story is worse. . . .

" There is a sort of cant," said Sir Richmond in a fierce parenthesis, " that the supplies of oil are inexhaustible—that you can muddle about with oil anyhow. . . . Optimism of knaves and imbeciles. . . . They don't want to be pulled up by any sane considerations. . . ."

For some moments he kept silence—as if in unspeakable commination.

" Here I am with some clearness of vision, my only gift, not very clever, with a natural bad temper—and a strong sexual bias, doing what I can to get a broader handling of the fuel question as a common interest for all mankind. And I find myself up against a lot of men, subtle men, sharp men, obstinate men, prejudiced men, able to get round me, able to get over me, able to blockade me. . . . Clever men—Yes, and all of them ultimately damned, oh ! utterly damned, fools. Coal owners who think only of themselves, solicitors who think backwards, politicians who think like a game of cat's-cradle, not a gleam of generosity—not a gleam."

" What particularly are you working for ? " asked the doctor.

" I want to get the whole business of the world's fuel discussed and reported upon as one affair—so that some day it may be handled as one affair—in the general interest."

" The world, did you say ?   You meant the empire ? "

" No, the world. It is all one system now. You can't work it in bits. I want to call in foreign representatives from the beginning."

" Advisory—consultative ? "

" No. With powers. These things interlock now internationally both through labour and finance. The sooner we scrap this nonsense about an autonomous British empire complete in itself, *contra mundum*, the better for us. A world control is fifty years overdue. Hence these disorders."

" Still — it's rather a difficult proposition, as things are."

" Oh, Lord ! don't I know it's difficult ! " cried Sir Richmond in the tone of one who swears. " Don't I know that perhaps it's impossible ! But it's the only way to do it. Therefore, I say, let's try to get it done. And everybody says, ' difficult difficult,' and nobody lifts a finger to try. And the only real difficulty is that everybody for one reason or another says that it's difficult. It's against human nature. Granted ! Every decent thing is. It's socialism. Who cares ? Along this line of comprehensive scientific control the world has to go or it will retrogress, it will muddle and rot. . . ."

" I agree," said Dr. Martineau.

" So I want a report to admit that distinctly. I want it to go further than that. I want to get the beginnings, the germ, of a world administration. I want to set up a permanent world commission of scientific men and economists—with powers, just as considerable powers as I can give them—they'll be feeble powers at the best—but still some sort of *say* in the whole fuel supply of the world. A say—that may grow at last to a control. A right to collect reports and receive accounts, for example, to begin with. And then the right to make recommendations. . . . You see ? . . . No, the international part is not the most difficult part of it. But my beastly owners and their beastly lawyers won't relinquish a scrap of what they call their freedom of action. And my labour men, because I'm a fairly big coal owner myself, sit and watch and suspect me, too stupid to grasp what I am driving at and too incompetent to get out a scheme of their own. They want a world control on scientific lines even less than the owners. They try to think that fuel production can carry an unlimited wages bill and the owners try to think that it can pay unlimited profits, and when I say : ' This business is something more than a scramble for profits and wages ; it's a service and a common interest,' they stare at me——" Sir Richmond was at a loss for an image. " Like a committee in a thieves' kitchen when some one has casually mentioned the law."

" But will you ever get your Permanent Commission ? "

" It can be done. If I can stick it out."

" But with the whole Committee against you ! "

" The curious thing is that the whole Committee isn't against me. Every individual is . . ."

Sir Richmond found it difficult to express. " The psychology of my Committee ought to interest you. . . . It is probably a fair sample of the way all sorts of things are going nowadays. It's curious. . . . There is not a man on that Committee who is quite comfortable within himself about the particular individual end he is there to serve. It's there I get them. They pursue their own ends bitterly and obstinately I admit, but they are bitter and obstinate because they pursue them against an internal opposition—which is on my side.

They are terrified to think, if once they stopped fighting me, how far they might not have to go with me."

" A suppressed world conscience in fact. This marches very closely with my own ideas——"

" A world conscience ? World conscience ? I don't know. But I do know that there is this drive in nearly every member of the Committee, some drive anyhow, towards the decent thing. It is the same drive that drives me. But I am the most driven. It has turned me round. It hasn't turned them. I go East and they go West. And they don't want to be turned round. Tremendously, they don't."

" Creative undertow," said Dr. Martineau, making notes as it were. " An increasing force in modern life. In the psychology of a new age—strengthened by education—it may play a directive part."

" They fight every little point. But, you see, because of this creative undertow—if you liked to call it that—we do get along. I am leader or whipper in, it is hard to say which, of a bolting flock. . . . I believe they will report for a permanent world commission ; I believe I have got them up to that ; but they will want to make it a bureau of this League of Nations, and I have the profoundest distrust of this League of Nations. It may turn out to be a sort of side-tracking arrangement for all sorts of important world issues. And they will find they have to report for some sort of control. But there again they will shy. They will report for it and then they will do their utmost to whittle it down again. They will refuse it the most reasonable powers. They will alter the composition of the Committee so as to make it innocuous."

" How ? "

" Get rid of the independent scientific men, load it up so far as Britain is concerned with muck of the colonial politician type and tame labour representatives, balance with shady new adventurer millionaires, get in still shadier stuff from abroad, let these gentry appoint their own tame experts after their own hearts—experts who will make merely advisory reports which will not be published. . . ."

" They want in fact to keep the old system going under the cloak of *your* Committee, reduced to a cloak and nothing more ? "

" That is what it amounts to. They want to have the air of doing right—indeed they do want to have the *feel* of doing right—and still leave things just exactly what they were before. And as I suffer under the misfortune of seeing the thing rather more clearly, I have to shepherd the conscience of the whole Committee. . . . But there is a conscience there. If I can hold out myself, I can hold the Committee."

He turned appealingly to the doctor. " Why should I have to be the conscience of that damned Committee ? Why should I do this exhausting inhuman job ? . . . In their hearts these others know. . . . Only they won't know. . . . Why should it fall on me ? "

"You have to go through with it," said Dr. Martineau.

"I have to go through with it, but it's a hell of utterly inglorious squabbling. They bait me. They have been fighting the same fight within themselves that they fight with me. They know exactly where I am, that I too am doing my job against internal friction. The one thing before all others that they want to do is to bring me down off my moral high horse. And I loathe the high horse. I am in a position of special moral superiority to men who are on the whole as good men as I am or better. That shows all the time. You see the sort of man I am. I've a broad streak of personal vanity. I fag easily. I'm short tempered. I've other things, as you perceive. When I fag I become obtuse, I repeat and bore, I get viciously ill tempered, I suffer from an intolerable sense of ill usage. Then that ass, Wagstaffe, who ought to be working with me steadily, sees his chance to be pleasantly witty. He gets a laugh round the table at my expense. Young Dent, the more intelligent of the labour men, reads me a lecture in Committee manners. Old Cassidy sees *his* opening and jabs some ridiculous petty accusation at me and gets me spluttering self-defence like a fool. All my stock goes down and as my stock goes down, the chances of a good report dwindle. Young Dent grieves to see me injuring my own case. Too damned a fool to see what will happen to the report ! You see if only they can convince themselves I am just a prig and an egotist and an impractical bore, they escape from a great deal more than my poor propositions. They escape from the doubt in themselves. By dismissing me they dismiss their own consciences. And then they can scamper off and be sensible little piggy-wigs and not bother any more about what is to happen to mankind in the long run. . . . Do you begin to realise the sort of fight, upside down in a dustbin, that that Committee is for me ? "

"You have to go through with it," Dr. Martineau repeated.

"I have. If I can. But I warn you I have been near breaking point. And if I tumble off the high horse, if I can't keep going regularly there to ride the moral high horse, that Committee will slump into utter scoundrelism. It will turn out a long, inconsistent, botched, unreadable report that will back up all sorts of humbugging bargains and sham settlements. It will contain some half-baked scheme to pacify the miners at the expense of the general welfare. It won't even succeed in doing that. But in the general confusion old Cassidy will get away with a series of hauls that may run into millions. Which will last his time—damn him ! And that is where we are. . . . Oh ! I know ! I know ! . . . I must do this job. I don't need any telling that my life will be nothing and mean nothing unless I bring this thing through. . . .

" But the thanklessness of playing this lone hand ! "

The doctor watched his friend's resentful black silhouette against the lights on the steely river, and said nothing for awhile.

" Why did I ever undertake to play it ? " Sir Richmond appealed. " Why has it been put upon me ? Seeing what a poor thing I am, why am I not a poor thing altogether ? "

§ 8

" I think I understand that loneliness of yours," said the doctor after an interval.

" I am *intolerable* to myself."

" And I think it explains why it is that you turn to women as you do. You want help ; you want reassurance. And you feel they can give it."

" I wonder if it has been quite like that," Sir Richmond reflected.

By an effort Dr. Martineau refrained from mentioning the mother complex. " You want help and reassurance as a child does," he said. " Women and women alone seem capable of giving that, of telling you that you are surely right, that notwithstanding your blunders you are right ; that even when you are wrong it doesn't so much matter, you are still in spirit right. They can show their belief in you as no man can. With all their being they can do that."

" Yes, I suppose they could."

" They can. You have said already that women are necessary to make things real for you."

" Not my work," said Sir Richmond. " I admit that it might be like that, but it isn't like that. It has not worked out like that. The two drives go on side by side in me. They have no logical connection. All I can say is that for me, with my bifid temperament, one makes a rest from the other, and is so far refreshment and a renewal of energy. But I do not find women coming into my work in any effectual way."

The doctor reflected further. " I suppose," he began and stopped short.

He heard Sir Richmond move in his chair, creaking an interrogation.

" You have never," said the doctor, " turned to the idea of God ? "

Sir Richmond grunted and made no other answer for the better part of a minute.

As Dr. Martineau waited for his companion to speak, a falling star streaked the deep blue above them.

" I can't believe in a God," said Sir Richmond.

" Something after the fashion of a God," said the doctor insidiously.

" No," said Sir Richmond. " Nothing that reassures."

" But this loneliness, this craving for companionship——"

" We have all been through that," said Sir Richmond. " We have all in our time lain very still in the darkness with our souls crying out for the fellowship of God, demanding some sign, some personal response. The faintest feeling of assurance would have satisfied us."

" And there has never been a response ? "

" Have *you* ever had a response ? "

" Once I seemed to have a feeling of exaltation and security."

" Well ? "

" Perhaps I only persuaded myself that I had. I had been reading William James on religious experiences and I was thinking very much of ' Conversion.' . . . I tried to experience Conversion. . . ."

" Yes ? "

" It faded."

" It always fades," said Sir Richmond with anger in his voice. " I wonder how many people there are nowadays who have passed through this last experience of ineffectual invocation, this appeal to the fading shadow of a vanished God. In the night. In utter loneliness. ' Answer me ! Speak to me ! ' Does he answer ? In the silence you hear the little blood vessels whisper in your ears. You see a faint glow of colour on the darkness. . . ."

Dr. Martineau sat without a word.

" I can believe that over all things Righteousness rules. I can believe that. But Righteousness is not friendliness nor mercy nor comfort nor any such dear and intimate things. This cuddling up to Righteousness ! It is a dream, a delusion and a phase. I've tried all that long ago. I've given it up long ago. I've grown out of it. Men do—after forty. Our souls were made in the squatting-place of the submen of ancient times. They are made out of primitive needs, and they die before our bodies as those needs are satisfied. Only young people have souls, complete. The need for a personal God, feared but reassuring is a youth's need. I no longer fear the Old Man nor want to propitiate the Old Man nor believe he matters any more. I'm a bit of an Old Man myself I discover. Yes. . . . But the other thing still remains."

" The Great Mother of the Gods," said Dr. Martineau—still clinging to his theories.

" The need of the woman," said Sir Richmond. " I want mating, because it is my nature to mate. I want fellowship because I am a social animal—and I want it from another social animal. Not from any God—any inconceivable God Who fades and disappears. No. . .

" Perhaps that other need will fade presently. I do not know. Perhaps it lasts as long as life does. How can I tell ? . . ."

He was silent for a little while. Then his voice sounded in the night, as if he spoke to himself. " But as for the God of All Things consoling and helping ! Imagine it ! That up there—having fellowship with me ! I would as soon think of cooling my throat with the Milky Way or shaking hands with those stars."

CHAPTER FIVE

§ 1

A GUST of confidence on the part of a person naturally or habitually reserved will often be followed by a phase of recoil. At breakfast next morning their overnight talk seemed to both Sir Richmond and Dr. Martineau like something each had dreamt about the other, a quite impossible excess of intimacy. They discussed the weather, which seemed to be settling down to the utmost serenity of which the English spring is capable, they talked of Sir Richmond's coming car and of the possible routes before them. Sir Richmond produced the Michelin maps which he had taken out of the pockets of the little Charmeuse. The Bath Road lay before them, he explained, Reading, Newbury, Hungerford, Marlborough, Silbury Hill which overhangs Avebury. Both travellers discovered a common excitement at the mention of Avebury and Silbury Hill. Both took an intelligent interest in archæology. Both had been greatly stimulated by the recent work of Elliot Smith and Rivers upon what was then known as the Heliolithic culture. It had revived their interest in Avebury and Stonehenge. The doctor moreover had been reading Hippisley Cox's *Green Roads of England*.

Neither gentleman had ever seen Avebury, but Dr. Martineau had once visited Stonehenge.

"Avebury is much the oldest," said the doctor. "They must have made Silbury Hill long before 2000 B.C. It may be five thousand years old or even more. It is the most important historical relic in the British Isles. And the most neglected."

They exchanged archæological facts. The secret places of the heart rested until the afternoon.

Then Sir Richmond saw fit to amplify his confessions in one particular.

§ 2

The doctor and his patient had discovered a need for exercise as the morning advanced. They had walked by the road to Marlow and had lunched at a riverside inn, returning after a restful hour in an arbour on the lawn of this place to tea at Maidenhead. It was as they returned that Sir Richmond took up the thread of their overnight conversation again.

"In the night," he said, " I was thinking over the account I tried to give you of my motives. A lot of it was terribly out of drawing."

" Facts ? " asked the doctor.

" No, the facts were all right. It was the atmosphere, the proportions. . . . I don't know if I gave you the effect of something Don Juanesque ? . . ."

" Vulgar poem," said the doctor remarkably. " I discounted that."

" Vulgar ! "

" Intolerable. Byron in sexual psychology is like a stink in a kitchen."

Sir Richard perceived he had struck upon the sort of thing that used to be called a pet aversion.

" I don't want you to think that I run about after women in an habitual and systematic manner. Or that I deliberately hunt them in the interests of my work and energy. Your questions had set me theorising about myself. And I did my best to improvise a scheme of motives yesterday. It was, I perceive, a jerry-built scheme, run up at short notice. My nocturnal reflections convinced me of that. I put reason into things that are essentially instinctive. The truth is that the wanderings of desire have no single drive. All sorts of motives come in, high and low, down to sheer vulgar imitativeness and competitiveness. What was true in it all was this, that a man with any imagination in a fatigue phase falls naturally into these complications because they are more attractive to his type and far easier and more refreshing to the mind, at the outset, than anything else. And they do work a sort of recovery in him. They send him back to his work refreshed —so far, that is, as his work is concerned."

" At the *outset* they are easier," said the doctor.

Sir Richmond laughed. " When one is fagged it is only the outset counts. The more tired one is the more readily one moves along the line of least resistance. . . .

" That is one footnote to what I said. So far as the motive of my work goes, I think we got something like the spirit of it. What I said about that was near the truth of things. . . .

" But there is another set of motives altogether," Sir Richmond went on with an air of having cleared the ground for his real business, " that I didn't go into at all yesterday."

He considered. " It arises out of these other affairs. Before you realise it your affections are involved. I am a man much swayed by my affections."

Dr. Martineau glanced at him. There was a note of genuine self-reproach in Sir Richmond's voice.

" I get fond of people. It is quite irrational, but I get fond of them. Which is quite a different thing from the admiration and excitement of falling in love. Almost the opposite thing. They cry or they come some mental or physical cropper and hurt themselves, or they do something distressingly little and human and suddenly I find they've *got* me. I'm distressed. I'm filled with something between pity and an impulse of responsibility. I become tender towards them. I am impelled to take care of them. I want to ease them off, to reassure them, to make them stop hurting at any cost. I don't see why it should be the weak and sickly and seamy side of people that grips me most, but it is. I don't know why it should be their failures that gives them power over me, but it is. I told you of this girl, this mistress of mine, who is ill just now. *She's* got me in that way ; she's got me tremendously."

" You did not speak of her yesterday with any morbid excess of pity," the doctor was constrained to remark.

" I abused her very probably. I forget exactly what I said. . . ."

The doctor offered no assistance.

" But the reason why I abuse her is perfectly plain. I abuse her because she distresses me by her misfortunes, and instead of my getting anything out of her, I go out to her. But I *do* go out to her. All this time at the back of my mind I am worrying about her. She has that gift of making one feel for her. I am feeling that damned carbuncle almost as if it had been my affair instead of hers.

" That carbuncle has made me suffer—*frightfully*. . . . Why should I ? It isn't mine."

He regarded the doctor earnestly. The doctor controlled a strong desire to laugh.

" I suppose the young lady——" he began.

" Oh ! *she* puts in suffering all right. I've no doubt about that.

" I suppose," Sir Richmond went on, " now that I have told you so much of this affair, I may as well tell you all. It is a sort of comedy, a painful comedy, of irrelevant affections. . . ."

The doctor was prepared to be a good listener. Facts he would always listen to ; it was only when people told him their theories that he would interrupt with his " Exactly."

" This young woman is a person of considerable genius. I don't know if you have seen in the illustrated papers a peculiar sort of humorous illustrations usually with a considerable amount of bite in them over the name of Martin Leeds ? "

" Extremely amusing stuff."

" It is that Martin Leeds. I met her at the beginning of her career. She talks almost as well as she draws. She amused me immensely. I'm not the sort of man who waylays and besieges women and girls. I'm not the pursuing type. But I perceived that in some odd way I attracted her, and I was neither wise enough nor generous enough not to let the thing develop."

" H'm," said Dr. Martineau.

" I'd never had to do with an intellectually brilliant woman before. I see now that the more imaginative force a woman has, the more likely she is to get into a state of extreme self-abandonment with any male thing upon which her imagination begins to crystallise. Before I came along she'd mixed chiefly with a lot of young artists and students, all doing nothing at all except talk about the things they were going to do. I suppose I profited by the contrast, being older and with my hands full of affairs. Perhaps something had happened that had made her recoil towards my sort of thing. I don't know. But she just let herself go at me."

" And you ? "

" Let myself go too. I'd never met anything like her before. It was her wit took me. It didn't occur to me that she wasn't my contemporary and as able as I was. As able to take care of herself. All sorts of considerations that I should have shown to a sillier woman I never dreamt of showing to her. I had never met any one so mentally brilliant before or so helpless and headlong. And so here we are on each other's hands ! "

" But the child ? "

" It happened to us. For four years now things have just happened to us. All the time I have been overworking, first at explosives and now at this fuel business. She too is full of her work. Nothing stops that though everything seems to interfere with it. And in a distraught, preoccupied way we are abominably fond of each other. ' Fond ' is the word. But we are both too busy to look after either ourselves or each other.

" She is much more incapable than I am," said Sir Richmond, as if he delivered a weighed and very important judgment.

" You see very much of each other ? "

" She has a flat in Chelsea and a little cottage in South Cornwall, and we sometimes snatch a few days together, away somewhere in Surrey or up the Thames or at such a place as Southend where one is lost in a crowd of inconspicuous people. When things go well—they usually go well at the start—we are glorious companions. She is happy, she is creative, she will light up a new place with flashes of humour, with a keenness of appreciation. . . ."

" But things do not always go well ? "

" Things," said Sir Richmond with the deliberation of a man who measures his words, " are apt to go wrong. . . . At the flat there is constant trouble with the servants ; they bully her. A woman is more entangled with servants than a man. Women in that position seem to resent the work and freedom of other women. Her servants won't leave her in peace as they would leave a man ; they make trouble for her. . . . And when we have had a few days anywhere away, even if nothing in particular has gone wrong——"

Sir Richmond stopped short.

" When they go wrong it is generally her fault ? " the doctor sounded.

" Almost always."

" But if they don't ? " said the psychiatrist.

" It is difficult to describe. . . . The essential incompatibility of the whole thing comes out."

The doctor maintained his expression of intelligent interest.

" She wants to go on with her work. She is able to work anywhere. All she wants is just cardboard and ink. My mind on the other hand turns back to the Fuel Commission. . . ."

" Then any little thing makes trouble."

" Any little thing makes trouble. And we always drift round to the same discussion ; whether we ought really to go on together."

" It is you begin that ? "

" Yes, I start that. You see she is perfectly contented when I am about. She is as fond of me as I am of her."

" Fonder perhaps."

" I don't know. But she is—adhesive. Emotionally adhesive. All she wants to do is just to settle down when I am there and go on with her work. But then, you see, there is *my* work."

" Exactly. . . . After all it seems to me that your great trouble is not in yourselves but in social institutions. Which haven't yet fitted themselves to people like you two. It is the sense of uncertainty makes her, as you say, adhesive. Nervously so. If we were indeed living in a new age instead of the moral ruins of a shattered one——"

" We can't alter the age we live in," said Sir Richmond a little testily.

" No. Exactly. But we *can* realise, in any particular situation, that it is not the individuals to blame but the misfit of ideas and forms and prejudices."

" No," said Sir Richmond, obstinately rejecting this pacifying suggestion ; " she could adapt herself. If she cared enough."

" But how ? "

" She will not take the slightest trouble to adjust herself to the peculiarities of our position. . . . She could be cleverer. Other women are cleverer. Any other woman almost would be cleverer than she is."

" But if she was cleverer, she wouldn't be the genius she is. She would just be any other woman."

" Perhaps she would," said Sir Richmond darkly and desperately. " Perhaps she would. Perhaps it would be better if she was."

Dr. Martineau raised his eyebrows in a furtive aside.

" But here you see that it is that in my case, the fundamental incompatibility between one's affections and one's wider conception of duty and work comes in. We cannot change social institutions in a year or a lifetime. We can never change them to suit an individual case. That would be like suspending the laws of gravitation in order to move a piano. As things are Martin is no good to me, no help to me. She is a rival to my duty. She feels that. She is hostile to my duty. A definite antagonism has developed. She feels and treats fuel and everything to do with fuel as a bore. It is an attack. We quarrel on that. It isn't as though I found it so easy to stick to my work that I could disregard her hostility. And I can't bear to part from her. I threaten it, I distress her excessively and then I am overcome by sympathy for her and I go back to her. . . . In the ordinary course of things I should be with her now."

" If it were not for the carbuncle ? "

" If it were not for the carbuncle. She does not care for me to see her disfigured. She does not understand——" Sir Richmond was at a loss for a phrase—" that it is not her good looks."

" She won't let you go to her ? "

" It amounts to that. . . . And soon there will be all the trouble about educating the girl. Whatever happens, she must have as good a chance as—any one. . . ."

" Ah ! That is worrying you too ! "

" Frightfully at times. If it were a boy it would be easier. It needs constant tact and dexterity to fix things up. Neither of us have any. It needs attention. . . ."

Sir Richmond mused darkly.

Dr. Martineau thought aloud. " An incompetent delightful person with Martin Leeds' sense of humour. And her powers of expression. She must be attractive to many people. She could probably do without you. If once you parted."

Sir Richmond turned on him eagerly.

" You think I ought to part from her ? On her account ? "

" On her account. It might pain her. But once the thing was done——"

" I want to part. I believe I ought to part."

" Well ? "

" But then my affection comes in."

" That extraordinary—*tenderness* of yours ? "

" I'm afraid."

" Of what ? "

" Any one might get hold of her—if I let her down. She hasn't a tithe of the ordinary cool-headed calculation of an average woman. . . . I've a duty to her genius. I've got to take care of her."

To which the doctor made no reply.

" Nevertheless the idea of parting has been very much in my mind lately."

" Letting her go free ? "

" You can put it in that way if you like."

" It might not be a fatal operation for either of you."

" And yet there are moods when parting is an intolerable idea. When one is invaded by a flood of affection. . . . And old habits of association."

Dr. Martineau thought. Was that the right word—affection ? Perhaps it was.

They had come out on the towing path close by the lock and they found themselves threading their way through a little crowd of boating people and lookers-on. For a time their conversation was broken. Sir Richmond resumed it.

" But this is where we cease to be Man on his Planet and all the rest of it. This is where the idea of a definite task, fanatically followed to the exclusion of all minor considerations, breaks down. When the work is good, when we are sure we are all right, then we may carry off things with a high hand. But the work isn't always good, we aren't always sure. We blunder, we make a muddle, we are fatigued. Then the sacrificed affections come in as accusers. Then it is that we want to be reassured."

" And then it is that Miss Martin Leeds—— ? "

" Doesn't," Sir Richmond snapped.

Came a long pause.

" And yet——

" It is extraordinarily difficult to think of parting from Martin."

§ 3

In the evening after dinner Dr. Martineau sought, rather unsuccessfully, to go on with the analysis of Sir Richmond.

But Sir Richmond was evidently a creature of moods. Either he regretted the extent of his confidences or the slight irrational irritation that he felt at waiting for his car affected his attitude towards his companion, or Dr. Martineau's tentatives were ill-chosen. At any rate he would not rise to any conversational bait that the doctor could devise. The doctor found this the more regrettable because it seemed to him that there was much to be worked upon in this Martin Leeds affair. He was inclined to think that she and Sir Richmond were unduly obsessed by the idea that they had to stick together because of the child, because of the look of the thing and so forth, and that really indeed each might be struggling against a very strong impulse indeed to break off the affair. It seemed evident to the doctor that they jarred upon and annoyed each other extremely. On the whole separating people appealed to the doctor's mind more strongly than bringing them together. Accordingly he framed his inquiries so as to make the revelation of a latent antipathy as easy as possible.

He made several not very well devised beginnings. At the fifth Sir Richmond was suddenly conclusive. " It's no use,"

he said. " I can't fiddle about any more with my motives
to-day."

An awkward silence followed. On reflection Sir Richmond
seemed to realise that this sentence needed some apology.
" I admit," he said, " that this expedition has already been a
wonderfully good thing for me. These confessions have made
me look into all sorts of things—squarely. But——

" I'm not used to talking about myself or even thinking
directly about myself. What I say, I afterwards find disconcerting to recall. I want to alter it. I can feel myself wallow-
ing into a mess of modifications and qualifications."

" Yes, but——"

" I want a rest anyhow. . . ."

There was nothing for Dr. Martineau to say to that.

The two gentlemen smoked for some time in a slightly
uncomfortable silence. Dr. Martineau cleared his throat
twice and lit a second cigar. They then agreed to admire the
bridge and think well of Maidenhead. Sir Richmond com-
municated hopeful news about his car, which was to arrive the
next morning before ten—he'd just ring the fellow up presently
to make sure—and Dr. Martineau retired early and went
rather thoughtfully to bed. The spate of Sir Richmond's
confidences, it was evident, was over.

§ 4

Sir Richmond's car arrived long before ten, brought down
by a young man in a state of scared alacrity—Sir Richmond
had done some vigorous telephoning before turning in—the
Charmeuse set off in a repaired and chastened condition to
town, and after a leisurely breakfast our two investigators
into the springs of human conduct were able to resume their
westward journey. They ran through scattered Twyford
with its pleasant-looking inns and through the commonplace
urbanities of Reading, by Newbury and Hungerford's pretty
bridge and up long wooded slopes to Savernake forest, where
they found the road heavy and dusty, still in its war-time
state, and so down a steep hill to the wide market street which
is Marlborough. They lunched in Marlborough and went on
in the afternoon to Silbury Hill, that British pyramid, the
largest artificial mound in Europe. They left the car by the
roadside and clambered to the top, and were very learned and
inconclusive about the exact purpose of this vast heap of
chalk and earth, this heap that men had made before the
temples at Karnak were built or Babylon had a name.

Then they returned to the car and ran round by a winding
road into the wonder of Avebury. They found a clean little
inn there kept by pleasant people, and they garaged the car
in the cowshed and took two rooms for the night that they
might the better get the atmosphere of the ancient place.

Wonderful indeed it is, a vast circumvallation that was already two thousand years old before the dawn of British history ; a great wall of earth with its ditch most strangely on its inner and not on its outer side ; and within this enclosure gigantic survivors of the great circles of unhewn stone that, even as late as Tudor days, were almost complete. A whole village, a church, a pretty manor house have been built, for the most part, out of the ancient megaliths ; the great wall is sufficient to embrace them all with their gardens and paddocks ; four cross-roads meet at the village centre. There are drawings of Avebury before these things arose there, when it was a lonely wonder on the plain, but for the most part the destruction was already done before the *Mayflower* sailed. To the southward stands the cone of Silbury Hill ; its shadow creeps up and down the intervening meadows as the seasons change. Around this lonely place rise the Downs, now bare sheep pastures, in broad undulations, with a wart-like barrow here and there, and from it radiate, creeping up to gain and hold the crests of the hills, the abandoned trackways of that forgotten world. These trackways, these green roads of England, these roads already disused when the Romans made their highway past Silbury Hill to Bath, can still be traced for scores of miles through the land, running to Salisbury and the English Channel, eastward to the crossing at the Straits and westward to Wales, to ferries over the Severn, and southwestward into Devon and Cornwall.

The doctor and Sir Richmond walked round the walls surveyed the shadow cast by Silbury upon the river flats, strolled up the down to the northward to get a general view of the village, had tea and smoked round the walls again in the warm April sunset. The matter of their conversation remained prehistoric. Both were inclined to find fault with the archæological work that had been done on the place. " Clumsy treasure hunting," Sir Richmond said. " They bore into Silbury Hill and expect to find a mummified chief or something sensational of that sort and they don't, and they report—nothing. They haven't sifted finely enough ; they haven't thought subtly enough. These walls of earth ought to tell what these people ate, what clothes they wore, what woods they used. Was this a sheep land then as it is now, or a cattle land ? Were these hills covered by forests ? I don't know. These archæologists don't know. Or if they do they haven't told me—which is just as bad. I don't believe they know.

" What trade came here along these tracks ? So far as I know, they had no beasts of burthen. But suppose one day some one were to find a potsherd here from early Knossos or a fragment of glass from Pepi's Egypt."

The place had stirred up his imagination. He wrestled with his ignorance as if he thought that by talking he might presently worry out some picture of this forgotten world, without metals, without beasts of burthen, without letters, without any sculpture that has left a trace, and yet with a sense of astronomical fact clear enough to raise the great gnomon of Silbury, and with a social system complex enough to give the large and orderly community to which the size of Avebury witnesses and the traffic to which the green roads testify.

The doctor had not realised before the boldness and liveliness of his companion's mind. Sir Richmond insisted that the climate must have been moister and milder in those days ; he covered all the downlands with woods as Savernake was still covered ; beneath the trees he restored a thicker, richer soil. These people must have done an enormous lot with wood. This use of stones here was a freak. It was the very strangeness of stones here that had made them into sacred things. One thought too much of the stones of the Stone Age. Who would carve these lumps of quartzite when one could carve good oak ? Or beech—a most carvable wood. Especially when one's sharpest chisel was a flint. " It's wood we ought to look for," said Sir Richmond. " Wood and fibre." He declared that these people had their tools of wood, their homes of wood, their gods and perhaps their records of wood. " A peat bog here, even a few feet of clay, might have pickled some precious memoranda. . . . No such luck. . . ." Now in Glastonbury marshes one found the life of the early iron age—half-way to our own times—quite beautifully pickled.

Though they wrestled mightily with the problem, neither Sir Richmond nor the doctor could throw a gleam of light upon the riddle why the ditch was inside and not outside the great wall.

" And what was our Mind like in those days ? " said Sir Richmond. " That, I suppose, is what interests you. A vivid childish mind, I guess, with not a suspicion as yet that it was Man ruling his Planet or anything of that sort."

The doctor pursed his lips. " None," he delivered judicially. " If one were able to recall one's childhood—at the age of about twelve or thirteen—when the artistic impulse so often goes into abeyance and one begins to think in a troubled, monstrous way about God and Hell, one might get something like the mind of this place."

" Thirteen. You put them at that—already ? . . . These people, you think, were religious ? "

" Intensely. In that personal way that gives death a nightmare terror. And as for the fading of the artistic impulse, they've left not a trace of the paintings and drawings and scratchings of the Old Stone people who came before them."

" Adults with the minds of thirteen-year-old children. Thirteen-year-old children with the strength of adults—and no one to slap them or tell them not to. . . . After all, they probably only thought of death now and then. And they never thought of fuel. They supposed there was no end to that. So they used up their woods and kept goats to nibble and kill the new undergrowth. . . . *Did* these people have goats ? "

" I don't know," said the doctor. " So little is known."

" Very like children they must have been. The same unending days. They must have thought that the world went on for ever—just as they knew it—like my damned Committee does. . . . With their fuel wasting away and the climate changing imperceptibly, century by century. . . . Kings and important men followed one another here for centuries and centuries. . . . They had lost their past and had no idea of any future. . . . They had forgotten how they came into the land. . . . When I was a child I believed that my father's garden had been there for ever. . . .

" This is very like trying to remember some game one played when one was a child. It is like coming on something that one built up with bricks and stones in some forgotten part of the garden. . . ."

" The life we lived here," said the doctor, " has left its traces in traditions, in mental predispositions, in still un-analysed fundamental ideas."

" Archæology is very like remembering," said Sir Richmond. " Presently we shall remember a lot more about all this. We shall remember what it was like to live in this place, and the long journey hither, age by age, out of the south. We shall remember the sacrifices we made and the crazy reasons why we made them. We sowed our corn in blood here. We had strange fancies about the stars. Those we brought with us out of the south where the stars are brighter. And what like were those wooden gods of ours ? I don't remember. . . . But I could easily persuade myself that I had been here before."

They stood on the crest of the ancient wall and the setting sun cast long shadows of them athwart a field of springing wheat.

" Perhaps we shall come here again," the doctor carried on Sir Richard's fancy ; " after another four thousand years or so, with different names and fuller minds. And then I suppose that this ditch won't be the riddle it is now."

" Life didn't seem so complicated then," Sir Richmond mused. " Our muddles were unconscious. We drifted from mood to mood and forgot. There was more sunshine then, more laughter perhaps, and blacker despair. Despair like the despair of children that can weep itself to sleep. . . . It's over. . . . Was it battle and massacre that ended that long afternoon here ? Or did the woods catch fire some exception-ally dry summer, leaving black hills and famine ? Or did strange men bring a sickness—measles, perhaps, or the black death ? Or was it cattle pest ? Or did we just waste our woods and dwindle away before the new peoples that came into the land across the southern sea ? I can't remember. . . ."

Sir Richmond turned about. " I would like to dig up the bottom of this ditch here foot by foot—and dry the stuff and sift it—very carefully. . . . Then I might begin to remember things."

§ 5

In the evening, after a pleasant supper, they took a turn about the walls with the moon sinking over beyond Silbury, and then went in and sat by lamplight before a brightly fussy wood fire and smoked. There were long intervals of friendly silence.

" I don't in the least want to go on talking about myself," said Sir Richmond abruptly.

" Let it rest then," said the doctor, generously.

" To-day, among these ancient memories, has taken me out of myself wonderfully. I can't tell you how good Avebury has been for me. This afternoon half my consciousness has seemed to be a tattooed creature wearing a knife of stone. . . ."

" The healing touch of history."

" And for the first time my damned Committee has mattered scarcely a rap."

Sir Richmond stretched himself in his chair and blinked cheerfully at his cigar smoke.

" Nevertheless," he said, " this confessional business of yours has been an excellent exercise. It has enabled me to get outside myself, to look at myself as a Case. Now I can even see myself as a remote Case. That I needn't bother about further. . . . So far as that goes, I think we have done all that there is to be done."

" I shouldn't say that—quite—yet," said the doctor.

" I don't think I'm a subject for real psycho-analysis at all. I'm not an overlaid sort of person. When I spread myself out there is not much indication of a suppressed wish or of anything masked or buried of that sort. What you get is a quite open and recognised discord of two sets of motives."

The doctor considered. " Yes, I think that is true. Your *libido* is, I should say, exceptionally free. Generally you are doing what you want to do—overdoing, in fact, what you want to do—and getting simply tired."

" Which is the theory I started with. I am a case of fatigue under irritating circumstances with very little mental complication or concealment."

" Yes," said the doctor. " I agree. You are not a case for psycho-analysis, strictly speaking, at all. You are in open conflict with yourself upon moral and social issues. Practically open. Your problems are problems of conscious conduct."

" As I said."

" Of what renunciations you have consciously to make."

Sir Richmond did not answer that. . . .

" This pilgrimage of ours," he said, presently, " has made for magnanimity. This day particularly has been a good day. When we stood on this old wall here in the sunset I seemed to be standing outside myself in an immense still sphere of past and future. I stood with my feet upon the Stone Age and saw myself four thousand years away and all my distresses as very little incidents in that perspective. Away there in London the case is altogether different ; after three hours or so of the Committee one concentrates into one little inflamed moment of personality. There is no past any longer, there is no future, there is only the rankling dispute. For all those three hours, perhaps, I have been thinking of just what I had to say, just how I had to say it, just how I looked while I said it, just how much I was making myself understood, how I might be misunderstood, how I might be misrepresented, challenged, denied. One draws in more and more as one is used up. At last one is reduced to a little, raw, bleeding, desperately fighting pin-point of *self*. . . . One goes back to one's home unable to recover. Fighting it over again. All night sometimes. . . . I get up and walk about the room and curse. . . . Martineau, how is one to get the Avebury frame of mind to Westminster ? "

" When Westminster is as dead as Avebury," said the doctor, unhelpfully. He added after some seconds, " Milton knew of these troubles. ' Not without dust and heat,' he wrote—a great phrase."

" But the dust chokes me," said Sir Richmond.

He took up a copy of *The Green Roads of England* that lay beside him on the table. But he did not open it. He held it in his hand and said the thing he had had in mind to say all that evening. " I do not think that I shall stir up my motives any more for a time. Better to go on into the west country cooling my poor old brain in these wide shadows of the past."

" I can prescribe nothing better," said Dr. Martineau. " Incidentally, we may be able to throw a little more light on one or two of your minor entanglements."

" I don't want to think of them," said Sir Richmond. " Let me get right away from everything. Until my skin has grown again."

CHAPTER SIX

THE ENCOUNTER AT STONEHENGE

§ 1

NEXT day in the early afternoon after a farewell walk over the downs round Avebury they went by way of Devizes and Netheravon and Amesbury to Stonehenge. Dr. Martineau had seen this ancient monument before, but now, with Avebury fresh in his mind, he found it a poorer thing than he had remembered it to be. Sir Richmond was frankly disappointed. After the real greatness and mystery of the older place, it seemed a poor little heap of stones ; it did not even dominate the landscape ; it was some way from the crest of the swelling down on which it stood, and it was further dwarfed by the colossal air-ship hangars and clustering offices of the air station that the great war had called into existence upon the slopes to the south-west. " It looks," Sir Richmond said, " as though some old giantess had left a discarded set of teeth on the hillside." Far more impressive than Stonehenge itself were the barrows that capped the neighbouring crests.

The sacred stones were fenced about, and our visitors had to pay for admission at a little kiosk by the gate. At the side of the road stood a travel-stained middle-class automobile, with a miscellany of dusty luggage, rugs and luncheon things therein—a family automobile with father no doubt at the wheel. Sir Richmond left his own trim coupé at its tail.

They were impeded at the entrance by a difference of opinion between the keeper of the turnstile and a small but resolute boy of perhaps five or six who proposed to leave the enclosure. The custodian thought that it would be better if his nurse or his mother came out with him.

" She keeps on looking at it," said the small boy. " It isunt anything. I want to go and clean the car."

" You won't see Stonehenge every day, young man," said the custodian, a little piqued.

" It's only an old beach," said the small boy, with extreme conviction. " It's rocks like the seaside. And there isunt no sea."

The man at the turnstile mutely consulted the doctor.

" I don't see that he can get into any harm here," the doctor advised, and the small boy was released from archæology.

He strolled to the family automobile, produced an *en-tout-cas* pocket-handkerchief and set himself to polish the lamps with great assiduity. The two gentlemen lingered at the turnstile for a moment or so to watch his proceedings. " Modern child," said Sir Richmond. " Old stones are just old stones to him. But motor-cars are gods."

" You can hardly expect him to understand — at his age," said the custodian, jealous for the honour of Stonehenge. . . .

" Reminds me of Martin's little girl," said Sir Richmond, as he and Dr. Martineau went on towards the circle. " When she encountered her first dragon-fly she was greatly delighted. ' Oh, dee' lill' a'eplane," she said."

As they approached the grey old stones they became aware of a certain agitation among them. A voice, an authoritative bass voice was audible, crying, " Anthony ! " A nurse appeared remotely, going in the direction of the aeroplane sheds, and her cry of " Master Anthony " came faintly on the breeze. An extremely pretty young woman of five- or six-and-twenty became visible standing on one of the great prostrate stones in the centre of the place. She was a black-haired, sun-burnt individual, and she stood with her arms akimbo, quite frankly amused at the disappearance of Master Anthony, and offering no sort of help for his recovery. On the green-sward before her stood the paterfamilias of the family auto-mobile, and he was making a trumpet with his hands in order to repeat the name of Anthony with greater effect. A short lady in grey emerged from among the encircling megaliths, and one or two other feminine personalities produced effects of movement rather than of individuality as they flitted among the stones. " Well," said the lady in grey, with that rising intonation of humorous conclusion which is so distinctively American, " those Druids have got him."

" He's hiding," said the automobilist, in a voice that promised chastisement to a hidden hearer. " That's what he's doing. He ought not to play tricks like this. A great boy who is almost six."

" If you are looking for a small, resolute boy of six," said Sir Richmond, addressing himself to the lady on the rock rather than to the angry parent below, " he's perfectly safe and happy. The Druids haven't got him. Indeed, they've failed altogether to get him. ' Stonehenge,' he says, ' is no good.' So he's gone back to clean the lamps of your car."

" Aa-oo. So *that's* it ! " said papa. " Winnie, go and tell Price he's gone back to the car. . . . They oughtn't to have let him out of the enclosure. . . ."

The . excitement about Master Anthony collapsed. The rest of the people in the circles crystallised out into the central space as two apparent sisters and an apparent aunt and the nurse, who was packed off at once to supervise the lamp cleaning. The head of the family found some difficulty, it would seem, in readjusting his mind to the comparative innocence of Anthony, and Sir Richmond and the young lady on the rock sought as if by common impulse to establish a general conversation. There were faint traces of excitement in her manner, as though there had been some controversial passage between herself and the family gentleman.

" We were discussing the age of this old place," she said, smiling in the frankest and friendliest way. " How old do *you* think it is ? "

The father of Anthony intervened, also with a shadow of controversy in his manner ; " I was explaining to the young lady that it dates from the early Bronze Age. Before chronology existed. . . . But she insists on dates."

" Nothing of bronze has ever been found here," said Sir Richmond.

" Well, when was this early Bronze Age, anyhow ? " said the young lady.

Sir Richmond sought a recognisable datum. " Bronze got to Britain somewhere between the times of Moses and Solomon."

" Ah ! " said the young lady, as who should say, ' This man at least talks sense.'

" But these stones are all shaped," said the father of the family. " It is difficult to see how that could have been done without something harder than stone."

" I don't *see* the place," said the young lady on the stone. " I can't imagine how they did it up—not one bit."

" *Did it up !* " exclaimed the father of the family in the tone of one accustomed to find a gentle sport in the intellectual frailties of his womankind.

" It's just the bones of a place. They hung things round it. They draped it."

" But what things ? " asked Sir Richmond.

" Oh ! they had things all right. Skins perhaps. Mats of rushes. Bast cloth. Fibre of all sorts. Wadded stuff."

" Stonehenge draped ! It's really a delightful idea," said the father of the family, enjoying it.

" It's quite a possible one," said Sir Richmond.

" Or they may have used wicker," the young lady went on, undismayed. She seemed to concede a point. " Wicker *is* likelier."

" But surely," said the father of the family, with the ex-postulatory voice and gesture of one who would recall erring wits to sanity ; " it is far more impressive standing out bare and noble as it does. In lonely splendour."

" But all this country may have been wooded then," said Sir Richmond. " In which case it wouldn't have stood out. It doesn't stand out so very much even now."

" You came to it through a grove," said the young lady, eagerly picking up the idea.

" Probably beech," said Sir Richmond.

" Which may have pointed to the midsummer sunrise," said Dr. Martineau, unheeded.

" These are *novel* ideas," said the father of the family in the reproving tone of one who never allows a novel idea inside *his* doors if he can prevent it.

" Well," said the young lady, " I guess there was some sort of show here anyhow. And no human being ever had a show yet without trying to shut people out of it in order to make them come in. I guess this was covered in all right. A dark hunched old place in a wood. Beech stems, smooth, like pillars. And they came to it at night, in procession, beating drums, and scared half out of their wits. They came in *there* and went round the inner circle with their torches. And so they were shown. The torches were put out and the priests did their mysteries. Until dawn broke. That's how they worked it."

" But even you can't tell what the show was, V.V.," said the lady in grey, who was standing now at Martineau's elbow.

" Something horrid," said Anthony's younger sister to her elder in a stage whisper.

" *Bluggy*," agreed Anthony's elder sister to the younger, in a noiseless voice that certainly did not reach father. " *Squeals !* " . . .

This young lady who was addressed as " V.V." was perhaps one- or two-and-twenty, Dr. Martineau thought—he was not very good at feminine ages. She had a clear sun-browned complexion, with dark hair and smiling lips. Her features were finely modelled, with just that added touch of breadth in the brow and softness in the cheek bones, that faint flavour of the Amerindian, one sees at times in American women. Her voice was a very soft and pleasing voice, and she spoke persuasively and not assertively as so many American women do. Her determination to make the dry bones of Stonehenge live shamed the doctor's disappointment with the place. And when she had spoken, Dr. Martineau noted that she looked at Sir Richmond as if she expected him at least to confirm her vision. Sir Richmond was evidently prepared to confirm it.

With a queer little twinge of infringed proprietorship, the doctor saw Sir Richmond step up on the prostrate megalith and stand beside her, the better to appreciate her point of view. He smiled down at her. " Now why do you think they came in *there* ? " he asked.

The young lady was not very clear about her directions. She did not know of the roadway running to the Avon river, nor of the alleged race-course to the north, nor had she ever heard that the stones were supposed to be of two different periods and that some of them might possibly have been brought from a very great distance.

§ 2

Neither Dr. Martineau nor the father of the family found the imaginative reconstruction of the Stonehenge rituals quite so exciting as the two principals. The father of the family endured some further particulars with manifest impatience, no longer able, now that Sir Richmond was encouraging the girl, to keep her in check with the slightly derisive smile proper to her sex. Then he proclaimed in a fine loud tenor, "All this is very imaginative, I'm afraid." And to his family, "Time we were pressing on. Turps, we must go-o. Come, Phœbe ! "

As he led his little flock towards the exit his voice came floating back. " Talking wanton nonsense. . . . Any professional archæologist would laugh, simply laugh. . . ."

He passed out of the world.

With a faint intimation of dismay Dr. Martineau realised that the two talkative ladies were not to be removed in the family automobile with the rest of the party. Sir Richmond and the younger lady went on very cheerfully to the population, agriculture, housing and general scenery of the surrounding Downland during the later Stone Age. The shorter, less attractive lady, whose accent was distinctly American, came now and stood at the doctor's elbow. She seemed moved to play the part of chorus to the two upon the stone.

" When V.V. gets going," she remarked, " she makes things come alive."

Dr. Martineau hated to be addressed suddenly by strange ladies. He started, and his face assumed the distressed politeness of the moon at its full. " Your friend," he said, " interested in archæology ? "

" Interested ! " said the stouter lady. " Why ! She's a fiend at it. Ever since we came on Carnac."

" You've visited Carnac ? "

" That's where the bug bit her," said the stout lady with a note of querulous humour. " Directly V.V. set eyes on Carnac, she just turned against all her up-bringing. ' Why wasn't I told of this before ? ' she said. ' What's Notre Dame to this ? This is where we came from. This is the real starting-point of the *Mayflower*. Belinda,' she said, ' we've got to see all we can of this sort of thing before we go back to America. They've been keeping this from us.' And that's why we're here right now instead of being shopping in Paris or London like decent American women."

The younger lady looked down on her companion with something of the calm expert attention that a plumber gives to a tap that is misbehaving, and like a plumber refrained from precipitate action. She stood with the backs of her hands resting on her hips.

" Well," she said slowly, giving most of the remark to Sir Richmond and the rest to the doctor, " it *is* nearer the beginnings of things than London or Paris."

" And nearer to us," said Sir Richmond.

" I call that—just paradoxical," said the shorter lady, who appeared to be called Belinda.

" Not paradoxical," Dr. Martineau contradicted gently. " Life is always beginning again. And this is a time of fresh beginnings."

" Now that's after V.V.'s own heart," cried the stout lady in grey. " She'll agree to all that. She's been saying it right across Europe. Rome, Paris, London ; they're simply just done. They don't signify any more. They've got to be cleared away."

" You let me tell my own opinions, Belinda," said the young lady who was called V.V. " I said that if people went on building with fluted pillars and Corinthian capitals for two thousand years, it was time they were cleared up and taken away."

" Corinthian capitals ? " Sir Richmond considered it and laughed cheerfully. " I suppose Europe does rather overdo that sort of thing."

" The way she went on about the Victor Emmanuele Monument ! " said the lady who answered to the name of Belinda. " It gave me cold shivers to think that those Italian officers might understand English."

The lady who was called V.V. smiled as if she smiled at herself, and explained herself to Sir Richmond. " When one is travelling about, one gets to think of history and politics in terms of architecture. I do anyhow. And those columns with Corinthian capitals have got to be a sort of symbol for me for everything in Europe that I don't want and have no sort of use for. It isn't a bad sort of capital in its way, florid and pretty, but not a patch on the Doric ;—and that a whole continent should come up to it and stick at it and never get past it ! . . ."

" It's the classical tradition."

" It puzzles me."

" It's the Roman Empire. That Corinthian column is a weed spread by the Romans all over western Europe."

" And it smothers the history of Europe. You can't see Europe because of it. Europe is obsessed by Rome. Everywhere Marble Arches and *Arcs de Triomphe*. You never get away from it. It is like some old gentleman who has lost his way in a speech and keeps on repeating the same thing. And can't sit down. ' The empire, gentlemen—Empire. Empire.' Rome itself is perfectly frightful. It stares at you with its great round stupid arches as though it couldn't imagine that you could possibly want anything else for ever. Saint Peter's and that frightful Monument are just the same stuff as the

Baths of Caracalla and the palaces of the Cæsars. Just the same. They will make just the same sort of ruins. It goes on and goes on."

"*Ave Roma Immortalis*," said Dr. Martineau.

"This Roman empire seems to be Europe's first and last idea. A fixed idea. And such a poor idea ! . . . America never came out of that. It's no good telling me that it did. It escaped from it. . . . So I said to Belinda here, 'Let's burrow, if we can, under all this marble and find out what sort of people we were before this Roman empire and its acanthus weeds got hold of us.' "

"I seem to remember at Washington, something faintly Corinthian, something called the Capitol," Sir Richmond reflected. "And other buildings. A Treasury."

"That's different," said the young lady, so conclusively that it seemed to leave nothing more to be said on that score.

"A last twinge of Europeanism," she vouchsafed. "We were young in those days."

"You are well beneath the marble here."

She assented cheerfully.

"A thousand years before it."

"Happy place ! Happy people ! "

'But even this place isn't the beginning of things here. Carnac was older than this. And older still is Avebury. Have you heard in America of Avebury ? It may have predated this place, they think, by another thousand years."

"Avebury ? " said the lady who was called Belinda.

"But what is this Avebury ? " asked V.V. "I've never heard of the place.

"I thought it was a lord," said Belinda.

Sir Richmond, with occasional appeals to Dr. Martineau, embarked upon an account of the glory and wonder of Avebury. Possibly he exaggerated Avebury. . . .

It was Dr. Martineau who presently brought this disquisition upon Avebury to a stop by a very remarkable gesture. He looked at his watch. He drew it out ostentatiously, a thick, respectable gold watch, for the doctor was not the sort of man to wear his watch upon his wrist. He clicked it open and looked at it. Thereby he would have proclaimed his belief this encounter was an entirely unnecessary interruption of his healing duologue with Sir Richmond, which must now be resumed.

But this action had scarcely the effect he had intended it to have. It set the young lady who was called Belinda asking about ways and means of getting to Salisbury ; it brought to light the distressing fact that V.V. had the beginnings of a chafed heel. Once he had set things going they moved much too quickly for the doctor to deflect their course. He found himself called upon to make personal sacrifices to facilitate the painless transport of the two ladies to Salisbury, where their luggage awaited them at the Old George Hotel. In some way too elusive to trace, it became evident that he and Sir Richmond were to stay at this same Old George Hotel. The luggage was to be shifted to the top of the coupé, the young lady called V.V. was to share the interior of the car with Sir Richmond, while the lady named Belinda, for whom Dr. Martineau was already developing a very strong dislike, was to be thrust into an extreme proximity with him and the balance of the luggage in the dicky seat behind.

Sir Richmond had never met with a young woman with a genuine historical imagination before, and he was evidently very greatly excited and resolved to get the utmost that there was to be got out of this encounter.

§ 3

Sir Richmond displayed a complete disregard of the sufferings of Dr. Martineau, shamefully compressed behind him. Of these he was to hear later. He ran his overcrowded little car, overcrowded so far as the dicky went, over the crest of the Down and down into Amesbury and on to Salisbury, stopping to alight and stretch the legs of the party when they came in sight of Old Sarum.

"Certainly they can do with a little stretching," said Dr. Martineau grimly.

This charming young woman had seized upon the imagination of Sir Richmond to the temporary exclusion of all other considerations. The long Downland gradients, quivering very slightly with the vibration of the road, came swiftly and easily to meet and pass the throbbing little car as he sat beside her and talked to her. He fell into that expository manner which comes so easily to the native entertaining the visitor from abroad.

"In England, it seems to me there are four main phases of history. Four. Avebury, which I would love to take you to see to-morrow. Stonehenge. Old Sarum, which we shall see in a moment as a great grassy mound on our right as we come over one of these crests. Each of them represents about a thousand years. Old Sarum was Keltic ; it saw the Romans and the Saxons through, and for a time it was a Norman city. Now it is pasture for sheep. Latest as yet is Salisbury— English, real English. It may last a few centuries still. It is little more than seven hundred years old. But when I think of those great hangars back there by Stonehenge, I feel that the next phase is already beginning. Of a world one will fly to the ends of, in a week or so. Our world still. Our people, your people and mine, who are going to take wing so soon now, were made in all these places. We are visiting the old homes.

I am glad I came back to it just when you were doing the same thing."

" I'm lucky to have found a sympathetic fellow traveller," she said ; " with a car."

" You're the first American I've ever met whose interest in history didn't seem——" He sought for an inoffensive word.

" Silly ? Oh ! I admit it. It's true of a lot of us. Most of us. We come over to Europe as if it hadn't anything to do with us except to supply us with old pictures and curios generally. We come sight-seeing. It's romantic. It's picturesque. We stare at the natives—like visitors at a Zoo. We don't realise that we belong. . . . I know our style. . . . But we aren't all like that. Some of us are learning a bit better than that. We had one or two teachers over there to lighten our darkness. There's Professor Breasted for instance. He comes sometimes to my father's house. And there's James Harvey Robinson and Professor Hutton Webster. They've been trying to restore our memory."

" I've never heard of any of them," said Sir Richmond.

" You hear so little of America over here. It's quite a large country and all sorts of interesting things happen there nowadays. And we are waking up to history. Quite fast. We shan't always be the most ignorant people in the world. We are beginning to realise that quite a lot of things happened between Adam and the *Mayflower* that we ought to be told about. I allow it's a recent revival. The United States has been like one of those men you read about in the papers who go away from home and turn up in some distant place with their memories gone. They've forgotten what their names were or where they lived or what they did for a living ; they've forgotten everything that matters. Often they have to begin again and settle down for a long time before their memories come back. That's how it has been with us. Our memory is just coming back to us."

" And what do you find you are ? "

" Europeans. Who came away from kings and churches—and Corinthian capitals."

" You feel all this country belongs to you ? "

" As much as it does to you."

Sir Richmond smiled radiantly at her. " But if I say that America belongs to me as much as it does to you ? "

" We are one people," she said.

" We ? "

" Europe. These parts of Europe anyhow. And ourselves."

" You are the most civilised person I've met for weeks and weeks."

" Well you are the first civilised person I've met in Europe for a long time. If I understand you."

" There are multitudes of reasonable, civilised people in Europe."

" I've heard or seen very little of them."

" They're scattered, I admit."

" And hard to find."

" So ours is a lucky meeting. I've wanted a serious talk to an American for some time. I want to know very badly what you think you are up to with the world—our world."

" I'm equally anxious to know what England thinks she is doing. Her ways recently have been a little difficult to understand. On any hypothesis—that is honourable to her."

" H'm," said Sir Richmond.

" I assure you we don't like it. This Irish business. We feel a sort of ownership in England. It's like finding your dearest Aunt torturing the cat."

" We must talk of that," said Sir Richmond.

" I wish you would."

" It is a cat and a dog—and they have been very naughty animals. And poor Aunt Britannia almost deliberately lost her temper. But I admit she hits about in a very nasty fashion."

" And favours the dog ? "

" She does."

" I want to know all you admit."

" You shall. And incidentally my friend and I may have the pleasure of showing you Salisbury and Avebury ? If you are free ? "

" We're travelling together, just we two. We're wandering about the south of England on our way to Falmouth. Where I join a father in a few days' time, and go on with him to Paris. And if you and your friend are coming to the Old George——? "

" We are," said Sir Richmond.

" I see no great scandal in talking right on to bedtime. And seeing Avebury to-morrow. Why not ? Perhaps if we did as the Germans do and gave our names now, it might mitigate something of the extreme informality of our be-haviour."

" My name is Hardy. I've been a munition manufacturer. I was slightly wounded by a stray shell near Arras while I was inspecting some plant I had set up, and also I was hit by a stray knighthood. So my name is now Sir Richmond Hardy. My friend is a very distinguished Harley Street physician. Chiefly nervous and mental cases. His name is Dr. Martineau. He is quite as civilised as I am. He is also a philosophical writer. He is really a very wise and learned man indeed. He is full of ideas. He stimulated me tremendously. You must talk to him."

Sir Richmond glanced over his shoulder at the subject of these commendations. Through the oval window glared an expression of malignity that made no impression whatever on his preoccupied mind.

"My name," said the young lady, "is Grammont. The war whirled me over to Europe on Red Cross work and since the peace I've been settling up things and travelling about Europe. My father is rather a big business man in New York."

"The oil Grammont ? "

"He is rather deep in oil, I believe. He is coming over to Europe because he does not like the way your people are behaving in Mesopotamia. He is on his way to Paris now. Paris it seems is where everything is to be settled against you. Belinda is a sort of companion I have acquired for the purposes of independent travel. She was Red Cross too. I must have somebody and I cannot bear a maid. Her name is Belinda Seyffert. From Philadelphia originally. You have that ?   Seyffert, Grammont ? "

"And Hardy ? "

"Sir Richmond and Dr. Martineau."

"And—Ah !—That great green bank there just coming into sight must be Old Sarum. The little ancient city that faded away when Salisbury lifted its spire into the world. We will stop here for a little while. . . ."

Then it was that Dr. Martineau was grim about the stretching of his legs.

§ 4

The sudden prospect which now opened out before Sir Richmond of talking about history and such like topics with a charming companion for perhaps two whole days instead of going on with this tiresome, shamefaced, egotistical business of self-examination was so attractive to him that it took immediate possession of his mind, to the entire exclusion and disregard of Dr. Martineau's possible objections to any such modification of their original programme. When they arrived in Salisbury, the doctor did make some slight effort to suggest a different hotel from that in which the two ladies had engaged their rooms, but on the spur of the moment and in their presence he could produce no sufficient reason for refusing the accommodation the Old George had ready for him. He was reduced to a vague : " We don't want to inflict ourselves——" He could not get Sir Richmond aside for any adequate expression of his feelings about Miss Seyffert before the four of them were seated together at tea amidst the mediæval modernity of the Old George smoking-room. And only then did he begin to realise the depth and extent of the engagements to which Sir Richmond had committed himself.

" I was suggesting that we run back to Avebury to-morrow," said Sir Richmond. " These ladies were nearly missing it."

The thing took the doctor's breath away. For the moment he could say nothing. He stared over his tea-cup dour faced.

An objection formulated itself very slowly. " But that dicky," he whispered.

His whisper went unnoted. Sir Richmond was talking of the completeness of Salisbury. From the very beginning it had been a cathedral city ; it was essentially and purely that. The church at its best, in the full tide of its mediæval ascendency, had called it into being. He was making some extremely loose and inaccurate generalisations about the buildings and ruins each age had left for posterity, and Miss Grammont was countering with equally unsatisfactory qualifications. " Our age will leave the ruins of hotels," said Sir Richmond. " Railway arches and hotels."

" Baths and aqueducts," Miss Grammont compared. " Rome of the Empire comes nearest to it. . . ."

As soon as tea was over, Dr. Martineau realised, they meant to walk round and about Salisbury. He foresaw that walk with the utmost clearness. In front and keeping just a little beyond the range of his intervention, Sir Richmond would go with Miss Grammont ; he himself and Miss Seyffert would bring up the rear. " If I do," he muttered, " I'll be damned ! " an unusually strong expression for him.

" You said—— ? " asked Miss Seyffert.

" That I have some writing to do—before the post goes," said the doctor brightly.

" Oh ! come and see the cathedral ! " cried Sir Richmond with ill-concealed dismay. He was, if one may put it in such a fashion, not looking at Miss Seyffert in the directest fashion when he said this.

" I'm afraid," said the doctor mulishly. " Impossible."

(With the unspoken addition of, " You try her for a bit.")

Miss Grammont stood up. Everybody stood up. " We can go first to look for shops," she said. " There's those things you want to buy, Belinda ; a fountain pen and the little books. We can all go together as far as that. And while you are shopping if you wouldn't mind getting one or two things for me. . . ."

It became clear to Dr. Martineau that Sir Richmond was to be let off Belinda. It seemed abominably unjust. And it was also clear to him that he must keep closely to his own room or he might find Miss Seyffert drifting back alone to the hotel and eager to resume with him. . . .

Well, a quiet time in his room would not be disagreeable. He could think over his notes. . . .

But in reality he thought over nothing but the little speeches

he would presently make to Sir Richmond about the unwarrantable, the absolutely unwarrantable, alterations that
were being made without his consent in their common programme. . . .

For a long time Sir Richmond had met no one so interesting
and amusing as this frank-minded young woman from America.
" Young woman " was how he thought of her ; she didn't
correspond to anything so prim and restrained and extensively
reserved and withheld as a " young lady " ; and though he
judged her no older than five-and-twenty, the word " girl "
with its associations of virginal ignorance, invisible purdah,
and trite ideas newly discovered, seemed even less appropriate
for her than the word " boy." She had an air of having
in some obscure way graduated in life, as if so far she had lived
each several year of her existence in a distinctive and conclusive
manner with the utmost mental profit and no particular
tarnish or injury. He could talk with her as if he talked
with a man like himself—but with a zest no man could
give him.

It was evident that the good things she had given at first
came as the natural expression of a broad stream of alert
thought ; they were no mere display specimens from one of
those jackdaw collection of bright things so many clever
women waste their wits in accumulating. She was not talking for effect at all, she was talking because she was tremendously interested in her discovery of the spectacle of history,
and delighted to find another person as possessed as she
was.

Belinda having been conducted to her shops, the two made
their way through the bright evening sunlight to the compact
gracefulness of the cathedral. A glimpse through a wrought-
iron gate of a delightful garden of spring flowers, alyssum,
aubrietia, snow-upon-the-mountains, daffodils, narcissus and
the like, held them for a time, and then they came out upon
the level grassy space, surrounded by little ripe old houses, on
which the cathedral stands. They stood for some moments
surveying it.

" It's a perfect little lady of a cathedral," said Sir Richmond. " But why, I wonder, did we build it ? "

" Your memory ought to be better than mine," she said,
with her half-closed eyes blinking at the sunlit spire sharp
against the blue. " I've been away for so long—over there—
that I forget altogether. Why *did* we build it ? "

She had fallen in quite early with this freak of speaking and
thinking as if he and she were all mankind. It was as if her
mind had been prepared for it by her own eager exploration
of Europe. " My friend, the philosopher," he had said, " will
not have it that we are really the individuals we think we are.
You must talk to him—he is a very curious and subtle thinker.
We are just thoughts in the Mind of the Race, he says, passing

thoughts. We are—what does he call it?—Man on his Planet, taking control of life."

" Man and woman," she had amended.

But just as man on his planet taking control of life had failed altogether to remember why the ditch at Avebury was on the inside instead of the outside of the vallum, so now Miss Grammont and Sir Richmond found very great difficulty in recalling why they had built Salisbury Cathedral.

" We built temples by habit and tradition," said Sir Richmond. " But the impulse was losing its force."

She looked up at the spire and then at him with a faintly quizzical expression.

But he had his reply ready.

" We were beginning to feel our power over matter. We were already very clever engineers. What interested us here wasn't the old religion any more. We wanted to exercise and display our power over stone. We made it into reeds and branches. We squirted it up in all these spires and pinnacles. The priest and his altar were just an excuse. Do you think people have ever feared and worshipped in this—this artist's lark—as they did in Stonehenge ? "

" I certainly do not remember that I ever worshipped here," she said.

Sir Richmond was in love with his idea. " The spirit of the Gothic cathedrals," he said, " is the spirit of the sky-scrapers. It is architecture in a mood of flaming ambition. The Freemasons on the building could hardly refrain from jeering at the little priest they had left down below there, performing antiquated puerile mysteries at his altar. He was just their excuse for doing it all."

" Sky-scrapers ? " she conceded. " An early display of the sky-scraper spirit. . . . You are doing your best to make me feel thoroughly at home."

" You are more at home here still than in that new country of ours over the Atlantic. But it seems to me now that I do begin to remember building this cathedral—and all the other cathedrals we built in Europe. . . . It was the fun of building made us do it. . . ."

" H'm," she said. " And my sky-scrapers ? "

" Still the fun of building. That is the thing I envy most about America. It's still large enough, mentally and materially, to build all sorts of things. . . . Over here, the sites are frightfully crowded. . . ."

" And what do you think we are building now ? And what do you think you are building over here ? "

" What are we building now ? I believe we have almost grown up. I believe it is time we began to build in earnest. For good. . . ."

" But are we building anything at all ? "

" A new world."

" Show it me," she said.

" We're still only at the foundations," said Sir Richmond. " Nothing shows as yet."

" I wish I could believe they were foundations."

" But can you doubt we are scrapping the old ? . . ."

It was too late in the afternoon to go into the cathedral, so they strolled to and fro round and about the west end and along the path under the trees towards the river, exchanging their ideas very frankly and freely about the things that had recently happened to the world and what they thought they ought to be doing in it.

§ 5

After dinner our four tourists sat late and talked in a corner of the smoking-room. The two ladies had vanished hastily at the first dinner gong and reappeared at the second, mysteriously and pleasantly changed from tweedy pedestrians to indoor company. They were quietly but definitely " dressed," pretty alterations had happened to their coiffure, a silver band and deep red stones lit the dusk of Miss Grammont's hair and a necklace of the same colourings kept the peace between her jolly sunburnt cheek and her soft untanned neck. It was evident her recent uniform had included a collar of great severity. Miss Seyffert had revealed a plump fore-arm and proclaimed it with a clash of bangles. Dr. Martineau thought her evening throat much too confidential.

The conversation drifted from topic to topic. It had none of the steady continuity of Sir Richmond's duologue with Miss Grammont. Miss Seyffert's methods were too discursive and exclamatory. She broke every thread that appeared. The Old George at Salisbury is really old ; it shows it, and Miss Seyffert laced the entire evening with her recognition of the fact. " Just look at that old beam ! " she would cry suddenly. " To think it was exactly where it is before there was a Cabot in America ! "

Miss Grammont let her companion pull the talk about as she chose. After the animation of the afternoon a sort of lazy contentment had taken possession of the younger lady. She sat deep in a basket chair and spoke now and then. Miss Seyffert gave her impressions of France and Italy. She talked of the cabmen of Naples and the beggars of Amalfi.

Apropos of beggars, Miss Grammont from the depths of her chair threw out the statement that Italy was frightfully over-populated. " In some parts of Italy it is like mites on a cheese. Nobody seems to be living. Every one is too busy keeping alive."

" Poor old women carrying loads big enough for mules," said Miss Seyffert.

" Little children working like slaves," said Miss Grammont.

"And everybody begging. Even the people at work by the roadside. Who ought to be getting wages—sufficient . . ."

"Begging—from foreigners—is just a sport in Italy," said Sir Richmond. "It doesn't imply want. But I agree that a large part of Italy is frightfully overpopulated. The whole world is. Don't you think so, Martineau ? "

"Well—yes—for its present social organisation."

"For any social organisation," said Sir Richmond.

"I've no doubt of it," said Miss Seyffert, and added amazingly : "I'm out for Birth Control all the time."

A brief but active pause ensued. Dr. Martineau in a state of sudden distress attempted to drink out of a cold and empty coffee-cup.

"The world swarms with cramped and undeveloped lives," said Sir Richmond. "Which amount to nothing. Which do not even represent happiness. And which help to use up the resources, the fuel and surplus energy of the world."

"I suppose they have a sort of liking for their lives," Miss Grammont reflected.

"Does that matter ? They do nothing to carry life on. They are just vain repetitions—imperfect—dreary, blurred repetitions of one common life. All that they feel has been felt, all that they do has been done better before. Because they are crowded and hurried and underfed and under-educated. And as for liking their lives, they need never have had the chance."

"How many people are there in the world ? " she asked abruptly.

"I don't know. Twelve hundred, fifteen hundred millions perhaps."

"And in *your* world ? "

"I'd have two hundred and fifty millions, let us say. At most. It would be quite enough for this little planet, for a time, at any rate. Don't you think so, doctor ? "

"I don't *know*," said Dr. Martineau. "Oddly enough, I have never thought about that question before. At least, not from this angle."

"But could you pick out two hundred and fifty million aristocrats ? " began Miss Grammont. "My native instinctive democracy——"

"Need not be outraged," said Sir Richmond. "Any two hundred and fifty million would do. They'd be able to develop fully, all of them. As things are, only a minority can do that. The rest never get a chance."

"That's what *I* always say," said Miss Seyffert.

"A New Age," said Dr. Martineau ; "a New World. We may be coming to such a stage, when population, as much as fuel, will be under a world control. If one thing, why not the other? I admit that the movement of thought is away from haphazard towards control——"

" I'm, for control all the time," Miss Seyffert injected, following up her previous success.

" I admit," the doctor began his broken sentence again with marked patience, " that the movement of thought is away from haphazard towards control—in things generally. But is the movement of events ? "

" The eternal problem of man," said Sir Richmond. " Can our wills prevail ? "

There came a little pause.

Miss Grammont smiled an inquiry at Miss Seyffert. " If *you* are," said Belinda.

" I wish I could imagine your world," said Miss Grammont, rising, " of two hundred and fifty millions of fully developed human beings with room to live and breathe in and no need for wars. Will they live in palaces ? Will they all be healthy ? . . . Machines will wait on them. No ! I can't imagine it. Perhaps I shall dream of it. My dreaming self may be cleverer."

She held out her hand to Sir Richmond. Just for a moment they stood hand in hand, appreciatively. . . .

" Well ! " said Dr. Martineau, as the door closed behind the two Americans, " this is a curious—encounter."

" That young woman has brains," said Sir Richmond, standing before the fireplace.

There was no doubt whatever which young woman he meant. But Dr. Martineau grunted.

" I don't like the American type," the doctor pronounced judicially.

" I do," Sir Richmond countered.

The doctor thought for a moment or so. " You are committed to the project of visiting Avebury ? " he said.

" They ought to see Avebury," said Sir Richmond.

" H'm," said the doctor, ostentatiously amused by his thoughts and staring at the fire. " Birth Control ! I *never* did."

Sir Richmond smiled down on the top of the doctor's head and said nothing.

" I think," said the doctor and paused . . . " I shall leave this Avebury expedition to you."

" We can be back in the early afternoon," said Sir Richmond. " To give them a chance of seeing the cathedral. The chapter house here is not one to miss. . . ."

" And then I suppose we shall go on ? "

" As you please," said Sir Richmond insincerely.

" I must confess that four people makes the car at any rate seem tremendously over-populated. And to tell the truth, I do not find this encounter so amusing as you seem to do. . . . I shall not be sorry when we wave good-bye to those young ladies, and resume our interrupted conversation."

Sir Richmond considered something mulish in the doctor's averted face.

" I find Miss Grammont an extremely interesting—and stimulating human being."

" Evidently."

The doctor sighed, stood up and found himself delivering one of the sentences he had engendered during his solitary meditations in his room before dinner. He surprised himself by the plainness of his speech. " Let me be frank," he said, regarding Sir Richmond squarely. " Considering the general situation of things and your position, I do not care very greatly for the part of an accessory to what may easily develop, as you know very well, into a very serious—flirtation. An absurd, mischievous, irrelevant flirtation. You may not like the word. You may pretend it is a conversation, an ordinary intellectual conversation. That is not the word. Simply that is not the word. You people eye one another. . . . Flirtation. I give the affair its proper name. That is all. Merely that. When I think—— But we will not discuss it now. . . . Good-night. . . . Forgive me if I put before you, rather bluntly, my particular point of view."

Sir Richmond found himself alone. With his eyebrows raised.

§ 6

After twenty-four eventful hours our two students of human motives found themselves together again by the fireplace in the Old George smoking-room. They had resumed their over-night conversation, in a state of considerable tension.

" If you find the accommodation of the car insufficient," said Sir Richmond in a tone of extreme reasonableness, " and I admit it is, we can easily hire a larger car in a place like this."

" I would not care if you hired an omnibus," said Dr. Martineau. " I am not coming on if these young women are."

" But if you consider it scandalous—and really, Martineau, really ! as one man to another, it does seem to me to be a bit pernickety of you, a broad and original thinker as you are——"

" Thought is one matter. Rash, inconsiderate action quite another. And above all, if I spend another day in or near the company of Miss Belinda Seyffert I shall—I shall be extremely rude to her."

" But," said Sir Richmond, and bit his lower lip and considered.

" We might drop Belinda," he suggested—turning to his friend and speaking in low, confidential tones. " She is quite a manageable person. Quite. She could—for example—

be left behind with the luggage and sent on by train. I do not know if you realise how the land lies in that quarter. It needs only a word to Miss Grammont."

There was no immediate reply. For a moment he had a wild hope that his companion would agree, and then he perceived that the doctor's silence meant only the preparation of an ultimatum.

"I object to Miss Grammont and—that side of the thing, more than I do to Miss Seyffert."

Sir Richmond said nothing.

"It may help you to see this affair from a slightly different angle if I tell you that twice to-day Miss Seyffert has asked me if you were a married man."

"And of course you told her I was."

"On the second occasion."

Sir Richmond smiled again.

"Frankly," said the doctor, "this adventure is altogether uncongenial to me. It is the sort of thing that has never happened in my life. This highway coupling——"

"Don't you think," said Sir Richmond, "that you are attaching rather too much—what shall I say ?—romantic ?—flirtatious ?—meaning to this affair. I don't mind that after my rather lavish confessions you should consider me a rather oversexed person, but isn't your attitude rather unfair—unjust, indeed, and almost insulting, to this Miss Grammont ? After all, she's a young lady of very good social position indeed. She doesn't strike you, does she ? as an undignified or helpless human being. Her manners suggest a person of considerable self-control. And knowing less of me than you do, she probably regards me as almost as safe as—a maiden aunt, say. I'm twice her age. We are a party of four. There are conventions, there are considerations. . . . Aren't you really, my dear Martineau, overdoing all this side of this very pleasant little enlargement of our interests ? "

"*Am* I ? " said Dr. Martineau and brought a scrutinising eye to bear on Sir Richmond's face.

"I want to go on talking to Miss Grammont for a day or so," Sir Richmond admitted.

"Then I shall prefer to leave your party."

There were some moments of silence.

"I am really very sorry to find myself in this dilemma," said Sir Richmond with a note of genuine regret in his voice.

"It is not a dilemma," said Dr. Martineau, with a corresponding loss of asperity. "I grant you we discover we differ —upon a question of taste and convenience. But before I suggested this trip, I had intended to spend a little time with my old friend Sir Kenelm Latter at Bournemouth. Nothing simpler than to go to him now. . . ."

"I shall be sorry all the same."

"I could have wished," said the doctor, "that these ladies had happened a little later. . . ."

The matter was settled. Nothing more of a practical nature remained to be said. But neither gentleman wished to break off with a harsh and bare decision.

"When the New Age is here," said Sir Richmond, "then, surely, a friendship between a man and a woman will not be subjected to the—the inconveniences your present code would set about it ? They would travel about together as they chose ? "

"The fundamental principle of the New Age," said the doctor, "will be *Honi soit qui mal y pense.* In these matters. With perhaps *Fay ce que vouldras* as its next injunction. So long as other lives are not affected. In matters of personal behaviour the world will probably be much more free and individuals much more open in their conscience and honour than they have ever been before. In matters of property, economics and public conduct it will probably be just the reverse. Then, there will be much more collective control and much more insistence, legal insistence, upon individual responsibility. But we are not living in a new age yet ; we are living in the patched-up ruins of a very old one. And you—if you will forgive me—are living in the patched-up remains of a life that has already had its complications. This young lady, whose charm and cleverness I admit, behaves as if the new age were already here. Well, that may be a very dangerous mistake both for her and for you. . . . This affair, if it goes on for a few days more , may involve very serious consequences indeed, with which I for one, do not wish to be involved."

Sir Richmond, upon the hearth-rug, had a curious feeling that he was back in the head-master's study at Caxton.

Dr. Martineau went on with a lucidity that Sir Richmond found rather trying, to give his impression of Miss Grammont and her position in life.

"She is," he said, "manifestly a very expensively educated girl. And in many ways—interesting. I have been watching her. I have not been favoured with very much of her attention, but that fact has enabled me to see her in profile. Miss Seyffert is a fairly crude mixture of frankness, insincerity and self-explanatory egotism, and I have been able to disregard a considerable amount of the conversation she has addressed to me. Now I guess this Miss Grammont has had no mother since she was quite little."

"Your guesses, doctor, are apt to be pretty good," said Sir Richmond.

"You know that ? "

"She has told me as much."

"H'm. Well—— She impressed me as having the air of a girl who has had to solve many problems for which the normal

mother provides ready-made solutions. That is how I in-
ferred that there was no mother. I don't think there has been
any stepmother, either friendly or hostile ? There hasn't
been. I thought not. She has had various governesses and
companions, ladies of birth and education, engaged to look
after her, and she has done exactly what she liked with them.
Her manner with Miss Seyffert, an excellent manner for Miss
Seyffert, by the bye, isn't the sort of manner any one acquires
in a day. Or for one person only. She is a very sure and
commanding young woman."

Sir Richmond nodded.

" I suppose her father adores and neglects her, and whenever
she has wanted a companion or governess butchered, the thing
has been done. . . . These business Americans, I am told,
neglect their womenkind, give them money and power, let
them loose on the world. . . . It is a sort of moral laziness
masquerading as affection. . . . Still I suppose custom and
tradition kept this girl in her place and she was petted,
honoured, amused, talked about but not in a harmful way, and
rather bored right up to the time when America came into the
war. Theoretically she had a tremendously good time."

" I think this must be near the truth of her biography," said
Sir Richmond.

" I suppose she has lovers."

" You don't mean—— ? "

" No I don't. Though that is a matter that ought to have
no special interest for you. I mean that she was surrounded
by a retinue of men who wanted to marry her or who behaved
as though they wanted to marry her or who made her happiness
and her gratifications and her condescensions seem a matter of
very great importance to them. She had the flattery of an
extremely uncritical and unexacting admiration. That is the
sort of thing that gratifies a silly woman extremely. Miss
Grammont is not silly, and all this homage and facile approval
probably bored her more than she realised. To any one too
intelligent to be steadily excited by buying things and wearing
things and dancing and playing games and going to places of
entertainment, and being given flowers, sweets, jewellery,
pet animals, and books bound in a special sort of leather, the
prospect of being a rich man's only daughter until such time
as it becomes advisable to change into a rich man's wealthy
wife, is probably not nearly so amusing as envious people
might suppose. I take it Miss Grammont has got all she could
out of that sort of thing some time before the war, and that she
had already read and thought rather more than most young
women in her position. Before she was twenty I guess she
was already looking for something more interesting in the way
of men than a rich admirer with an automobile full of presents.
Those who seek find."

" What do you think she found ? "

" What would a rich girl find out there in America ?   I don't know.   I haven't the material to guess with.   In London a girl might find a considerable variety of active, interesting men, rising politicians, university men of distinction, artists and writers even, men of science, men—there are still such men—active in the creative work of the empire.

" In America I suppose there is at least an equal variety, made up of rather different types.   She would find that life was worth while to such people in a way that made the ordinary entertainments and amusements of her life a monstrous silly waste of time.   With the facility of her sex she would pick up from one of them the idea that made life worth while for him.   I am inclined to think there was some one in her case who did seem to promise a sort of life that was worth while.   And that somehow the war came to alter the look of that promise."

" How ? "

" I don't know.   Perhaps I am only romancing.   But for this young woman I am convinced this expedition to Europe has meant—experience, harsh educational experience and very profound mental disturbance.   There have been love experiences ;   experiences that were something more than the treats and attentions and proposals that made up her life when she was sheltered over there.   And something more than that.   What it is I don't know.   The war has turned an ugly face to her.   She has seen death and suffering and ruin.   Perhaps she has seen people she knew killed.   Perhaps the man has been killed.   Or she has met with cowardice or cruelty or treachery where she didn't expect it.   She has been shocked out of the first confidence of youth.   She has ceased to take the world for granted. . . . It hasn't broken her but it has matured her. . . . That I think is why history has become real to her.   Which so attracts you in her.   History, for her, has ceased to be a fabric of picturesque incidents ;   it is the study of a tragic struggle that still goes on.   She sees history as you see it and I see it.   She is a very grown-up young woman. . . ."

" It's just that," said Sir Richmond.   " It's just that. If you see as much in Miss Grammont as all that, why don't you want to come on with us ?   You see the interest of her."

" I see a lot more than that.   You don't know what an advantage it is to be as I am, rather cold and unresponsive to women and unattractive and negligible—negligible, that is the exact word—to them.   *You* can't look at a woman for five minutes without losing sight of her in a mist of imaginative excitement.   Because she looks back at you.   I have the privilege of the negligible—which is a cool head.   Miss Grammont has a startled and matured mind, an original mind.   Yes. And there is something more to be said.   Her intelligence is better than her character."

" I don't quite see what you are driving at."

" The intelligence of all intelligent women is better than their characters. Goodness in a woman, as we understand it, seems to imply necessarily a certain imaginative fixity. Miss Grammont has an impulsive and adventurous character. And as I have been saying she was a spoilt child, with no discipline. . . . You also are a person of high intelligence and defective controls. She is very much at loose ends. You— on account of the illness of that rather forgotten lady, Miss Martin Leeds——"

" Aren't you rather abusing the secrets of the confessional ? "

" This *is* the confessional. It closes to-morrow morning but it is the confessional still. Look at the thing frankly. You, I say, are also at loose ends. Can you deny it ? My dear Sir, don't we both know that ever since we left London you have been ready to fall in love with any pretty thing in petticoats that seemed to promise you three ha'porth of kindness. A lost dog looking for a master ! You're a stray man looking for a mistress. Miss Grammont being a woman is a little more selective than that. But if she's at a loose end as I suppose, she isn't protected by the sense of having made her selection. And she has no preconceptions of what she wants. You are a very interesting man in many ways. You carry marriage and—entanglements lightly. With an air of being neither married nor entangled. She is quite prepared to fall in love with you."

" But you don't really think that ? " said Sir Richmond, with an ill-concealed eagerness.

Dr. Martineau rolled his face towards Sir Richmond. " These miracles—grotesquely—happen," he said. " She knows nothing of Martin Leeds. . . . You must remember that. . . .

" And then," he added, " if she and you fall in love, as the phrase goes, what is to follow ? "

There was a pause.

Sir Richmond looked at his toes for a moment or so as if he took counsel with them and then decided to take offence.

" Really ! " he said ; " this is preposterous. You talk of falling in love as though it was impossible for a man and woman to be deeply interested in each other—without that. And the gulf in our ages—in our quality ! From the Psychologist of a New Age I find this amazing. Are men and women to go on for ever—separated by this possibility into two hardly communicating and yet inter-penetrating worlds ? Is there never to be friendship and companionship between men and women without passion ? "

" You ought to know even better than I do that there is not. For such people as you two anyhow. And at present the world is not prepared to tolerate friendship and companionship *with* that accompaniment. That is the core of this situation."

A pause fell between the two gentlemen. They had smoothed over the extreme harshness of their separation and there was very little more to be said.

"Well," said Sir Richmond in conclusion, "I am very sorry indeed, Martineau, that we have to part like this."

CHAPTER SEVEN

COMPANIONSHIP

§ 1

"WELL," said Dr. Martineau, extending his hand to Sir Richmond on the Salisbury station platform ; " I leave you to it."

His round face betrayed little or no vestiges of his overnight irritation.

" Ought you to leave me to it ? " smiled Sir Richmond.

" I shall be interested to learn what happens."

" But if you won't stay to see ! "

" Now, Sir, please," said the guard respectfully but firmly, and Dr. Martineau got in.

Sir Richmond walked thoughtfully down the platform towards the exit.

" What else could I do ? " he asked aloud to nobody in particular.

For a little while he thought confusedly of the collapse of his expedition into the secret places of his own heart with Dr. Martineau, and then his prepossession with Miss Grammont resumed possession of his mind. Dr. Martineau was forgotten.

§ 2

For the better part of the forty hours, Sir Richmond had either been talking to Miss Grammont or carrying on imaginary conversations with her in her absence, or sleeping and dreaming dreams in which she never failed to play a part, even if at times it was an altogether amazing and incongruous part. And as they were both very frank and expressive people, they already knew a very great deal about each other.

For an American Miss Grammont was by no means auto-biographical. She gave no sketches of her idiosyncrasies, and she repeated no remembered comments and prophecies of her contemporaries about herself. She either concealed or she had lost any great interest in her own personality. But she was interested in and curious about the people she had met in life, and her talk of them reflected a considerable amount of light upon her own upbringing and experiences. And her liking for Sir Richmond was pleasingly manifest. She liked his turn of thought, she watched him with a faint smile on her lips as he spoke, and she spread her opinions before him carefully in that soft voice of hers like a shy child showing its treasures to some suddenly trusted and favoured visitor.

Their ways of thought harmonised. They talked at first chiefly about the history of the world, and the extraordinary situation of aimlessness in a phase of ruin to which the Great

War had brought all Europe, if not all mankind. The world excited them both in the same way, as a crisis in which they were called upon to do something—they did not yet clearly know what. Into this topic they peered as into some deep pool, side by side, and in it they saw each other reflected.

The visit to Avebury had been a great success. It had been a perfect springtime day, and the little inn had been delighted at the reappearance of Sir Richmond's car so soon after its departure. Its delight was particularly manifest in the cream and salad it produced for lunch. Both Miss Grammont and Miss Seyffert displayed an intelligent interest in their food. After lunch they had all gone out to the stones and the wall. Half a dozen sunburnt children were putting one of the partially overturned megaliths to a happy use by clambering to the top of it and sliding on their little behinds down its smooth and sloping side amidst much mirthful squealing.

Sir Richmond and Miss Grammont had walked round the old circumvallation together, but Belinda Seyffert had strayed away from them, professing an interest in flowers. It was not so much that she felt they had to be left together that made her do this as her own consciousness of being possessed by a devil who interrupted conversations. When Miss Grammont was keenly interested in a conversation, then Belinda had learnt from experience that it was wiser to go off with her devil out of the range of any temptation to interrupt.

" You really think," said Miss Grammont, " that it would be possible to take this confused old world and reshape it, set it marching towards that new world of yours—of two hundred and fifty million fully developed, beautiful and happy people? "

" Why not ? Nobody is doing anything with the world except muddle about. Why not give it a direction ? "

" You'd take it in your hands like clay ? "

" Obdurate clay with a sort of recalcitrant unintelligent life of its own."

Her imagination glowed in her eyes and warmed her voice. " I believe what you say is possible. If people dare."

" I am tired of following little motives that are like flames that go out when you get to them. I am tired of seeing all the world doing the same. I am tired of a world in which there is nothing great but great disasters. Here is something mankind can attempt, that we can attempt."

" And will ? "

" I believe that as Mankind grows up this is the business Man has to settle down to and will settle down to."

She considered that.

" I've been getting to believe something like this. But—— . . . it frightens me. I suppose most of us have this same sort of dread of taking too much upon ourselves."

" So we just live like pigs. Sensible little piggy-wiggys. I've got a Committee full of that sort of thing. We live like little modest pigs. And let the world go hang. And pride ourselves upon our freedom from the sin of presumption."

" Not quite that ! "

" Well ! How do you put it ? "

" We are afraid," she said. " It's too vast. We want bright little lives of our own."

" Exactly—sensible little piggy-wiggs."

" We have a right to life—and happiness."

" First," said Sir Richmond ; " as much right as a pig has to food. But whether we get life and happiness or fail to get them we human beings who have imaginations want something more nowadays. . . . Of course we want bright lives, of course we want happiness. Just as we want food, just as we want sleep. But when we have eaten, when we have slept, when we have jolly things about us—it is nothing. We have been made an exception of—and got our rations. The big thing confronts us still. It is vast, I agree, but vast as it is it is the thing we have to think about. I do not know why it should be so, but I am compelled by something in my nature to want to serve this idea of a new age for mankind. I want it as my culminating want. I want a world in order, a disciplined mankind going on to greater things. Don't you ? "

" Now you tell me of it," she said with a smile, " I do."

" But before—— ? "

" No. You've made it clear. It wasn't clear before."

" I've been talking of this sort of thing with my friend Dr. Martineau. And I've been thinking as well as talking. That perhaps is why I'm so clear and positive."

" I don't complain that you are clear and positive. I've been coming along the same way. . . . It's refreshing to meet you."

" I found it refreshing to meet Martineau." A twinge of conscience about Dr. Martineau turned Sir Richmond into a new channel. " He's a most interesting man," he said. " Rather shy in some respects. Devoted to his work. And he's writing a book which has saturated him in these ideas. Only two nights ago we stood here and talked about it. *The Psychology of a New Age.* The world, he believes, is entering upon a new phase in its history, the adolescence, so to speak, of mankind. It is an idea that seizes the imagination. There is a flow of new ideas abroad, he thinks, widening realisations, unprecedented hopes and fears. There is a consciousness of new powers and new responsibilities. We are sharing the adolescence of our race. It is giving history a new and more intimate meaning for us. It is bringing us into directer relation with public affairs—making them matter as formerly they didn't seem to matter. That idea of the bright little private life has to go by the board."

" I suppose it has," she said, meditatively, as though she had been thinking over some such question before.

" The private life," she said, " has a way of coming aboard
again."

Her reflections travelled fast and broke out now far ahead
of him.

" You have some sort of work cut out for you," she said,
abruptly.

" Yes. Yes, I have."

" I haven't," she said.

" So that I go about," she added, " like some one who is
looking for something. I'd like to know—if it's not jabbing
too searching a question at you—what you have found."

Sir Richmond considered. " Incidentally," he smiled, " I
want to get a lasso over the neck of that very forcible and
barbaric person, your father. I am doing my best to help lay
the foundations of a scientific world control of fuel production
and distribution. We have a Fuel Commission in London
with rather wide powers of inquiry into the whole world
problem of fuel. We shall come out to Washington presently
with proposals."

Miss Grammont surveyed the landscape. " I suppose,"
she said, " poor father *is* rather like an unbroken mule in
business affairs. So many of our big business men in America
are. He'll lash out at you."

" I don't mind if only he lashes out openly in the sight of
all men."

She considered and turned on Sir Richmond gravely.

" Tell me what you want to do to him. You find out so
many things for me that I seem to have been thinking about
in a sort of almost invisible half-conscious way. I've been
suspecting for a long time that Civilisation wasn't much good
unless it got people like my father under some sort of control.
But controlling father—as distinguished from managing
him ! " She reviewed some private and amusing memories.
" He is a most intractable man."

§ 3

They had gone on to talk of her father and of the types of
men who controlled international business. She had had
plentiful opportunities for observation in their homes and her
own. Gunter Lake, the big banker, she knew particularly
well, because it seemed she had been engaged or was engaged to
marry him. " All these people," she said, " are pushing things
about, affecting millions of lives, hurting and disordering
hundreds of thousands of people. They don't seem to know
what they are doing. They have no plans in particular. . . .
And you are getting something going that will be a plan and a
direction and a conscience and a control for them ? You will
find my father extremely difficult, but some of our younger
men would love it.

" And," she went on, " there are American women who'd love it too. We're petted. We're kept out of things. We aren't placed. We don't get enough to do. We're spenders and wasters—not always from choice. While these fathers and brothers and husbands of ours play about with the fuel and power and life and hope of the world as though it was a game of poker. With all the empty unspeakable solemnity of the male. And treat us as though we ought to be satisfied if they bring home part of the winnings.

" That can't go on," she said.

Her eyes went back to the long, low, undulating skyline of the downs. She spoke as though she took up the thread of some controversy that had played a large part in her life. " That isn't going on," she said with an effect of conclusive decision.

Sir Richmond recalled that little speech now as he returned from Salisbury station to the Old George after his farewell to Martineau. He recalled too the soft firmness of her profile and the delicate line of her lifted chin. He felt that this time at any rate he was not being deceived by the outward shows of a charming human being. This young woman had real firmness of character to back up her free and independent judgments. He smiled at the idea of any facile passion in the composition of so sure and gallant a personality. Martineau was very fine-minded in many respects, but he was an old maid ; and like all old maids he saw man and woman in every encounter. But passion was a thing men and women fell back upon when they had nothing else in common. When they thought in the pleasantest harmony and every remark seemed to weave a fresh thread of common interest then it wasn't so necessary. It might happen, but it wasn't so necessary. . . . If it did it would be a secondary thing to companionship. . . . That's what she was—a companion.

But a very lovely and wonderful companion, the companion one would not relinquish until the very last moment one could keep with her.

Her views about America and about her own place in the world seemed equally fresh and original to Sir Richmond.

" I realise I've got to be a responsible American citizen," she had said. That didn't mean that she attached very much importance to her recently acquired vote. She evidently classified voters into the irresponsible who just had votes and the responsible who also had a considerable amount of property as well. She had no illusions about the power of the former class. It didn't exist. They were steered to their decisions by people employed, directed or stimulated by " father " and his friends and associates, the owners of America, the real " responsible citizens." Or they fell a prey to the merely adventurous leading of " revolutionaries." But anyhow they were steered. She herself, it was clear, was bound to become a very responsible citizen indeed. She would some day, she laughed, be " swimming in oil and suchlike property." Her interest in Sir Richmond's schemes for a scientific world management of fuel was therefore, she realised, a very direct one. But it was remarkable to find a young woman seeing it like that.

Father, it seemed, varied very much in his attitude towards her. He despised and distrusted women generally, and it was evident he had made it quite clear to her how grave an error it was on her part to persist in being a daughter and not a son. At moments it seemed to Sir Richmond that she was disposed to agree with father upon that. When Mr. Grammont's sense of her regrettable femininity was uppermost, then he gave his intelligence chiefly to schemes for tying her up against the machinations of adventurers by means of trustees, partners, lawyer advisers, agreements and suchlike complications, or for acquiring a workable son by marriage. To this last idea it would seem the importance in her life of the rather heavily named Gunter Lake was to be ascribed. But another mood of the old man's was distrust of anything that could not be spoken of as his " own flesh and blood," and then he would direct his attention to a kind of masculinisation of his daughter and to schemes for giving her the completest control of all he had to leave her provided she never married nor fell under masculine sway. " After all," he would reflect as he hesitated over the practicability of this life's ideal : " there was Hetty Green."

This latter idea had reft her suddenly at the age of seventeen from the educational care of an English gentlewoman warranted to fit her for marriage with any Prince in Europe, and thrust her for the mornings and a moiety of the afternoons of the better part of a year, after a swift but competent training into a shirt waist and an office down town. She had been entrusted at first to a harvester concern independent of Mr. Grammont, because he feared his own people wouldn't train her hard. She had worked for ordinary wages and ordinary hours, and at the end of the day, she mentioned casually, a large automobile with two menservants and a trustworthy secretary used to pick her out from the torrent of undistinguished workers that poured out the Synoptical Building. This masculinisation idea had also sent her on a commission of inquiry into Mexico. There apparently she had really done responsible work.

But upon the question of labour Mr. Grammont was fierce, even for an American business man, and one night at a dinner party he discovered his daughter displaying what he considered an improper familiarity with socialist ideas. This had produced a violent revulsion towards the purdah system and the idea of a matrimonial alliance with Gunter Lake. Gunter Lake, Sir Richmond gathered, wasn't half a bad fellow.

Generally it would seem Miss Grammont liked him, and she had a way of speaking about him that suggested that in some way Mr. Lake had been rather hardly used and had acquired merit by his behaviour under bad treatment. There was some story, however, connected with her war services in Europe upon which Miss Grammont was evidently indisposed to dwell. About that story Sir Richmond was left at the end of his Avebury day and after his last talk with Dr. Martineau, still quite vaguely guessing.

So much fact about Miss Grammont as we have given had floated up in fragments and pieces itself together in Sir Richmond's mind in the course of a day and a half. The fragments came up as allusions or by way of illustration. The sustaining topic was this New Age Sir Richmond foreshadowed, this world under scientific control, the Utopia of fully developed people fully developing the resources of the earth. For a number of trivial reasons Sir Richmond found himself ascribing the project of this New Age almost wholly to Dr. Martineau, and presenting it as a much more complete scheme than he was justified in doing. It was true that Dr. Martineau had not said many of the things Sir Richmond ascribed to him, but also it is true that they had not crystallised out in Sir Richmond's mind before his talks with Dr. Martineau. The idea of a New Age necessarily carries with it the idea of fresh rules of conduct and of different relationships between human beings. And it throws those who talk about it into the companionship of a common enterprise. To-morrow the New Age will be here no doubt, but to-day it is the hope and adventure of only a few human beings.

So that it was natural for Miss Grammont and Sir Richmond to ask : " What are *we* to do with such types as father ? " and to fall into an idiom that assumed a joint enterprise. They had agreed by a tacit consent to a common conception of the world they desired as a world scientifically ordered, an immense organisation of mature common sense, healthy and secure, gathering knowledge and power for creative adventures as yet beyond dreaming. They were prepared to think of the makers of the Avebury dyke as their yesterday selves, of the Stone Age savages as a phase in their late childhood, and of this great world order Sir Richmond foresaw as a day where dawn was already at hand. And in such long perspectives, the states, governments and institutions of to-day became very temporary-looking and replaceable structures indeed. Both these two people found themselves thinking in this fashion with an unwonted courage and freedom because the other one had been disposed to think in this fashion before. Sir Richmond was still turning over in his mind the happy mutual release of the imagination this chance companionship had brought about when he found himself back again at the threshold of the Old George.

§ 4

Sir Richmond Hardy was not the only man who was thinking intently about Miss Grammont at that particular moment. Two gentlemen were coming towards her across the Atlantic whose minds, it chanced, were very busily occupied by her affairs. One of these was her father, who was lying in his brass bed in his commodious cabin on the *Hollandia*, regretting his diminishing ability to sleep in the early morning now, even when he was in the strong and soothing air of mid-Atlantic, and thinking of V.V. because she had a way of coming into his mind when it was undefended ; and the other was Mr. Gunter Lake on the *Megantic*, one day out from Sandy Hook, who found himself equally sleepless and preoccupied. And although Mr. Lake was a man of vast activities and complicated engagements, he was coming now to Europe for the express purpose of seeing V.V. and having things out with her fully and completely because, in spite of all that had happened, she made such an endless series of delays in coming to America.

Old Grammont, as he appeared upon the pillow of his bed by the light of a rose-shaded bedside lamp, was a small-headed grey-haired gentleman with a wrinkled face and sunken brown eyes. Years of business experience, mitigated only by such exercise as the game of poker affords, had intensified an instinctive inexpressiveness. Under the most solitary circumstances old Grammont was still inexpressive, and the face that stared at the ceiling of his cabin and the problem of his daughter, might have been the face of a pickled head in a museum for any indication it betrayed of the flow of thought within. He lay on his back and his bent knees lifted the bedclothes into a sharp mountain. He was not even trying to sleep.

Why, he meditated, had V.V. stayed on in Europe so much longer than she need have done ? And why Gunter Lake suddenly got into a state of mind about her ? Why didn't the girl confide in her father at least about these things ? What was afoot ? She had thrown over Lake once and it seemed she was going to turn him down again. Well, if she was an ordinary female person that was a silly sort of thing to do. With her fortune and his—you could buy the world. But suppose she was not an ordinary female person. . . . Her mother hadn't been ordinary anyhow, whatever else you called her, and no one could call Grammont blood an ordinary fluid. . . . Old Grammont had never had any delusions about Lake. If Lake's father hadn't been a big man Lake would never have counted for anything at all. Suppose she did turn him down. In itself that wasn't a thing to break her father's heart.

What did matter was not whether she threw Lake over but

what she threw him over for. If it was because he wasn't
man enough, well and good. But if it was for some other
lover, some good-looking, worthless impostor, some European
title or suchlike folly—— !

At the thought of a lover for V.V. a sudden flood of anger
poured across the old man's mind, behind the still mask of his
face. It infuriated him even to think of V.V., his little V.V.
his own girl, entertaining a lover, being possibly—most
shameful thought—*in love!* Like some ordinary silly female
sinking to kisses, to the deeds one could buy and pay for
His V.V. ! The idea infuriated and disgusted him. He fought
against it as a possibility. Once some woman in New York
had ventured to hint something to him of some fellow, some
affair with an artist, Caston ; she had linked this Caston with
V.V.'s Red Cross nursing in Europe. . . . Old Grammont
had made that woman sorry she spoke. Afterwards he had
caused inquiries to be made about this Caston, careful inquiries. It seems that he and V.V. had known each other
there had been something——. But nothing that V.V. need be
ashamed of. When old Grammont's inquiry man had come
back with his report, old Grammont had been very particular
about that. At first the fellow had not been very clear, rather
muddled indeed as to how things were—no doubt he had
wanted to make out there was something just to seem to earn
his money. Old Grammont had struck the table sharply and
the eyes that looked out of his mask had blazed. " What
have you found out against her ? " he had asked in a low even
voice. " Absolutely nothing, Sir," said the agent, suddenly
white to the lips. . . .

Old Grammont stared at his memory of that moment for a
while ! That affair was all right, quite all right. Of course
it was all right. And also, happily, Caston was among the
dead. But it was well her broken engagement with Lake had
been resumed as though it had never been broken off. If
there had been any talk that fact answered it. And now that
Lake had served his purpose old Grammont did not care in the
least if he was shelved. V.V. could stand alone.

Old Grammont had got a phrase in his mind that looked like
dominating the situation. He dreamt of saying to V.V.
" V.V., I'm going to make a man of you—if you're man
enough." That was a large proposition ; it implied—oh !
it implied all sorts of things. It meant that she would care a
little for philandering as an able young business man. Perhaps some day, a long time ahead, she might marry. There
wasn't much reason for it, but it might be she would not wish
to be called a spinster. " Take a husband," thought old
Grammont, " when I am gone, as one takes a butler, to make
the household complete." In previous meditations on his
daughter's outlook old Grammont had found much that was
very suggestive in the precedent of Queen Victoria. She had

had no husband of the lord and master type, so to speak, but only a Prince Consort, well in hand. Why shouldn't the Grammont heiress dominate her male belonging, if it came to that, in the same fashion ? Why shouldn't one tie her up and tie the whole thing up, so far as any male belonging was concerned, leaving V.V. in all other respects free ? How could one do it ?

The speculative calm of the sunken brown eyes deepened. His thoughts went back to the white face of the private inquiry agent. "Absolutely nothing, Sir." What had the fellow thought of hinting ? Nothing of that kind in V.V.'s composition—never fear. Yet it was a curious anomaly that while one had a thousand ways of defending one's daughter and one's property against that daughter's husband, there was no power on earth by which a father could stretch his dead hand between that daughter and the undue influence of a lover. Unless you tied her up for good and all, lover or none. . . .

One was left at the mercy of V.V.'s character. . . .

"I ought to see more of her," he thought. "She gets away from me. Just as her mother did." A man need not suspect his womenkind but he should know what they are doing. It is duty, his protective duty to them. These companions, these Seyffert women and so forth were all very well in their way ; there wasn't much they kept from you if you got them cornered and asked them intently. But a father's eye is better. He must go about with the girl for a time, watch her with other men, give her chances to talk business with him and see if she took them. "V.V., I'm going to make a man of you," the phrase ran through his brain. The deep instinctive jealousy of the primordial father was still strong in old Grammont's blood. It would be pleasant to go about with her on his right hand in Paris, *his* girl, straight and lovely, desirable and unapproachable—above that sort of nonsense, above all other masculine subjugation.

"V.V., I'm going to make a man of you." . . .

His mind grew calmer. Whatever she wanted in Paris should be hers. He'd just let her rip. They'd be like sweethearts together, he and his girl.

Old Grammont dozed off into dreamland.

§ 5

The imaginations of Mr. Gunter Lake, two days behind Mr. Grammont upon the Atlantic, were of a gentler, more romantic character. In them V.V. was no longer a daughter in the fierce focus of a father's jealousy, but the goddess enshrined in a good man's heart. Indeed the figure that the limelight of the reverie fell upon was not V.V. at all but Mr. Gunter Lake himself, in his favourite rôle of the perfect lover.

An interminable speech unfolded itself. " I ask for nothing in return. I've never worried you about that Caston business and I never will. Married to me you shall be as free as if you were unmarried. Don't I know, my dear girl, that you don't love me yet. Let that be as you wish. I want nothing you are not willing to give me, nothing at all. All I ask is the privilege of making life happy—and it shall be happy—for you. . . . All I ask. . . . All I ask. . . . Protect, guard, cherish. . . ."

For to Mr. Gunter Lake it seemed there could be no lovelier thing in life than a wife " in name only " slowly warmed into a glow of passion by the steadfast devotion and the strength and wisdom of a mate at first despised. Until at last a day would come. . . . .

" My darling ! " Mr. Gunter Lake whispered to the darkness. " My little guurl. *It has been worth the waiting.* . . ."

§ 6

Miss Grammont met Sir Richmond in the bureau of the Old George with a telegram in her hand. " My father reported his latitude and longitude by wireless last night. The London people think he will be off Falmouth in four days' time. He wants me to join his liner there and go to Cherbourg and Paris. He's arranged that. He's the sort of man who can arrange things like that. There'll be some one at Falmouth to look after us and put us aboard the liner. I must wire them where I can pick up a telegram to-morrow."

" Wells in Somerset," said Sir Richmond.

His plans were already quite clear. He explained that he wanted her first to see Shaftesbury, a little old Wessex town that was three or four hundred years older than Salisbury, perched on a hill, a Saxon town, where Alfred had gathered his forces against the Danes and where Canute, who had ruled over all Scandinavia and Iceland and Greenland, and had come near ruling a patch of America, had died. It was a little sleepy place now, looking out dreamily over beautiful views. They would lunch in Shaftesbury and walk round it. Then they would go in the afternoon through the pleasant west country where the Celts had prevailed against the old folk of the Stonehenge temple and the Romans against the Celts and the Saxons against the Romanised Britons and the Danes against the Saxons, a war-scarred landscape, abounding in dykes and entrenchments and castles, sunken now into the deepest peace, to Glastonbury to see what there was to see of a marsh village the Celts had made for themselves three or four hundred years before the Romans came. And at Glastonbury also there were the ruins of a great Benedictine church and abbey that had once rivalled Salisbury. Thence they would go on to Wells to see yet another great cathedral and to dine and sleep. Glastonbury Abbey and Wells Cathedral brought the story of Europe right up to Reformation times.

"That will be a good day for us," said Sir Richmond. "It will be like turning over the pages of the history of our family, to and fro. There will be nothing nearly so old as Avebury in it, but there will be something from almost every chapter that comes after Stonehenge. Rome will be poorly represented, but that may come the day after at Bath. And the next day, too, I want to show you something of our old River Severn. We will come right up to the present if we go through Bristol. There we shall have a whiff of America, our new find, from which the tobacco comes, and we shall be reminded of how we set sail thither—was it yesterday or the day before ? You will understand at Bristol how it is that the energy has gone out of this dreaming land—to Africa and America and the whole wide world. It was the good men of Bristol, by the bye, with their trade from Africa to America, who gave you your colour problem. Bristol we may go through to-morrow and Gloucester, mother of I don't know how many American Gloucesters. Bath we'll get in somehow. And then as an Anglo-American showman I shall be tempted to run you northward a little way past Tewkesbury, just to go into a church here and there and show you monuments bearing little shields with the stars and stripes upon them, a few stars and a few stripes, the Washington family monuments."

"It was not only from England that America came," said Miss Grammont.

"But England takes an American memory back most easily and most fully—to Avebury and the Baltic Northmen, past the emperors and the Corinthian columns that smothered Latin Europe. . . . For you and me anyhow this is our past, this was our childhood, and this is our land."

He interrupted laughing as she was about to reply. "Well, anyhow," he said, "it is a beautiful day and a pretty country before us with the ripest history in every grain of its soil. So we'll send a wire to your London people and tell them to send their instructions to Wells."

"I'll tell Belinda," she said, "to be quick with her packing."

§ 7

As Miss Grammont and Sir Richmond Hardy fulfilled the details of his excellent programme and revised their impressions of the past and their ideas about the future in the springtime sunlight of Wiltshire and Somerset, with Miss Seyffert acting the part of an almost ostentatiously discreet chorus, it was inevitable that their conversation should become, by imperceptible gradations, more personal and intimate. They kept up the pose, which was supposed to represent Dr. Martineau's philosophy, of being Man and Woman on their Planet considering its Future, but insensibly they developed the idiosyncrasies of their position. They might profess to be Man and Woman in the most general terms, but the facts that she was the daughter not of Everyman but old Grammont and that Sir Richmond was the angry leader of a minority upon the Fuel Commission became more and more important. " What shall we do with this planet of ours ? " gave way by the easiest transitions to " What are you and I doing and what have we got to do ? How do you feel about it all ? What do you desire and what do you dare ? "

It was natural that Sir Richmond should talk of his Fuel Commission to a young woman whose interests in fuel were even greater than his own. He found that she was very much better read than he was in the recent literature of socialism, and that she had what he considered to be a most unfeminine grasp of economic ideas. He thought her attitude towards socialism a very sane one because it was also his own. So far as socialism involved the idea of a scientific control of natural resources as a common property administered in the common interest, she and he were very greatly attracted by it, but so far as it served as a form of expression for the merely insubordinate discontent of the many with the few, under any conditions, so long as it was a formula for class jealousy, and warfare, they were both repelled by it. If she had had any illusions about the working class possessing as a class any profounder political wisdom or more generous public impulses than any other class, those illusions had long since departed. People were much the same, she thought, in every class ; there was no stratification of either rightness or righteousness.

He found he could talk to her of his work and aims upon the Fuel Commission and of the conflict and failure of motives he found in himself, as freely as he had done to Dr. Martineau and with a surer confidence of understanding. Perhaps his talks with the doctor had got his ideas into order and made them more readily expressible than they would have been otherwise. He argued against the belief that any class could be good as a class or bad as a class, and he instanced the conflict of motives he found in all the members of his Committee and most so in himself. He repeated the persuasion he had already confessed to Dr. Martineau that there was not a single member of the Fuel Commission but had a considerable drive towards doing the right thing about fuel, and not one who had a single-minded unencumbered drive towards the right thing. " That," said Sir Richmond, " is what makes life so interesting and, in spite of a thousand tragic disappointments, so hopeful. Every man is a bad man, every man is a feeble man, and every man is a good man. My motives come and go. Yours do the same. We vary in response to the circumstances about us. Given a proper atmosphere, most men will be public-spirited, right-living, generous. Given perplexities and darkness, most of us can be cowardly and vile. People say you cannot change human nature, and perhaps that is true, but you can change its responses endlessly. The other day I was in Bohemia, discussing Silesian coal with Benes, and I went to see the Festival of the Bohemian Sokols. Opposite to where I sat, far away across the arena, was a great bank of men of the Sokol organisations, an unbroken brown mass wrapped in their brown uniform cloaks. Suddenly the sun came out and at a word the whole body flung back their cloaks, showed their Garibaldi shirts, and became one solid blaze of red. It was an amazing transformation until one understood what had happened. Yet nothing material had changed—but the sunshine. And given a change in laws and prevailing ideas, and the very same people who are greedy traders, grasping owners and revolting workers to-day will all throw their cloaks aside and you will find them working together, cheerfully, even generously, for a common end. They aren't traders and owners and workers and so forth by any inner necessity. Those are just the ugly parts they play in the present drama. Which is nearly at the end of its run."

" That's a hopeful view," said Miss Grammont.   " I don't see the flaw in it—if there is a flaw."

" There isn't one," said Sir Richmond.   " It is my chief discovery about life. I began with the question of fuel and the energy it affords mankind, and I have found that my generalisation applies to all human affairs. Human beings are fools, weaklings, cowards, passionate idiots—I grant you. That is the brown cloak side of them, so to speak. But they are not such fools and so forth that they can't do pretty well materially if once we hammer out a sane collective method of getting and using fuel. Which people generally will understand—in the place of our present methods of snatch and wrangle. Of that I am absolutely convinced. Some work some help, some willingness you can get out of everybody. That's the red. And the same principle applies to most labour and property problems, to health, to education, to population, social relationships and war and peace. We haven't got the right system, we have inefficient half-baked systems, or no system at all, and a wild confusion and war of ideas, in all these respects. But there is a right system possible none the less. Let us only hammer our way through to the sane and reasonable organisation in this and that and the other human affairs, and once we have got it we shall have got it for good. We may not live to see even the beginnings of success, but the spirit of order, the spirit that has already produced organised science, if only there are a few faithful persistent people to stick to the job, will in the long run certainly save mankind and make human life—clean and splendid, happy work in a clear mind. If I could live to see it ! "

" And as for us—in our time ? "

" Measured by the end we serve, we don't matter. You know we don't matter."

" We have to find our fun in the building and in our confidence that we do really build."

" So long as our confidence lasts there is no great hardship," said Sir Richmond.

" So long as our confidence lasts," she repeated after him.

" Ah ! " cried Sir Richmond. " There it is ! So long as our confidence lasts ! So long as one keeps one's mind steady. That is what I came away with Dr. Martineau to discuss. I went to him for advice. I haven't known him for more than a month. It's amusing to find myself preaching forth to you. It was just faith I had lost. Suddenly I had lost my power of work. My confidence in the rightness of what I was doing evaporated. My will failed me. I don't know if you will understand what that means. It wasn't that my reason didn't assure me just as certainly as ever that what I was trying to do was the right thing to try to do. But somehow that seemed a cold and personally unimportant proposition. The life had gone out of it. . . ."

He paused as if arrested by a momentary doubt . " I don't know why I tell you these things," he said.

" You tell them me," she said.

" It's a little like a patient in a hydropath retailing his ailments."

" No. No. Go on."

" I begin to think now that what took the go out of me as my work went on was the lack of any real fellowship in what I was doing. It was the pressure of the opposition in the Committee, day after day. It was being up against men who didn't reason against me but who just showed by everything they did that the things I wanted to achieve didn't matter to them one rap. It was going back to a home, lunching in clubs, reading papers, going about a world in which all the organisation, all the possibility of the organisation I dream of is tacitly denied. I don't know if it seems an extraordinary confession of weakness to you, but that steady refusal of the majority of my Committee to come into co-operation with me has beaten me—or at any rate has come very near to beating me. Most of them you know are such *able* men. You can *feel* their knowledge and common sense. They—and everybody about me, seemed busy and intent upon more immediate things, that seemed more real to them than this remote, theoretical, *priggish* end I have set for myself. . . ."

He paused.

" Go on," said Miss Grammont. " I think I understand this."

" And yet I know I am right."

" I know you are right. I'm certain. Go on."

" If one of those ten thousand members of the Sokol Society had thrown back his brown cloak and shown red when all the others still kept themselves cloaked—if he was a normal sensitive man—he might have felt something of a fool. He might have felt premature and presumptuous. Red he was and the others he knew were red also, but why show it ? That is the peculiar distress of people like ourselves, who have some sense of history and some sense of a larger life within us than our merely personal life. We don't want to go on with the old story merely. We want to live somehow in that large life and to live for its greater ends and lose something unbearable of ourselves, and in wanting to do that we are only wanting to do what nearly everybody perhaps is ripe to do and will presently want to do. When the New Age Martineau talks about begins to come, it may come very quickly—as the red came at Prague. But for the present every one hesitates about throwing back the cloak."

" Until the cloak becomes unbearable," she said, repeating his word.

" I came upon this holiday in the queerest state. I thought I was ill. I thought I was overworked. But the real trouble was a loneliness that robbed me of all driving force. Nobody seemed thinking and feeling with me. . . . I have never realised until now what a gregarious beast man is. It needed only a day or so with Martineau, in the atmosphere of ideas and beliefs like my own, to begin my restoration. Now as I talk to you—— That is why I have clutched at your company. Because here you are, coming from thousands of miles away, and you talk my ideas, you fall into my ways of thought as though we had gone to the same school."

" Perhaps we *have* gone to the same school," she said.

" You mean ? "

" Disappointment. Disillusionment. Having to find something better in life than the first things it promised us."

" But you—— ? Disappointed ? I thought that in America people might be educating already on different lines—— "

" Even in America," Miss Grammont said, " crops only grow on the ploughed land."

§ 8

Glastonbury in the afternoon was wonderful, they talked of Avalon and of that vanished legendary world of King Arthur and his knights, and in the early evening they came to Wells and a pleasant inn, with a quaint little garden before its front door that gave directly upon the Cathedral. The three tourists devoted a golden half-hour before dinner to the sculptures on the western face. The great screen of wrought stone rose up warmly, grey and clear and distinct against a clear blue sky in which the moon hung, round and already bright. That western façade with its hundreds of little figures, tells the whole story of God and Man from Adam to the Last Judgment, as the mediæval mind conceived it. It is an even fuller exposition than the carved Bible history that goes round the chapter-house at Salisbury. It presented the universe, said Sir Richmond, as a complete crystal globe. It explained everything in life in a simple and natural manner, hope, heaven, devil and despair. Generations had lived and died mentally within that crystal globe, convinced that it was all and complete.

" And now," said Miss Grammont, " we are in limitless space and time. The crystal globe is broken."

" And," said Belinda amazingly—for she had been silent for some time, " the goldfish are on the floor, V.V. Free to flop about. Are they any happier ? "

It was one of those sudden rhetorical triumphs that are best left alone. " I trow not," said Belinda, giving the last touch to it.

After dinner Sir Richmond and Miss Grammont walked round the cathedral and along by the moat of the bishop's palace, and Miss Seyffert stayed in the hotel to send off post-cards to her friends, a duty she had neglected for some days. The evening was warm and still and the moon was approaching its full and very bright. Insensibly the soft afterglow passed into moonlight.

At first the two companions talked very little. Sir Richmond was well content with this tacit friendliness and Miss Grammont was preoccupied because she was very strongly moved to tell him things about herself that hitherto she had told to no one. It was not merely that she wanted to tell him these things but also that for reasons she did not put as yet very clearly to herself she thought they were things he ought to know. She talked of herself at first in general terms. " Life comes on any one with a rush, childhood seems lasting for ever and then suddenly one tears into life," she said. It was even more so for women than it was for men. You are shown life, a crowded vast spectacle full of what seems to be intensely interesting activities and endless delightful and frightful and tragic possibilities, and you have hardly had time to look at it before you are called upon to make decisions. And there is something in your blood that urges you to decisive acts. Your mind, your reason resists. " Give me time," it says. " They clamour at you with treats, crowds, shows, theatres, all sorts of things ; lovers buzz at you, each trying to fix you part of his life when you are trying to get clear to live a little of your own." Her father had had one merit at any rate. He had been jealous of her lovers and very ready to interfere.

" I wanted a lover to love," she said. " Every girl of course wants that. I wanted to be tremendously excited. . . . And at the same time I dreaded the enormous interference. . . .

" I wasn't temperamentally a cold girl. Men interested and excited me, but there were a lot of men about, and they clashed with each other. Perhaps way down in some out of the way place I should have fallen in love quite easily with the one man who came along. But no man fixed his image. After a year or so I think I began to lose the power which is natural to a young girl of falling very easily into love. I became critical of the youths and men who were attracted to me, and I became analytical about myself. . . .

" I suppose it is because you and I are going to part so soon that I can speak so freely to you. . . . But there are things about myself that I have never had out even with myself. I can talk to myself in you——"

She paused baffled. " I know exactly," said Sir Richmond.

" In my composition I perceive there have always been two ruling strains. I was a spoilt child at home, a rather reserved girl at school, keen on my dignity. I like respect. I didn't give myself away. I suppose one would call that personal pride. Anyhow it was that streak made me value the position of being a rich married woman in New York. That was why I became engaged to Lake. He seemed to be as good a man as there was about. He said he adored me and wanted me to crown his life. He wasn't ill-looking or ill-mannered. The second main streak in my nature wouldn't however fit in with that."

She stopped short.

" The second streak," said Sir Richmond.

" Oh !—— Love of beauty, love of romance. I want to give things their proper names ; I don't want to pretend to you. . . . It was more or less than that. . . . It was— imaginative sensuousness. Why should I pretend it wasn't in me ? I believe that streak is in all women."

" I believe so too. In all properly constituted women."

" I tried to devote that streak to Lake," she said. " I did my best for him. But Lake was much too much of a gentle- man or an idealist about women, or what you will, to know his business as a lover. And that side of me fell in love, the rest of me protesting, with a man named Caston. It was a notorious affair. Everybody in New York couples my name with Caston. Except when my father is about. His jealousy has blasted an area of silence—in that matter—all round him. He will not know of that story. And they dare not tell him. I should pity any one who tried to tell it him."

" What sort of man was this Caston ? "

Miss Grammont seemed to consider. She did not look at Sir Richmond ; she kept her profile to him.

" He was," she said deliberately, " a very rotten sort of man."

She spoke like one resolved to be exact and judicial. " I
believe I always knew he wasn't right. But he was very
handsome. And ten years younger than Lake. And nobody
else seemed to be all right, so I swallowed that. He was an
artist, a painter. Perhaps you know his work." Sir Richmond shook his head. " He could make American business
men look like characters out of *The Three Musketeers*, they said,
and he was beginning to be popular. He made love to me. In
exactly the way Lake didn't. If I shut my eyes to one or two
things, it was delightful. I liked it. But my father would have
stood a painter as my husband almost as cheerfully as he would
a man of colour. I made a fool of myself, as people say, about
Caston. Well—— When the war came, he talked in a way
that irritated me. He talked like an East Side Annunzio,
about art and war. It made me furious to know it was all talk
and that he didn't mean business. I made him go."

She paused for a moment. " He hated to go.

" Then I relented. Or I missed him and I wanted to be
made love to. Or I really wanted to go on my own account.
I forget. I forget my motives altogether now. That early
war time was a queer time for every one. A kind of wildness
got into the blood. . . . I threw over Lake. All the time
things had been going on in New York—I had still been
engaged to Lake. I went to France. I did good work. I
did do good work. And also things were possible that would
have seemed fantastic in America. You know something of
the war-time atmosphere. There was death everywhere and
people snatched at gratifications. Caston made 'To-morrow
we die,' his text. We contrived three days in Paris together—
not very cleverly. All sorts of people know about it. . . .
We went very far."

She stopped short.

" Well ? " said Sir Richmond.

" He did die. . . ."

Another long pause. " They told me Caston had been killed.
But some one hinted—or I guessed—that there was more in it
than an ordinary casualty.

" Nobody, I think, realises that I know. This is the first
time I have ever confessed that I do know. He was shot.
He was shot for cowardice."

" That might happen to any man," said Sir Richmond
presently. " No man is a hero all round the twenty-four
hours. Perhaps he was caught by circumstances, unprepared.
He may have been taken by surprise."

" It was the most calculated, cold-blooded cowardice
imaginable. He let three other men go on and get killed. . . .
" No. It is no good your inventing excuses for a man you
know nothing about. It was vile, contemptible cowardice—
and meanness. It fitted in with a score of ugly little things
I remembered. It explained them all. I know the evidence

and the judgment against him were strictly just and true, because they were exactly in character. . . . And that, you see, was my man. That was the lover I had chosen. That was the man to whom I had given myself with both hands."

Her soft unhurrying voice halted for a time, and then resumed in the same even tones of careful statement. " I wasn't disgusted, not even with myself. About him I was chiefly sorry, intensely sorry, because I had made him come out of a life that suited and protected him, to the war. About myself, I was stunned and perplexed. I had the clearest realisation that what you and I have been calling the bright little personal life had broken off short and was spoilt and over and done with. I felt as though it was my body they had shot. And there I was, with fifty years of life left in me and nothing particular to do with them."

" That was just the prelude to life," said Sir Richmond.

" It didn't seem so at the time. I felt I had to get hold of something or go to pieces. I couldn't turn to religion. I had no religion. And Duty ? What is Duty ? I set myself to that. I had a kind of revelation one night. ' Either I find out what all this world is about,' I said, ' or I perish.' I have lost myself and I must forget myself—by getting hold of something bigger than myself. And becoming that. That's why I have been making a sort of historical pilgrimage. . . . That's my story, Sir Richmond. That's my education. . . . Somehow though your troubles are different, it seems to me that my little muddle makes me understand how it is with you. What you've got, this idea of a scientific ordering of the world, is what I, in my younger, less experienced way, have been feeling my way towards. I want to join on. I want to get hold of this idea of a great fuel control in the world and of a still greater economic and educational control of which it is a part. I want to make that idea a part of myself. Rather I want to make myself a part of it. When you talk of it I believe in it altogether."

" And I believe in it, when I talk of it to you."

§ 9

Sir Richmond was stirred very deeply by Miss Grammont's confidences. His dispute with Dr. Martineau was present in his mind, so that he did not want to make love to her. But he was extremely anxious to express his vivid sense of the value of her friendship. And while he hesitated over this difficult and unfamiliar task she began to talk again of herself, and in such a way as to give a new turn to Sir Richmond's thoughts.

" Perhaps I ought to tell you a little more about myself," she said ; " now that I have told you so much. I did a thing that still puzzles me. I was filled with a sense of hopeless disaster in France and I suppose I had some sort of desperate idea of saving something out of the situation. . . . I renewed my correspondence with Gunter Lake. He made the suggestion I knew he would make, and I renewed our engagement."

" To go back to wealth and dignity in New York."

" Yes."

" But you don't love him ? "

" That's always been plain to me. But what I didn't realise, until I had given my promise over again, was that I dislike him—acutely."

" You hadn't realised that before ? "

" I hadn't thought about him sufficiently. But now I had to think about him a lot. The other affair had given me an idea perhaps of what it means to be married to a man. And here I am drifting back to him. The horrible thing about him is the steady—*enveloping* way in which he has always come at me. Without fellowship. Without any community of ideas. Ready to make the most extraordinary bargains. So long as he can in any way fix me and get me. What does it mean ? What is there behind those watching soliciting eyes of his ? I don't in the least love him, and this desire and service and all the rest of it he offers me—it's not love. It's not even such love as Caston gave me. It's a game he plays with his imagination."

She had released a flood of new ideas in Sir Richmond's mind. " This is—illuminating," he said. " You dislike Lake acutely. You always have disliked him."

" I suppose I have. But it's only now I admit it to myself."

" Yes. And—— You might, for example, have married him in New York before the war."

" It came very near to that."

" And then probably you wouldn't have discovered you disliked him. You wouldn't have admitted it to yourself."

" I suppose I shouldn't. I suppose I should have tried to believe I loved him."

" Women do this sort of thing. Odd ! I never realised it before. And there are endless wives suppressing an acute dislike. My wife does. I see now quite clearly that she detests me. Reasonably enough. From her angle I'm entirely detestable. But she won't admit it, won't know of it. She never will. To the end of my life, always, she will keep that detestation unconfessed. She puts a face on the matter. We both do. And this affair of yours. . . . Have you thought how unjust it is to Lake ? "

" Not nearly so much as I might have done."

" It is unfair to him. Atrociously unfair. He's not my sort of man, perhaps, but it will hurt him cruelly according to the peculiar laws of his being. He seems to me a crawling sort of lover—with an immense self-conceit at the back of his crawlingness."

" He has," she endorsed.

" He backs himself to crawl—until he crawls triumphantly right over you. . . . I don't like to think of the dream he has. . . . I take it, he will lose. Is it fair to go into this game with him ? "

" In the interests of Lake," she said, smiling softly at Sir Richmond in the moonlight. " But you are perfectly right."

" And suppose he doesn't lose ! "

Sir Richmond found himself uttering sentiments.

" There is only one decent way in which a civilised man and a civilised woman may approach one another. Passionate desire is not enough. What is called love is not enough. Pledges, rational considerations, all these things are worthless. All these things are compatible with hate. The primary essential is friendship, clear understanding, absolute confidence. Then within that condition, in that elect relationship, love is permissible, mating, marriage or no marriage, as you will—all things are permissible. . . ."

Came a long pause between them.

" Dear old cathedral," said Miss Grammont, a little irrelevantly. She had an air of having concluded something that to Sir Richmond seemed scarcely to have begun. She stood looking at the great dark façade edged with moonlight for some moments and then turned towards the hotel, which showed a pink lit window.

" I wonder," she said, " if Belinda is still up. And what she will think when I tell her of the final extinction of Mr. Lake. I think she rather looked forward to being the intimate friend, secrets and everything, of Mrs. Gunter Lake."

§ 10

Sir Richmond woke up at dawn and he woke out of an extraordinary dream. He was saying to Miss Grammont : " There is no other marriage than the marriage of true minds. There is no other marriage than the marriage of true minds." He saw her as he had seen her the evening before, light and cool, coming towards him in the moonlight from the hotel. But also in the inconsistent way of dreams he was very close to her kind, faintly smiling face, and his eyes were wet with tears and he was kissing her hand. "My dear wife and mate," he was saying, and suddenly he was kissing her cool lips.

He woke up and stared at this dream which faded out only very slowly before the fresh sunrise upon the red tiles and tree boughs outside the open window, and before the first stir and clamour of the birds.

He felt like a court in which some overwhelmingly revolutionary piece of evidence had been tendered. All the elaborate defence had broken down at one blow.   He sat up on the edge of his bed, facing the new fact.

" This is monstrous and ridiculous," he said, " and Martineau judged me exactly.   I am in love with her.   I have never been so much in love or so truly in love with any one before."

§ 11

That was the dawn of a long day of tension for Sir Richmond and Miss Grammond.   Because each was now vividly aware of being in love with the other and so neither was able to see how things were with the other.   They were afraid of each other.   A restraint had come upon them both, a restraint that was greatly enhanced by their sense of Belinda, acutely observant, ostentatiously tactful and self-effacing, and pre-pared at the slightest encouragement to be overwhelmingly romantic and sympathetic.   Their talk waned, and was revived to an artificial activity and waned again.   The his-torical interest had evaporated from the west of England and left only an urgent and embarrassing present.

But the loveliness of the weather did not fail, and the whole day was set in Severn landscapes.   They first saw the great river like a sea with the Welsh mountains hanging in the sky behind as they came over the Mendip crest above Shipham. They saw it again as they crossed the hill before Clifton Bridge, and so they continued, climbing to hill crests for views at Alveston and near Dursley, and so to Gloucester and the lowest bridge, and thence back down stream again through fat meadow lands at first and much apple-blossom and then over gentle hills through wide, pale Newnham and Lidney and Alvington and Woolaston to old Chepstow and its brown castle, always with the widening estuary to the left of them and its foaming shoals and shining sandbanks.   From Chepstow they turned back north along the steep Wye gorge to Tintern, and there at the snug little Beaufort Arms with its prim lawn and flower garden they ended the day's journey.

Tintern Abbey they thought a poor graceless mass of ruin down beside the river, and it was fenced about jealously and locked up from their invasion.   After dinner Sir Richmond and Miss Grammont went for a walk in the mingled twilight and moonlight up the hill towards Chepstow.   Both of them were absurdly and nervously pressing to Belinda to come with them, but she was far too wise to take this sudden desire for her company seriously.   Her dinner shoes, she said, were too thin.   Perhaps she would change and come out a little later. " Yes, come later," said Miss Grammont and led the way to the door.

They passed through the garden.   " I think we go up the hill ? " said Sir Richmond.

" Yes," she agreed, " up the hill."

Followed a silence.

Sir Richmond made an effort, but after some artificial and disconnected talk about Tintern Abbey, concerning which she had no history ready, and then, still lamer, about whether Monmouthshire is in England or Wales, silence fell again. The silence lengthened, assumed a significance, a dignity that no common words might break.

Then Sir Richmond spoke. " I love you," he said, " with all my heart."

Her soft voice came back after a stillness. " I love you," she said. " With all myself."

" I had long ceased to hope," said Sir Richmond, "that I should ever find a friend . . . a lover . . . perfect companionship. . . ."

They went on walking side by side, without touching each other or turning to each other.

" All the things I wanted to think I believe have come alive in me," she said. . . .

" Cool and sweet," said Sir Richmond. " Such happiness as I could not have imagined."

The light of a silent bicycle appeared above them up the hill and swept down upon them, lit their two still faces brightly and passed.

" My dear," she whispered in the darkness between the high hedges.

They stopped short and stood quite still, trembling. He saw her face, dim and tender, looking up to his.

Then he took her in his arms and kissed her lips as he had desired in his dream. . . .

When they returned to the inn Belinda Seyffert offered flat explanations of why she had not followed them, and enlarged upon the moonlight effect of the Abbey ruins from the inn lawn. But the scared congratulations in her eyes betrayed her recognition that momentous things had happened between the two.

CHAPTER EIGHT

§ 1

SIR RICHMOND had talked in the moonlight and shadows of having found such happiness as he could not have imagined. But when he awoke in the night that happiness had evaporated. He awoke suddenly out of this love dream that had lasted now for nearly four days, and he awoke in a mood of astonishment and dismay.

He had thought that when he parted from Dr. Martineau he had parted also from that process of self-exploration that they had started together, but now he awakened to find it established and in full activity in his mind. Something or some one, a sort of etherealised Martineau-Hardy, an abstracted intellectual conscience, was demanding what he thought he was doing with Miss Grammont and whither he thought he was taking her, how he proposed to reconcile the close relationship with her that he was now embarked upon with, in the first place, his work upon and engagements with the Fuel Commission, and, in the second place, Martin Leeds. Curiously enough Lady Hardy didn't come into the case at all. He had done his utmost to keep Martin Leeds out of his head throughout the development of this affair. Now in an unruly and determined way that was extremely characteristic of her she seemed resolute to break in.

She appeared as an advocate, without affection for her client but without any hostility, of the claims of Miss Grammont to be let alone. The elaborate pretence that Sir Richmond had maintained to himself that he had not made love to Miss Grammont, that their mutual attraction had been irresistible and had achieved its end in spite of their resolute and complete detachment, collapsed and vanished from his mind. He admitted to himself that driven by a kind of instinctive necessity he had led their conversation step by step to a realisation and declaration of love, and that it did not exonerate him in the least that Miss Grammont had been quite ready and willing to help him and meet him half-way. She wanted love as a woman does, more than a man does, and he had steadily presented himself as a man free to love, able to love and loving.

" She wanted a man to love, she wanted perfected fellowship, and you have made her that tremendous promise. That was implicit in your embrace. And how can you keep that promise ? "

It was as if Martin spoke ; it was her voice, it was the very quality of her thought.

" You belong to this work of yours, which must needs be interrupted or abandoned if you take her. Whatever is not mortgaged to your work is mortgaged to me. For the strange thing in all this is that you and I love one another—and have no power to do otherwise. In spite of all this.

" You have nothing to give her but stolen goods," said the shadow of Martin. " You have nothing to give any one personally any more. . . .

" Think of the love that she desires and think of this love that you can give. . . .

" Is there any new thing in you that you can give her that you haven't given me ? You and I know each other very well ; perhaps I know *you* too well. Haven't you loved me as much as you can love any one ? Think of all that there has been between us that you are ready now, eager now to set aside and forget as though it had never been. For four days you have kept me out of your mind in order to worship her. Yet you have known I was there—for all you would not know. No one else will ever be so intimate with you as I am. We have quarrelled together, wept together, jested happily and jested bitterly. You have spared me not at all. Pitiless and cruel you have been to me. You have reckoned up all my faults against me as though they were sins. You have treated me at times unlovingly—never was lover treated so unlovingly as you have sometimes treated me. And yet I have your love—as no other woman can ever have it. Even now when you are wildly in love with this girl's freshness and boldness and cleverness I come into your mind by right and necessity— *your* Martin. What are you offering her ? "

" She is different," argued Sir Richmond.

" But you are the same," said the shadow of Martin with Martin's unsparing return. " Your love has never been a steadfast thing. It comes and goes—like the wind. You are an extravagantly imperfect lover. But I have learnt to accept you, as people accept the English weather. . . . Never in all your life have you loved, wholly, fully, steadfastly—as people deserve to be loved ; not your mother nor your father, not your wife nor your children, nor me, nor our child, nor any living thing. Pleasant to all of us at times—at times bitterly disappointing. You do not even love this work of yours steadfastly, this work to which you sacrifice us all in turn. You do not love enough. That is why you have these moods and changes, that is why you have these lassitudes. So it is you are made. . . .

" And that is why you must not take this brave young life, so much simpler and braver than your own, and exalt it— as you can do—and then fail it, as you will do. . . ."

Sir Richmond's mind and body lay very still for a time.

" Should I fail her ? . . ."

For a time Martin Leeds passed from the foreground of his mind.

He was astonished to think how planless, instinctive and

unforeseeing his treatment of Miss Grammont had been. It had been just a blind drive to get hold of her and possess her. . . .

Suddenly his passion for her became active in its defence again.

" But is there such a thing as a perfect love ? Is *yours* a perfect love, my dear Martin, with its insatiable jealousy, its ruthless criticism ? Has the world ever seen a perfect lover yet ? Isn't it our imperfection that brings us together in a common need ? Is Miss Grammont, after all, likely to get a more perfect love in all her life than this poor love of mine ? And isn't it good for her that she should love ? "

" Perfect love cherishes. Perfect love foregoes."

Sir Richmond found his mind wandering far away from the immediate question. " Perfect love," the phrase was his point of departure. Was it true that he could not love passionately and completely ? Was that fundamentally what was the matter with him ? Was that perhaps what was the matter with the whole world of mankind ? It had not yet come to that power of loving which makes action full and simple and direct and unhesitating. Man upon his planet has not grown up to love, is still an eager, egotistical and fluctuating adolescent. He lacks the courage to love and the wisdom to love. Love is here. But it comes and goes, it is mixed with greeds and jealousies and cowardice and cowardly reservations. One hears it only in snatches and single notes It is like something tuning up before the music begins. . . . The metaphor altogether ran away with Sir Richmond's half-dreaming mind. Some day perhaps all life would go to music.

Love was music and power. If he had loved enough he need never have drifted away from his wife. Love would have created love, would have tolerated and taught and inspired. Where there is perfect love there is neither greed nor impatience. He would have done his work calmly. He would have won his way with his Committee instead of fighting and quarrelling with it perpetually. . . .

" Flimsy creatures," he whispered. " Uncertain health. Uncertain strength. A will that comes and goes. Moods of baseness. Moods of utter beastliness. . . . Love like April sunshine. April ? . . ."

He dozed and dreamt for a time of spring passing into a high summer sunshine, into a continuing music of love. He thought of a world like some great playhouse in which players and orchestra and audience all co-operate in a noble production without dissent or conflict. He thought he was the savage of thirty thousand years ago dreaming of the great world that is still perhaps thirty thousand years ahead. His effort to see more of that coming world than indistinct and cloudy pinnacles and to hear more than a vague music, dissolved his dream and left him awake again and wrestling with the problem of Miss Grammont.

§ 2

The shadow of Martin stood over him, inexorable. He had to release Miss Grammont from the adventure into which he had drawn her. This decision stood out stern and inevitable in his mind with no conceivable alternative.

As he looked at the task before him he began to realise its difficulty. He was profoundly in love with her, he was still only learning how deeply, and it was evident she was not going to play a merely passive part in this affair. She was perhaps as deeply in love with him. . . .

He could not bring himself to the idea of confessions and disavowals. He could not bear to think of her disillusionment. He felt that he owed it to her not to disillusion her, to spoil things for her in that fashion. " To turn into something mean and ugly after she has believed in me. . . . It would be like playing a practical joke upon her. It would be like taking her into my arms and suddenly making a grimace at her. . . . It would scar her with a second humiliation. . . ."

Should he take her on to Bath or Exeter to-morrow and contrive by some sudden arrival of telegrams that he had to go from her suddenly ? But a mere sudden parting would not end things between them now unless he went off abruptly without explanations or any arrangements for further communications. At the outset of this escapade there had been a tacit but evident assumption that it was to end when she joined her father at Falmouth. It was with an effect of discovery that Sir Richmond realised that now it could not end in that fashion, that with the whisper of love and the touching of lips, something had been started that would go on, that would develop. To break off now and go away without a word would leave a raw and torn end, would leave her perplexed and perhaps even more humiliated with an aching mystery to distress her. " Why did he go ? Was it something I said ?—something he found out or imagined ? "

Parting had disappeared as a possible solution of this problem. She and he had got into each other's lives to stay : the real problem was the terms upon which they were to stay in each other's lives. Close association had brought them to the point of being, in the completest sense, lovers ; that could not be, and the real problem was the transmutation of their relationship to some form compatible with his honour and her happiness. A word, an idea, from some recent reading floated into Sir Richmond's head. " Sublimate," he whispered. " We have to sublimate this affair. We have to put this relationship upon a Higher Plane."

His mind stopped short at that.

Presently his voice sounded out of the depths of his heart. " God ! How I loathe the Higher Plane ! . . .

" God has put me into this Higher Plane business like some poor little kid who has to wear irons on its legs.

" I *want* her. . . .

" Do you hear, Martin ? I want her."

As if by a lightning flash he saw his car with himself and Miss Grammont—Miss Seyffert had probably fallen out—traversing Europe and Asia in headlong flight. To a sunlit beach in the South Seas. . . .

His thoughts presently resumed as though these unmannerly and fantastic interruptions had not occurred.

" We have to carry the whole affair on to a Higher Plane, and keep it there. We two love one another—that has to be admitted now. (I ought never to have touched her. I ought never to have thought of touching her.) But we two are too high, our aims and work and obligations are too high for any ordinary love making. That sort of thing would embarrass us, would spoil everything.

" Spoil everything," he repeated, rather like a small boy who learns an unpalatable lesson.

For a time Sir Richmond, exhausted by moral effort, lay staring at the darkness.

" It has to be done. I believe I can carry her through with it if I can carry myself. She's a finer thing than I am. . . . On the whole I am glad it's only one more day. Belinda will be about. . . . Afterwards we can write to each other. . . . If we can get over the next day it will be all right. Then we can write about fuel and politics—and there won't be her voice and her presence. We shall really *sublimate*. . . . First-class idea—sublimate ! . . . And I will go back to dear old Martin who's all alone there and miserable ; I'll be kind to her and tell her her Carbuncle scar rather becomes her. . . And in a little while I shall be altogether in love with her again. . . .

" Queer what a brute I've always been to Martin.

" Queer that Martin can come in a dream to me and take the upper hand with me. . . .

" Queer that *now*—I love Martin.

He thought still more profoundly. " By the time the Committee meets again I shall have been tremendously refreshed."

He repeated : " Put things on the Higher Plane and keep them there. Then go back to Martin. And so to the work. That's it. . . ."

Nothing so pacifies the mind as a clear-cut purpose. Sir Richmond fell asleep during the fourth recapitulation of this programme.

§ 3

When Miss Grammont appeared at breakfast Sir Richmond saw at once that she too had had a restless night. When she came into the little long breakfast room of the inn with its brown screens and its neat white tables it seemed to him that the Miss Grammont of his nocturnal speculations, the beautiful young lady who had to be protected and managed and loved unselfishly, vanished like some exorcised intruder. Instead was this real dear young woman, who had been completely forgotten during the reign of her simulacrum and who now returned completely remembered, familiar, friendly remembered, familiar, friendly, intimate. She touched his hand for a moment, she met his eyes with the shadow of a smile in her own.

" Oranges ! " said Belinda from the table by the window. " Beautiful oranges."

She had been preparing them, poor Transatlantic exile, after the fashion in which grape fruits are prepared upon liners and in the civilised world of the west. " He's getting us tea-spoons," said Belinda, as they sat down.

" This is realler England than ever," she said. " I've been up an hour. I found a little path down to the river bank. It's the greenest morning world and full of wild flowers. Look at these."

" That's lady's-smock," said Sir Richmond. " It's not really a flower ; it's a quotation from Shakespeare."

" And there are cowslips ! "

" *Cuckoo buds of yellow hue Do paint the meadows with delight*. All the English flowers come out of Shakespeare. I don't know what we did before his time."

The waiter arrived with the tea-spoons for the oranges.

Belinda having distributed these, resumed her discourse of enthusiasm for England. She asked a score of questions about Gloucester and Chepstow, the Severn and the Romans and the Welsh, and did not wait for the answers. She did not want answers ; she talked to keep things going. Her talk masked a certain constraint that came upon her companions after the first morning's greetings were over.

Sir Richmond as he had planned upstairs produced two Michelin maps. " To-day," he said, " we will run back to Bath—from which it will be easy for you to train to Falmouth. We will go by Monmouth and then turn back through the Forest of Dean, where you will get glimpses of primitive coal mines still worked by two men and a boy with a windlass and a pail. Perhaps we will go through Cirencester. I don't know. Perhaps it is better to go straight to Bath. In the very heart of Bath you will find yourselves in just the same world you visited at Pompeii. Bath is Pompeii overlaid by Jane Austen's England."

He paused for a moment. " We can wire to your agents from here before we start and we can pick up their reply at Gloucester or Nailsworth or even Bath itself. So that if your father is nearer than we suppose—— But I think to-morrow afternoon will be soon senough for Falmouth, anyhow."

He stopped interrogatively.

Miss Grammont's face was white. " That will do very well," she said.

§ 4

They started, but presently they came to high banks that showed such masses of bluebells, ragged Robin, great stitch-wort and the like that Belinda was not to be restrained. She clamoured to stop the car and go up the bank and pick her hands full, and so they drew up by the roadside and Sir Richmond and Miss Grammont sat down near the car while Belinda carried her enthusiastic onslaught on the flowers up the steep bank and presently out of earshot.

The two lovers said unheeded things about the flowers to each other and then fell silent. Then Miss Grammont turned her head and seemed deliberately to measure her companion's distance. Evidently she judged her out of earshot.

" Well," said Miss Grammont in her soft even voice. " We love one another. Is that so still ? "

" I could not love you more."

" It wasn't a dream ? "

" No."

" And to-morrow we part ? "

He looked her in the eyes. "I have been thinking of that all night," he said at last.

" I too."

" And you think—— ? "

" That we must part. Just as we arranged it—when was it ? Three days or three ages ago ? There is nothing else in the world to do except for us to go our ways. . . . I love you. That means for a woman—— It means that I want to be with you. But that is impossible. . . . Don't doubt whether I love you because I say—impossible. . . ."

Sir Richmond, faced with his own nocturnal decision, was now moved to oppose it flatly. " Nothing that one can do is impossible."

She glanced again at Belinda and bent down towards him. " Suppose," she said, " you got back into that car with me ; suppose that instead of going on as we have planned, you took me—away. How much of us would go ? "

" You would go," said Sir Richmond, " and my heart."

" And this work of yours ? And your honour ? For the honour of a man in this New Age of yours will be first of all in the work he does for the world. And you will leave your work—to be just a lover. And the work that I might do—because of my father's wealth ; all that would vanish too. We should leave all of that, all our usefulness, all that much

of ourselves. But what has made me love you ? Just your
breadth of vision, just the sense that you mattered. What has
made you love me ? Just that I have understood the dream
of your work. All that we should have to leave behind. We
should specialise—in our own scandal. We should run away
just for one thing. To think, by sharing the oldest, simplest,
dearest indulgences in the world, that we had got each other.
When really we had lost each other, lost all that mattered. . . ."

Her face was flushed with the earnestness of her conviction.
Her eyes were bright with tears. " Don't think I don't love
you. It's so hard to say all this. Somehow it seems like
going back on something—something supreme. Our instincts
have got us. . . . Don't think I'd hold myself from you,
dear. I'd give myself to you with both hands. I love
you—— When a woman loves—I at any rate—she loves
altogether. But this thing—I am convinced—cannot be.
I must go my own way, the way I have to go. My father is
the strangest man, obstinate, more than half a savage. For
me—I know it—he has the jealousy of ten husbands. If you
take me—— If our secret becomes manifest—— If you
are to take me and keep me then his life and your life will
become wholly this Feud, nothing but this Feud. You have
to fight him anyhow—that is why I of all people must keep
out of the quarrel. For him, it would be an immense excitement, full of the possibility of fierce satisfactions ; for you,
whether you won me or lost me, it would be utter waste and
ruin."

She paused and then went on : " And for me too, waste
and ruin. I shall be a woman fought over. I shall be fought
over as dogs fight over a bone. I shall sink back to the level
of Helen of Troy. I shall cease to be a free citizen, a responsible
free person. Whether you win me or lose me it will be waste
and ruin for us both. Your Fuel Commission will go to pieces,
all the wide, enduring work you have set me dreaming about
will go the same way. We shall just be another romantic
story. . . . No ! "

Sir Richmond sat still, a little like a sullen child, she thought.
" I hate all this," he said slowly. " I didn't think of your
father before, and now I think of him it sets me bristling for a
fight. It makes all this harder to give up. And yet, do you
know, in the night I was thinking, I was coming to conclusions, very like yours. For quite other reasons. I thought
we ought not to—— We have to keep friends anyhow and
hear of each other ? "

" That goes without saying."

" I thought we ought not to go on to be lovers in any way
that would affect you, touch you too closely. . . . I was
sorry—I had kissed you."

" Not I. No. Don't be sorry for that. I am glad we
have fallen in love, more glad than I have been of anything else

in my life, and glad we have spoken plainly. . . . Though we have to part. . . . And——"

Her whisper came close to him. "For a whole day yet, all round the clock twice, you and I have one another."

Miss Seyffert began speaking as soon as she was well within earshot.

"I don't know the name of a single one of these flowers," she cried, "except the bluebells. Look at this great handful I've gotten ! Spring-time in Italy doesn't compare with it, not for a moment."

§ 5

Because Belinda Seyffert was in the dicky behind them with her alert interest in their emotions all too thinly and obviously veiled, it seemed more convenient to Sir Richmond and Miss Grammont to talk not of themselves but of Man and Woman and of that New Age according to the prophet Martineau, which Sir Richmond had partly described and mainly invented and ascribed to his departed friend. They talked anthropologically, philosophically, speculatively, with an absurd pretence of detachment, they sat side by side in the little car, scarcely glancing at one another, but side by side and touching each other, and all the while they were filled with tenderness and love and hunger for one another.

In the course of a day or so they had touched on nearly every phase in the growth of Man and Woman from that remote and brutish past which has left its traces in human bones mingled with the bones of hyænas and cave bears beneath the stalagmites of Wookey Hole near Wells. In those nearly forgotten days the mind of man and woman had been no more than an evanescent succession of monstrous and infantile imaginations. That brief journey in the west country had lit up phase after phase in the long teaching and discipline of man as he had developed depth of memory and fixity of purpose out of these raw beginnings, through the dreaming childhood of Avebury and Stonehenge and the crude boyhood of ancient wars and massacres. Sir Richmond recalled those phases now and how, as they had followed one another, man's idea of woman and woman's idea of man had changed with them, until nowadays in the minds of civilised men brute desire and possession and a limitless jealousy had become almost completely overlaid by the desire for fellowship and a free mutual loyalty. "Overlaid," he said. "The older passions are still there like the fires in an engine." He invented a saying for Dr. Martineau that the Man in us to-day was still the old man of Palæolithic times, with his will, his wrath against the universe increased rather than diminished. If to-day he ceases to crack his brother's bones and rape and bully his women-kind, it is because he has grown up to a greater game, and means to crack this world and feed upon its marrow and wrench their secrets from the stars.

And furthermore it would seem that the prophet Martineau had declared that in this New Age that was presently to dawn for mankind, jealousy was to be disciplined even as we had disciplined lust and anger ; instead of ruling our law it was to be ruled by law and custom. No longer were the jealousy of strange peoples, the jealousy of ownership and the jealousy of sex to determine the framework of human life. There was to be one peace and law throughout the world, one economic scheme and a universal freedom for men and women to possess and give themselves.

" And how many generations yet must there be before we reach that Utopia ? " Miss Grammont asked.

" I wouldn't put it at a very great distance."

" But think of all the confusions of the world ! "

" Confusions merely. The world is just a muddle of states and religions and theories and stupidities. There are great lumps of disorderly strength in it, but as a whole it is a weak world. It goes on by habit. There's no great idea in possession, and the only possible great idea is this one. The New Age may be nearer than we dare to suppose."

" If I could believe that ! "

" There are many more people think as we do than you suppose. Are you and I such very strange and wonderful and exceptional people ? "

" No. I don't think so."

" And yet the New World is already completely established in our hearts. What has been done in our minds can be done in most minds. In a little while the muddled angry mind of Man upon his Planet will grow clear and it will be this idea that will have made it clear. And then life will be very different for every one. That tyranny of disorder which oppresses every life on earth now will be lifted. There will be less and less insecurity, less and less irrational injustice. It will be a better instructed and a better behaved world. We shall live at our ease, not perpetually anxious, not resentful and angry. And that will alter all the rules of love. Then we shall think more of the loveliness of other people because it will no longer be necessary to think so much of the dangers and weaknesses and pitifulnesses of other people. We shall not have to think of those who depend upon us for happiness and self-respect. We shall not have to choose between a wasteful fight for a personal end or the surrender of our heart's desire."

" Heart's desire," she whispered. " Am I indeed your heart's desire ? "

Sir Richmond sank his head and voice in response.

" You are the best of all things. And I have to let you go."

I

Sir Richmond suddenly remembered Miss Seyffert and half turned his face towards her. Her forehead was just visible over the hood of the open coupé. She appeared to be intelligently intent upon the scenery. Then he broke out suddenly into a tirade against the world. "But I am bored by this jostling unreasonable world. At the bottom of my heart I am bitterly resentful to-day. This is a world of fools and brutes in which we live, a world of idiotic traditions, imbecile limitations, cowardice, habit, greed and mean cruelty. It is a slum of a world, a congested district, an insanitary jumble of souls and bodies. Every good thing, every sweet desire is thwarted—every one. I have to lead the life of a slum missionary, a sanitary inspector, an underpaid teacher. I am bored. Oh God! how I am bored! I am bored by our laws and customs. I am bored by our rotten empire and its empty monarchy. I am bored by its parades and its flags and its sham enthusiasms. I am bored by London and its life, by its smart life and by its servile life alike. I am bored by theatres and by books and by every sort of thing that people call pleasure. I am bored by the brag of people and the claims of people and the feelings of people. Damn people! I am bored by profiteers and by the snatching they call business enterprise. Damn every business man! I am bored by politics and the universal mismanagement of everything. I am bored by France, by Anglo-Saxondom, by German self-pity, by Bolshevik fanaticism. I am bored by these fools' squabbles that devastate the world. I am bored by Ireland, Orange and Green. Curse the Irish—north and south together! Lord! how I *hate* the Irish from Carson to the last Sinn Feiner! And I am bored by India and by Egypt. I am bored by Poland and by Islam. I am bored by any one who professes to have rights. Damn their rights! Curse their rights! I am bored to death by this year and by last year and by the prospect of next year. I am bored—I am horribly bored by my work. I am bored by every sort of renunciation. I want to live with the woman I love and I want to work within the limits of my capacity. Curse all—— Hullo! Damn his eyes!—Steady, ah! The spark! . . . Good! No skid."

He had come round a corner at five-and-twenty miles an hour and had stopped his spark and pulled up neatly within a yard of the fore-wheel of a waggon that was turning in the road so as to block the way completely.

"That almost had me." . . .

"And now you feel better?" said Miss Grammont.

"Ever so much," said Sir Richmond and chuckled.

The waggoner cleared the road and the car started up again. For a minute or so neither spoke.

"You ought to be smacked hard for that outbreak—my dear," said Miss Grammont.

" I ought—*my* dear. I have no right to be ill-tempered. We two are among the supremely fortunate ones of our time. We have no excuse for misbehaviour. Got nothing to grumble at. Always I am lucky. *That*—with the waggon—was a very near thing. God spoils us.

" We two," he went on, after a pause, " are among the most fortunate people alive. We are both rich and easily rich. That gives us freedoms few people have. We have a vision of the whole world in which we live. It's in a mess—but that is by the way. The mass of mankind never gets enough education to have even a glimpse of the world as a whole. They never get a chance to get the hang of it. It is really possible for us to do things that will matter in the world. All our time is our own ; all our abilities we are free to use. Most people, most intelligent and educated people, are caught in cages of pecuniary necessity ; they are tied to tasks they can't leave, they are driven and compelled and limited by circumstances they can never master. But we, if we have tasks, have tasks of our own choosing. We may not like the world but anyhow we are free to do our best to alter it. If I were a clerk in Hoxton and you were a city typist, then we *might* swear."

" It was you who swore," smiled Miss Grammond.

" It's the thought of that clerk in Hoxton and that city typist who really keep me at my work. Any smacking ought to come from them. I couldn't do less than I do in the face of their helplessness. Nevertheless a day will come—through what we do and what we refrain from doing—when there will be no bound and limited clerks in Hoxton and no captive typists in the city. And nobody at all to consider."

" According to the prophet Martineau," said Miss Grammont.

" And then you and I must contrive to be born again."

" Heighho ! " cried Miss Grammont. " A thousand years ahead ! When fathers are civilised. When all these phantom people who intervene on your side—no ! I don't want to know anything about them, but I know of them by instinct—when they also don't matter."

" Then you and I can have things out with each other— *thoroughly*," said Sir Richmond, with a surprising ferocity in his voice, charging the little hill before him as though he charged at Time.

§ 6

They had to wait at Nailsworth for a telegram from Mr. Grammont's agents ; they lunched there and drove on to Bath in the afternoon. They came into the town through unattractive and unworthy outskirts, and only realised the charm of the place after they had garaged their car at the Pulteney Hotel and walked back over the Pulteney Bridge to see the Avon and the Pump Room and the Roman Baths.

The Pulteney they found hung with pictures and adorned with sculpture to an astonishing extent ; some former proprietor must have had a mania for replicas and the place is eventful with white marble fauns and sylphs and lions and Cæsars and Queen Victorias and packed like an exhibition with memories of Rome, Florence, Milan, Paris, the National Gallery and the Royal Academy, amidst which splendours a competent staff administers modern comforts with an old-fashioned civility. But round and about the Pulteney one has still the scenery of Georgian England, the white faintly classical terraces and houses of the days of Fielding, Smollett, Fanny Burney and Jane Austen, the graceful bridge with the bright little shops full of " presents from Bath " ; the Pump Room with its water drinkers and a fine array of the original Bath chairs.

Down below the Pump Room our travellers explored the memories of the days when the world was Latin from York to the Tigris, and the Corinthian capital flourished like a weed from Bath to Baalbek. And they considered a little doubtfully the seventeenth-century statue of Bladud, who is said to have been healed by the Bath waters and to have founded the city in the days when Stonehenge still flourished, eight hundred years before the Romans came.

In the afternoon Miss Seyffert came with Sir Richmond and Miss Grammont and was very enthusiastic about everything, but in the evening after dinner it was clear that her rôle was to remain in the hotel. Sir Richmond and Miss Grammont went out into the moonlit gloaming ; they crossed the bridge again and followed the road beside the river towards the old Abbey Church, that Lantern of the West. Away in some sunken gardens ahead of them a band was playing, and a cluster of little lights about the bandstand showed a crowd of people down below dancing on the grass. These little lights, these bobbing black heads and the lilting music, this little inflamed centre of throbbing sounds and ruddy illumination, made the dome of the moonlit world about it seem very vast and cool and silent. Our visitors began to realise that Bath could be very beautiful. They went to the parapet above the river and stood there, leaning over it elbow to elbow and smoking cigarettes. Miss Grammont was moved to declare the Pulteney Bridge with its noble arch, its effect of height over the swirling river, and the cluster of houses above, more beautiful than the Ponte Vecchio at Florence. Down below was a man in waders with a fishing-rod going to and fro along the foaming weir, and a couple of boys paddled a boat against the rush of the water lower down the stream.

" Dear England ! " said Miss Grammont, surveying this gracious spectacle. " How full it is of homely and lovely and kindly things ! "

" It is the home we come from."

' You belong to it still."

" No more than you do. I belong to a big overworking modern place called London which stretches its tentacles all over the world. I am as much a home-coming tourist as you are. Most of this western country I am seeing for the first time."

She said nothing for a space. " I've not a word to say to-night," she said. " I'm just full of a sort of animal satisfaction in being close to you. . . . And in being with you among lovely things. . . . Somewhere—— Before we part to-night—— . . ."

" Yes ? " he said to her pause, and his face came very near to hers.

" I want you to kiss me."

" Yes," he said awkwardly, glancing over his shoulder, acutely aware of the promenaders passing close to them.

" It's a promise ? "

" Yes."

Very timidly and guiltily his hand sought hers beside it and gripped it and pressed it. " My dear ! " he whispered, tritest and most unavoidable of expressions. It was not very like Man and Woman loving upon their Planet ; it was much more like the shy endearments of the shop boys and work girls who made the darkling populous about them with their silent interchanges.

" There are a thousand things I want to talk about to you," she said. " After we have parted to-morrow I shall begin to think of them. But now—every rational thing seems dissolved in this moonlight." . . .

Presently she made an effort to restore the intellectual dignity of their relationship.

" I suppose I ought to be more concerned to-night about the work I have to do in the world and anxious for you to tell me this and that, but indeed am not concerned at all about it. I seem to have it in outline all perfectly clear. I mean to play a man's part in the world just as my father wants me to do. I mean to win his confidence and work with him —like a partner. Then some day I shall be a power in the world of fuel. And at the same time I must watch and read and think and learn how to be the servant of the world. . . . We two have to live like trusted servants who have been made guardians of a helpless minor. We have to put things in order and keep them in order against the time when Man—Man whom we call in America the Common Man—can take hold of his world——"

" And release his servants," said Sir Richmond.

" All that is perfectly clear in my mind. That is what I am going to live for ; that is what I have to do."

She stopped abruptly. " All that is about as interesting to-night—in comparison with the touch of your dear fingers— as next month's railway time-table."

But later she found a topic that could hold their attention for a time.

" We have never said a word about religion," she said.

Sir Richmond paused for a moment. " I am a godless man," he said. " The stars and space and time overwhelm my imagination. I cannot imagine anything above or beyond them."

She thought that over. " But there are divine things," she said.

" *You* are divine. . . . I'm not talking lover's nonsense," he hastened to add. " I mean that there is something about human beings—not just the everyday stuff of them—but something that appears intermittently—as though a light shone through some thing translucent. If I believe in any divinity at all it is the divinity revealed to me by other people—— And even by myself in my own heart.

" I'm never surprised at the badness of human beings," said Sir Richmond ; " seeing how they have come about and what they are ; but I have been surprised time after time by fine things. . . . Often in people I disliked or thought little of. . . . I can understand that I find you full of divine quality, because I am in love with you and all alive to you. Necessarily I keep on discovering loveliness in you. But I have seen divine things—in dear old Martineau, for example. A vain man, fussy, timid—and yet filled with a passion for truth, ready to make great sacrifices and to toil tremendously for that. And in those men I am always cursing, my Committee, it is astonishing at times to discover what streaks of goodness even the really bad men can show. . . . But one can't make use of just any one's divinity. I can see the divinity of Martineau but it leaves me cold. He tried me and bored me. . . . But I live on you. It's only through love that the God can reach over from one human being to another. All real love is a divine thing, a reassurance, a release of courage. It is wonderful enough that we should take food and drink and turn them into imagination, invention and creative energy ; it is still more wonderful that we should take an animal urging and turn it into a light to discover beauty and an impulse towards the utmost achievements of which we are capable. All love is a sacrament and all lovers are priests to each other. You and I——"

Sir Richmond broke off abruptly. " I spent three days trying to tell this to Dr. Martineau. But he wasn't the priest I had to confess to and the words wouldn't come. I can confess it to you readily enough. . . ."

" I cannot tell," said Miss Grammont, " whether this is the last **wis**dom in life or—moonshine. I cannot tell whether I am thinking or feeling ; but the noise of the water going over the weir below is like the stir in my heart. And I am swimming in love and happiness. Am I awake or am I dreaming

you, and are we dreaming one another ? Hold my hand—
hold it hard and tight. I'm trembling with love for you and
all the world. . . . If I say more I shall be weeping."

For a long time they stood side by side saying not a word
to one another.

Presently the band down below and the dancing ceased and
the little lights were extinguished. The silent moon seemed
to grow brighter and larger and the whisper of the waters
louder. A crowd of young people flowed out of the gardens
and passed by on their way home. Sir Richmond and Miss
Grammont strolled through the dispersing crowd and over the
Toll Bridge, and went exploring down a little staircase that
went down from the end of the bridge to the dark river and
then came back to their old position at the parapet looking
upon the weir and the Pulteney Bridge. The gardens that
had been so gay were already dark and silent as they returned,
the streets echoed emptily to the few people who were still
abroad.

"It's the most beautiful bridge in the world," said Miss
Grammont, and gave him her hand again.

Some deep-toned clock close by proclaimed the hour
eleven.

The silence healed again.

" Well ? " said Sir Richmond.

" Well ? " said Miss Grammont, smiling very faintly.

" I suppose we must go out of all this beauty now, back to
the lights of the hotel and the watchful eyes of your dragon."

" She has not been a very exacting dragon so far, has she ? "

" She is a miracle of tact."

" She does not really watch. But she is curious—and very
sympathetic."

" She is wonderful." . . .

" That man is still fishing," said Miss Grammont.

For a time she peered down at the dark figure wading in the
foam below as though it was the only thing of interest in the
world. Then she turned to Sir Richmond.

" I would trust Belinda with my life," she said. " And
anyhow—now—we need not worry about Belinda."

§ 7

At the breakfast table it was Belinda who was the most
nervous of the three, the most moved, the most disposed to
throw a sacramental air over their last meal together. Her
companions had passed beyond the idea of separation ; it was
as if they now cherished a secret satisfaction at the high
dignity of their parting. Belinda in some way perceived they
had become different. They were no longer tremulous lovers ;
they seemed sure of one another and with a new pride in their
bearing. It would have pleased Belinda better, seeing how

soon they were to be torn apart, if they had not made quite such excellent breakfasts. She even suspected them of having slept—well. Yet yesterday they had been deeply stirred. They had stayed out late last night, so late that she had not heard them come in. Perhaps then they had passed the climax of their emotions. Sir Richmond, she learnt, was to take the party to Exeter, where there would be a train for Falmouth a little after two. If they started from Bath about nine that would give them an ample margin of time in which to deal with a puncture or any such misadventure.

They crested the Mendips above Shepton Mallet, ran through Ilchester and Ilminster into the lovely hill country about Up-Ottery and so to Honiton and the broad level road to Exeter. Sir Richmond and Miss Grammont were in a state of happy gravity; they sat contentedly, side by side, talking very little. They had already made their arrangements for writing to one another. There was to be no stream of love letters or protestations. That might prove a mutual torment. Their love was to be implicit. They were to write at intervals about political matters, and their common interests, and to keep each other informed of their movements about the world.

" We shall be working together," she said, speaking suddenly out of a train of thought she had been following, " we shall be closer together than many a couple who have never spent a day apart for twenty years."

Then presently she said : " In the New Age all lovers will have to be accustomed to meeting and parting. We women will not be tied very much by domestic needs. Unless we see fit to have children. We shall be going about our business like men—we shall have world-wide businesses—many of us— just as men will. . . .

" It will be a world full of lovers' meetings. Some day— somewhere—we two will certainly meet again."

" Even you have to force circumstances a little," said Sir Richmond.

" We shall meet," she said, " without doing that."

" But where ? " he asked, unanswered. . . .

" Meetings and partings," she said. " Women will be used to seeing their lovers go away. Even to seeing them go away to other women who have borne them children and who have a closer claim on them."

" No one——" began Sir Richmond, startled.

" But I don't mind very much. It's how things are. If I were a perfectly civilised woman I shouldn't mind at all. If men and women are not to be tied to each other there must needs be such things as this."

" But you," said Sir Richmond. " I at any rate am not like that. I cannot bear the thought that *you*——"

" You need not bear it, my dear. I was just trying to

imagine this world that is to be. Women I think are different from men—in their jealousy. Men are jealous of the other man ; women are jealous for their man—and careless about the other woman. What I love in you I am sure about. My mind was empty when it came to you and now it is full to overflowing. I shall feel you moving about in the same world with me. I'm not likely to think of any one else for a very long time. . . . Later on, who knows ? I may marry. I make no vows. But I think until I know certainly that you do not want me any more it will be impossible for me to marry or to have a lover. I don't know, but that is how I believe it will be with me. And my mind feels beautifully clear now and settled. I've got your idea and made it my own, your idea that we matter scarcely at all, but that the work we do matters supremely. I'll find my rope and tug it, never fear. Half-way round the world perhaps some day you will feel me tugging."

"I shall feel you're there," he said, "whether you tug or not. . . ."

"Three miles left to Exeter," he reported presently.

She glanced back at Belinda.

"It is good that we have loved, my dear," she whispered. "Say it is good."

"The best thing in all my life," he said, and lowered his head and voice to say : "My dearest dear."

"Heart's desire—still ? "

"Heart's delight. . . . Priestess of life. . . . Divinity."

She smiled and nodded, and suddenly Belinda, up above their lowered heads, accidentally and irrelevantly no doubt, coughed.

At Exeter station there was not very much time to spare after all. Hardly had Sir Richmond secured a luncheon basket for the two travellers before the train came into the station. He parted from Miss Grammont with a hand clasp. Belinda was flushed and distressed at the last but her friend was quiet and still. "Au revoir," said Belinda without conviction when Sir Richmond shook her hand.

§ 8

Sir Richmond stood quite still on the platform as the train ran out of the station. He did not move until it had disappeared round the bend. Then he turned, lost in a brown study, and walked very slowly towards the station exit.

"The most wonderful thing in my life," he thought. "And already—it is unreal.

"She will go on to her father—whom she knows ten thousand times more thoroughly than she knows me ; she will go on to Paris, she will pick up all the threads of her old story, be reminded of endless things in her life, but never except in

the most casual way of these days ; they will be cut off from
everything else that will serve to keep them real ; and as for
me—this connects with nothing else in my life at all. . . . It
is as disconnected as a dream. . . . Already it is hardly more
substantial than a dream. . . .

" We shall write letters. Do letters breathe faster or slower
as you read them ?

" We may meet."

" Where are we likely to meet again ? . . . I never realised
before how improbable it is that we shall meet again ? And
if we meet ? . . .

" Never in all our lives shall we be really *together* again.
It's over—— With a completeness. . . .

" Like death."

He came opposite the bookstalls and stopped short and
stared with unseeing eyes at the display of popular literature.
He was wondering now whether after all he ought to have let
her go. He experienced something of the blank amazement
of a child who has burst its toy balloon. His golden globe of
satisfaction in an instant had gone. An irrational sense of
loss was flooding every other feeling about V.V. If she had
loved him truly and altogether could she have left him like
this ? Neither of them surely had intended so complete a
separation. He wanted to go back and recall that train.

A few seconds more, he realised, and he would give way to
anger. Whatever happened that must not happen. He
pulled himself together. What was it he had to do now ? He
had not to be angry, he had not even to be sorry. They had
done the right thing. Outside the station his car was waiting.

He went outside the station and stared at his car. He had
to go somewhere. Of course ! down into Cornwall to Martin's
cottage. He had to do down to her and be kind and comforting about that carbuncle. To be kind ? . . . If this
thwarted feeling broke out into anger he might be tempted
to take it out of Martin. That at any rate he must not do.
He had always for some inexplicable cause treated Martin
badly. Nagged her and blamed her and threatened her.
That must stop now. No shadow of this affair must lie on
Martin. . . . And Martin must never have a suspicion of any
of this. . . .

The image of Martin became very vivid in his mind. He
thought of her as he had seen her many times, with the tears
close, fighting with her back to the wall, with all her wit and
vigour gone, because she loved him more steadfastly than he
did her. Whatever happened he must not take it out of
Martin. It was astonishing how real she had become now—as
V.V. became a dream.

Yes, Martin was astonishingly real. And if only he could
go now and talk to Martin—face the facts of life with her,
even as he had with that phantom Martin in his dream. . . .

But things were not like that.

He looked to see if his car was short of water or petrol ; both needed replenishing, and so he would have to go up the hill into Exeter town again. He got into his car and sat with his fingers on the electric starter.

Martin ! Old Friend ! Eight days were still left before the Commission met again, eight days for golden kindness. He would distress Martin by no clumsy confession. He would just make her happy as she loved to be made happy. . . . Nevertheless. Nevertheless. . . .

Was it Martin who failed him or he who failed Martin ?

Incessant and insoluble dispute. Well, the thing now was to go to Martin. . . . And then the work !

He laughed suddenly.

" I'll take it out of the damned Commission. I'll make old Rumford Brown sit up."

He was astonished to find himself thinking of the affairs of the Commission with a lively interest and no trace of fatigue. He had had his change ; he had taken his rest ; he was equal to his task again already. He started his engine and steered his way past a van and a waiting cab.

" Fuel," he said.

CHAPTER NINE

THE LAST DAYS OF SIR RICHMOND HARDY

§ 1

THE Majority and Minority Reports of the Fuel Commission were received on their first publication with much heat and disputation, but there is already a fairly general agreement that they are great and significant documents, broadly conceived and historically important. They do lift the questions of fuel supply and distribution high above the level of parochial jealousies and above the petty and destructive profiteering of private owners and traders, to a view of a general human welfare. They form an important link in a series of private and public documents that are slowly opening out a prospect of new economic methods, methods conceived in the generous spirit of scientific work, that may yet arrest the drift of our western civilisation towards financial and commercial squalor and the social collapse that must ensue inevitably on that. In view of the composition of the Committee, the Majority Report is in itself an amazing triumph of Sir Richmond's views; it is astonishing that he was able to drive his opponents so far and then leave them there securely advanced while he carried on the adherents he had altogether won, including of course the labour representatives, to the further altitudes of the Minority Report.

After the summer recess the Majority Report was discussed and adopted. Sir Richmond had shown signs of flagging energy in June but he had come back in September in a state of exceptional vigour ; for a time he completely dominated the Committee by the passionate force of his convictions and the illuminating scorn he brought to bear on the various subterfuges and weakening amendments by which the meaner interests sought to save themselves in whole or in part from the common duty of sacrifice. But towards the end he fell ill. He had worked to the pitch of exhaustion. He neglected a cold that settled on his chest. He began to cough persistently and betray an increasingly irritable temper. In the last fights in the Committee his face was bright with fever, and he spoke in a voiceless whisper, often a vast angry whisper. His place at table was marked with scattered lozenges and scraps of paper torn to the minutest shreds. Such good manners as had hitherto mitigated his behaviour on the Committee departed from him. He carried his last points, gesticulating and coughing and wheezing rather than speaking. But he had so hammered his ideas into the Committee that they took the effect of what he was trying to say.

He died of pneumonia at his own house three days after

the passing of the Majority Report. The Minority Report, his own especial creation, he never signed. It was completed by Wast and Carmichael. . . .

After their parting at Salisbury station Dr. Martineau heard very little of Sir Richmond for a time except through the newspapers, which contained frequent allusions to the Committee. Some one told him that Sir Richmond had been staying at Ruan in Cornwall where Martin Leeds had a cottage, and some one else had met him at Bath on his way, he said, in his car from Cornwall to a conference with Sir Peter Davis in Glamorganshire.

But in the interim Dr. Martineau had the pleasure of meeting Lady Hardy at a luncheon party. He was seated next to her, and he found her a very pleasing and sympathetic person indeed. She talked to him freely and simply of her husband and of the journey the two men had taken together. Either she knew nothing of the circumstances of their parting or if she did she did not betray her knowledge. " That holiday did him a world of good," she said. " He came back to his work like a giant. I feel very grateful to you."

Dr. Martineau said it was a pleasure to have helped Sir Richmond's work in any way. He believed in him thoroughly. Sir Richmond was inspired by great modern creative ideas.

" Forgive me if I keep you talking about him," said Lady Hardy. " I wish I could feel as sure that I had been of use to him."

Dr. Martineau insisted. " I know very well that you are."

" I do what I can to help him carry his enormous burthen of toil," she said. " I try to smooth his path. But he is a strange silent creature at times."

Her eye scrutinised the doctor's face.

It was not the doctor's business to supplement Sir Richmond's silences. Yet he wished to meet the requirements of this lady if he could. " He is one of those men," he said, " who are driven by forces they do not fully understand. A man of genius."

" Yes," she said in an undertone of intimacy. " Genius. . . . A great irresponsible genius. . . . Difficult to help. . . . I wish I could do more for him."

A very sweet and charming lady. It was with great regret that the doctor found the time had come to turn to his left-hand neighbour.

§ 2

It was with some surprise that Dr. Martineau received a fresh appeal for aid from Sir Richmond. It was late in October and Sir Richmond was already seriously ill. But he was still going about his business as though he was perfectly wel . He had not mistaken his man. Dr. Martineau received him as though there had never been a shadow of offence between them.

He came straight to the point. " Martineau," he said, " I must have those drugs I asked you for when first I came to you now. I must be bolstered up. I can't last out unless I am. I'm at the end of my energy. I come to you because you will understand. The Commission can't go on now for more than another three weeks. Whatever happens afterwards I must keep going until then."

The doctor did understand. He made no vain objections. He did what he could to patch up his friend for his last struggles with the opposition in the Committee. " Pro forma," he said, stethoscope in hand, " I must order you to bed. You won't go. But I order you. You must know that what you are doing is risking your life. Your lungs are congested, the bronchial tubes already. That may spread at any time. If this open weather lasts you may go about and still pull through. But at any time this may pass into pneumonia. And there's not much in you just now to stand up against pneumonia. . . ."

" I'll take all reasonable care."

" Is your wife at home ? "

" She is in Wales with her people. But the household is well trained. I can manage."

" Go in a closed car from door to door. Wrap up like a mummy. I wish the Committee room wasn't down those abominable House of Commons corridors. . . ."

They parted with an affectionate handshake.

§ 3

Death approved of Sir Richmond's determination to see the Committee through. Our universal creditor gave this particular debtor grace to the very last meeting. Then he brushed a gust of chilly rain across the face of Sir Richmond as he stood waiting for his car outside the strangers' entrance to the House. For a couple of days Sir Richmond felt almost intolerably tired, but scarcely noted the changed timbre of the wheezy notes in his throat. He rose later each day and with ebbing vigour, jotted down notes and corrections upon the proofs of the Minority Report. He found it increasingly difficult to make decisions ; he would correct and alter back and then repeat the correction perhaps half a dozen times. On the evening of the second day his lungs became painful and his breathing difficult. His head ached, and a sense of some great impending evil came upon him. His skin was suddenly a detestable garment to wear. He took his temperature with a little clinical thermometer he kept by him and found it was a hundred and one. He telephoned hastily for

Dr. Martineau and without waiting for his arrival, took a hot bath and got into bed. He was already thoroughly ill when the doctor arrived.

"Forgive my sending for you," he said. "Not your line, I know. . . . My wife's G.P.—an exasperating sort of ass. Can't stand him. No one else."

He was lying on a narrow little bed with a hard pillow that the doctor replaced by one from Lady Hardy's room. He had twisted the bed-clothes into a hopeless muddle, the sheet was on the floor.

Sir Richmond's bedroom was a large apartment in which sleep seemed to have been an admitted necessity rather than a principal purpose. On one hand it opened into a business-like dressing and bath room, on the other into the day study. It bore witness to the nocturnal habits of a man who had long lived a life of irregular impulses to activity and dislocated hours and habits. There was a desk and reading lamp for night work near the fireplace, an electric kettle for making tea at night, a silver biscuit tin ; all the apparatus for the lonely intent industry of the small hours. There was a book-case of bluebooks, books of reference and suchlike material, and some files. Over the mantelpiece was an enlarged photograph of Lady Hardy and a plain office calendar. The desk was littered with the galley proofs of the Minority Report upon which Sir Richmond had been working up to the moment of his hasty retreat to bed. And lying among the proofs, as though it had been taken out and looked at quite recently, was the photograph of a girl. For a moment Dr. Martineau's mind hung in doubt, and then he knew it for the young American of Stonehenge. How that affair had ended he did not know. And now it was not his business to know.

These various observations printed themselves on Dr. Martineau's mind after his first cursory examination of his patient and while he cast about for anything that would give this large industrious apartment a little more of the restful-ness and comfort of a sick-room. "I must get in a night nurse at once," he said. "We must find a small table somewhere to put near the bed.

"I am afraid you are very ill," he said, returning to the bedside. "This is not, as you say, my sort of work. Will you let me call in another man, a man we can trust thoroughly, to consult ? "

"I'm in your hands," said Sir Richmond. "I want to pull through."

"He will know better where to get the right sort of nurse for the case—and everything. . . ."

The second doctor presently came, with the right sort of nurse hard on his heels. Sir Richmond submitted almost silently to his expert handling and was sounded and looked to and listened at.

" H'm," said the second doctor, and then encouragingly to
Sir Richmond : " We've got to take care of you."

" There's a lot about this I don't like," said the second
doctor and drew Dr. Martineau by the arm towards the study.
For a moment or so Sir Richmond listened to the low murmur
of their voices, but he did not feel very deeply interested in
what they were saying. He began to think what a decent
chap Dr. Martineau was, how helpful and fine and forgiving
his professional training had made him ; how completely he
had ignored the smothered incivilities of their parting at
Salisbury. All men ought to have some such training. Not
a bad idea to put every boy and girl through a year or so of
hospital service. . . . Sir Richmond must have dozed for his
next perception was of Dr. Martineau standing over him and
saying, " I am afraid, my dear Hardy, that you are very
ill indeed. Much more so than I thought you were at
first."

Sir Richmond's raised eyebrows conveyed that he accepted
this fact.

" I think Lady Hardy ought to be sent for."

Sir Richmond shook his head with unexpected vigour.

" Don't want her about," he said, and after a pause, " Don't
want anybody about."

" But if anything happens—— ? "

" Send then."

An expression of obstinate calm overspread Sir Richmond's
face. He seemed to regard the matter as settled. He closed
his eyes.

For a time Dr. Martineau desisted. He went to the window
and turned to look again at the impassive figure on the bed.
Did Sir Richmond fully understand ? He made a step
towards his patient and hesitated. Then he brought a chair
and sat down at the bedside.

Sir Richmond opened his eyes and regarded him with a
slight frown.

" A case of pneumonia," said the doctor, " after great
exertion and fatigue, may take very rapid and unexpected
turns."

Sir Richmond, cheek on pillow, seemed to assent.

" I think if you want to be sure that Lady Hardy sees you
again—— . . . If you don't want to take risks about
that—— . . . One never knows in these cases. Probably
there is a night train."

Sir Richmond manifested no surprise at the warning. But
he stuck to his point. His voice was faint but firm. " Couldn't
make up anything to say to her. Anything she'd like."

Dr. Martineau rested on that for a little while. Then he
said : " If there is any one else ? "

" Not possible," said Sir Richmond, with his eyes on the
ceiling.

" But to see ? "

Sir Richmond turned his head to Dr. Martineau. His face puckered like a peevish child's. "They'd want things said to them. . . . Things to remember. . . . I *can't*. I'm tired out."

"Don't trouble," whispered Dr. Martineau, suddenly remorseful.

But Sir Richmond also was remorseful. "Give them my love," he said. "Best love. . . . Old Martin. Love."

Dr. Martineau was turning away when Sir Richmond spoke again in a whisper. "Best love. . . . Poor at the best. . . ."

He dozed for a time. Then he made a great effort. "I can't see them, Martineau, until I've something to say. It's like that. Perhaps I shall think of some kind things to say— after a sleep. But if they came now . . . I'd say something wrong. Be cross perhaps. Hurt some one. I've hurt so many. . . . People exaggerate. . . . People exaggerate— importance these occasions."

"Yes, yes," whispered Dr. Martineau. "I quite understand."

§ 4

For a time Sir Richmond dozed. Then he stirred and muttered. "Second rate. . . . Poor at the best. . . . Love. . . . Work. All. . . ."

"It has been splendid work," said Dr. Martineau, and was not sure that Sir Richmond heard.

"Those last few days . . . lost my grip. . . . Always lose my damned grip.

"Ragged them. . . . Put their backs up. . . . Silly. . . ."

"Never. . . . Never done anything—*well*. . . .

"It's done. Done. Well or ill. . . .

"Done."

His voice sank to the faintest whisper. "Done for ever and ever . . . and ever . . . and ever."

Again he seemed to doze.

Dr. Martineau stood up softly   Something beyond reason told him that this was certainly a dying man. He was reluctant to go, and he had an absurd desire that some one, some one for whom Sir Richmond cared should come and say good-bye to him, and for Sir Richmond to say good-bye to some one. He hated this lonely launching from the shores of life of one who had sought intimacy so persistently and vainly. It was extraordinary—he saw it now for the first time—he loved this man. If it had been in his power, he would at that moment have anointed him with kindness.

The doctor found himself standing in front of the untidy writing desk, littered like a recent battlefield. The photograph of the American girl drew his eyes. What had happened?

Was there not perhaps some word for her ?   He turned about as if to enquire of the dying man and found Sir Richmond's eyes open and regarding him.   In them he saw an expression he had seen there once or twice before, a faint but excessively irritating gleam of amusement,

" Oh—*Well !* " said Dr. Martineau and turned away.   He went to the window and stared out as his habit was.

Sir Richmond continued to smile dimly at the doctor's back until his eyes closed again.

It was their last exchange.   Sir Richmond died that night in the small hours, so quietly that for some time the night nurse did not observe what had happened.   She was indeed roused to that realisation by the ringing of the telephone bell in the adjacent study.

§ 5

For a long time that night Dr. Martineau had lain awake unable to sleep.   He was haunted by the figure of Sir Richmond lying on his uncomfortable little bed in his big bedroom and by the curious effect of loneliness produced by the nocturnal desk and by the evident dread felt by Sir Richmond of any death-bed partings.   He realised how much this man, who had once sought so feverishly for intimacies, had shrunken back upon himself, how solitary his motives had become, how rarely he had taken counsel with any one in his later years. His mind now dwelt apart.   Even if people came about him he would still be facing death alone.

And so it seemed he meant to slip out of life, as a man might slip out of a crowded assembly, unobserved.   Even now he might be going.   The doctor recalled how he and Sir Richmond had talked of the rage of life in a young baby, how we drove into life in a sort of fury, how that rage impelled us to do this and that, how we fought and struggled until the rage spent itself and was gone.   That eddy of rage that was Sir Richmond was now perhaps very near its end.   Presently it would fade and cease, and the stream that had made it and borne it would know it no more.

Dr. Martineau's thoughts relaxed and passed into the picture-land of dreams.   He saw the figure of Sir Richmond, going as it were away from him along a narrow path, a path that followed the crest of a ridge, between great darknesses, enormous cloudy darknesses, above him and below.   He was going along this path without looking back, without a thought for those he left behind, without a single word to cheer him on his way, walking as Dr. Martineau had sometimes watched him walking, without haste or avidity, walking as a man might along some great picture gallery with which he was perhaps even over familiar.   His hands would be in his pockets, his indifferent eyes upon the clouds about him.   And as he strolled along that path, the darkness closed in upon him. His figure became dim and dimmer.

Whither did that figure go ? Did that enveloping darkness hide the beginnings of some strange long journey or would it just dissolve that figure into itself ?

Was that indeed the end ?

Dr. Martineau was one of that large class of people who can neither imagine nor disbelieve in immortality. Dimmer and dimmer grew the figure but still it remained visible. As one can continue to see a star at dawn until one turns away. Or one blinks or nods and it is gone.

Vanished now are the beliefs that held our race for countless generations. Where now was that Path of the Dead, mapped so clearly, faced with such certainty, in which the heliolithic peoples believed from Avebury to Polynesia ? Not always have we had to go alone and unprepared into uncharted darknesses. For a time the dream artist used a palette of the doctor's vague memories of things Egyptian, he painted a new roll of the Book of the Dead, at a copy of which the doctor had been looking a day or so before. Sir Richmond became a brown naked figure, crossing a bridge of danger, passing between terrific monsters, ferrying a dark and dreadful stream. He came to the scales of judgment before the very throne of Osiris and stood waiting while dog-headed Anubis weighed his conscience, and that evil monster, the Devourer of the Dead, crouched ready if the judgment went against him. The doctor's attention concentrated upon the scales. A memory of Swedenborg's *Heaven and Hell* mingled with the Egyptian fantasy. Now at last it was possible to know something real about this man's soul, now at last one could look into the Secret Places of his Heart. Anubis and Thoth, the god with the ibis head, were reading the heart as if it were a book, reading aloud from it to the supreme judge.

Suddenly the doctor found himself in his own dreams. His anxiety to plead for his friend had brought him in. He too had become a little painted figure and he was bearing a book in his hand. He wanted to show that the laws of the new world could not be the same as those of the old, and the book he was bringing as evidence was his own *Psychology of a New Age*.

The clear thought of that book broke up his dream by releasing a train of waking troubles. . . . You have been six months on Chapter Ten ; will it ever be ready for Osiris ? . . . Will it ever be ready for print ? . . .

Dream and waking thoughts were mingled like sky and cloud upon a windy day in April. Suddenly he saw again that lonely figure on the narrow way with darknesses above and darknesses below and darknesses on every hand. But this time it was not Sir Richmond. . . . Who was it ? Surely it was Everyman. Everyman had to travel at last along that selfsame road, leaving love, leaving every task and

every desire. But was it Everyman ? . . . A great fear and
horror came upon the doctor. That little figure was himself !
And the book which was his particular task in life was still
undone. He himself stood in his turn upon that lonely path
with the engulfing darknesses about him. . . .

He seemed to wrench himself awake.

He lay very still for some moments and then he sat up in
bed. An overwhelming conviction had arisen in his mind
that Sir Richmond was dead. He felt he must know for
certain. He switched on his electric light, mutely interrogated
his round face reflected in the looking-glass, got out of bed,
shuffled on his slippers and went along the passage to the
telephone. He hesitated for some seconds and then lifted the
receiver. It was his call which aroused the nurse to the fact
of Sir Richmond's death.

§ 6

Lady Hardy arrived home in response to Dr. Martineau's
telegram late on the following evening. He was with her
next morning, comforting and sympathetic. Her big blue
eyes, bright with tears, met his very wistfully ; her little body
seemed very small and pathetic in its simple black dress.
And yet there was a sort of bravery about her. When he
came into the drawing-room she was in one of the window
recesses talking to a serious-looking woman of the dressmaker
type. She left her business at once to come to him. "Why
did I not know in time ? " she cried.

"No one, dear lady, had any idea until late last night,"
he said, taking both her hands in his for a long friendly
sympathetic pressure.

"I might have known that if it had been possible you
would have told me," she said.

"You know," she added, "I don't believe it yet. I don't
realise it. I go about these formalities——"

"I think I can understand that."

"He was always, you know, not quite here. . . . It is as if
he were a little more not quite here. . . . I can't believe it is
over. . . ."

She asked a number of questions and took the doctor's
advice upon various details of the arrangements. "My
daughter Helen comes home to-morrow afternoon," she explained. "She is in Paris. But our son is far, far away in
the Punjab. I have sent him a telegram. . . . It is so kind
of you to come in to me."

Dr. Martineau went more than half-way to meet Lady
Hardy's disposition to treat him as a friend of the family.
He had conceived a curious, half-maternal affection for Sir
Richmond that had survived even the trying incident of the
Salisbury parting and revived very rapidly during the last

few weeks. This affection extended itself now to Lady Hardy
Hers was a type that had always appealed to him. He could
understand so well the perplexed loyalty with which she was
now setting herself to gather together some preservative and
reassuring evidences of this man who had always been, as she
put it, "never quite here." It was as if she felt that now it
was at last possible to make a definite reality of him. He
could be fixed. And as he was fixed he would stay. Never
more would he be able to come in and with an almost ex-
pressionless glance wither the interpretation she had imposed
upon him. She was finding much comfort in this task of reconstruction. She had gathered together in the drawing-room
every presentable portrait she had been able to find of him.
He had never, she said, sat to a painter, but there was an
early pencil sketch done within a couple of years of their
marriage ; there was a number of photographs, several of
which—she wanted the doctor's advice upon this point—she
thought might be enlarged ; there was a statuette done by
some woman artist who had once beguiled him into a sitting.
There was also a painting she had had worked up from a
photograph and some notes. She flitted among these
memorials, going from one to the other, undecided which to
make the standard portrait. "That painting, I think, is
most like," she said ; "as he was before the war. But the
war and the Commission changed him—worried him and
aged him. . . . I grudged him to that Commission. He let
it worry him frightfully."

"It meant very much to him," said Dr. Martineau.

"It meant too much to him. But of course his ideas were
splendid. You know it is one of my hopes to get some sort
of book done, explaining his ideas. He would never write.
He despised it—unreasonably. A real thing done, he said,
was better than a thousand books. Nobody read books, he
said, but women, parsons and idle people. But there must
be books. And I want one. Something a little more real
than the ordinary official biography. . . . I have thought of
young Leighton, the secretary of the Commission. He seems
thoroughly intelligent and sympathetic and really anxious to
reconcile Richmond's views with those of the big business men
on the Committee. He might do. . . . Or perhaps I might
be able to persuade two or three people to write down their
impressions of him. A sort of memorial volume. . . . But
he was shy of friends. There was no man he talked to very
intimately about his ideas unless it was to you. . . . I wish I
had the writer's gift, doctor."

§ 7

It was on the second afternoon that Lady Hardy summoned
Dr. Martineau by telephone. "Something rather disagreeable,"

she said. " If you could spare the time. If you could come round."

" It is frightfully distressing," she said when he got round to her, and for a time she could tell him nothing more. She was having tea and she gave him some. She fussed about with cream and cakes and biscuits. He noted a crumpled letter under the edge of the silver tray.

" He talked, I know, very intimately with you," she said, coming to it at last. " He probably went into things with you that he never talked about with any one else. Usually he was very reserved. Even with me there were things about which he said nothing."

" We did," said Dr. Martineau with discretion, " deal a little with his private life."

" There was some one——"

Dr. Martineau nodded and then, not to be too portentous, took and bit a biscuit.

" Did he by any chance ever mention some one called Martin Leeds ? "

Dr. Martineau seemed to reflect. Then realising that this was a mistake, he said : " He told me the essential facts."

The poor lady breathed a sigh of relief. " I'm glad," she said simply. She repeated, " Yes, I'm glad. It makes things easier now."

Dr. Martineau looked his enquiry.

" She wants to come and see him."

" Here ? "

" Here ! And Helen here ! And the servants noticing everything ! I've never met her. Never set eyes on her. For all I know she may want to make a scene." There was infinite dismay in her voice.

Dr. Martineau was grave. " You would rather not receive her ? "

" I don't want to refuse her. I don't want even to seem heartless. I understand, of course, she has a sort of claim." She sobbed her reluctant admission. " I know it. I know. . . . There was much between them."

Dr. Martineau pressed the limp hand upon the little tea-table. " I understand, dear lady," he said. " I understand. Now . . . suppose I were to write to her and arrange—— I do not see that you need be put to the pain of meeting her. Suppose I were to meet her here myself ? "

" If you *could* ! "

The doctor was quite prepared to save the lady any further distresses, no matter at what trouble to himself. " You are so good to me," she said, letting the tears have their way with her.

" I am silly to cry," she said, dabbing her eyes.

" We will get it over to-morrow," he reassured her. " You need not think of it again."

He took over Martin's brief note to Lady Hardy and set to work by telegram to arrange for her visit. She was in London at her Chelsea flat and easily accessible. She was to come to the house at midday on the morrow and to ask not for Lady Hardy, but for him. He would stay by her while she was in the house and it would be quite easy for Lady Hardy to keep herself and her daughter out of the way. They could, for example, go out quietly to the dressmakers in the closed car, for many little things about the mourning still remained to be seen to.

§ 8

Miss Martin Leeds arrived punctually, but the doctor was well ahead of his time and ready to receive her. She was ushered into the drawing-room where he awaited her. As she came forward the doctor first perceived that she had a very sad and handsome face, the face of a sensitive youth rather than the face of a woman. She had fine grey eyes under very fine brows ; they were eyes that at other times might have laughed very agreeably, but which were now full of an un-restrained sadness. Her brown hair was very untidy and parted at the side like a man's. Then he noted that she seemed to be very untidily dressed as if she was that rare and, to him, very offensive thing, a woman careless of her beauty. She was short in proportion to her broad figure and her broad forehead.

" You are Dr. Martineau ? " she said. " He talked of you." As she spoke her glance went from him to the pictures that stood about the room. She walked up to the painting and stood in front of it with her distressed gaze wandering about her. " Horrible ! " she said. " Absolutely horrible ! . . . Did *she* do this ? "

Her question disconcerted the doctor very much. " You mean Lady Hardy ? " he asked. " She doesn't paint."

" No, no. I mean, did she get all these things together ? "

" Naturally," said Dr. Martineau.

" None of them are a bit like him. They are like blows aimed at his memory. Not one has his life in it. How could she do it ? Look at that idiot statuette ! . . . He was extraordinarily difficult to get. I have burnt every photo-graph I had of him. For fear that this would happen ; that he would go stiff and formal—just as you have got him there. I have been trying to sketch him almost all the time since he died. But I can't get him back. He's gone."

She turned to the doctor again. She spoke to him, not as if she expected him to understand her, but because she had to say these things which burthened her mind to some one. " I have done hundreds of sketches. My room is littered with them. When you turn them over he seems to be lurking among them. But not one of them is like him."

She was trying to express something beyond her power. " It is as if some one had suddenly turned out the light."

She followed the doctor upstairs. " This was his study," the doctor explained.

" I know it. I came here once," she said.

They entered the big bedroom in which the coffined body lay. Dr. Martineau, struck by a sudden memory, glanced nervously at the desk, but some one had made it quite tidy and the portrait of Miss Grammont had disappeared. Miss Leeds walked straight across to the coffin and stood looking down on the waxen inexpressive dignity of the dead. Sir Richmond's brows and nose had become sharper and more clear-cut than they had ever been in life and his lips had set into a faint inane smile. She stood quite still for a long time. At length she sighed deeply.

She spoke, a little as though she thought aloud, a little as though she talked at that silent presence in the coffin. " I think he loved," she said. " Sometimes I think he loved me. But it is hard to tell. He was kind. He could be intensely kind and yet he didn't seem to care for you. He could be intensely selfish and yet he certainly did not care for himself. . . . Anyhow, I loved *him*. . . . There is nothing left in me now to love any one else—for ever. . . ."

She put her hands behind her back and looked at the dead man with her head a little on one side. " Too kind," she said very softly.

" There was a sort of dishonesty in his kindness. He would not let you have the bitter truth. He would not say he did not love you. . . .

" He was too kind to life ever to call it the foolish thing it is. He took it seriously because it takes itself seriously. He worked for it and killed himself with work for it. . . ."

She turned to Dr. Martineau and her face was streaming with tears. " And life, you know, isn't to be taken seriously. It is a joke—a bad joke—made by some cruel little god who has caught a neglected planet. . . . Like torturing a stray cat. . . . But he took it seriously and he gave up his life for it.

" There was much happiness he might have had. He was very capable of happiness. But he never seemed happy. This work of his came before it. He overworked and fretted our happiness away. He sacrificed his happiness and mine."

She held out her hands towards the doctor. " What am I to do now with the rest of my life? Who is there to laugh with me now and jest?

" I don't complain of him. I don't blame him. He did his best—to be kind. . . .

" But all my days now I shall mourn for him and long for him. . . ."

She turned back to the coffin. Suddenly she lost every

vestige of self control. She sank down on her knees beside the trestle. " Why have you left me ? " she cried.

" Oh ! Speak to me, my darling ! Speak to me, *I tell you !* Speak to me ! "

It was a storm of passion, monstrously childish and dreadful. She beat her hands upon the coffin. She wept loudly and fiercely as a child does. . . .

Dr. Martineau drifted feebly to the window.

He wished he had locked the door. The servants might hear and wonder what it was all about.

Always he had feared love for the cruel thing it was, but now it seemed to him for the first time that he realised its monstrous cruelty.

GOD THE INVISIBLE KING

"Nec erit alia lex Romæ, alia Athenis, alia nunc, alia posthac; sed et omnes gentes et omni tempore una lex, et sempiterna et immortalis continebit, unusque erit communis quasi magister et Imperator omnium DEUS."

CICERO, DE REPUBLICA.

PREFACE

THIS book sets out as forcibly and exactly as possible the religious belief of the writer. That belief is not orthodox Christianity ; it is not, indeed, Christianity at all ; its core, nevertheless, is a belief in a personal and intimate God. There is nothing in its statements that need shock or offend any one who is prepared for the expression of a faith different from and perhaps in several particulars opposed to his own. The writer will be found to be sympathetic with all sincere religious feeling. Nevertheless it is well to prepare the prospective reader for statements that may jar harshly against deeply rooted mental habits. It is well to warn him at the outset that the departure from accepted beliefs is here no vague scepticism, but a quite sharply defined objection to dogmas very widely revered. Let the writer state the most probable occasion of trouble forthwith. An issue upon which this book will be found particularly uncompromising is the dogma of the Trinity. The writer is of opinion that the Council of Nicæa, which forcibly crystallised the controversies of two centuries and formulated the creed upon which all the existing Christian churches are based, was one of the most disastrous and one of the least venerable of all religious gatherings, and he holds that the Alexandrine speculations which were then conclusively imposed upon Christianity merit only disrespectful attention at the present time. There you have a chief possibility of offence. He is quite unable to pretend any awe for what he considers the spiritual monstrosities established by that undignified gathering. He makes no attempt to be obscure or propitiatory in this connection. He criticises the creeds explicitly and frankly, because he believes it is particularly necessary to clear them out of the way of those who are seeking religious consolation at this present time of exceptional religious need. He does little to conceal his indignation at the rôle played by these dogmas in obscuring, perverting and preventing the religious life of mankind. After this warning such readers from among the various Christian churches and sects as are accessible to storms of theological fear or passion, to whom the Trinity is an ineffable mystery and the name of God almost unspeakably awful, read on at their own risk. This is a religious book written by a believer, but so far as their beliefs and religion go it may seem to them more sceptical and more antagonistic than blank atheism. That the writer cannot tell. He is not simply denying their God. He is declaring that there is a living God, different altogether from that Triune God and nearer to the heart of man. The spirit of this book is like that of a missionary who would only too gladly overthrow and smash some Polynesian divinity of shark's teeth and painted wood and mother-of-pearl. To the writer such elaborations as " begotten of the Father before all worlds " are no better than intellectual shark's teeth and oyster shells. His purpose, like the purpose of that missionary, is not primarily to shock and insult ; but he is zealous to liberate, and he is impatient with a reverence that stands between man and God. He gives this fair warning and proceeds with his matter.

His matter is modern religion as he sees it. It is only incidentally and because it is unavoidable that he attacks doctrinal Christianity.

In *First and Last Things* he has stated his convictions upon certain general ideas of life and thought as clearly as he could. All of philosophy, all of metaphysics that is, seems to him to be a discussion of the relations of class and individual. The antagonism of the Nominalist and the Realist, the opposition of the One and the Many, the contrast of the Ideal and the Actual, all these oppositions express a certain structural and essential duality in the activity of the human mind. From an imperfect recognition of that duality ensue great masses of misconception. That was the substance of *First and Last Things*. In this present book there is no further attack on philosophical or metaphysical questions. Here we work at a less fundamental level and deal with religious feeling and religious ideas. But just as the writer was inclined to attribute a whole world of disputation and inexactitudes to confused thinking about the exact value of classes and terms, so here he is disposed to think that interminable controversies and conflicts arise out of a confusion of intention due to a double meaning of the word " God " ; that the word " God " conveys not one idea or set of ideas, but several essentially different ideas, incompatible one with another, and falling mainly into one or other of two divergent groups ; and that people slip carelessly from one to the other of these groups of ideas and so get into ultimately inextricable confusions.

The writer believes that the centuries of fluid religious thought that preceded the violent ultimate crystallisation of Nicæa was essentially a struggle—obscured, of course, by many complexities—to reconcile and get into a relationship these two separate main series of God-ideas.

Putting the leading idea of this book very roughly, these two antagonistic typical conceptions of God may be best contrasted by speaking of one of them as God-as-Nature or the Creator, and of the other as God-as-Christ or the Redeemer. One is the great Outward God ; the other is the Inmost God. The first idea was perhaps developed most highly and completely in the God of Spinoza. It is a conception of God tending to pantheism, to an idea of a comprehensive God as ruling with justice rather than affection, to a conception of aloofness and awe-striking worshipfulness. The second idea, which is opposed to this idea of an absolute God, is the God of the human heart. The writer would suggest that the great outline of the theological struggle of that phase of civilisation and world unity which produced Christianity, was a persistent but unsuccessful attempt to get these two different ideas of God into one focus. It was an attempt to make the God of Nature accessible and the God of the Heart invincible, to bring the former into a conception of love and to vest the latter with the beauty of stars and flowers and the dignity of inexorable justice. There could be no finer metaphor for such a correlation than Fatherhood and Sonship. But the trouble is that it seems impossible to most people to continue to regard the relations of the Father to the Son as being simply a mystical metaphor. Presently some materialistic bias swings them in a moment of intellectual carelessness back to the idea of sexual filiation.

And it may further be suggested that the extreme aloofness and inhumanity, which is logically necessary in the idea of a Creator God, of an Infinite God, was the reason, so to speak, for the invention of a Holy Spirit, as something proceeding from— as something bridging—the great gulf, a Comforter, a mediator, descending into the sphere of the human understanding. That, and the suggestive influence of the Egyptian Trinity that was then being worshipped at the Serapeum, and which had saturated the thought of Alexandria with the conception of a trinity in unity, are probably the realities that account for the Third Person of the Christian Trinity. At any rate the present writer believes that the discussions that shaped the Christian theology we know were dominated by such natural and fundamental thoughts. These discussions were, of course, complicated from the outset ; and particularly were they complicated by the identification of the man Jesus with the theological Christ, by materialistic expectations of his second coming, by materialistic inventions about his " miraculous " begetting, and by the morbid speculations about virginity and the like that arose out of such grossness. They were still further complicated by the idea of the textual inspiration of the scriptures, which presently swamped though in texual interpretation. That swamping came very early in the development of Christianity. The writer of St. John's gospel appears still to be thinking with a considerable freedom, but Origen is already hopelessly in the net of the texts. The writer of St. John's gospel was a free man, but Origen was a superstitious man. He was emasculated mentally as well as bodily through his bibliolatry. He quotes ; his predecessor thinks.

But the writer throws out these guesses at the probable intentions of early Christian thought in passing. His business here is the definition of a position. The writer's position here in this book is, firstly, complete Agnosticism in the matter of God the Creator, and secondly, entire faith in the matter of God the Redeemer. That, so to speak, is the key of his book.

He cannot bring the two ideas under the same term God. He used the word God therefore for the God in our hearts only, and he uses the term the Veiled Being for the ultimate mysteries of the universe, and he declares that we do not know and perhaps cannot know in any comprehensible terms, the relation of the Veiled Being to that living reality in our lives who is, in his terminology, the true God. Speaking from the point of view of practical religion, he is restricting and defining the word God, as meaning only the personal God of mankind, he is restricting it so as to exclude all cosmogony and ideas of providence from our religious thought and leave nothing but the essentials of the religious life.

Many people, whom one would class as rather liberal Christians of an Arian or Arminian complexion, may find the larger part of this book acceptable to them if they will read "the Christ God" where the writer has written "God." They will then differ from him upon little more than the question whether there is an essential identity in aim and quality between the Christ God and the Veiled Being who answer to their Creator God. This the orthodox post-Nicæan Christians assert, and many pre-Nicæans and many heretics (as the Cathars) contradicted with its exact contrary. The Cathars, Paulicians, Albigenes and so on held, with the Manichæans, that the God of Nature, God the Father, was evil. The Christ God was his antagonist. This was the idea of the poet Shelley. And, passing beyond Christian theology altogether, a clue can still be found to many problems in comparative theology in this distinction between the Being of Nature (*cf.* Kant's "starry vault above") and the God of the heart (Kant's "moral law within"). The idea of an antagonism seems to have been cardinal in the thought of the Essenes and the Orphic cult and in the Persian dualism. So, too, Buddhism seems to be "antagonistic." On the other hand, the Moslem teaching and modern Judaism seem absolutely to combine and identify the two ; God the Creator is altogether and without distinction also God the King of Mankind. Christianity stands somewhere between such complete identification and complete antagonism. It admits a difference in attitude between Father and Son in its distinction between the Old Dispensation (of the Old Testament) and the New. Every possible change is rung in the great religions of the world between identification, complete separation, equality, and disproportion of these Beings ; but it will be found that these two ideas are, so to speak, the basal elements of all theology in the world. The writer is chary of assertion or denial in these matters. He believes that they are speculations not at all necessary to salvation. He believes that men may differ profoundly in their opinions upon these points and still be in perfect agreement upon the essentials of religion. The reality of religion he believes deals wholly and exclusively with the God of the

Heart. He declares as his own opinion, as and the opinion which seems most expressive of modern thought, that there is no reason to suppose the Veiled Being either benevolent or malignant towards men. But if the reader believes that God is Almighty and every way Infinite the practical outcome is not very different. For the purposes of human relationship it is impossible to deny that God *presents himself as finite*, as struggling and taking a part against evil. The writer believes that these dogmas of relationship are not merely extraneous to religion, but an impediment to religion. His aim in this book is to give a statement of religion which is no longer entangled in such speculations and disputes.

CONTENTS

CHAPTER ONE

THE COSMOGONY OF MODERN RELIGION

§ 1

Modern Religion has no Founder

PERHAPS all religions, unless the flaming onset of Moham-medanism be an exception, have dawned imperceptibly upon the world. A little while ago and the thing was not ; and then suddenly it has been found in existence, and already in a state of diffusion. People have begun to hear of the new belief first here and then there. It is interesting, for example, to trace how Christianity drifted into the conscious-ness of the Roman world. But when a religion has been in-terrogated it has always had hitherto a tale of beginnings, the name, and story of a founder. The renascent religion that is now taking shape, it seems, had no founder ; it points to no origins. It is the Truth, its believers declare ; it has always been here ; it has always been visible to those that had eyes to see. It is perhaps plainer than it was and to more people—that is all.

It is as if it still did not realise its own difference. Many of those who hold it still think of it as if it were a kind of Chris-tianity. Some, catching at a phrase of Huxley's, speak of it as Christianity without Theology. They do not know the creed they are carrying. It has, as a matter of fact, a very fine and subtle theology, flatly opposed to any belief that could, except by great stretching of charity and the imagination, be called Christianity. One might find, perhaps, a parallelism with the system ascribed to some Gnostics, but that is far more probably an accidental rather than a sympathetic coincidence. Of that the reader shall presently have an opportunity of judging.

This indefiniteness of statement and relationship is probably only the opening phase of the new faith. Christianity also began with an extreme neglect of definition. It was not at first anything more than a sect of Judaism. It was only after three centuries, amidst the uproar and emotions of the Council of Nicæa, when the more enthusiastic Trinitarians stuffed their fingers in their ears in affected horror at the argu-ments of old Arius, that the cardinal mystery of the Trinity was established as the essential fact of Christianity. Through-out those three centuries, the centuries of its greatest achieve-ments and noblest martyrdoms, Christianity had not defined its God. And even to-day it has to be noted that a large majority of those who possess and repeat the Christian creeds have come into the practice so insensibly from unthinking childhood that only in the slightest way do they realise the nature of the statements to which they subscribe. They will speak and think of both Christ and God in ways flatly incompatible with the doctrine of the Triune deity upon which, theoretically, the entire fabric of all the churches rests. They will show themselves as frankly Arians as though that damnable heresy had not been washed out of the world for ever after centuries of persecution in torrents of blood. But whatever the present state of Christendom in these matters may be, there can be no doubt of the enormous pains taken in the past to give Christian beliefs the exactest, least ambiguous statement possible. Christianity knew itself clearly for what it was in its maturity, whatever the indecisions of its childhood or the confusions of its decay. The renascent religion that one finds now, a thing active and sufficient in many minds, has still scarcely come to self-consciousness. But it is so coming, and this present book is very largely an attempt to state the shape it is assuming and to compare it with the beliefs and imperatives and usages of the various Christian, pseudo-Christian, philosophical, and agnostic cults amidst which it has appeared.

The writer's sympathies and convictions are entirely with this that he speaks of as renascent or modern religion ; he is neither Atheist nor Buddhist nor Mohammedan nor Christian. He will make no pretence, therefore, to impartiality and detachment. He will do his best to be as fair as possible and as candid as possible, but the reader must reckon with this bias. He has found this faith growing up in himself ; he has found it, or something very difficult to distinguish from it, growing independently in the minds of men and women he has met. They have been people of very various origins : English, Americans, Bengalis, Russians, French, people brought up in a " Catholic atmosphere," Positivists, Baptists, Sikhs, Mohammedans. Their diversity of source is as remarkable as their convergence of tendency. A miscellany of minds thinking upon parallel lines has come out to the same light. The new teaching is also traceable in many professedly Christian religious books, and it is to be heard from Christian pulpits. The phase of definition is manifestly at hand.

§ 2

Modern Religion has a Finite God

Perhaps the most fundamental difference between this new faith and any recognised form of Christianity is that, knowingly or unknowingly, it worships *a finite God*. Directly the believer is fairly confronted with the plain questions of the case, the vague identifications that are still care-

lessly made with one or all of the persons of the Trinity dissolve away. He will admit that his God is neither all-wise
nor all-powerful, nor omnipresent ; that he is neither the maker
of heaven nor earth, and that he has little to identify him with
that hereditary God of the Jews who became the " Father " in
the Christian system. On the other hand he will assert that
his God is a god of salvation, that he is a spirit, a person,
a strongly marked and knowable personality, loving, inspiring,
and lovable, who exists or strives to exist in every human soul.
He will be much less certain in his denials that his God has a
close resemblance to the Pauline (as distinguished from the
Trinitarian) " Christ." . . .

The modern religious man will almost certainly profess a
kind of universalism ; he will assert that whensoever men
have called upon any God and have found fellowship and
comfort and courage and that sense of God within them, that
inner light which is the quintessence of the religious experience, it was the True God that answered them. For the True
God is a generous God, not a jealous God ; the very antithesis
of that bickering monopolist who " will have none other gods
but Me " ; and when a human heart cries out—to what name
it matters not—for a larger spirit and a stronger help than the
visible things of life can give, straightway the nameless Helper
is with it and the God of Man answers to the call. The True
God has no scorn nor hate for those who have accepted the
many-handed symbols of the Hindu or the lacquered idols of
China. Where there is faith, where there is need, there is the
True God ready to clasp the hands that stretch out seeking
for him into the darkness behind the ivory and gold.

The fact that God is *finite* is one upon which those who think
clearly among the new believers are very insistent. He is,
above everything else, a personality, and to be a personality
is to have characteristics, to be limited by characteristics ;
he is a Being, not us but dealing with us and through us, he has
an aim and that means he has a past and future, he is within
time and not outside it. And they point out that this is really
what every one who prays sincerely to God or gets help from
God, feels and believes. Our practice with God is better
than our theory. None of us really pray to that fantastic,
unqualified *danse à trois*, the Trinity, which the wranglings
and disputes of the worthies of Alexandria and Syria declared
to be God. We pray to one single understanding person.
But so far the tactics of those Trinitarians at Nicæa, who stuck
their fingers in their ears, have prevailed in this world ; this
was no matter for discussion, they declared ; it was a Holy
Mystery full of magical terror and few religious people have
thought it worth while to revive these terrors by a definite
contradiction. The truly religious have been content to
lapse quietly into the comparative sanity of an unformulated
Arianism, they have left it to the scoffing Atheist to mock at the

patent absurdities of the official creed. But one magnificent protest against this theological fantasy must have been the work of a sincerely religious man, the cold, superb humour of that burlesque creed, ascribed—at first no doubt facetiously and then quite seriously—to Saint Athanasius the Great, which, by an irony far beyond its original intention, has become at last the accepted creed of the church.

The long truce in the criticism of Trinitarian theology is drawing to its end. It is when men most urgently need God that they become least patient with foolish presentations and dogmas. The new believers are very definitely set upon a thorough analysis of the nature and growth of the Christian creeds and ideas. There has grown up a practice of assuming that, when God is spoken of, the Hebrew-Christian God of Nicæa is meant. But that God trails with him a thousand misconceptions and bad associations ; his alleged infinite nature, his jealousy, his strange preferences, his vindictive Old Testament past. These things do not even make a caricature of the True God ; they compose an altogether different and antagonistic figure.

It is a very childish and unphilosophical set of impulses that has led the theologians of nearly every faith to claim infinite qualities for their deity. One has to remember the poorness of the mental and moral quality of the churchmen of the third, fourth, and fifth centuries who saddled Christendom with its characteristic dogmas, and the extreme poverty and confusion of the circle of ideas within which they thought. Many of these makers of Christianity, like Saint Ambrose of Milan (who had even to be baptized after his election to his bishopric), had been pitchforked into the church from civil life ; they lived in a time of pitiless factions and personal feuds ; they had to conduct their disputations amidst the struggles of would-be emperors ; court eunuchs and favourites swayed their counsels, and popular rioting clinched their decisions. There was less freedom of discussion then in the Christian world than there is at present (1916) in Belgium, and the whole audience of educated opinion by which a theory could be judged did not equal, either in numbers or accuracy of information, the present population of Constantinople. To these conditions we owe the claim that the Christian God is a magic god, very great medicine in battle, " *in hoc signo vinces*," and the argument so natural to the minds of those days and so absurd to ours, that since he had *all* power, *all* knowledge, and existed for ever and ever, it was no use whatever to set up any other god against him. . . .

By the fifth century Christianity had adopted as its fundamental belief, without which every one was to be " damned everlastingly," a conception of God and of Christ's relation to God, of which even by the Christian account of his teaching, Jesus was either totally unaware or so negligent and careless of the future comfort of his disciples as scarcely to make mention. The doctrine of the Trinity, so far as the relationship of the Third Person goes, hangs almost entirely upon one ambiguous and disputed utterance in St. John's gospel (xv. 26). Most of the teachings of Christian orthodoxy resolve themselves to the attentive student into assertions of the nature of contradiction and repartee. Some one floats an opinion in some matter that has been hitherto vague, in regard, for example, to the sonship of Christ or to the method of his birth. The new opinion arouses the hostility and alarm of minds unaccustomed to so definite a statement, and in the zeal of their recoil they fly to a contrary proposition. The Christians would neither admit that they worshipped more gods than one because of the Greeks, nor deny the divinity of Christ because of the Jews. They dreaded to be polytheistic ; equally did they dread the least apparent detraction from the power and importance of their Saviour. They were forced into the theory of the Trinity by the necessity of those contrary assertions, and they had to make it a mystery protected by curses to save it from a *reductio ad absurdum*. The entire history of the growth of the Christian doctrine in those disordered early centuries is a history of theology by committee ; a history of furious wranglings, of hasty compromises, and still more hasty attempts to clinch matters by anathema. When the muddle was at its very worst, the church was confronted by enormous political opportunities. In order that it should seize these, one chief thing appeared imperative : doctrinal uniformity. The emperor himself, albeit unbaptized and very ignorant of Greek, came and seated himself in the midst of Christian thought upon a golden throne. At the end of it all Eusebius, that supreme Trimmer, was prepared to damn everlastingly all those who doubted that consubstantiality he himself had doubted at the beginning of the conference. It is quite clear that Constantine did not care who was damned or for what period, so long as the Christians ceased to wrangle among themselves. The practical unanimity of Nicæa was secured by threats, and then, turning upon the victors, he sought by threats to restore Arius to communion. The imperial aim was a common faith to unite the empire. The crushing out of the Arians and of the Paulicians and such-like heretics, and more particularly the systematic destruction by the orthodox of all heretical writings, had about it none of that quality of honest conviction which comes to those who have a real knowledge of God ; it was a bawling down of dissensions that, left to work themselves out, would have spoiled good business ; it was the fist of Nicolas of Myra over again, except that after the days of Ambrose the sword of the executioner and the fires of the book-burner were added to the weapon of the human voice. Priscillian was the first human sacrifice formally offered up under these improved conditions to the greater glory of the reinforced Trinity. Thereafter, the blood of the heretics was the cement of Christian unity.

It is with these things in mind that those who profess the new faith are becoming so markedly anxious to distinguish God from the Trinitarian's deity. At present if any one who has left the Christian communion declares himself a believer in God, priest and parson swell with self-complacency. There is no reason why they should do so. That many of us have gone from them and found God is no concern of theirs. It is not that we who went out into the wilderness which we thought to be a desert, away from their creeds and dogmas, have turned back and are returning. It is that we have gone on still further, and are beyond that desolation. Never more shall we return to those who gather under the cross. By faith we disbelieved and denied. By faith we said of that stuffed scarecrow of divinity, that incoherent accumulation of antique theological notions, the Nicene deity, " This is certainly no God." And by faith we have found God. . . .

§ 3

The Infinite Being is not God

There has always been a demand upon the theological teacher that he should supply a cosmogony. It has always been an effective propagandist thing to say : " *Our* God made the whole universe. Don't you think that it would be wise to abandon *your* deity, who did not, as you admit, do anything of the sort ? "

The attentive reader of the lives of the Saints will find that this style of argument did in the past bring many tribes and nations into the Christian fold. It was second only to the claim of magic advantages, demonstrated by a free use of miracles. Only one great religious system, the Buddhist, seems to have resisted the temptation to secure for its divinity the honour and title of Creator. Modern religion is like Buddhism in that respect. It offers no theory whatever about the origin of the universe. It does not reach behind the appearances of space and time. It sees only a featureless presumption in that playing with superlatives which has entertained so many minds from Plotinus to the Hegelians with the delusion that such negative terms as the Absolute or the Unconditioned can assert anything at all. At the back of all known things there is an impenetrable curtain ; the ultimate of existence is a Veiled Being, which seems to know nothing of life or death or good or ill. Of that Being, whether it is simple or complex or divine, we know nothing ; to us it is no more than the limit of understanding, the unknown beyond.

It may be of practically limitless intricacy and possibility. The new religion does not pretend that the God of its life is that Being, or that he has any relation of control or association with that Being.   It does not even assert that God knows all or much more than we do about that ultimate Being.

For us life is a matter of our personalities in space and time. Human analysis probing with philosophy and science towards the Veiled Being reveals nothing of God, reveals space and time only as necessary forms of consciousness, glimpses a dance of atoms, of whirls in the ether.   Some day in the end-less future there may be a knowledge, an understanding of relationship, a power and courage that will pierce into those black wrappings.   To that it may be our God, the Captain of Mankind, will take us.

That now is a mere speculation.   The veil of the unknown is set with the stars ;   its outer texture is ether and atom and crystal.   The Veiled Being, enigmatical and incomprehensible, broods over the mirror upon which the busy shapes of life are moving.   It is as if it waited in a great stillness.   Our lives do not deal with it, and cannot deal with it.   It may be that they may never be able to deal with it.

§ 4

The Life Force is not God

So it is that comprehensive setting of the universe presents itself to the modern mind.   It is altogether outside good and evil and love and hate.   It is outside God, who is love and goodness.   And coming out of this Veiled Being, proceeding out of it in a manner altogether inconceivable, is another lesser being, an impulse thrusting through matter and clothing itself in continually changing material forms, the maker of our world, Life, the Will to Be.   It comes out of that inscrutable being as a wave comes rolling to us from beyond the horizon. It is as it were a great wave rushing through matter and possessed by a spirit.   It is a breeding, fighting thing ;   it pants through the jungle track as the tiger and lifts itself towards heaven as the tree ;   it is the rabbit bolting for its life and the dove calling to her mate ;   it crawls, it flies, it dives, it lusts and devours, it pursues and eats itself in order to live still more eagerly and hastily ;   it is every living thing, of it are our passions and desires and fears.   And it is aware of itself not as a whole, but dispersedly as individual self-consciousness, starting out dispersedly from every one of the sentient creatures it has called into being.   They look out for their little moments, red-eyed and fierce, full of greed, full of the passions of acquisition and assimilation and repro-duction, submitting only to brief fellowships of defence or

aggression. They are beings of strain and conflict and competition. They are living substance still mingled painfully
with the dust. The forms in which this being clothes itself
bear thorns and fangs and claws, are soaked with poison and
bright with threats or allurements, prey slyly or openly on
one another, hold their own for a little while, breed savagely
and resentfully, and pass. . . .

This second Being men have called the Life Force, the Will
to Live, the Struggle for Existence. They have figured it too
as Mother Nature. We may speculate whether it is not what
the wiser among the Gnostics meant by the Demiurge, but
since the Christians destroyed all the Gnostic books,˙that must
remain a mere curious guess. We may speculate whether
this heat and haste and wrath of life about us is the Dark God
of the Manichees, the evil spirit of the sun-worshippers. But
in contemporary thought there is no conviction apparent that
this Demiurge is either good or evil ; it is conceived of as both
good and evil. If it gives all the pain and conflict of life, it
gives also the joy of the sunshine, the delight and hope of
youth, the pleasures. If it has elaborated a hundred thousand
sorts of parasite, it has also moulded the beautiful limbs of
man and woman ; it has shaped the slug and the flower. And
in it, as part of it, taking its rewards, responding to its goads,
struggling against the final abandonment to death, do we
all live, as the beasts live, glad, angry, sorry, revengeful,
hopeful, weary, disgusted, forgetful, lustful, happy, excited,
bored, in pain, mood after mood but always fearing death,
with no certainty and no coherence within us, until we find
God. And God comes to us neither out of the stars nor out
of the pride of life, but as a still, small voice within.

§ 5

God is Within

God comes, we know not whence, into the conflict of life.
He works in men and through men. He is a spirit, a single
spirit and a single person ; he has begun and he will never
end. He is the immortal part and leader of mankind. He
has motives, he has characteristics, he has an aim. He is by
our poor scales of measurement boundless love, boundless
courage, boundless generosity. He is thought and a steadfast
will. He is our friend and brother and the light of the world.
That briefly is the belief of the modern mind with regard to
God. There is no very novel idea about this God, unless it
be the idea that he had a beginning. This is the God that
men have sought and found in all ages, as God or as the
Messiah or the Saviour. The finding of him is salvation from
the purposelessness of life. The new religion has but dis-

entangled the idea of him from the absolutes and infinities and mysteries of the Christian theologians ; from mythological virgin births and the cosmogonies and intellectual pretentiousness of a vanished age.

Modern religion appeals to no revelation, no authoritative teaching, no mystery. The statement it makes is, it declares, a mere statement of what we may all perceive and experience. We all live in the storm of life, we all find our understandings limited by the Veiled Being ; if we seek salvation and search within for God, presently we find him. All this is in the nature of things. If every one who perceives and states it were to be instantly killed and blotted out, presently other people would find their way to the same conclusions ; and so on again and again. To this all true religion, casting aside its hulls of misconception, must ultimately come. To it indeed much religion is already coming. Christian thought struggles towards it, with the millstones of Syrian theology and an outrageous mythology of incarnation and resurrection about its neck. When at last our present bench of bishops join the early fathers of the church in heaven there will be, I fear, a note of reproach in their greeting of the ingenious person who saddled them with *omnipotens*. Still more disastrous for them has been the virgin birth, with the terrible fascination of its detail for unpoetic minds. How rich is the literature of authoritative Christianity with decisions upon the continuing virginity of Mary and the virginity of Joseph—ideas that first arose in Arabia as a Moslem gloss upon Christianity—and how little have these peepings and pryings to do with the needs of the heart and the finding of God !

Within the last few years there have been a score or so of such volumes as that recently compiled by Dr. Foakes Jackson, entitled *The Faith and the War*, a volume in which the curious reader may contemplate deans and canons, divines and church dignitaries, men intelligent and inquiring and religiously disposed, all lying like overladen camels, panting under this load of obsolete theological responsibility, groaning great articles, outside the needle's eye that leads to God.

§ 6

The Coming of God

Modern religion bases its knowledge of God and its account of God entirely upon experience. It has encountered God. It does not argue about God ; it relates without any of those wrappings of awe and reverence that fold so necessarily about imposture, it relates as one tells of a friend and his assistance, of a happy adventure, of a beautiful thing found and picked up by the wayside.

So far as its psychological phases go the new account of personal salvation tallies very closely with the account of " conversion " as it is given by other religions. It has little to tell that is not already familiar to the reader of William James's *Varieties of Religious Experience*. It describes an initial state of distress with the aimlessness and cruelties of life, and particularly with the futility of the individual life, a state of helpless self-disgust, of inability to form any satisfactory plan of living. This is the common prelude known to many sorts of Christians as " conviction of sin " ; it is, at any rate, a conviction of hopeless confusion. . . . Then in some way the idea of God comes into the distressed mind, at first simply as an idea, without substance or belief. It is read about or it is remembered ; it is expounded by some teacher or some happy convert. In the case of all those of the new faith with whose personal experience I have any intimacy, the idea of God has remained for some time simply as an idea floating about in a mind still dissatisfied. God is not believed in, but it is realised that if there were such a being he would supply the needed consolation and direction, his continuing purpose would knit together the scattered effort of life, his immortality would take the sting from death. Under this realisation the idea is pursued and elaborated. For a time there is a curious resistance to the suggestion that God is truly a person ; he is spoken of preferably by such phrases as the Purpose in Things, as the Racial Consciousness, as the Collective Mind.

I believe that the resistance in so many contemporary minds to the idea of God as a person is due very largely to the enormous prejudice against divine personality created by the absurdities of the Christian teaching and the habitual monopoly of the Christian idea. The picture of Christ as the Good Shepherd thrusts itself before minds accustomed to the idea that they are lambs. The cross in the twilight bars the way. It is a novelty and an enormous relief to such people to realise that one may think of God without being committed to think of either the Father, the Son, or the Holy Ghost, or of all of them at once. That freedom had not seemed possible to them. They had been hypnotised and obsessed by the idea that the Christian God is the only thinkable God. They had heard so much about that God and so little of any other. With that release their minds become, as it were, nascent and ready for the coming of God.

Then suddenly, in a little while, in his own time, God comes. This cardinal experience is an undoubting, immediate sense of God. It is the attainment of an absolute certainty that one is not alone in oneself. It is as if one was touched at every point by a being akin to oneself, sympathetic, beyond measure wiser, steadfast and pure in aim. It is completer and more intimate, but it is like standing side by side with and touching some one that we love very dearly and trust completely. It is as if this being bridged a thousand misunderstandings and brought us into fellowship with a great multitude of other people. . . .

"Closer he is than breathing, and nearer than hands and feet."

The moment may come while we are alone in the darkness, under the stars, or while we walk by ourselves or in a crowd, or while we sit and muse. It may come upon the sinking ship or in the tumult of the battle. There is no saying when it may not come to us. . . . But after it has come our lives are changed. God is with us and there is no more doubt of God. Thereafter one goes about the world like one who was lonely and has found a lover, like one who was perplexed and has found a solution. One is assured that there is a Power that fights with us against the confusion and evil within us and without. There comes into the heart an essential and enduring happiness and courage.

There is but one God, there is but one true religious experience, but under a multitude of names, under veils and darknesses, God has in this manner come into countless lives. There is scarcely a faith, however mean and preposterous, that has not been a way to holiness. God who is himself finite, who himself struggles in his great effort from strength to strength, has no spite against error. Far beyond half-way he hastens to meet the purblind. But God is against the darkness in their eyes. The faith which is returning to men girds at veils and shadows, and would see God plainly. It has little respect for mysteries. It rends the veil of the temple in rags and tatters. It has no superstitious fear of this huge friendliness, of this great brother and leader of our little beings. To find God is but the beginning of wisdom, because then for all our days we have to learn his purpose with us and to live our lives with him.

CHAPTER TWO

HERESIES ; OR THE THINGS THAT GOD IS NOT

§ I

Heresies are Misconceptions of God

RELIGION is not a plant that has grown from one seed : it is like a lake that has been fed by countless springs. It is a great pool of living water, mingled from many sources and tainted with much impurity. It is synthetic in its nature ; it becomes simpler from original complexities ; the sediment subsides.

A life perfectly adjusted to its surroundings is a life without mentality ; no judgment is called for, no inhibition, no disturbance of the instinctive flow of perfect reactions. Such a life is bliss, or nirvana. It is unconsciousness below dreaming. Consciousness is discord evoking the will to adjust ; it is inseparable from need. At every need consciousness breaks into being. Imperfect adjustments, needs, are the rents and tatters in the smooth dark veil of being through which the light of consciousness shines—the light of consciousness and will of which God is the sun.

So that every need of human life, every disappointment and dissatisfaction and call for help and effort is a means whereby men may and do come to the realisation of God.

There is no cardinal need, there is no sort of experience in human life from which there does not come or has not come a contribution to men's religious ideas. At every challenge men have to put forth effort, feel doubt of adequacy, be thwarted, perceive the chill shadow of their mortality. At every challenge comes the possibility of help from without, the idea of eluding frustration, the aspiration towards immortality. It is possible to classify the appeals men make for God under the headings of their chief system of effort, their efforts to understand, their fear and their struggles for safety and happiness, the craving of their restlessness for peace, their angers against disorder and their desire for the avenger ; their sexual passions and perplexities.

Each of these great systems of needs and efforts brings its own sort of sediment into religion. Each, that is to say, has its own kind of heresy, its distinctive misapprehension of God. It is only in the synthesis and mutual correction of many divergent ideas that the idea of God grows clear. The effort to understand completely, for example, leads to the endless Heresies of Theory. Men trip over the inherent infirmities of the human mind. But in these days one does not argue

greatly about dogma. Almost every conceivable error about
unity, about personality, about time and quantity and genus
and species, about begetting and beginning and limitation and
similarity and every kink in the difficult mind of man, has
been thrust forward in some form of dogma. Beside the
errors of thought are the errors of emotion. Fear and feebleness go straight to the heresies that God is magic or that
God is Providence ; restless egotism at leisure and unchal-
lenged by urgent elementary realities breeds the heresies
of Mysticism ; anger and hate call for God's judgments,
and the stormy emotions of sex gave mankind the Phallic
God. Those who find themselves possessed by the new
Spirit in religion, realise very speedily the necessity of
clearing the mind of all these exaggerations, transferences,
and overflows of feeling. The search for divine truth is
like gold washing ; nothing is of any value until most has
been swept away.

§ 2

Heresies and Speculation

One sort of heresies stands apart from the rest. It is
infinitely the most various sort. It includes all those heresies
which result from wrong-headed mental elaboration, as distinguished from those which are the result of hasty and imperfect
apprehension, the heresies of the clever rather than the
heresies of the obtuse. The former are of endless variety
and complexity ; the latter are in comparison natural, simple
confusions. The former are the errors of the study, the
latter the superstitions that spring by the wayside, or are
brought down to us in our social structure out of a barbaric
past.

To the heresies of thought and speculation belong the
elaborate doctrine of the Trinity, dogmas about God's absolute
qualities, such odd deductions as the accepted Christian
teachings about the virginity of Mary and Joseph and the like.
All these things are parts of orthodox Christianity. Yet none
of them did Christ, even by the Christian account, expound
or recommend. He treated them as negligible. It was left
for the Alexandrians, for Alexander, for little, red-haired,
busy, wire-pulling Athanasius, to find out exactly what their
Master was driving at, three centuries after their Master was
dead. . . .

Men still sit at little desks remote from God or life, and rack
their inadequate brains to meet fancied difficulties and state
unnecessary perfections. They seek God by logic, ignoring
the marginal errors that creep into every syllogism. Their
conceit blinds them to the limitations upon their thinking.

They weave spider-like webs of muddle and disputation across
the path by which men come to God. It would not matter
very much if it were not that simpler souls are caught in these
webs. Every great religious system in the world is choked by
such webs ; each system has its own. Of all the blood-
stained, tangled heresies which make up doctrinal Christianity
and imprison the mind of the western world to-day, not one
seems to have been known to the nominal founder of Christianity. Jesus Christ never certainly claimed to be the
Messiah ; never spoke clearly of the Trinity ; was vague
upon the scheme of salvation and the significance of his
martyrdom. We are asked to suppose that he left his apostles
without instructions that were necessary to their eternal
happiness, that he could give them the Lord's Prayer, but
leave them to guess at the all-important Creed,[1] and that the
Church staggered along blindly, putting its foot in and out of
damnation, until the " experts " of Nicæa, that " garland of
priests," marshalled by Constantine's officials, came to its
rescue. . . . From the conversion of Paul onward, the heresies
of the intellect multiplied about Christ's memory and hid
him from the sight of men. We are no longer clear about
the doctrine he taught nor about the things he said and
did. . . .

We are all so weary of this theology of the Christians, we
are all at heart so sceptical about their Triune God, that it is
needless here to spend any time or space upon the twenty
thousand different formulæ in which the orthodox have
attempted to believe in something of the sort. There are
several useful encyclopædias of sects and heresies, compact
but still bulky, to which the curious may go. There are ten
thousand different expositions of orthodoxy. No one who
really seeks God thinks of the Trinity, either the Trinity of
the Trinitarian or the Trinity of the Sabellian or the Trinity
of the Arian, any more than one thinks of those theories made
stone, those gods with three heads and seven hands, who sit
on lotus leaves and flourish lingams and what not, in the
temples of India. Let us leave, therefore, these morbid
elaborations of the human intelligence to drift to limbo,
and come rather to the natural heresies that spring from
fundamental weaknesses of the human character, and
which are common to all religions. Against these it is
necessary to keep constant watch. They return very
insidiously.

---

[1] Even the " Apostles' Creed " is not traceable earlier than the fourth century. It is
manifestly an old, patched formulary. Rufinus explains that it was not written down for
a long time, but transmitted orally, kept secret, and used as a sort of password among the
elect.

§ 3

God is not Magic

One of the most universal of these natural misconceptions of God is to consider him as something magic serving the ends of men.

It is not easy for us to grasp at first the full meaning of giving our souls to God. The missionary and teacher of any creed is all too apt to hawk God for what he will fetch ; he is greedy for the poor triumph of acquiescence ; and so it comes about that many people who have been led to believe themselves religious, are in reality still keeping back their own souls and trying to use God for their own purposes. God is nothing more for them as yet than a magnificent fetish. They did not really want him, but they have heard that he is potent stuff ; their unripe souls think to make use of him. They call upon his name, they do certain things that are supposed to be peculiarly influential with him, such as saying prayers and repeating gross praises of him, or reading in a blind, industrious way that strange miscellany of Jewish and early Christian literature, the Bible, and such-like mental mortification, or making the Sabbath dull and uncomfortable. In return for these fetishistic propitiations God is supposed to interfere with the normal course of causation in their favour. He becomes a celestial log-roller. He remedies unfavourable accidents, cures petty ailments, contrives unexpected gifts of medicine, money, or the like, he averts bankruptcies, arranges profitable transactions, and does a thousand such services for his little clique of faithful people. The pious are represented as being constantly delighted by these little surprises, these bouquets and chocolate boxes from the divinity. Or contrariwise he contrives spiteful turns for those who fail in their religious attentions. He murders Sabbath-breaking children, or disorganises the careful business schemes of the ungodly. He is represented as going Sabbath-breakering on Sunday morning as a Staffordshire worker goes ratting. Ordinary, everyday Christianity is saturated with this fetishistic conception of God. It may be disowned in *The Hibbert Journal* but it is unblushingly advocated in the parish magazine. It is an idea taken over by Christianity with the rest of the qualities of the Hebrew God. It is natural enough in minds so self-centred that their recognition of weakness and need brings with it no real self-surrender, but it is entirely inconsistent with the modern conception of the True God.

There has dropped upon the table as I write a modest periodical called *The Northern British Israel Review*, illustrated with portraits of various clergymen of the Church of England, and of ladies and gentlemen who belong to the little school of thought which this magazine represents ; it is, I should judge, a sub-sect entirely within the Established Church of England, that is to say within the Anglican communion of the Trinitarian Christians. It contains among other papers a very entertaining summary by a gentleman entitled—I cite the unusual title-page of the periodical—" Landseer Mackenzie, Esq.," of the views of Isaiah, Ezekiel, and Obadiah upon the Kaiser Wilhelm. They are distinctly hostile views. Mr. Landseer Mackenzie discourses not only upon these anticipatory condemnations but also upon the relations of the weather to this war. He is convinced quite simply and honestly that God has been persistently rigging the weather against the Germans. He points out that the absence of mist on the North Sea was of great help to the British in the autumn of 1914, and declares that it was the wet state of the country that really held up the Germans in Flanders in the winter of 1914–15. He ignores the part played by the weather in delaying the relief of Kut-el-Amara, and he has not thought of the difficult question why the Deity, having once decided upon intervention, did not, instead of this comparatively trivial meteorological assistance, adopt the more effective course of, for example, exploding or spoiling the German stores of ammunition by some simple atomic miracle, or misdirecting their gunfire by a sudden local modification of the laws of refraction or gravitation. . . .

Since these views of God come from Anglican vicarages I can only conclude that this kind of belief is quite orthodox and permissible in the established church, and that I am charging orthodox Christianity here with nothing that has ever been officially repudiated. I find indeed the essential assumptions of Mr. Landseer Mackenzie repeated in endless official Christian utterances on the part of German and British and Russian divines. The Bishop of Chelmsford, for example, has recently ascribed our difficulties in the war to our impatience with long sermons—among other similar causes. Such Christians are manifestly convinced that God can be invoked by ritual—for example by special days of national prayer or an increased observance of Sunday—or made malignant by neglect or levity. It is almost fundamental in their idea of him. The ordinary Mohammedan seems as confident of this magic pettiness of God, and the belief of China in the magic propitiations and resentments of " Heaven " is at least equally strong.

But the True God as those of the new religion know him is no such God of luck and intervention. He is not to serve men's ends or the ends of nations or associations of men ; he is careless of our ceremonies and invocations. He does not lose his temper with our follies and weaknesses. It is for us to serve him. He captains us, he does not coddle us. He has his own ends for which he needs us. . . .

§ 4

God is not Providence

Closely related to this heresy that God is magic is the heresy that calls him Providence, that declares the apparent adequacy of cause and effect to be a sham, and that all the time, incalculably, he is pulling about the order of events for our personal advantages.

The idea of Providence was very gaily travestied by Daudet in *Tartarin in the Alps*. You will remember how Tartarin's friend assured him that all Switzerland was one great Trust, intent upon attracting tourists and far too wise and kind to permit them to venture into real danger, that all the precipices were netted invisibly, and all the loose rocks guarded against falling, that the avalanches were prearranged spectacles and the crevasses at their worst slippery ways down into kindly catchment bags. If the mountaineer tried to get into real danger he was turned back by specious excuses. Inspired by this persuasion Tartarin behaved with incredible daring. . . . That is exactly the Providence theory of the whole world. There can be no doubt that it does enable many a timid soul to get through life with a certain recklessness. And, provided there is no slip into a crevasse, the Providence theory works well. It would work altogether well if there were no crevasses.

Tartarin was reckless because of his faith in Providence, and escaped. But what would have happened to him if he had fallen into a crevasse ?

There exists a very touching and remarkable book by Sir Francis Younghusband called *Within* (Williams & Norgate). It is the confession of a man who lived with a complete confidence in Providence until he was already well advanced in years. He went through battles and campaigns, he filled positions of great honour and responsibility, he saw much of the life of men, without altogether losing his faith. The loss of a child, an Indian famine, could shake it but not overthrow it. Then, coming back one day from some races in France, he was knocked down by an automobile and hurt very cruelly. He suffered terribly in body and mind. His sufferings caused much suffering to others. He did his utmost to see the hand of a loving Providence in his and their disaster and the torment it inflicted and, being a man of sterling honesty and a fine essential simplicity of mind, he confessed at last that he could not do so. His confidence in the benevolent intervention of God was altogether destroyed. His book tells of this shattering, and how laboriously he reconstructed his religion upon less confident lines. It is a book typical of an age and of a very English sort of mind, a book well worth reading.

That he came to a full sense of the True God cannot be asserted, but how near he came to God let one quotation witness.

" The existence of an outside Providence," he writes, " who created us, who watches over us, and who guides our lives like a Merciful Father, we have found impossible longer to believe in. But of the existence of a Holy Spirit radiating upward through all animate beings, and finding its fullest expression in man in love, and in the flowers in beauty, we can be as certain as of anything in the world. This fiery spiritual impulsion at the centre and the source of things, ever burning in us, is the supremely important factor in our existence. It does not always attain to light. In many directions it fails ; the conditions are too hard and it is utterly blocked. In others it only partially succeeds. But in a few it bursts forth into radiant light. There are few who in some heavenly moment of their lives have not been conscious of its presence. We may not be able to give it outward expression, but we know that it is there."

God does not guide our feet. He is no sedulous governess restraining and correcting the wayward steps of men. If you would fly into the air, there is no God to bank your aeroplane correctly for you or keep an ill-tended engine going ; if you would cross a glacier, no God nor angel guides your steps amidst the slippery places. He will not even mind your innocent children for you if you leave them before an unguarded fire. Cherish no delusions ; for yourself and others you challenge danger and chance on your own strength ; no talisman, no God, can help you or those you care for. Nothing of such things will God do ; it is an idle dream. But God will be with you nevertheless. In the reeling aeroplane or the dark ice-cave God will be your courage. Though you suffer or are killed, it is not an end. He will be with you as you face death ; he will die with you as he has died already countless myriads of brave deaths. He will come so close to you that at the last you will not know whether it is you or he who dies, and the present death will be swallowed up in his victory.

§ 5

The Heresy of Quietism

God comes to us within and takes us for his own. He releases us from ourselves ; he incorporates us with his own undying experience and adventure ; he receives us and gives himself. He is a stimulant ; he makes us live immortally and more abundantly. I have compared him to the sensation of a dear, strong friend who comes and stands quietly beside one, shoulder to shoulder.

The finding of God is the beginning of service. It is not an escape from life and action ; it is the release of life and action from the prison of the mortal self. Not to realise that is the heresy of Quietism, of many mystics. Commonly such people are people of some wealth, able to command services for all their everyday needs. They make religion a method of indolence. They turn their back on the toil and stresses of existence and give themselves up to a delicious reverie in which they flirt with the divinity. They will recount their privileges and ecstasies, and how ingeniously and wonderfully God has tried and proved them. But indeed the True God was not the lover of Madame Guyon. The True God is not a spiritual troubadour wooing the hearts of men and women to no purpose. The True God goes through the world like fifes and drums and flags, calling for recruits along the street. We must go out to him. We must accept his discipline and fight his battle. The peace of God comes not by thinking about it but by forgetting oneself in him.

§ 6

God does not Punish

Man is a social animal, and there is in him a great faculty for moral indignation. Many of the early Gods were mainly Gods of Fear. They were more often " wrath " than not. Such was the temperament of the Semitic deity who, as the Hebrew Jehovah, proliferated, perhaps under the influence of the Alexandrian Serapeum, into the Christian Trinity and who became also the Moslem God.[1] The natural hatred of un-regenerate men against everything that is unlike themselves, against strange people and cheerful people, against unfamiliar usages and things they do not understand, embodied itself in this conception of a malignant and partisan Deity, perpetually " upset " by the little things people did, and contriving murder and vengeance. Now this God would be drowning everybody in the world, now he would be burning Sodom and

[1] It is not so generally understood as it should be among English and American readers, that a very large proportion of early Christians, before the creeds established and regularised the doctrine of the Trinity, denied absolutely that Jehovah was God ; they regarded Christ as a rebel against Jehovah and a rescuer of humanity from him, just as Prometheus was a rebel against Jove. These beliefs survived for a thousand years throughout Christendom ; they were held by a great multitude of persecuted sects, from the Albigenses and Cathars to the eastern Paulicians. The Catholic Church found it necessary to prohibit the circulation of the Old Testament among laymen very largely on account of the polemics of the Cathars against the Hebrew God. But in this book, be it noted, the word Christian, when it is not otherwise defined, is used to indicate only the Trinitarians who accept the official creeds.

Gomorrah, now he would be inciting his congenial Israelites to the most terrific pogroms. This divine " frightfulness " is of course the natural human dislike and distrust for queer practices or for too sunny a carelessness, a dislike reinforced by the latent fierceness of the ape in us, liberating the latent fierceness of the ape in us, giving it an excuse and pressing permission upon it, handing the thing hated and feared over to its secular arm. . . .

It is a human paradox that the desire for seemliness, the instinct for restraints and fair disciplines, and the impulse to cherish sweet, familiar things, that these things of the True God should so readily liberate cruelty and tyranny. It is like a woman going with a light to tend and protect her sleeping child, and setting the house on fire. None the less, right down to to-day, the heresy of God the Revengeful, God the Perse-cutor and Avenger, haunts religion. It is only in quite recent years that the growing gentleness of everyday life has begun to make men a little ashamed of a Deity less tolerant and gentle than themselves. The recent literature of the Anglicans abounds in the evidence of this trouble.

Bishop Colenso of Natal was prosecuted and condemned in 1863 for denying the irascibility of his God and teaching " the Kaffirs of Natal " the dangerous heresy that God is all mercy. " We cannot allow it to be said," the Dean of Cape Town insisted, " that God was not angry and was not ap-peased by punishment." He was angry " on account of Sin, which is a great evil and a great insult to His Majesty." The case of the Rev. Charles Voysey, which occurred in 1870, was a second assertion of the church's insistence upon the fierceness of her God. This case is not to be found in the ordinary church histories nor is it even mentioned in the latest edition of the *Encyclopædia Britannica* : nevertheless, it appears to have been a very illuminating case. It is doubtful if the church would prosecute or condemn either Bishop Colenso or Mr. Voysey to-day.

§ 7

God and the Nursery-Maid

Closely related to the heresy of God the Avenger is that kind of miniature God the Avenger to whom the nursery-maid and the overtaxed parents are so apt to appeal. You stab your children with such a God and he poisons all their lives. For many of us the word " God " first came into our lives to denote a wanton, irrational restraint, as Bogey, as the All-seeing and quite ungenerous Eye. God Bogey is a great convenience to the nursery-maid who wants to leave Fear to mind her charges and enforce her disciplines, while she goes off upon her own aims. But, indeed, the teaching of God Bogey is an outrage upon the soul of a child scarcely less dreadful than an indecent assault. The reason rebels and is crushed under this horrible and pursuing suggestion. Many minds never rise again from their injury. They remain for the rest of life spiritually crippled and debased, haunted by a fear, stained with a persuasion of relentless cruelty in the ultimate cause of all things.

I, who write, was so set against God, thus rendered. He and his Hell were the nightmare of my childhood ; I hated him while I still believed in him, and who could help but hate ? I thought of him as a fantastic monster perpetually spying, perpetually listening, perpetually waiting to condemn and to "strike me dead " ; his flames as ready as a grill-room fire. He was over me and about my feebleness and silliness and forgetfulness as the sky and sea would be about a child drowning in mid-Atlantic. When I was still only a child of thirteen, by the grace of the True God in me, I flung this Lie out of my mind, and for many years, until I came to see that God himself had done this thing for me, the name of God meant nothing to me but the hideous scar in my heart where a fearful demand had been.

I see about me to-day many dreadful moral and mental cripples with this Bogey God of the nursery-maid, with his black, insane revenges, still living like a horrible parasite in their hearts in the place where God should be. They are afraid, afraid, afraid ; they dare not be kindly to formal sinners, they dare not abandon a hundred foolish observances ; they dare not look at the cause of things. They are afraid of sunshine, of nakedness, of health, of adventure, of science, lest that old watching spider take offence. The voice of the True God whispers in their hearts, echoes in speech and writing, but they avert themselves, fear-driven. For the True God has no lash of fear. And how the foul-minded bigot, with his ill-shaven face, his greasy skin, his thick, gesticulating hands, his bellowings and threatenings, loves to reap this harvest of fear the ignorant cunning of the nursery-girl has sown for him ! How he loves the importance of denunciation, and, himself a malignant cripple, to rally the company of these crippled souls to persecute and destroy the happy children of God ! . . .

Christian priestcraft turns a dreadful face to children. There is a real wickedness of the priest that is different from other wickedness, and that affects a reasonable mind just as cruelty and strange perversions of instinct affect it. Let a former Archbishop of Canterbury speak for me. This that follows is the account given by Archbishop Tait in a debate in the Upper House of Convocation (July 3rd, 1877) of one of the publications of a certain *Society of the Holy Cross.*

" I take this book, as its contents show, to be meant for the instruction of very young children. I find, in one of the pages of it, the statement that between the ages of six and six and a half years would be the proper time for the inculcation of the teaching which is to be found in the book. Now, six to six and a half is certainly a very tender age, and to these children I find these statements addressed in this book :—

" ' It is to the priest, and to the priest only, that the child must acknowledge his sins, if he desires that God should forgive him.'

" I hope and trust the person, the three clergymen, or however many there were, did not exactly realise what they were writing ; that they did not mean to say that a child was not to confess its sins to God direct ; that it was not to confess its sins, at the age of six, to its mother, or to its father, but was only to have recourse to the priest. But the words, to say the least of them, are rash. Then comes the very obvious question :—

" ' Do you know why ? It is because God, when he was on earth, gave to his priests, and to them alone, the Divine Power of forgiving men their sins. It was to priests alone that Jesus said : " Receive ye the Holy Ghost." . . . Those who will not confess will not be cured. Sin is a terrible sickness, and casts souls into hell.'

" That is addressed to a child six years of age.

" ' I have known,' the book continues, ' poor children who concealed their sins in confession for years ; they were very unhappy, were tormented with remorse, and if they had died in that state they would certainly have gone to the everlasting fires of hell.' " . . .

Now there is something against nature, something that I have seen time after time in the faces and bearing of priests and heard in their preaching. It is a distinct lust. Much nobility and devotion there are among priests, saintly lives and kindly lives, lives of real worship, lives no man may better ; this that I write is not of all, perhaps not of many priests. But there has been in all ages that have known sacerdotalism this terrible type of the priest ; priestcraft and priestly power release an aggressive and narrow disposition to a recklessness of suffering and a hatred of liberty that surely exceeds the badness of any other sort of men.

§ 8

The Children's God

Children do not naturally love God. They have no great capacity for an idea so subtle and mature as the idea of God.

While they are still children in a home and cared for, life is too kind and easy for them to feel any great need of God. All things are still something Godlike. . . .

The True God, our modern minds insist upon believing, can have no appetite for unnatural praises and adoration. He does not clamour for the attention of children. He is not like one of those senile uncles who dream of glory in the nursery, who love to hear it said, " The children adore him." If children are loved and trained to truth, justice, and mutual forbearance, they will be ready for the True God as their needs bring them within his scope. They should be left to their innocence, and to their trust in the innocence of the world, as long as they can be. They should be told only of God as a Great Friend whom some day they will need more and understand and know better. That is as much as most children need. The phrases of religion put too early into their mouths may become a cant, something worse than blasphemy.

Yet children are sometimes very near to God. Creative passion stirs in their play. At times they display a divine simplicity. But it does not follow that therefore they should be afflicted with theological formulæ or inducted into cere-monies and rites that they may dislike or misinterpret. If by any accident, by the death of a friend or a distressing story, the thought of death afflicts a child, then he may begin to hear of God, who takes those that serve him out of their slain bodies into his shining immortality. Or if by some menial treachery, through some prowling priest, the whisper of Old Bogey reaches our children, then we may set their minds at ease by the assurance of his limitless charity. . . .

With adolescence comes the desire for God and to know more of God, and that is the most suitable time for religious talk and teaching.

§ 9

God is not Sexual

In the last two or three hundred years there has been a very considerable disentanglement of the idea of God from the com-plex of sexual thought and feeling. But in the early days of religion the two things were inseparably bound together ; the fury of the Hebrew prophets, for example, is continually proclaiming the extraordinary " wrath " of their God at this or that little dirtiness or irregularity or breach of the sexual tabus. The ceremony of circumcision is clearly indicative of the original nature of the Semitic deity who developed into the Trinitarian God. So far as Christianity dropped this rite, so far Christianity disavowed the old associations. But to this day the representative Christian churches still make marriage into a mystical sacrament, and, with some exceptions, the Roman communion exacts the sacrifice of celibacy from its priesthood, regardless of the mischievousness and maliciousness that so often ensue. Nearly every Christian church inflicts as much discredit and injustice as it can contrive upon the illegitimate child. They do not treat illegitimate children as unfortunate children, but as children with a mystical and incurable taint of *sin*. Kindly, easy-going Christians may resent this statement because it does not tally with their own attitudes, but let them consult their orthodox authorities.

One must distinguish clearly here between what is held to be sacred or sinful in itself and what is held to be one's duty or a nation's duty because it is in itself the wisest, cleanest, clearest, best thing to do. By the latter tests and reasonable arguments most or all of our institutions regulating the relations of the sexes may be justifiable. But my case is not whether they can be justified by these tests, but that it is not by these tests that they are judged, even to-day, by the professors of the chief religions of the world. It is the temper and not the conclusions of the religious bodies that I would criticise. These sexual questions are guarded by a holy irascibility, and the most violent efforts are made—with a sense of complete righteousness—to prohibit their discussion. That fury about sexual things is only to be explained on the hypothesis that the Christian God remains a sex God in the minds of great numbers of his exponents. His disentanglement from that plexus is incomplete. Sexual things are still, to the orthodox Christian, sacred things.

Now the God whom those of the new faith are finding is only mediately concerned with the relations of men and women. He is no more sexual essentially than he is essentially dietetic or hygienic. The God of Leviticus was all these things. He is represented as prescribing the most petty and intimate observances—many of which are now habitually disregarded by the Christians who profess him. . . . It is part of the evolution of the idea of God that we have now so largely disentangled our conception of him from the dietary and regimen and meticulous sexual rules that were once inseparably bound up with his majesty. Christ himself was one of the chief forces in this disentanglement; there is the clearest evidence in several instances of his disregard of the rule and his insistence that his disciples should seek for the spirit underlying and often masked by the rule. His Church, being made of baser matter, has followed him as reluctantly as possible and no further than it was obliged. But it has followed him far enough to admit this principle that in all these matters there is no need for superstitious fear, that the interpretation of the divine purpose is left to the unembarrassed intelligence of men. The church has followed him far enough to make the harsh threatenings of priests and ecclesiastics against what they are pleased to consider impurity or sexual impiety a profound inconsistency. One seems to hear their distant protests when one reads of Christ and the Magdalen, or of Christ eating with publicans and sinners. The clergy of our own days play the part of the New Testament Pharisees with the utmost exactness and complete unconsciousness. One cannot imagine a modern ecclesiastic conversing with a Magdalen in terms of ordinary civility, unless she was in a very high social position indeed, or blending with disreputable characters without a dramatic sense of condescension and much explanatory by-play. Those who profess modern religion do but follow in these matters a course entirely compatible with what has survived of the authentic teachings of Christ, when they declare that God is not sexual, and that religious passion and insult and persecution upon the score of sexual things are a barbaric inheritance.

But lest any one should fling off here with some hasty assumption that those who profess the religion of the True God are sexually anarchistic, let stress be laid at once upon the opening sentence of the preceding paragraph, and let me a little anticipate a section which follows. We would free men and women from exact and superstitious rules and observances, not to make them less the instruments of God but more wholly his. The claim of modern religion is that one should give oneself unreservedly to God, that there is no other salvation. The believer owes all his being and every moment of his life to God, to keep mind and body as clean, fine, wholesome, active and completely at God's service as he can. There is no scope for indulgence or dissipation in such a consecrated life. It is a matter between the individual and his conscience or his doctor or his social understanding what exactly he may do or not do, what he may eat or drink or so forth, upon any occasion. Nothing can exonerate him from doing his utmost to determine and perform the right act. Nothing can excuse his failure to do so. But what is here being insisted upon is that none of these things has immediately to do with God or religious emotion, except only the general will to do right in God's service. The detailed interpretation of that "right" is for the dispassionate consideration of the human intelligence.

All this is set down here as distinctly as possible. Because of the emotional reservoirs of sex, sexual dogmas are among the most obstinately recurrent of all heresies, and sexual excitement is always tending to leak back into religious feeling. Amongst the sex-tormented priesthood of the Roman communion in particular, ignorant of the extreme practices of the Essenes and of the Orphic cult and such-like predecessors of Christianity, there seems to be an extraordinary belief that chastity was not invented until Christianity came, and that the religious life is largely the propitiation of God by feats of sexual abstinence. But a superstitious abstinence that scars and embitters the mind, distorts the imagination, makes the body gross and keeps it unclean, is just as offensive to God as any positive depravity.

CHAPTER THREE

THE LIKENESS OF GOD

§ 1

God is Courage

Now, having set down what those who profess the new religion regard as the chief misconceptions of God, having put these systems of ideas aside from our explanations, the path is cleared for the statement of what God is. Since language springs entirely from material, spatial things, there is always an element of metaphor in theological statement. So that I have not called this chapter the Nature of God, but the Likeness of God.

And firstly, GOD IS COURAGE.

§ 2

God is a Person

And next, GOD IS A PERSON.

Upon this point those who are beginning to profess modern religion are very insistent. It is, they declare, the central article, the axis, of their religion. God is a person who can be known as one knows a friend, who can be served and who receives service, who partakes of our nature ; who is, like us, a being in conflict with the unknown and the limitless and the forces of death ; who values much that we value and is against much that we are pitted against. He is our king to whom we must be loyal ; he is our captain, and to know him is to have a direction in our lives. He feels us and knows us ; he is helped and gladdened by us. He hopes and attempts. . . . God is no abstraction nor trick of words, no Infinite. He is as real as a bayonet thrust or an embrace.

Now this is where those who have left the old creeds and come asking about the new realisations find their chief difficulty. They say, Show us this person ; let us hear him. (If they listen to the silences within, presently they will hear him.) But when one argues, one finds oneself suddenly in the net of those ancient controversies between species and individual, between the one and the many, which arise out of the necessary imperfect methods of the human mind. Upon these matters there has been much pregnant writing during the last half-century. Such ideas as this writer has to offer are to be found in a previous little book of his *First and Last Things*, in which, writing as one without authority or specialisation in logic and philosophy, as an ordinary man vividly interested, for others in a like case, he was at some pains to elucidate the imperfections of this instrument of ours, this mind, by which we must seek and explain and reach up to God. Suffice it here to say that theological discussion may very easily become like the vision of a man with a cataract, a mere projection of inherent imperfections. If we do not use our phraseology with a certain courage, and take that of those who are trying to convey their ideas to us with a certain politeness and charity, there is no end possible to any discussion in so subtle and intimate a matter as theology but assertions, denials, and wranglings. And about this word " person " it is necessary to be as clear and explicit as possible, though perfect clearness, a definition of mathematical sharpness, is by the very nature of the case impossible.

Now, when we speak of a person or an individual we think typically of a man and we forget that he was once an embryo and will presently decay ; we forget that he came of two people and may beget many, that he has forgotten much and will forget more, that he can be confused, divided against himself, delirious, drunken, drugged, or asleep. On the contrary we are, in our hasty way of thinking of him, apt to suppose him continuous, definite, acting consistently and never forgetting. But only abstract and theoretical persons are like that. We couple with him the idea of a body. Indeed, in the common use of the word " person " there is more thought of body than of mind. We speak of a lover possessing the person of his mistress. We speak of offences against the person as opposed to insults, libels, or offences against property. And the gods of primitive men and the earlier civilisations were quite of that quality of person. They were thought of as living in very splendid bodies and as acting consistently. If they were invisible in the ordinary world it was because they were aloof or because their " persons " were too splendid for weak human eyes. Moses was permitted a mitigated view of the person of the Hebrew God on Mount Horeb ; and Semele, who insisted upon seeing Zeus in the glories that were sacred to Juno, was utterly consumed. The early Islamic conception of God, like the conception of most honest, simple Christians to-day, was clearly, in spite of the theologians, of a very exalted anthropomorphic personality away somewhere in Heaven. The personal appearance of the Christian God is described in The Revelation, and, however much that description may be explained away by commentators as symbolical, it is certainly taken by most straightforward believers as a statement of concrete reality. Now if we are going to insist upon this primary meaning of person and individual, then, certainly, God as he is now conceived is not a person and not an individual. The True God will never promenade an Eden or a Heaven, nor sit upon a throne.

But current Christianity, modern developments of Islam, much Indian theological thought—that, for instance, which has found such delicate and attractive expression in the devotional poetry of Rabindranath Tagore—has long since abandoned this anthropomorphic insistence upon a body. From the earliest ages man's mind has found little or no difficulty in the idea of something essential to the personality, a soul or a spirit or both, existing apart from the body and continuing after the destruction of the body, and being still a person and an individual. From this it is a small step to the thought of a person existing independently of any existing or pre-existing body. That is the idea of theological Christianity, as distinguished from the Christianity of simple faith. The Triune Persons—omnipresent, omniscient, and omnipotent— exist for all time, superior to and independent of matter. They are supremely disembodied. One became incarnate— as a wind eddy might take up a whirl of dust. . . . Those who profess modern religion conceive that this is an excessive abstraction of the idea of spirituality, a disembodiment of the idea of personality beyond the limits of the conceivable ; nevertheless they accept the conception that a person, a spiritual individual, may be without an ordinary, mortal body. . . . They declare that God is without any specific body, that he is immaterial, that he can affect the material universe—and that means that he can only reach our sight, our hearing, our touch—through the bodies of those who believe in him and serve him.

His nature is of the nature of thought and will. Not only has he, in his essence, nothing to do with matter, but nothing to do with space. He is not of matter nor of space. He comes into them. Since the period when all the great theologies that prevail to-day were developed, there have been great changes in the ideas of men towards the dimensions of time and space. We owe to Kant the release from the rule of these ideas as essential ideas. Our modern psychology is alive to the possibility of Being that has no extension in space at all, even as our speculative geometry can entertain the possibility of dimensions—fourth, fifth, nth dimensions—outside the three-dimensional universe of our experience. And God, being non-spatial, is not thereby banished to an infinite remoteness but brought nearer to us ; he is everywhere immediately at hand, even as a fourth dimension would be everywhere immediately at hand. He is a Being of the minds and in the minds of men. He is in immediate contact with all who apprehend him. . . .

But modern religion declares that though he does not exist in matter or space, he exists in time just as a current of thought may do ; that he changes and becomes more even as a man's purpose gathers itself together ; that somewhere in the dawning of mankind he had a beginning, an awakening,

and that as mankind grows he grows. With our eyes he looks
out upon the universe he invades ; with our hands he lays
hands upon it. All our truth, all our intentions and achieve-
ments, he gathers to himself. He is the undying human
memory, the increasing human will.

But this, you may object, is no more than saying that God
is the collective mind and purpose of the human race. You
may declare that this is no God, but merely the sum of mankind. But those who believe in the new ideas very steadfastly deny that. God is, they say, not an aggregate but a
synthesis. He is not merely the best of all of us, but a Being
in himself, composed of that but more than that, as a temple
is more than a gathering of stones, or a regiment is more than
an accumulation of men. They point out that a man is made
up of a great multitude of cells, each equivalent to a unicellular
organism. Not one of those cells is he, nor is he simply just
the addition of all of them. He is more than all of them.
You can take away these and these and these, and he still
remains. And he can detach part of himself and treat it as
if it were not himself, just as a man may beat his breast or, as
Cranmer the martyr did, thrust his hand into the flames. A
man is none the less himself because his hair is cut or his
appendix removed or his leg amputated.

And take another image. . . . Who bears affection for this
or that spadeful of mud in my garden ? Who cares a throb
of the heart for all the tons of chalk in Kent or all the lumps
of limestone in Yorkshire ? But men love England, which is
made up of such things.

And so we think of God as a synthetic reality though he has
neither body nor material parts. And so too we may obey
him and listen to him, though we think but lightly of the men
whose hands or voices he sometimes uses. And we may think
of him as having moods and aspects—as a man has—and a
consistency we called his character.

These are theorisings about God. These are statements to
convey this modern idea of God. This, we say, is the nature
of the person whose will and thoughts we serve. No one,
however, who understands the religious life seeks conversion
by argument. First one must feel the need of God, then one
must form or receive an acceptable idea of God. That much
is no more than turning one's face to the east to see the coming
of the sun. One may still doubt if that direction is the east
or whether the sun will rise. The real coming of God is not
that. It is a change, an irradiation of the mind. Everything
is there as it was before, only now it is aflame. Suddenly the
light fills one's eyes, and one knows that God has risen and
that doubt has fled for ever.

§ 3

God is Youth

The third thing to be told of the True God, is that GOD IS YOUTH.

God, we hold, began and is always beginning. He looks for ever into the future.

Most of the old religions derive from a patriarchal phase. God is in those systems the Ancient of Days. I know of no Christian attempt to represent or symbolise God the Father which is not a bearded, aged man. White hair, beard, bearing, wrinkles : a hundred such symptoms of senile decay are there. These marks of senility do not astonish our modern minds in the picture of God, only because tradition and usage have blinded our eyes to the absurdity of a time-worn immortal. Jove, too, and Wotan are figures far past the prime of their vigour. These are gods after the ancient habit of the human mind, that turned perpetually backward for causes and reasons and saw all things to come as no more than the working out of Fate—

> " Of Man's first disobedience, and the fruit
> Of that forbidden tree, whose mortal taste
> Brought death into the world, and all our woe."

But the God of this new age, we repeat, looks not to our past but our future, and if a figure may represent him it must be the figure of a beautiful youth, already brave and wise, but hardly come to his strength. He should stand lightly on his feet in the morning time, eager to go forward, as though he had but newly arisen to a day that was still but a promise ; he should bear a sword, that clean, discriminating weapon, his eyes should be as bright as swords ; his lips should fall apart with eagerness for the great adventure before him, and he should be in very fresh and golden harness, reflecting the rising sun. Death should still hang like mists and cloudbanks and shadows in the valleys of the wide landscape about him. There should be dew upon the threads of gossamer and the little leaves and blades of the turf at his feet. . . .

§ 4

When We say God is Love

One of the sayings about God that have grown at the same time most trite and most sacred is that God is Love. This is a saying that deserves careful examination. Love is a word very loosely used ; there are people who will say they love new potatoes ; there are a multitude of loves of different colours and values. There is the love of a mother for her child, there is the love of brothers, there is the love of youth and maiden, and the love of husband and wife, there is illicit love and the love one bears one's home or one's country, there are dog-lovers and the loves of the Olympians, and love which is a passion of jealousy. Love is frequently a mere blend of appetite and preference ; it may be almost pure greed ; it may have scarcely any devotion nor be a whit self-forgetful nor generous. It is possible so to phrase things that the furtive craving of a man for another man's wife may be made out to be a light from God. Yet about all the better sorts of love, the sorts of love that people will call " true love," there is something of that same exaltation out of the narrow self that is the essential quality of the knowledge of God.

Only while the exaltation of the love passion comes and goes, the exaltation of the religious passion comes to remain. Loves are the windows by which we may look out of the prison of self, but God is the open door by which we freely go. And God never dies, nor disappoints, nor betrays.

The love of a woman and a man has usually, and particularly in its earlier phases of excitement, far too much desire, far too much possessiveness and exclusiveness, far too much distrust or forced trust, and far too great a kindred with jealousy to be like the love of God. The former is a dramatic relationship that drifts to a climax, and then again seeks presently a climax, and that may be satiated or fatigued. But the latter is far more like the love of comrades, or like the love of a man and a woman who have loved and been through much trouble together, who have hurt one another and forgiven, and come to a complete and generous fellowship. There is a strange and beautiful love that men tell of that will spring up on battlefields between sorely wounded men, and often they are men who have fought together, so that they will do almost incredibly brave and tender things for one another, though but recently they have been trying to kill each other. There is often a pure exaltation of feeling between those who stand side by side manfully in any great stress. These are the forms of love that perhaps come nearest to what we mean when we speak of the love of God.

That is man's love of God, but there is also something else : there is the love God bears for man in the individual believer. Now this is not an indulgent, instinctive, and sacrificing love like the love of a woman for her baby. It is the love of the captain for his men ; God must love his followers as a great captain loves his men, who are so foolish, so helpless in themselves, so confiding, and yet whose faith alone makes him possible. It is an austere love. The spirit of God will not hesitate to send us to torment and bodily death. . . .

And God waits for us, for all of us who have the quality to reach him. He has need of us as we of him. He desires us and desires to make himself known to us. When at last the individual breaks through the limiting darknesses to him, the irradiation of that moment, the smile and soul clasp, is in God as well as in men. He has won us from the enemy. We come staggering through into the golden light of his kingdom, to fight for his kingdom henceforth, until at last we are altogether taken up into his being.

CHAPTER FOUR

THE RELIGION OF ATHEISTS

§ I

The Scientific Atheist

IT is a curious thing that while most organised religions seem to drape about and conceal and smother the statement of the True God, the honest Atheist, with his passionate impulse to strip the truth bare, is constantly and unwittingly reproducing the divine likeness. It will be interesting here to call a witness or so to the extreme instability of absolute negation.

Here, for example, is a deliverance from Professor Metchnikoff, who was a very typical antagonist of all religion. He died only the other day. He was a very great physiologist indeed ; he was a man almost of the rank and quality of Pasteur or Charles Darwin. A decade or more ago he wrote a book called *The Nature of Man,* in which he set out very plainly a number of illuminating facts about life. They are facts so illuminating that presently, in our discussion of sin, they will be referred to again. But it is not Professor Metchnikoff's intention to provide material for a religious discussion. He sets out his facts in order to overthrow theology as he conceives it. The remarkable thing about his book, the thing upon which I would now lay stress, is that it betrays no inkling of the fact that he has no longer the right to conceive theology as he conceives it. The development of his science has destroyed that right.

He does not realise how profoundly modern biology has affected our ideas of individuality and species, and how the import of theology is modified through these changes. When he comes from his own world of modern biology to religion and philosophy he goes back in time. He attacks religion as he understood it when first he fell out with it fifty years or more ago.

Let us state as compactly as possible the nature of these changes that biological science has wrought almost imperceptibly in the general scheme and method of our thinking. The influence of biology upon thought in general consists essentially in diminishing the importance of the individual and developing the realisation of the species, as if it were a kind of super-individual, a modifying and immortal super-individual, maintaining itself against the outer universe by the birth and death of its constituent individuals. Natural History, which began by putting individuals into species as if the latter were mere classificatory divisions, has come to see that the species has its adventures, its history and drama, far exceeding in interest and importance the individual adventure. "The Origin of Species" was for countless minds the discovery of a new romance in life.

The contrast of the individual life and this specific life may be stated plainly and compactly as follows. A little while ago we current individuals, we who are alive now, were each of us distributed between two parents, then between four grandparents, and so on backward ; we are temporarily assembled, as it were, out of an ancestral diffusion ; we stand our trial, and presently our individuality is dispersed and mixed again with other individualities in an uncertain multitude of descendants. But the species is not like this ; it goes on steadily from newness to newness, remaining still a unity. The drama of the individual life is a mere episode, beneficial or abandoned, in this continuing adventure of the species. And Metchnikoff finds most of the trouble of life and the distresses of life in the fact that the species is still very painfully adjusting itself to the fluctuating conditions under which it lives. The conflict of life is a continual pursuit of adjustment, and the " ills of life," of the individual life that is, are due to its " disharmonies." Man, acutely aware of himself as an individual adventure and unawakened to himself as a species, finds life jangling and distressful, finds death frustration. He fails and falls as a person in what may be the success and triumph of his kind. He does not apprehend the struggle or the nature of victory, but only his own gravitation to death, and personal extinction.

Now Professor Metchnikoff is anti-religious, and he is anti-religious because to him, as to so many Europeans, religion is confused with priestcraft and dogmas, is associated with disagreeable impressions of irrational repression and misguidance. How completely he misconceives the quality of religion, how completely he sees it as an individual's affair, his own words may witness :—

" Religion is still occupied with the problem of death. The solutions which as yet it has offered cannot be regarded as satisfactory. A future life has no single argument to support it, and the non-existence of life after death is in consonance with the whole range of human knowledge. On the other hand, resignation as preached by Buddha will fail to satisfy humanity, which has a longing for life, and is overcome by the thought of the inevitability of death."

Now here it is clear that by death he means the individual death, and by a future life the prolongation of individuality. But Buddhism does not in truth appear ever to have been concerned with that, and modern religious developments are certainly not under that preoccupation with the narrower self.

Buddhism, indeed, so far from "preaching resignation" to death, seeks as its greater good a death so complete as to be absolute release from the individual's burthen of *karma*. Buddhism seeks an *escape from individual immortality*. The deeper one pursues religious thought the more nearly it approximates to a search for escape from the self-centred life and over-individuation, and the more it diverges from Professor Metchnikoff's assertion of its aims. Salvation is indeed to lose one's self. But Professor Metchnikoff, having roundly denied that this is so, is then left free to take the very essentials of the religious life as they are here conceived and present them as if they were the antithesis of the religious life. His book, when it is analysed, resolves itself into just that research for an escape from the painful accidents and chagrins of individuation, which is the ultimate of religion.

At times, indeed, he seems almost wilfully blind to the true solution round and about which his writing goes. He suggests, as his most hopeful satisfaction for the cravings of the human heart, such a scientific prolongation of life that the instinct for self-preservation will be at last extinct. If that is not the very "resignation" he imputes to the Buddhist I do not know what it is. He believes that an individual which has lived fully and completely may at last welcome death with the same instinctive readiness as, in the days of its strength, it shows for the embraces of its mate. We are to be glutted by living to six score and ten. We are to rise from the table at last as gladly as we sat down. We shall go to death as unresistingly as tired children go to bed. Men are to have a life far beyond the range of what is now considered their prime, and their last period (won by scientific self-control) will be a period of ripe wisdom (from seventy to eighty to a hundred and twenty or thereabouts) and public service !

(But why, one asks, public service ? Why not book-collecting or the simple pleasure of reminiscence so dear to aged egotists ? Metchnikoff never faces that question. And again, what of the man who is challenged to die for right at the age of thirty ? What does the prolongation of life do for him ? And where are the consolations for accidental misfortune, for the tormenting disease or the lost limb ?)

But in his peroration Professor Metchnikoff lapses into pure religiosity. The prolongation of life gives place to sheer self-sacrifice as the fundamental "remedy." And indeed what other remedy has ever been conceived for the general evil of life ?

"On the other hand," he writes, "the knowledge that the goal of human life can be attained only by the development of a high degree of solidarity amongst men will restrain actual egotism. The mere fact that the enjoyment of life according to the precepts of Solomon (Ecclesiastes ix. 7–10) [1] is opposed to the goal of human life, will lessen luxury and the evil that comes from luxury. Conviction that science alone is able to redress the disharmonies of the human constitution will lead directly to the improvement of education and to the solidarity of mankind.

"In progress towards the goal, nature will have to be consulted continuously. Already, in the case of the ephemerids, nature has produced a complete cycle of normal life ending in natural death. In the problem of his own fate, man must not be content with the gifts of nature ; he must direct them by his own efforts. Just as he has been able to modify the nature of animals and plants, man must attempt to modify his own constitution, so as to readjust its disharmonies. . . .

"To modify the human constitution, it will be necessary, first, to frame the ideal, and thereafter to set to work with all the resources of science.

"If there can be formed an ideal able to unite men in a kind of religion of the future, this ideal must be founded on scientific principles. And if it be true, as has been asserted so often, that man can live by faith alone, the faith must be in the power of science."

Now this, after all the flat repudiations that have preceded it of " religion " and " philosophy " as remedies for human ills, is nothing less than the fundamental proposition of the religious life translated into terms of materialistic science, the proposition that damnation is really over-individuation and that salvation is escape from self into the larger being of life. . . .

What can this " religion of the future " be but that devotion to the racial adventure under the captaincy of God which we have already found, like gold in the bottom of the vessel, when we have washed away the confusions and impurities of dogmatic religion ? By an inquiry setting out from a purely religious starting-point we have already reached conclusions identical with this ultimate refuge of an extreme materialist.

This altar to the Future of his, we can claim as an altar to our God—an altar rather indistinctly inscribed.

---

[1] Go thy way, eat thy bread with joy, and drink thy wine with a merry heart ; for God now accepteth thy works. Let thy garments be always white ; and let thy head lack no ointment. Live joyfully with the wife whom thou lovest all the days of the life of thy vanity, which he hath given thee under the sun, all the days of thy vanity ; for that is thy portion in this life, and in thy labour which thou takest under the sun. Whatsoever thy hand findeth to do, do it with thy might ; for there is no work, nor device, nor knowledge, nor wisdom, in the grave, whither thou goest.

§ 2

Sacrifice implies God

Almost all agnostic and atheistical writings that show any fineness and generosity of spirit have this tendency to become, as it were, the statement of an anonymous God. Everything is said that a religious writer would say—except that God is not named. Religious metaphors abound. It is as if they accepted the living body of religion but denied the bones that held it together—as they might deny the bones of a friend. It is true, they would admit, the body moves in a way that implies bones in its every movement, but—*we have never seen those bones.*

The disputes in theory—I do not say the difference in reality—between the modern believer and the atheist or agnostic—becomes at times almost as impalpable as that subtle discussion dear to students of physics, whether the scientific "ether" is real or a formula. Every material phenomenon is consonant with the helps to define this ether, which permeates and sustains and is all things, which nevertheless is perceptible to no sense, which is reached only by an intellectual process. Most minds are disposed to treat this ether as a reality. But the acutely critical mind insists that what is only so attainable by inference is not real ; it is no more than " a formula that satisfies all phenomena."

But if it comes to that, am I anything more than the formula that satisfies all my forms of consciousness ?

Intellectually there is hardly anything more than a certain will to believe, to divide the religious man who knows God to be utterly real from the man who says that God is merely a formula to satisfy moral and spiritual phenomena. The former has encountered him, the other has as yet felt only unassigned impulses. One says God's will is so ; the other that Right is so. One says God moves me to do this or that, the other the Good Will in me, which I share with you and all well-disposed men, moves me to do this or that. But the former makes an exterior reference and escapes a risk of self-righteousness.

I have recently been reading a book by Mr. Joseph McCabe called *The Tyranny of Shams* (Nash), in which he displays very typically this curious tendency to a sort of religion with God "blacked out." His is an extremely interesting case. He is a writer who was formerly a Roman Catholic priest, and in his reaction from Catholicism he displays a resolution, even sterner than Professor Metchnikoff's, to deny that anything religious or divine can exist, that there can be any aim in life except happiness, or any guide but "science." But—and here immediately he turns east again—he is careful not to say " individual happiness." And he says " Pleasure is, as Epicureans insisted, only a part of a large idea of happiness." So he lets the happiness of devotion and sacrifice creep in. So he opens indefinite possibilities of getting away from any merely materialistic rule of life. And he writes :—

" In every civilised nation the mass of the people are inert and indifferent. Some even make a pretence of justifying their inertness. Why, they ask, should we stir at all ? Is there such a thing as a duty to improve the earth ? What is the meaning or purpose of life ? Or has it a purpose ?

" One generally finds that this kind of reasoning is merely a piece of controversial athletics or a thin excuse for idleness. People tell you that the conflict of science and religion—it would be better to say the conflict of modern culture and ancient traditions—has robbed life of its plain significance. The men who, like Tolstoy, seriously urge this point, fail to appreciate the modern outlook on life. Certainly modern culture—science, history, philosophy and art—finds no purpose in life ; that is to say, no purpose eternally fixed and to be discovered by man. A great chemist said a few years ago that he could imagine ' a series of lucky accidents ' — the chance blowing by the wind of certain chemicals into pools on the primitive earth—accounting for the first appearance of life ; and one might not unjustly sum up the influences which have lifted those early germs to the level of conscious beings as a similar series of lucky accidents.

" But it is sheer affectation to say that this demoralises us. If there is no purpose impressed on the universe, or prefixed to the development of humanity, it follows only that humanity may choose its own purpose and set up its own goal ; and the most elementary sense of order will teach us that this choice must be social, not merely individual. In whatever measure ill-controlled individuals may yield to personal impulses or attractions, the aim of the race must be a collective aim. I do not mean an austere demand of self-sacrifice from the individual, but an adjustment—as genial and generous as possible—of individual variations for common good. Otherwise life becomes discordant and futile, and the pain and waste react on each individual. So we raise again, in the twentieth century, the old question of " the greatest good," which men discussed in the Stoa Poikile and the suburban groves of Athens, in the cool atria of patrician mansions on the Palatine and the Pincian, in the Museum at Alexandria, and the schools which Omar Khayyám frequented, in the straw-strewn schools of the Middle Ages and the opulent chambers of Cosimo dei Medici."

And again :—

" The old dream of a co-operative effort to improve life, to bring happiness to as many minds of mortals as we can reach, shines above all the mists of the day. Through the ruins of creeds and philosophies, which have for ages disdained it, we are retracing our steps toward that height—just as the Athenians did two thousand years ago. It rests on no meta-physic, no sacred legend, no disputable tradition—nothing that scepticism can corrode or advancing knowledge under-mine. Its foundations are the fundamental and unchanging impulses of our nature."

And again :—

" The revolt which burns in so much of the abler literature of our time is an unselfish revolt, or non-selfish revolt : it is an outcome of that larger spirit which conceives the self to be a part of the general social organism, and it is therefore neither egoistic nor altruistic. It finds a sanction in the new intelligence, and an inspiration in the finer sentiments of our generation, but the glow which chiefly illumines it is the glow of the great vision of a happier earth. It speaks of the claims of truth and justice, and assails untruth and injustice, for these are elemental principles of social life ; but it appeals more confidently to the warmer sympathy which is linking the scattered children of the race, and it urges all to co-operate in the restriction of suffering and the creation of happiness. The advance guard of the race, the men and women in whom mental alertness is associated with fine feeling, cry that they have reached Pisgah's slope ; and in increasing numbers men and women are pressing on to see if it be really the Promised Land."

" Pisgah—the Promised Land ! " Mr. McCabe in that passage sounds as if he were half-way to " Oh ! Beulah Land ! " and the tambourine.

That " larger spirit," we maintain, is God ; those " impulses " are the power of God, and Mr. McCabe serves a Master he denies. He has but to realise fully that God is not necessarily the Triune God of the Catholic Church, and banish his intense suspicion that he may yet be lured back to that altar he abandoned ; he has but to look up from that preoccupation, and immediately he will begin to realise the presence of Divinity.

§ 3

God is an External Reality

It may be argued that if atheists and agnostics, when they set themselves to express the good will that is in them, do shape out God, that if their conception of right living fall in so completely with the conception of God's service as to be broadly identical, that then indeed God, like the ether of scientific speculation, is no more than a theory, no more than an imaginative externalisation of man's inherent good will. Why trouble about God then ? Is not the declaration of a good disposition a sufficient evidence of salvation ? What is the difference between such benevolent unbelievers as Professor Metchnikoff or Mr. McCabe and those who have found God ?

The difference is this, that the benevolent atheist stands alone upon his own good will, without a reference, without a standard, trusting to his own impulse to goodness, relying upon his own moral strength. A certain immodesty, a certain self-righteousness, hangs like a precipice above him ; incalculable temptations open like gulfs beneath his feet. He has not really given himself or got away from himself. He has no one to whom he can give himself. He is still a masterless man. His exaltation is self-centred, is priggishness, his fall is unrestrained by any exterior obligation. His devotion is only the good will in himself, a disposition ; it is a mood that may change. At any moment it may change. He may have pledged himself to his own pride and honour, but who will hold him to his bargain ? He has no source of strength beyond his own amiable sentiments, his conscience speaks with an unsupported voice, and no one watches while he sleeps. He cannot pray ; he can but ejaculate. He has no real and living link with other men of good will.

And those whose acquiescence in the idea of God is merely intellectual are in no better case than those who deny God altogether. They may have all the forms of truth and not divinity. The religion of the atheist, with ¡a God-shaped blank at its heart, and the persuasion of the unconverted theologian are both like lamps unlit. The lit lamp has no difference in form from the lamp unlit. But the lit lamp is alive and the lamp unlit is asleep or dead.

The difference between the unconverted and the unbeliever and the servant of the true God is this ; it is that the latter has experienced a complete turning away from self. This only difference is all the difference in the world. It is the realisation that this goodness that I thought was within me and of myself, and upon which I rather prided myself, is without me and above myself, and infinitely greater and stronger than I. It is the immortal and I am mortal. It is invincible and steadfast in its purpose, and I am weak and insecure. It is no longer that I, out of my inherent and remarkable goodness, out of the excellence of my quality and the benevolence of my heart, give a considerable amount of time and attention to the happiness and welfare of others—

because I choose to do so. On the contrary I have come under a divine imperative, I am obeying an irresistible call, I am a humble and willing servant of the righteousness of God. That altruism which Professor Metchnikoff and Mr. McCabe would have us regard as the goal and refuge of a broad and free intelligence, is really the first simple commandment in the religious life.

§ 4

Another Religious Materialist

Now here is a passage from a book, *Evolution and the War* (Murray), by Professor Metchnikoff's translator, Dr. Chalmers Mitchell, which comes even closer to our conception of God as an immortal being arising out of man, and external to the individual man. He has been discussing that well-known passage of Kant's : " Two things fill my mind with ever-renewed wonder and awe the more often and deeper I dwell on them—the starry vault above me, and the moral law within me."

From that discussion, Dr. Chalmers Mitchell presently comes to this most definite and interesting statement :—

" Writing as a hard-shell Darwinian evolutionist, a lover of the scalpel and microscope, and of patient, empirical observation, as one who dislikes all forms of supernaturalism, and who does not shrink from the implications even of the phrase that thought is a secretion of the brain as bile is a secretion of the liver, I assert as a biological fact, that the moral law is as real and as external to man as the starry vault. It has no secure seat in any single man or in any single nation. It is the work of the blood and tears of long generations of men. It is not in man, inborn or innate, but is enshrined in his traditions, in his customs, in his literature and his religion. Its creation and sustenance are the crowning glory of man, and his consciousness of it puts him in a high place above the animal world. Men live and die, nations rise and fall, but the struggle of individual lives and of individual nations must be measured not by their immediate needs, but as they tend to the debasement or perfection of man's great achievement."

This is the same reality. This is the same Link and Captain that this book asserts. It seems to me a secondary matter whether we call him " Man's Great Achievement " or " The Son of Man " or the " God of Mankind " or " God." So far as the practical and moral ends of life are concerned, it does not matter how we explain or refuse to explain his presence in our lives.

There is but one possible gap left between the position of Dr. Chalmers Mitchell and the position of this book. In this book it is asserted that *God responds*, that he *gives* courage and the power of self-suppression to our weakness.

§ 5

A Note on a Lecture by Professor Gilbert Murray

Let me now quote and discuss a very beautiful passage from a lecture upon Stoicism (Watts) by Professor Gilbert Murray, which also displays the same characteristic of an involuntary shaping out of God in the forms of denial. It is a passage remarkable for its conscientious and resolute Agnosticism. And it is remarkable too for its blindness to the possibility of separating quite completely the idea of the Infinite Being from the idea of God. It is another striking instance of that obsession of modern minds by merely Christian theology of which I have already complained. Professor Murray has quoted Mr. Bevan's phrase for God, " the Friend behind phenomena," and he does not seem to realise that that phrase carries with it no obligation whatever to believe that this Friend is in control of the phenomena. He assumes that he is supposed to be in control as if it were a matter of course.

" We do seem to find," Professor Murray writes, " not only in all religions, but in practically all philosophies, some belief that man is not quite alone in the universe, but is met in his endeavours towards the good by some external help or sympathy. We find it everywhere in the unsophisticated man. We find it in the unguarded self-revelations of the most severe and conscientious atheists. Now, the Stoics, like many other schools of thought, drew an argument from this consensus of all mankind. It was not an absolute proof of the existence of the Gods or Providence, but it was a strong indication. The existence of a common instinctive belief in the mind of man gives at least a presumption that there must be a good cause for that belief.

" This is a reasonable position. There must be some such cause. But it does not follow that the only valid cause is the truth of the content of the belief. I cannot help suspecting that this is precisely one of those points on which Stoicism, in company with almost all philosophy up to the present time, has gone astray through not sufficiently realising its dependence on the human mind as a natural biological product. For it is very important in this matter to realise that the so-called belief is not really an intellectual judgment so much as a craving of the whole nature.

" It is only of very late years that psychologists have begun to realise the enormous dominion of those forces in man of which he is normally unconscious. We cannot escape as easily as these brave men dreamed from the grip of the blind powers beneath the threshold. Indeed, as I see philosophy after philosophy falling into this unproven belief in the Friend behind phenomena, as I find that I myself cannot, except for a moment and by an effort, refrain from making the same assumption, it seems to me that perhaps here too we are under the spell of a very old ineradicable instinct. We are gregarious animals ; our ancestors have been for countless ages. We cannot help looking out on the world as gregarious animals do ; we see it in terms of humanity and of fellowship. Students of animals under domestication have shown us how the habits of a gregarious creature, taken away from his kind, are shaped in a thousand details by reference to the lost pack which is no longer there—the pack which a dog tries to smell his way back to all the time he is out walking, the pack he calls to for help when danger threatens. It is a strange and touching thing, this eternal hunger of the gregarious animal for the herd of friends who are not there. And it may be, it may very possibly be, that, in the matter of this Friend behind pheno-mena, our own yearning and our own almost ineradicable instinctive conviction, since they are certainly not founded on either reason or observation, are in origin the groping of a lonely-souled gregarious animal to find its herd or its herd-leader in the great spaces between the stars.

" At any rate, it is a belief very difficult to get rid of."

There the passage and the lecture end.

I would urge that here again is an inadvertent witness to the reality of God.

Professor Murray writes of gregarious animals as though there existed solitary animals that are not gregarious, pure individualists, " atheists " so to speak, and as though this appeal to a life beyond one's own was not the universal dis-position of living things. His classical training disposes him to a realistic exaggeration of individual difference. But nearly every animal, and certainly every mentally considerable animal, begins under parental care, in a nest or a litter, mates to breed, and is associated for much of its life. Even the great carnivores do not go alone except when they are old and have done with the most of life. Every pack, every herd, begins at some point in a couple, it is the equivalent of the tiger's litter if that were to remain undispersed. And it is within the memory of men still living that in many districts the African lion has, with a change of game and conditions, lapsed from a " solitary " to a gregarious, that is to say a prolonged family habit of life.

Man, too, if in his ape-like phase he resembled the other higher apes, is an animal becoming more gregarious and not less. He has passed within the historical period from a tribal gregariousness to a nearly cosmopolitan tolerance. And he has his tribe about him. He is not, as Professor Murray seems to suggest, a solitary *lost* gregarious beast. Why should his desire for God be regarded as the overflow of an unsatisfied gregarious instinct, when he has home, town, society, companionship, trade union, state, *increasingly* at hand, to glut it ? Why should gregariousness drive a man to God rather than to the third-class carriage and the public-house ? Why should gregariousness drive men out of crowded Egyptian cities into the cells of the Thebaid ? Schopenhauer in a memorable passage (about the hedgehogs who assembled for warmth) is flatly opposed to Professor Murray, and seems far more plausible when he declares that the nature of man is sufficiently gregarious. The parallel with the dog is not a valid one.

Does not the truth lie rather in the supposition that it is not the Friend that is the instinctive delusion but the isolation ? Is not the real deception our belief that we are completely individualised, and is it not possible that this that Professor Murray calls " instinct " is really not a vestige but a new thing arising out of our increasing understanding, an intellectual penetration to that greater being of the species, that vine of which we are the branches ? Why should not the soul of the species, many-faceted indeed, be nevertheless a soul like our own ?

Here, as in the case of Professor Metchnikoff, and in many other cases of atheism, it seems to me that nothing but an inadequate understanding or individuation bars the way to at least the intellectual recognition of the True God.

§ 6

Religion as Ethics

And while I am dealing with rationalists let me note certain recent interesting utterances of Sir Harry Johnston's. You will note that, while in this book we use the word " God " to indicate the God of the Heart, Sir Harry uses " God " for that idea of God-of-the-Universe which we have spoken of as the Infinite Being. This use of the word " God " is of late theological origin ; the original identity of the words "good " and " god " and all the stories of the gods are against him. But Sir Harry takes up God only to define him away into incomprehensible necessity. Thus :—

" We know absolutely nothing concerning the Force we call God ; and, assuming such an intelligent ruling force to be in existence, permeating this universe of millions of stars and (no doubt) tens of millions of planets, we do not know under what conditions and limitations It works. We are quite entitled to assume that the end of such an influence is intended to be order out of chaos, happiness and perfection out of incompleteness and misery ; and we are entitled to identify the reactionary forces of brute Nature with the anthropomorphic Devil of primitive religions, the power of darkness resisting the power of light. But in these conjectures we must surely come to the conclusion that the theoretical potency we call ' God ' makes endless experiments, and scrap-heaps the failures. Think of the Dinosaurs and the expenditure of creative energy that went to their differentiation and their well-nigh incredible physical development. . . .

" To such a Divine Force as we postulate, the whole development and perfecting of life on this planet, the whole production of man, may seem little more than to any one of us would be the chipping out, the cutting, the carving, and the polishing of a gem ; and we should feel as little remorse or pity for the scattered dust and fragments as must the Creative Force of the immeasurably vast universe feel for the *disjecta membra* of perfected life on this planet. . . ."

But thence he goes on to a curiously imperfect treatment of the God of man as if he consisted in nothing more than some vague sort of humanitarianism. Sir Harry's ideas are much less thoroughly thought out than those of any other of these sceptical writers I have quoted. On that account they are perhaps more typical. He speaks as though Christ were simply an eminent but ill-reported and abominably served teacher of ethics—and yet of the only right ideal and ethics. He speaks as though religions were nothing more than ethical movements, and as though Christianity were merely some one remarking with a bright impulsiveness that everything was simply horrid, and so, " Let us instal loving-kindness as a cardinal axiom." He ignores altogether the fundamental essential of religion, which is *the development and synthesis of the divergent and conflicting motives of the unconverted life, and the identification of the individual life with the immortal purpose of God*. He presents a conception of religion relieved of its " nonsense " as the cheerful self-determination of a number of bright little individuals (much stirred but by no means overcome by Cosmic Pity) to the Service of Man. As he seems to present it, it is as outward a thing, it goes as little into the intimacy of their lives, as though they had after proper consideration agreed to send a subscription to a Red Cross Ambulance or take part in a public demonstration against the Armenian massacres, or do any other rather nice-spirited exterior thing. This is what he says :—

" I hope that the religion of the future will devote itself wholly to the Service of Man. It can do so without departing from the Christian ideal and Christian ethics. It need only drop all that is silly and disputable, and 'mattering not neither here nor there,' of Christian theology—a theology virtually absent from the direct teaching of Christ—and all of Judaistic literature or prescriptions not made immortal in their application by unassailable truth and by the confirmation of science. An excellent remedy for the nonsense which still clings about religion may be found in two books : Cotter Morrison's *Service of Man*, which was published as long ago as 1887, and has since been re-issued by the Rationalist Press Association in its well-known sixpenny series, and J. Allanson Picton's *Man and the Bible*. Similarly, those who wish to acquire a sane view of the relations between man and God would do well to read Winwood Reade's *Martyrdom of Man*."

Sir Harry in fact clears the ground for God very ably, and then makes a well-meaning gesture in the vacant space. There is no help nor strength in his gesture unless God is there. Without God, the *Service of Man* is no better than a hobby or a sentimentality or an hypocrisy in the undisciplined prison of the mortal life.

CHAPTER FIVE

THE INVISIBLE KING

§ I

Modern Religion a Political Religion

THE conception of a young and energetic God, an Invisible Prince, growing in strength and wisdom, who calls men and women to his service and who gives salvation from self and mortality only through self-abandonment to his service, necessarily involves a demand for a complete revision and fresh orientation of the life of the convert.

God faces the blackness of the Unknown and the blind joys and confusions and cruelties of Life, as one who leads mankind through a dark jungle to a great conquest. He brings mankind not rest but a sword. It is plain that he can admit no divided control of the world he claims. He concedes nothing to Cæsar. In our philosophy there are no human things that are God's and others that are Cæsar's. Those of the new thought cannot render unto God the things that are God's, and to Cæsar the things that are Cæsar's. Whatever claim Cæsar may make to rule men's lives and direct their destinies outside the will of God, is a usurpation. No king nor Cæsar has any right to tax or to service or to tolerance, except he claim as one who holds for and under God. And he must make good his claim. The steps of the altar of the God of Youth are no safe place for the sacrilegious figure of a king. Who claims " divine right " plays with the lightning.

The new conception does not tolerate either kings or aristocracies or democracies. Its implicit command to all its adherents is to make plain the way to the world theocracy. Its rule of life is the discovery and service of the will of God, which dwells in the hearts of men, and the performance of that will, not only in the private life of the believer but in the acts and order of the state and nation of which he is a part. I give myself to God not only because I am so and so, but because I am mankind. I become in a measure responsible for every evil in the world of men. I become a knight in God's service. I become my brother's keeper. I become a responsible minister of my King. I take sides against injustice, disorder, and against all those temporal kings, emperors, princes, landlords, and owners who set themselves up against God's rule and worship. Kings, owners, and all who claim rule and decision in the world's affairs, must either show themselves clearly the fellow-servants of the believer or become the objects of his steadfast antagonism.

§ 2

The Will of God

It is here that those who explain this modern religiosity will seem most arbitrary to the inquirer. For they relate of God, as men will relate of a close friend, his dispositions, his apparent intentions, the aims of his kingship. And just as they advance no proof whatever of the existence of God but their realisation of him, so with regard to these qualities and dispositions they have little argument but profound conviction. What they say is this : that if you do not feel God then there is no persuading you of him ; we cannot win over the incredulous. And what they say of his qualities is this :that if you feel God than you will know, you will realise more and more clearly, that thus and thus and no other is his method and intention.

It comes as no great shock to those who have grasped the full implications of the statement that God is Finite, to hear it asserted that the first purpose of God is the attainment of clear knowledge, of knowledge as a means to more knowledge, and of knowledge as a means to power. For that he must use human eyes and hands and brains.

And as God gathers power he uses it to an end that he is only beginning to apprehend, and that he will apprehend more fully as time goes on. But it is possible to define the broad outlines of the attainment he seeks. It is the conquest of death.

It is the conquest of death ; first the overcoming of death in the individual by the incorporation of the motives of his life into an undying purpose, and then the defeat of that death that seems to threaten our species upon a cooling planet beneath a cooling sun. God fights against death in every form, against the great death of the race, against the petty death of indolence, insufficiency, baseness, misconception, and perversion. He it is and no other who can deliver us " from the body of this death." This is the battle that grows plainer ; this is the purpose to which he calls us out of the animal's round of eating, drinking, lusting, quarrelling and laughing and weeping, fearing and failing, and presently of wearying and dying, which is the whole life that living without God can give us. And from these great propositions there follow many very definite maxims and rules of life for those who serve God. These we will immediately consider.

§ 3

The Crucifix

But first let me write a few words here about those who hold a kind of intermediate faith between the worship of the

God of Youth and the vaguer sort of Christianity. There are a number of people closely in touch with those who have found the new religion who, biased probably by a dread of too complete a break with Christianity, have adopted a theogony which is very reminiscent of Gnosticism and of the Paulician, Catharist, and kindred sects to which allusion has already been made. Him, who is called in this book God, they would call God-the-Son or Christ, or the Logos ; and what is here called the Darkness or the Veiled Being, they would call God-the-Father: And what we speak of here as Life, they would call, with a certain disregard of the poor brutes that perish, Man. And they would assert, what we of the new belief, pleading our profound ignorance, would neither assert nor deny, that the Darkness, out of which came Life and God, since it produced them must be ultimately sympathetic and of like nature with them. And that ultimately Man, being redeemed and led by Christ and saved from death by him would be reconciled with God the Father.[1] And this great adventurer out of the heart of man that we here call God, they would present as the same with that teacher from Galilee who was crucified at Jerusalem.

Now we of the modern way would offer the following criticisms upon this apparent compromise between our faith and the current religion. Firstly, we do not presume to theorise about the nature of the Veiled Being nor about that Being's relations to God and to Life. We do not recognise any consistent sympathetic possibilities between these outer beings and our God. Our God is, we feel, like Prometheus, a rebel. He is unfilial. And the accepted figure of Jesus, instinct with meek submission, is not in the tone of our worship. It is not by suffering that God conquers death, but by fighting. Incidentally our God dies a million deaths, but the thing that matters is not the deaths but the immortality. It may be he cannot escape in this person or that person being nailed to a cross or chained to be torn by vultures on a rock. These may be necessary sufferings, like hunger and thirst in a campaign ; they do not in themselves bring victory. They may be necessary, but they are not glorious. The symbol of the crucifixion, the drooping, pain-drenched figure of Christ, the sorrowful cry to his Father, " My God, my God, why hast thou forsaken me ? "—these things jar with our spirit. We little men may well fail and repent, but it is our faith that our God does not fail us nor himself. We cannot accept the Christian's crucifix, or pray to a pitiful God. We cannot accept the Resurrection as though it were an afterthought to a bitterly felt death. Our crucifix, if you must have a crucifix, would

<hr />

[1] This probably was the conception of Spinoza. Christ for him is the wisdom of God manifested in all things, and chiefly in the mind of man. Through him we reach the blessedness of an intuitive knowledge of God. Salvation is an escape from the " inadequate " ideas of the mortal human personality to the " adequate " and timeless ideas of God.

show God with a hand or a foot already torn away from its nail, and with eyes not downcast but resolute against the sky ; a face without pain, pain lost and forgotten in the surpassing glory of the struggle and the inflexible will to live and prevail. . . .

But we do not care how long the thorns are drawn, nor how terrible the wounds, so long as he does not droop. God is courage. God is courage beyond any conceivable suffering.

But when all this has been said, it is well to add that it concerns the figure of Christ only in so far as that professes to be the figure of God, and the crucifix only so far as that stands for divine action. The figure of Christ crucified, so soon as we think of it as being no more than the tragic memorial of Jesus, of the man who proclaimed the loving-kindness of God and the supremacy of God's kingdom over the individual life, and who, in the extreme agony of his pain and exhaustion, cried out that he was deserted, becomes something altogether distinct from a theological symbol. Immediately that we cease to worship, we can beg in to love and pity. Here was a being of extreme gentleness and delicacy and of great courage, of the utmost tolerance and the subtlest sympathy, a saint of non-resistance. . . .

We of the new faith repudiate the teaching of non-resistance. We are the militant followers of and participators in a militant God. We can appreciate and admire the greatness of Christ, this gentle being upon whose nobility the theologians trade. But submission is the remotest quality of all from our God, and a moribund figure is the completest inversion of his likeness as we know him. A Christianity which shows, for its daily symbol, Christ risen and trampling victoriously upon a broken cross would be far more in the spirit of our worship.[1]

---

[1] It is curious, after writing the above, to find in a letter written by Foss Westcott Bishop of Durham, to that pertinacious correspondent, the late Lady Victoria Welby, almost exactly the same sentiments I have here expressed. " If I could fill the Crucifix with life as you do," he says, " I would gladly look on it, but the fallen Head and the closed Eye exclude from my thought the idea of glorified humanity. The Christ to whom we are led is One who ' hath been crucified,' who hath passed the trial victoriously and borne the fruits to heaven. I dare not then rest on this side of the glory."

I find, too, a still more remarkable expression of the modern spirit in a tract, " The Call of the Kingdom," by that very able and subtle Anglican theologian, the Rev. W. Temple, who declares that under the vitalising stresses of the war we are winning " faith in Christ as an heroic leader. We have thought of Him so much as meek and gentle that there is no ground, in our picture of Him, for the vision which His disciple had of Him : ' His head and His hair were white as white wool, white as snow ; and His eyes were as a flame of fire ; and His feet like unto burnished brass, as if it had been refined in a furnace ; and His voice as the voice of many waters. And He had in His right hand seven stars ; and out of His mouth proceeded a sharp two-edged sword ; and His countenance was as the sun shineth in its strength.' "

These are both exceptional utterances, interesting as showing how clearly parallel are the tendencies within and without Christianity.

§ 4

The Primary Duties

Now it follows very directly from the conception of God as a finite intelligence of boundless courage and limitless possibilities of growth and victory, who has pitted himself against death, who stands close to our inmost beings ready to receive us and use us, to rescue us from the chagrins of egotism and take us into his immortal adventure, that we who have realised him, and given ourselves joyfully to him, must needs be equally ready and willing to give our energies to the task we share with him, to do our utmost to increase knowledge, to increase order and clearness, to fight against indolence, waste, disorder, cruelty, vice, and every form of his and our enemy, death, first and chiefest in ourselves but also in all mankind, and to bring about the establishment of his real and visible kingdom throughout the world.

And that idea of God as the Invisible King of the whole world means not merely that God is to be made and declared the head of the world, but that the kingdom of God is to be present throughout the whole fabric of the world, that the Kingdom of God is to be in the teaching at the village school, in the planning of the railway siding of the market town, in the mixing of the mortar at the building of the workman's house. It means that ultimately no effigy of intrusive king or emperor is to disfigure our coins and stamps any more ; God himself and no delegate is to be represented wherever men buy or sell, on our letters and our receipts, a perpetual witness, a perpetual reminder. There is no act altogether without significance, no power so humble that it may not be used for or against God, no life but can orient itself to him. To realise God in one's heart is to be filled with the desire to serve him, and the way of his service is neither to pull up one's life by the roots nor to continue it in all its essentials unchanged, but to turn it about, to turn everything that there is in it round into his way.

The outward duty of those who serve God must vary greatly with the abilities they possess and the positions in which they find themselves, but for all there are certain fundamental duties ; a constant attempt to be utterly truthful with oneself, a constant sedulousness to keep oneself fit and bright for God's service, and to increase one's knowledge and powers, and a hidden persistent watchfulness of one's baser motives, a watch against fear and indolence, against vanity, against greed and lust, against envy, malice, and uncharitableness. To have found God truly does in itself make God's service one's essential motive, but these evils lurk in the shadows, in the lassitudes, and unwary moments. No one escapes them

altogether ; there is no need for tragic moods on account
of imperfections. We can no more serve God without blunders
and set-backs than we can win battles without losing men.
But the less of such loss the better. The servant of God must
keep his mind as wide and sound and his motives as clean as
he can, just as an operating surgeon must keep his nerves
and muscles as fit and his hands as clean as he can. Neither
may righteously evade exercise and regular washing—of
mind as of hands. An incessant watchfulness of one's
self and one's thoughts and the soundness of one's thoughts,
cleanliness, clearness, a wariness against indolence and prejudice, careful truth, habitual frankness, fitness and steadfast
work ; these are the daily fundamental duties that every
one who truly comes to God will, as a matter of course, set
before himself.

§ 5

The Increasing Kingdom

Now, of the more intimate and personal life of the believer
it will be more convenient to write a little later. Let us for the
present pursue the idea of this world-kingdom of God, to
whose establishment he calls us. This kingdom is to be a
peaceful and co-ordinated activity of all mankind upon
certain divine ends. These, we conceive, are first, the maintenance of the racial life ; secondly, the exploration of the external
being of nature as it is and as it has been, that is to say history
and science ; thirdly, that exploration of inherent human
possibility which is art ; fourthly, that clarification of thought
and knowledge which is philosophy, and finally, the progressive
enlargement and development of the racial life under these
lights, so that God may work through a continually better
body of humanity and through better and better equipped
minds, that he and our race may increase for ever, working
unendingly upon the development of the powers of life and
the mastery of the blind forces of matter throughout the deeps
of space. He sets out with us, we are persuaded, to conquer
ourselves and our world and the stars. And beyond the stars
our eyes can as yet see nothing, our imaginations reach and
fail. Beyond the limits of our understanding is the Veiled
Being of Fate, whose face is hidden from us. . . .

It may be that minds will presently appear among us of such
a quality that the face of that Unknown will not be altogether
hidden. . . .

But the business of such ordinary lives as ours is the setting
up of this earthly kingdom of God. That is the form into
which our lives must fall and our consciences adapt themselves.

Belief in God as the Invisible King brings with it almost necessarily a conception of this coming kingdom of God on earth. Each believer, as he grasps this natural and immediate consequence of the faith that has come into his life will form at the same time a Utopian conception of this world changed in the direction of God's purpose. The vision will follow the realisation of God's true nature and purpose as a necessary second step. And he will begin to develop the latent citizen of this world-state in himself. He will fall in with the idea of the world-wide sanities of this new order being drawn over the warring outlines of the present, and of men falling out of relationship with the old order and into relationship with the new. Many men and women are already working to-day at tasks that belong essentially to God's kingdom, tasks that would be of the same essential nature if the world were now a theocracy ; for example, they are doing or sustaining scientific research or education or creative art ; they are making roads to bring men together, they are doctors working for the world's health, they are building homes, they are constructing machinery to save and increase the powers of men. . . .

Such men and women need only to change their orientation, as men will change about at a work-table when the light that was coming in a little while ago from the southern windows begins presently to come in chiefly from the west, to become open and confessed servants of God. This work that they were doing for ambition, or the love of men or the love of knowledge or what seemed the inherent impulse to the work itself, or for money or honour or country or king, they will realise they are doing for God and by the power of God. Self-transformation into a citizen of God's kingdom and a new realisation of all earthly politics as no more than the struggle to define and achieve the kingdom of God on the earth, follow on, without any need for a fresh spiritual impulse, from the moment when God and the believer meet and clasp one another.

This transfiguration of the world into a theocracy may seem a merely fantastic idea to any one who comes to it freshly without such general theological preparation as the preceding pages have made. But to any one who has been at the pains to clear his mind even a little from the obsession of existing but transitory things, it ceases to be a mere suggestion and becomes more and more manifestly the real future of mankind. From the phase of " so things should be," the mind will pass very rapidly to the realisation that " so things will be." Towards this the directive wills among men have been drifting more and more steadily and perceptibly and with fewer eddyings and retardations, for many centuries. The purpose of mankind will not be always thus confused and fragmentary. This dissemination of will-power is a phase. The age of warring tribes and kingdoms and empires that began a hundred centuries or so ago, draws to its close. The kingdom of God on earth is not a metaphor, not a mere spiritual state, not a dream, not an uncertain project ; it is the thing before us, it is the close and inevitable destiny of mankind.

In a few score years the faith of the True God will be spreading about the world. The few halting confessions of God that one hears here and there to-day, like that little twittering of birds which comes before the dawn, will have swollen to a choral unanimity. In but a few centuries the whole world will be openly, confessedly, preparing for the kingdom. In but a few centuries God will have led us out of the dark forest of these present wars and confusions into the open brotherhood of his rule.

§ 6

What is My Place in the Kingdom

This conception of the general life of mankind as a transformation at thousands of points of the confused, egotistical, proprietary, partisan, nationalist, life-wasting chaos of human life to-day into the coherent development of the world-kingdom of God, provides the form into which every one who comes to the knowledge of God will naturally seek to fit his every thought and activity. The material greeds, the avarice, fear, rivalries, and ignoble ambitions of a disordered world will be challenged and examined under one general question : " What am I in the kingdom of God ? "

It has already been suggested that there is a great and growing number of occupations that belong already to God's kingdom, research, teaching, creative art, creative administration, cultivation, construction, maintenance, and the honest satisfaction of honest, practical human needs. For such people conversion to the intimacy of God means at most a change in the spirit of their work, a refreshed energy, a clearer understanding, a new zeal, a completer disregard to gains and praises and promotion. Pay, honours, and the like cease to be the inducement of effort. Service, and service alone, is the criterion that the quickened conscience will recognise.

Most of such people will find themselves in positions in which service is mingled with activities of a baser sort, in which service is a little warped and deflected by old traditions and usage, by mercenary and commercial considerations, by some inherent or special degradation of purpose. The spirit of God will not let the believer rest until his life is readjusted and as far as possible freed from the waste of these base diversions.

For example, a scientific investigator, lit and inspired by great
inquiries, may be hampered by the conditions of his professor-
ship or research fellowship, which exacts an appearance of
"practical results." Or he may be obliged to lecture or conduct classes. He may be able to give but half his possible gift
to the work of his real aptitude, and that at a sacrifice of money
and reputation among short-sighted but influential contemporaries. Well, if he is by nature an investigator he will
know that the research is what God needs of him. He cannot
continue it at all if he leaves his position, and so he must needs
waste something of his gift to save the rest. But should a
poorer or a humbler post offer him better opportunity, there
lies his work for God. There one has a very common and
simple type of the problems that will arise in the lives of men
when they are lit by sudden realisation of the immediacy of
God.

Akin to that case is the perplexity of any successful physician
between the increase of knowledge and the public welfare on
the one hand and the lucrative possibilities of his practice
among wealthy people on the other. He belongs to a profession that is crippled by a mediæval code, a profession which
was blind to the common interest of the Public Health and regarded its members merely as skilled practitioners employed
to "cure" individual ailments. Very slowly and tortuously
do the methods of the profession adapt themselves to the
modern conception of an army of devoted men working as a
whole under God for the health of mankind as a whole,
broadening out from the frowsy den of the "leech," with
its crocodile and bottles and hieroglyphic prescriptions, to
a skilled and illuminating co-operation with those who
deal with the food and housing and economic life of the
community.

And again quite parallel with these personal problems is the
trouble of the artist between the market and vulgar fame on
the one hand and his divine impulse on the other.

The presence of God will be a continual light and help in
every decision that must be made by men and women in these
more or less vitiated, but still fundamentally useful and
righteous positions.

The trouble becomes more marked and more difficult in the
case of a man who is a manufacturer or a trader, the financier
of business enterprise or the proprietor of great estates. The
world is in need of manufactures and that goods should be
distributed ; land must be administered and new economic
possibilities developed. The drift of things is in the direction
of state ownership and control, but in a great number of cases
the state is not ripe for such undertakings ; it commands
neither sufficient integrity nor sufficient ability, and the proprietor of factory, store, credit or land, must continue in
possession, holding as a trustee for God, and so far as lies in

his power, preparing for his supersession by some more public administration. Modern religion admits of no facile flights from responsibility. It permits no headlong resort to the wilderness and sterile virtue. It counts the recluse who fasts among scorpions in a cave as no better than a deserter in hiding. It unhesitatingly forbids any rich young man to sell all that he has and give to the poor. Himself and all that he has must be alike dedicated to God.

The plain duty that will be understood by the proprietor of land and of every sort of general need and service, so soon as he becomes aware of God, is so to administer his possessions as to achieve the maximum of possible efficiency, the most generous output, and the least private profit. He may set aside a salary for his maintenance ; the rest he must deal with like a zealous public official. And, if he perceives that the affair could be better administered by other hands than his own, then it is his business to get it into those hands with the smallest delay and the least profit to himself. . . .

The rights and wrongs of human equity are very different from right and wrong in the sight of God. In the sight of God no landlord has a *right* to his rent, no usurer has a *right* to his interest. A man is not justified in drawing the profits from an advantageous agreement nor free to spend the profits of a speculation as he will. God takes no heed of savings nor of abstinence. He recognises no right to the " rewards of abstinence," no right to any rewards. Those profits and comforts and consolations are the inducements that dangle before the eyes of the spiritually blind. Wealth is an embarrassment to the religious, for God calls them to account for it. The servant of God has no business with wealth or power except to use them immediately in the service of God. Finding these things in his hands he is bound to administer them in the service of God.

The tendency of modern religion goes far beyond the alleged communism of the early Christians, and far beyond the tithes of the Scribes and Pharisees. God takes all. He takes you, blood and bones and house and acres, he takes skill and influence and expectations. For all the rest of your life you are nothing but God's agent. If you are not prepared for so complete a surrender, then you are infinitely remote from God. You must go your way. Here you are merely a curious interloper. Perhaps you have been desiring God as an experience or coveting him as a possession. You have not begun to understand. This that we are discussing in this book is as yet nothing for you.

§ 7

Adjusting Life

This picturing of a human world more to the mind of God than this present world, and the discovery and realisation of one's own place and work in and for that kingdom of God, is the natural next phase in the development of the believer. He will set about revising and adjusting his scheme of life, his ways of living, his habits and his relationships in the light of his new convictions.

Most men and women who come to God will have already a certain righteousness in their lives ; these things happen like a thunderclap only in strange, exceptional cases, and the same movements of his mind that have brought them to God will already have brought their lives into a certain rightness of direction and conduct. Yet occasionally there will be some one to whom the self-examination that follows conversion will reveal an entirely wrong and evil way of living. It may be that the light has come to some rich idler doing nothing but follow a pleasurable routine. Or to some one following some highly profitable and amusing, but socially useless or socially mischievous occupation. One may be an advocate at the disposal of any man's purpose or an actor or actress ready to fall in with any theatrical enterprise. Or a woman may find herself a prostitute or a pet wife, a mere kept instrument of indulgence. These are lives of prey, these are lives of futility ; the light of God will not tolerate such lives. Here religion can bring nothing but a severance from the old way of life altogether, a break and a struggle towards use and service and dignity.

But even here it does not follow that because a life has been wrong the new life that begins must be far as the poles asunder from the old. Every sort of experience that has ever come to a human being is in the self that he brings to God, and there is no reason why a knowledge of evil ways should not determine the path of duty. No one can better devise protection against vices than those who have practised them ; none know temptations better than those who have fallen. If a man has followed an evil trade, it becomes him to use his knowledge of the tricks of that trade to help end it. He knows the charities it may claim and the remedies it needs. . . .

A very interesting case to discuss in relation to this question of adjustment is that of the barrister. A practising barrister under contemporary conditions does indeed give most typically the opportunity for examining the relation of an ordinary self-respecting worldly life to life under the dispensation of God discovered. A barrister is usually a man of some energy and ambition, his honour is moulded by the traditions of an ancient and antiquated profession, instinctively self-preserving and yet with a real desire for consistency and respect. As a profession it has been greedy and defensively conservative, but it has never been shameless nor has it ever broken faith with its own large and selfish, but quite definite, propositions. It has never, for instance, had the shamelessness of such a traditionless and undisciplined class as the early factory organisers. It has never had the dull, incoherent wickedness of the sort of men who exploit drunkenness and the turf. It offends within limits. Barristers can be, and are, disbarred. But it is now a profession extraordinarily out of date ; its code of honour derives from a time of cruder and lower conceptions of human relationships. It apprehends the State as a mere " ring " kept about private disputations ; it has not begun to move towards the modern conception of the collective enterprise as the determining criterion of human conduct. It sees its business as a mere play upon the rules of a game between man and man, or between men and men. They haggle, they dispute, they inflict and suffer wrongs, they evade dues, and are liable or entitled to penalties and compensations. The primary business of the law is held to be decision in these wrangles and, as wrangling is subject to artistic elaboration, the business of the barrister is the business of a professional wrangler ; he is a bravo in wig and gown who fights the duels of ordinary men because they are incapable, very largely on account of the complexities of legal procedure, of fighting for themselves. His business is never to explore any fundamental right in the matter. His business is to say all that can be said for his client, and to conceal or minimise whatever can be said against his client. The successful promoted advocate, who in Britain and the United States of America is the judge, and whose habits and interests all incline him to disregard the realities of the case in favour of the points in the forensic game, then adjudicates upon the contest. . . .

Now this condition of things is clearly incompatible with the modern conception of the world as becoming a divine kingdom. When the world is openly and confessedly the kingdom of God, the law court will exist only to adjust the differing views of men as to the manner of their service to God ; the only right of action one man will have against another will be that he has been prevented or hampered or distressed by the other in serving God. The idea of the law courts will have changed entirely from a place of dispute, exaction and vengeance, to a place of adjustment. The individual or some state organisation will plead *on behalf of the common good* either against some state official or state regulation, or against the actions or inaction of another individual. This is the only sort of legal proceedings compatible with the broad beliefs of the new faith.

. . . Every religion that becomes ascendant, in so far as it is not other-worldly, must necessarily set its stamp upon the methods and administration of the law. That this was not the case with Christianity is one of the many contributory aspects that lead one to the conviction that it was not Christianity that took possession of the Roman empire, but an imperial adventurer who took possession of an all too complaisant Christianity.

Reverting now from these generalisations to the problem of the religions from which they arose, it will have become evident that the essential work of any one who is conversant with the existing practice and literature of the law and whose natural abilities are forensic, will lie in the direction of reconstructing the theory and practice of the law in harmony with modern conceptions, of making that theory and practice clear and plain to ordinary men, of reforming the abuses of the profession by working for the separation of bar and judiciary, for the amalgamation of the solicitors and the barristers, and the like needed reforms. These are matters that will probably only be properly set right by a quickening of conscience among lawyers themselves. Of no class of men is the help and service so necessary to the practical establishment of God's kingdom, as of men learned and experienced in the law. And there is no reason why for the present an advocate should not continue to plead in the courts, provided he does his utmost only to handle cases in which he believes he can serve the right. Few righteous cases are ill-served by a frank disposition on the part of lawyer and client to put everything before the court. Thereby, of course, there arises a difficult case of conscience. What if a lawyer, believing his client to be in the right, discovers him to be in the wrong ? He cannot throw up the case unless he has been scandalously deceived, because so he would betray the confidence his client has put in him to " see him through." He has a right to " give himself away," but not to " give away " his client in this fashion. If he has a chance of a private consultation I think he ought to do his best to make his client admit the truth of the case and give in, but failing this he has no right to be virtuous on behalf of another. No man may play God to another ; he may remonstrate, but that is the limit of his right. He must respect a confidence, even if it is purely implicit and involuntary. I admit that here the barrister is in a cleft stick, and that he must see the business through according to the confidence his client has put in him— and afterwards be as sorry as he may be if injustice ensues. And also I would suggest a lawyer may with a fairly good conscience defend a guilty man as if he were innocent, to save him from unjustly heavy penalties. . . .

This comparatively full discussion of the barrister's problem has been embarked upon because it does bring in, in a very typical fashion, just those uncertainties and imperfections that abound in real life.   Religious conviction gives us a general direction, but it stands aside from many of these entangled struggles in the jungle of conscience.   Practice is often easier than a rule.   In practice a lawyer will know, far more accurately than a hypothetical case can indicate, how far he is bound to see his client through, and how far he may play the keeper of his client's conscience.   And nearly every day there happen instances where the most subtle casuistry will fail and the finger of conscience point unhesitatingly. One may have worried long in the preparation and preliminaries of the issue, one may bring the case at last into the final court of conscience in an apparently hopeless tangle.   Then suddenly comes decision.

The procedure of that silent, lit, and empty court in which a man states his case to God, is very simple and perfect.   The excuses and the special pleading shrivel and vanish.   In a little while the case lies bare and plain.

§ 8

The Oath of Allegiance

The question of oaths of allegiance, acts of acquiescence in existing governments, and the like, is one that arises at once with the acceptance of God as the supreme and real King of the Earth.   At the worst Cæsar is a usurper, a satrap claiming to be sovereign ;   at the best he is provisional.   Modern casuistry makes no great trouble for the believing public official.   The chief business of any believer is to do the work for which he is best fitted, and since all state affairs are to become the affairs of God's kingdom it is of primary importance that they should come into the hands of God's servants. It is scarcely less necessary to a believing man with administrative gifts that he should be in the public administration than that he should breathe and eat.   And whatever oath or the like to usurper church or usurper king has been set up to bar access to service is an oath imposed under duress.   If it cannot be avoided it must be taken rather than that a man should become unserviceable.   All such oaths are unfair and foolish things.   They exclude no scoundrels ; they are appeals to superstition.   Whenever an opportunity occurs for the abolition of an oath, the servant of God will seize it, but where the oath is unavoidable he will take it.

The service of God is not to achieve a delicate consistency of statement ; it is to do as much as one can of God's work.

§ 9

The Priest and the Creed

It may be doubted if this line of reasoning regarding the official and his oath can be extended to excuse the priest or pledged minister of religion who finds that faith in the True God has ousted his formal beliefs.

This has been a frequent and subtle moral problem in the intellectual life of the last hundred years. It has been increasingly difficult for any class of reading, talking, and discussing people such as are the bulk of the priesthoods of the Christian churches to escape hearing and reading the accumulated criticism of the Trinitarian theology and of the popularly accepted story of man's fall and salvation. Some have no doubt defeated this universal and insidious critical attack entirely, and honestly established themselves in a right-down acceptance of the articles and disciplines to which they have subscribed and of the creeds they profess and repeat. Some have recanted and abandoned their positions in the priesthood. But a great number have neither resisted the bacillus of criticism nor left the churches to which they are attached. They have adopted compromises, they have qualified their creeds with modifying foot-notes of essential repudiation ; they have decided that plain statements are metaphors and have undercut, transposed, and inverted the most vital points of the vulgarly accepted beliefs. One may find within the Anglican communion Arians, Unitarians, Atheists, disbelievers in immortality, attenuators of miracles ; there is scarcely a doubt or a cavil that has not found a lodgment within the ample charity of the English Establishment. I have been interested to hear one distinguished Canon deplore that " they " did not identify the Logos with the third instead of the second Person of the Trinity, and another distinguished Catholic apologist declare his indifference to the " historical Jesus." Within most of the Christian communions one may believe anything or nothing, provided only that one does not call too public an attention to one's eccentricity. The late Rev. Charles Voysey, for example, preached plainly in his church at Healaugh against the divinity of Christ, unhindered. It was only when he published his sermons under the provocative title of *The Sling and the Stone,* and caused an outcry beyond the limits of his congregation, that he was indicted and deprived.

Now the reasons why these men do not leave the ministry or priesthood in which they find themselves are often very plausible. It is probable that in very few cases is the retention of stipend or incumbency a conscious dishonesty. At the worst it is mitigated by thought for wife or child. It has only been during very exceptional phases of religious development and controversy that beliefs have been really sharp. A creed, like a coin, it may be argued, loses little in practical value because it is worn, or bears the image of a vanished king. The religious life is a reality that has clothed itself in many garments, and the concern of the priest or minister is with the religious life, and not with the poor symbols that may indeed pretend to express, but do as a matter of fact no more than indicate, its direction. It is quite possible to maintain that the church and not the creed is the real and valuable instrument of religion, that the religious life is sustained not by its propositions but by its routines. Any one who seeks the intimate discussion of spiritual things with professional divines will find this is the substance of the case for the ecclesiastical sceptic. His church, he will admit, mumbles its statement of truth, but where else is truth ? What better formulæ are to be found for ineffable things ? And meanwhile—he does good.

That may be a valid defence before a man finds God. But we who profess the worship and fellowship of the living God deny that religion is a matter of ineffable things. The way of God is plain and simple and easy to understand.

Therewith the whole position of the conforming sceptic is changed. If a professional religious has any justification at all for his professionalism it is surely that he proclaims the nearness and greatness of God. And these creeds and articles and orthodoxies are not proclamations but curtains ; they are a darkening and confusion of what should be crystal-clear. What compensatory good can a priest pretend to do when his primary business is the truth and his method a lie ? The oaths and incidental conformities of men who wish to serve God in the state are on a different footing altogether from the falsehood and mischief of one who knows the True God and yet recites to a trustful congregation a misleading and ill-phrased Levantine creed.

Such is the line of thought which will impose the renunciation of his temporalities and a complete cessation of services upon every ordained priest and minister as his first act of faith. Once that he has truly realised God, it becomes impossible for him ever to repeat his creed again. His course seems plain and clear. It becomes him to stand up before the flock he has led in error, and to proclaim the being and nature of the one True God. He must be explicit to the utmost of his powers. Then he may await his expulsion. It may be doubted whether it is sufficient for him to go away silently, making false excuses or none at all for his retreat. He has to atone for the implicit acquiescence of his conforming years.

§ 10

The Universalism of God

Are any sorts of people shut off as if by inherent necessity from God ?

This is, so to speak, one of the standing questions of theology ; it reappears with slight changes of form at every period of religious interest, it is, for example, the chief issue between the Arminian and the Calvinist. From its very opening proposition modern religion sweeps past and far ahead of the old Arminian teachings of Wesleyans and Methodists, in its insistence upon the entirely finite nature of God. Arminians seem merely to have insisted that God has conditioned himself, and by his own free act left men free to accept or reject salvation. To the realist type of mind— here as always I use " realist " in its proper sense as the opposite of nominalist—to the old-fashioned over-exact and over-accentuating type of mind, such ways of thinking seem vague and unsatisfying. Just as it distresses the more down-right kind of intelligence with a feeling of disloyalty to admit that God is not Almighty, so it troubles the same sort of intelligence to hear that there is no clear line to be drawn between the saved and the lost. Realists like an exclusive flavour in their faith. Moreover, it is a natural weakness of humanity to be forced into extreme positions by argument. It is probable, as I have already suggested, that the absolute attributes of God were forced upon Christianity under the stresses of propaganda, and it is probable that the theory of a superhuman obstinacy beyond salvation arose out of the irritations natural to theological debate. It is but a step from the realisation that there are people absolutely unable or absolutely unwilling to see God as we see him, to the conviction that they are, therefore, shut off from God by an invincible soul-blindness.

It is very easy to believe that other people are essentially damned.

Beyond the little world of our sympathies and comprehension there are those who seem inaccessible to God by any means within our experience. They are people answering to the " hard-hearted," to the " stiff-necked generation " of the Hebrew prophets. They betray and even confess to standards that seem hopelessly base to us. They show themselves incapable of any disinterested enthusiasm for beauty or truth or goodness. They are altogether remote from intelligent sacrifice. To every test they betray vileness of texture ; they are mean, cold, wicked. There are people who seem to cheat with a private self-approval, who are ever ready to do harsh and cruel things, whose use for social feeling is the malignant boycott, and for prosperity, monopolisation and humiliating display ; who seize upon religion and turn it into persecution, and upon beauty to torment it on the altars of some joyless vice. We cannot do with such souls ; we have no use for them, and it is very easy indeed to step from that persuasion to the belief that God has no use for them.

And besides these base people there are the stupid people and the people with minds so poor in texture that they cannot even grasp the few broad and simple ideas that seem necessary to the salvation we experience, who lapse helplessly into fetishistic and fearful conceptions of God, and are apparently quite incapable of distinguishing between what is practically and what is spiritually good.

It is an easy thing to conclude that the only way to God is our way to God, that he is the privilege of a finer and better sort to which we, of course, belong, that he is no more the God of the card-sharper or the pickpocket or the " smart " woman or the loan-monger or the village oaf than he is of the swine in the sty. But are we justified in thus limiting God to the measure of our moral and intellectual understandings ? Because some people seem to me steadfastly and consistently base or hopelessly and incurably dull and confused, does it follow that there are not phases, albeit I have never chanced to see them, of exaltation in the one case and illumination in the other ? And may I not be a little restricting my perception of Good ? While I have been ready enough to pronounce this or that person as being, so far as I was concerned, thoroughly damnable or utterly dull, I find a curious reluctance to admit the general proposition which is necessary for these instances. It is possible that the difference between Arminian and Calvinist is a difference of essential intellectual temperament rather than of theoretical conviction. I am temperamentally Arminian as I am temperamentally Nominalist. I feel that it must be in the nature of God to attempt all souls. There must be accessibilities of which I know nothing.

Yet here is a consideration pointing rather the other way. If you think, as you must think, that you yourself can be lost to God and damned, then I cannot see how you can avoid thinking that other people can be damned. But that is not to believe that there are people damned at the outset by their normal and intellectual insufficiency ; that is not to make out that there is a class of essential and incurable spiritual defectives. The religious life preceded clear religious understanding and extends far beyond its range.

In my own case I perceive that, in spite of the value I attach to true belief, the reality of religion is not an intellectual thing. The essential religious fact is in another than the mental sphere. I am passionately anxious to have the idea of God clear in my own mind, and to make my beliefs plain and clear to other people, and particularly to other people who may seem to be feeling with me ; I do perceive that error is evil if only because a faith based on confused conceptions and partial understandings may suffer irreparable injury through the collapse of its substratum of ideas. I doubt if faith can be complete and enduring if it is not secured by the definite knowledge of the True God. Yet I have also to admit that I find the form of my own religious emotion paralleled by people with whom I have no intellectual sympathy and no agreement in phrase or formula at all.

There is, for example, this practical identity of religious feeling and this discrepancy of interpretation between such an inquirer as myself and a convert of the Salvation Army. Here, clothing itself in phrases and images of barbaric sacrifice, of slaughtered lambs and fountains of precious blood, a most repulsive and incomprehensible idiom to me, and expressing itself by shouts, clangour, trumpeting, gesticulations, and rhythmic pacings that stun and dismay my nerves, I find the same object sought, release from self, and the same end, the end of identification with the immortal, successfully if, perhaps, rather insecurely achieved. I see God indubitably present in these excitements, and I see personalities I could easily have misjudged as too base or too dense for spiritual understandings, lit by the manifest reflection of divinity. One may be led into the absurdest underestimates of religious possibilities if one estimates people only coldly and in the light of everyday life. There is a subintellectual religious life which, very conceivably, when its utmost range can be examined, excludes nothing human from religious co-operation, which will use any words to its tune, which takes its phrasing ready-made from the world about it, as it takes the street for its temple, and yet which may be at its inner point in the directest contact with God. Religion may suffer from aphasia and still be religion ; it may utter misleading or nonsensical words and yet intend and convey the truth. The methods of the Salvation Army are older than doctrinal Christianity, and may long survive it. Men and women may still chant of Beulah Land and cry out in the ecstasy of salvation ; the tambourine, that modern revival of the thrilling Alexandrine sistrum, may still stir dull nerves to a first apprehension of powers and a call beyond the immediate material compulsion of life, when the creeds of Christianity are as dead as the lore of the Druids.

The emancipation of mankind from obsolete theories and formularies may be accompanied by great tides of moral and emotional release among types and strata that by the standards of a trained and explicit intellectual may seem spiritually hopeless. It is not necessary to imagine the whole world critical and lucid in order to imagine the whole world unified in religious sentiment, comprehending the same phrases and coming together, regardless of class and race and quality, in the worship and service of the True God. The coming king-ship of God, if it is to be more than hieratic tyranny, must have this universality of appeal. As the head grows clear the body will turn in the right direction. To the mass of men modern religion says, " This is the God it has always been in your nature to apprehend."

§ 11

God and the Love and Status of Women

Now that we are discussing the general question of individual conduct, it will be convenient to take up again, and restate in that relationship, propositions already made very plainly in the second and third chapters. Here there are several excellent reasons for a certain amount of deliberate repetition. . . .

All the mystical relations of chastity, virginity, and the like with religion, those questions of physical status that play so large a part in most contemporary religions, have disappeared from modern faith. Let us be as clear as possible upon this. God is concerned by the health and fitness and vigour of his servants; we owe him our best and utmost ; but he has no special concern and no special preferences or commandments regarding sexual things.

Christ, it is manifest, was of the modern faith in these matters ; he welcomed the Magdalen, neither would he con-demn the woman taken in adultery. Manifestly corruption and disease were not to stand between him and those who sought God in him. But the Christianity of the creeds, in this as in so many respects, does not rise to the level of its founder, and it is as necessary to repeat to-day as though the name of Christ had not been ascendant for nineteen centuries, that sex is a secondary thing to religion, and sexual status of no account in the presence of God. It follows quite logically that God does not discriminate between man and woman in any essential things. We leave our individuality behind us when we come into the presence of God. Sex is not dis-avowed but forgotten. Just as one's last meal is forgotten—which also is a difference between the religious moment of modern faith and certain Christian sacraments. You are a believer and God is at hand to you ; heed not your state ; reach out to him and he is there. In the moment of religion you are human ; it matters not what else you are, male or female, clean or unclean, Hebrew or Gentile, bond or free. It is *after* the moment of religion that we become concerned about our state and the manner in which we use ourselves.

We have to follow our reason as our sole guide in our individual treatment of all such things as food and health and sex. God is the king of the whole world ; he is the owner of our souls and bodies and all things. He is not particularly concerned about any aspect, because he is concerned about every aspect. We have to make the best use of ourselves for his kingdom ; that is our rule of life. That rule means neither painful nor frantic abstinences nor any forced way of living. Purity, cleanliness, health—none of these things are for themselves, they are for use ; none are magic, all are means. The sword must be sharp and clean. That does not mean that we are perpetually to sharpen and clean it—which would weaken and waste the blade. The sword must neither be drawn constantly nor always rusting in its sheath. Those who have had the wits and soul to come to God will have the wits and soul to find out and know what is waste, what is vanity, what is the happiness that begets strength of body and spirit, what is error, where vice begins, and to avoid and repent and recoil from all those things that degrade. These are matters not of the rule of life but of the application of life. They must neither be neglected nor made disproportionately important.

To the believer, relationship with God is the supreme relationship. It is difficult to imagine how the association of lovers and friends can be very fine and close and good unless the two who love are each also linked to God, so that through their moods and fluctuations and the changes of years they can be held steadfast by his undying steadfastness. But it has been felt by many deep-feeling people that there is so much kindred between the love and trust of husband and wife and the feeling we have for God, that it is reasonable to consider the former also as a sacred thing. They do so value that close love of mated man and woman, they are so intent upon its permanence and completeness, and to lift the dear relationship out of the ruck of casual and transitory things, that they want to bring it, as it were, into the very presence and assent of God. There are many who dream and desire that they are as deeply and completely mated as this, many more who would fain be so, and some who are. And from this comes the earnest desire to make marriage sacramental and the attempt to impose upon all the world the outward appearance, the restrictions, the pretence at least of such a sacramental union.

There may be such a quasi-sacramental union in many cases, but only after years can one be sure of it ; it is not to be brought about by vows and promises but by an essential kindred and cleaving of body and spirit ; and it concerns only the two who can dare to say they have it, and God. And the divine thing in marriage, the thing that is most like the love of God, is even then, not the relationship of the man and woman as man and woman, but the comradeship and trust and mutual help and pity that joins them. No doubt that from the mutual necessities of bodily love and the common adventure, the necessary honesties and helps of a joint life, there springs the stoutest, nearest, most enduring and best of human companionship ; perhaps only upon that root can the best of mortal comradeship be got ; but it does not follow that the mere ordinary coming together and pairing off of men and women is in itself divine or sacramental or anything of the sort. Being in love is a condition that may have its moments of sublime exaltation, but it is for the most part an experience far down the scale below divine experience ; it is often love only in so far as it shares the name with better things ; it is greed, it is admiration, it is desire, it is the itch for excitement, it is the instinct for competition, it is lust, it is curiosity, it is adventure, it is jealousy, it is hate. On a hundred scores " lovers " meet and part. Thereby some few find true love and the spirit of God in themselves or others.

Lovers may love God in one another ; I do not deny it. That is no reason why the imitation and outward form of this great happiness should be made an obligation upon all men and women who are attracted by one another, nor why it should be woven into the essentials of religion. For women much more than for men is this confusion dangerous, lest a personal love should shape and dominate their lives instead of God. " He for God only ; she for God in him," phrases the idea of Milton and of ancient Islam ; it is the formula of sexual infatuation, a formula quite easily inverted, as the end of Goethe's Faust (" The woman soul leadeth us upward and on ") may witness. The whole drift of modern religious feeling is against this exaggeration of sexual feeling, these moods of sexual slavishness, in spiritual things. Between the healthy love of ordinary mortal lovers in love and the love of God, there is an essential contrast and opposition in this, that preference, exclusiveness, and jealousy seem to be in the very nature of the former and are absolutely incompatible with the latter. The former is the intensest realisation of which our individualities are capable ; the latter is the way of escape from the limitations of individuality. It may be true that a few men and more women do achieve the completest unselfishness and self-abandonment in earthly love. So the poets and romancers tell us. If so, it is that by an imaginative perversion they have given to some attractive person a worship that should be reserved for God and a devotion that is normally evoked only by little children in their mother's heart. It is

not the way between most of the men amd women one meets
in this world.

But between God and the believer there is no other way,
there is nothing else, but self-surrender and the ending
of self.

CHAPTER SIX

MODERN IDEAS OF SIN AND DAMNATION

§ 1

The Biological Equivalent of Sin

IF the reader who is unfamiliar with scientific things will obtain and read Metchnikoff's *Nature of Man*, he will find there an interesting summary of the biological facts that bear upon and destroy the delusion that there is such a thing as individual perfection, that there is even ideal perfection for humanity. With an abundance of convincing instances Professor Metchnikoff demonstrates that life is a system of " disharmonies," capable of no perfect way, that there is no " perfect " dieting, no " perfect " sexual life, no " perfect " happiness, no " perfect " conduct. He releases one from the arbitrary but all too easy assumption that there is even an ideal " perfection " in organic life. He sweeps out of the mind, with all the confidence and conviction of a physiological specialist, any idea that there is a perfect man or a conceivable perfect man. It is in the nature of every man to fall short at every point from perfection. From the biological point of view we are as individuals a series of involuntary " tries " on the part of an imperfect species towards an unknown end.

Our spiritual nature follows our bodily, as a glove follows a hand. We are disharmonious beings and salvation no more makes an end to the defects of our souls than it makes an end to the decay of our teeth or to those vestigial structures of our body that endanger our physical welfare. Salvation leaves us still disharmonious, and adds not an inch to our spiritual and moral stature.

§ 2

What is Damnation ?

Let us now take up the question of what is Sin, and what we mean by the term " damnation," in the light of this view of human reality. Most of the great world religions are as clear as Professor Metchnikoff that life in the world is a tangle of disharmonies, and in most cases they supply a more or less myth-like explanation ; they declare that evil is one side of the conflict between Ahriman and Ormazd, or that it is the punishment of an act of disobedience, of the fall of man and world alike from a state of harmony. Their case, like his, is that *this* world is damned.

361

We do not find the belief that superposed upon the miseries of this world there are the still bitterer miseries of punishments after death so nearly universal. The endless punishments of hell appear to be an exploit of theory ; they have a super-added appearance even in the Christian system ; the same common tendency to superlatives and absolutes that makes men ashamed to admit that God is finite makes them seek to enhance the merits of their Saviour by the device of ever-lasting fire. Conquest over the sorrow of life and the fear of death does not seem to them sufficient for Christ's glory.

Now the turning round of the modern mind from a conception of the universe as something derived deductively from the past to a conception of it as something gathering itself adventurously towards the future involves a release from the supposed necessity to tell a story and explain why. Instead comes the inquiry, " To what end ? " We can say, without mental discomfort, these disharmonies are here, this damnation is here—inexplicably. We can, without any distressful inquiry into ultimate origins, bring our minds to the conception of a spontaneous and developing God arising out of those stresses in our hearts and in the universe, and arising to overcome them. Salvation for the individual is escape from the individual distress at disharmony, and the individual defeat by death, into the kingdom of God. And damnation can be nothing more and nothing less than the failure or inability or disinclination to make that escape.

Something of that idea of damnation as a lack of the will for salvation has crept at a number of points into contemporary religious thought. It was the fine fancy of Swedenborg that the damned go to their own hells of their own accord. It underlies a queer poem, " Simpson," by that interesting essayist upon modern Christianity, Mr. Clutton Brock, which I have recently read. Simpson dies and goes to hell—it is rather like the Cromwell Road—and approves of it very highly, and then, and then only, is he completely damned. Not to realise that one can be damned is certainly to be damned ; such is Mr. Brock's idea. It is his definition of damnation. Satisfaction with existing things is damnation. It is surrender to limitation ; it is acquiescence in " disharmony " ; it is making peace with that enemy against whom God fights for ever.

(But whether there are indeed Simpsons who acquiesce always and for ever remains for me, as I have already confessed in the previous chapter, a quite open question. My Arminian temperament turns me from the Calvinistic conclusion of Mr. Brock's satire.)

§ 3

Sin is not Damnation

Now the question of sin will hardly concern those damned and lost by nature, if such there be.   Sin is not the same thing as damnation, as we have just defined damnation.   Damnation is a state, but sin is an incident.   One is an essential and the other an incidental separation from God.   It is possible to sin without being damned ; and to be damned is to be in a state when sin scarcely matters, like ink upon a blackamoor. You cannot have questions of more or less among absolute things.

It is the amazing and distressful discovery of every believer so soon as the first exaltation of belief is past, that one does not remain always in touch with God.   At first it seems incredible that one should ever have any motive again that is not also God's motive.   Then one finds oneself caught unawares by a base impulse.   We discover that discontinuousness of our apparently homogeneous selves, the unincorporated and warring elements that seemed at first altogether absent from the synthesis of conversion.   We are tripped up by forgetfulness, by distraction, by old habits, by tricks of appearance.   There come dull patches of existence ; those mysterious obliterations of one's finer sense that are due at times to the little minor poisons one eats or drinks, to phases of fatigue, ill-health and bodily disorder, or one is betrayed by some unanticipated storm of emotion, brewed deep in the animal being and released by any trifling accident, such as personal jealousy or lust, or one is relaxed by contentment into vanity.   All these rebel forces of our ill-co-ordinated selves, all these " disharmonies " of the inner being, snatch us away from our devotion to God's service, carry us off to follies, offences, unkindness, waste, and leave us compromised, involved, and regretful, perplexed by a hundred difficulties we have put in our own way back to God.

This is the personal problem of Sin.   Here prayer avails ; here God can help us.   From God comes the strength to repent and make such reparation as we can, to begin the battle again farther back and lower down.   From God comes the power to anticipate the struggle with one's rebel self, and to resist and prevail over it.

§ 4

The Sins of the Insane

An extreme case is very serviceable in such a discussion as this.

It happens that the author carries on a correspondence with

several lunatics in asylums. There is a considerable freedom of note-paper in these institutions ; the outgoing letters are no doubt censored or selected in some way, but a proportion at any rate are allowed to go out to their addresses. As a journalist who signs his articles and as the author of various books of fiction, as a frequent *name*, that is, to any one much forced back upon reading, the writer is particularly accessible to this type of correspondent. The letters come, some manifesting a hopeless disorder that permits of no reply, but some being the expression of minds overlaid not at all offensively by a web of fantasy, and some (and these are the more touching ones and the ones that most concern us now) as sanely conceived and expressed as any letters could be. They are written by people living lives very like the lives of us who are called " sane," except that they lift to a higher excitement and fall to a lower depression, and that these extremer phases of mania or melancholia slip the leash of mental consistency altogether and take abnormal forms. They tap deep founts of impulse, such as we of the safer ways of mediocrity do but glimpse under the influence of drugs, or in dreams and rare moments of controllable extravagance. Then the insane become " glorious," or they become murderous, or they become suicidal. All these letter-writers in confinement have convinced their fellow-creatures by some extravagance that they are a danger to themselves or others.

The letters that come from such types, written during their sane intervals, are entirely sane. Some, who are probably unaware—I think they should know—of the offences or possibilities that justify their incarceration, write with a certain resentment at their position ; others are entirely acquiescent ; but one or two complain of the neglect of friends and relations. But all are as manifestly capable of religion and of the religious life as any other intelligent persons during the lucid interludes that make up nine-tenths perhaps of their lives. . . . Suppose now one of these cases, and suppose that the infirmity takes the form of some cruel, disgusting or destructive disposition that may become at times overwhelming, and you have our universal trouble with sinful tendency, as it were magnified for examination. It is clear that the mania which defines his position must be the primary if not the cardinal business in the life of a lunatic, but his problem with that is different not in kind but merely in degree from the problem of lusts, vanities, and weaknesses in what we call normal lives. It is an unconquered tract, a great rebel province in his being, which refuses to serve God and tries to prevent him serving God and succeeds at times in wresting his capital out of his control. But his relationship to that is the same relationship as ours to the backward and insubordinate parishes, criminal slums, and disorderly houses in our own private texture.

It is clear that the believer who is a lunatic is, as it were, only the better part of himself. He serves God with this unconquered disposition in him, like a man who, whatever else he is and does, is obliged to be the keeper of an untrustworthy and wicked animal. His beast gets loose. His only resort is to warn those about him when he feels that jangling or excitement of the nerves which precedes its escapes, to limit its range, to place weapons beyond its reach. And there are plenty of human beings very much in his case, whose beasts have never got loose or have got caught back before their essential insanity was apparent. And there are those uncertifiable lunatics we call men and women of "impulse" and "strong passions." If perhaps they have more self-control than the really mad, yet it happens oftener with them that the whole intelligent being falls under the dominion of evil. The passion scarcely less than the obsession may darken the whole moral sky. Repentance and atonement ; nothing less will avail them after the storm has passed, and the sedulous preparation of defences and palliatives against the return of the storm.

This discussion of the lunatic's case gives us, indeed, usefully coarse and large, the lines for the treatment of every human weakness by the servants of God. A " weakness," just like the lunatic's mania, becomes a particular charge under God, a special duty for the person it affects. He has to minimise it, to isolate it, to keep it out of mischief. If he can he must adopt preventive measures. . . .

These passions and weaknesses that get control of us hamper our usefulness to God, they are an incessant anxiety and distress to us, they wound our self-respect and make us incomprehensible to many who would trust us, they discredit the faith we profess. If they break through and break through again, it is natural and proper that men and women should cease to believe in our faith, cease to work with us or to meet us frankly. . . . Our sins do everything evil to us and through us except separate us from God.

Yet let there be no mistake about one thing. Here prayer is a power. Here God can indeed work miracles. A man with the light of God in his heart can defeat vicious habits, rise again combative and undaunted after a hundred falls, escape from the grip of lusts and revenges, make head against despair, thrust back the very onset of madness. He is still the same man he was before he came to God, still with his libidinous, vindictive, boastful, or indolent vein ; but now his will to prevail over those qualities can refer to an exterior standard and an external interest, he can draw upon a strength, almost boundless, beyond his own.

§ 5

Believe, and You are Saved

But, be a sin great or small, it cannot damn a man once he has found God. You may kill and hang for it, you may rob or rape ; the moment you truly repent and set yourself to such atonement and reparation as is possible there remains no barrier between you and God. Directly you cease to hide or deny or escape, and turn manfully towards the consequences and the setting of things right, you take hold again of the hand of God. Though you sin seventy times seven times, God will still forgive the poor rest of you. Nothing but utter blindness of the spirit can shut a man off from God.

There is nothing one can suffer, no situation so unfortunate, that it can shut off one who has the thought of God, from God. If you but lift up your head for a moment out of a stormy chaos of madness and cry to him, God is there, God will not fail you. A convicted criminal, frankly penitent, and neither obdurate nor abject, whatever the evil of his yesterdays, may still die well and bravely on the gallows to the glory of God. He may step straight from that death into the immortal being of God.

This persuasion is the very essence of the religion of the True God. There is no sin, no state that, being regretted and repented of, can stand between God and man.

CHAPTER SEVEN

THE IDEA OF A CHURCH

§ 1

The World Dawn

As yet those who may be counted as belonging definitely to the new religion are few and scattered and unconfessed. Their realisations are still uncertain and incomplete. But that is no augury for the continuance of this state of affairs even for the next few decades. There are many signs that the revival is coming very swiftly; it may be coming as swiftly as the morning comes after a tropical night. It may seem at present as though nothing very much were happening, except for the fact that the old familiar constellations of theology have become a little pallid and lost something of their multitude of points. But nothing fades of itself. The deep stillness of the late night is broken by a stirring, and the morning star of creedless faith, the last and brightest of the stars, the star that owes its light to the coming sun, is in the sky.

There is a stirring and a movement. There is a stir, like the stir before a breeze. Men are beginning to speak of religion without the bluster of the Christian formulæ; they have begun to speak of God without any reference to Omnipresence, Omniscience, Omnipotence. The Deists and Theists of an older generation, be it noted, never did that. Their "Supreme Being" repudiated nothing. He was merely the whittled stump of the Trinity. It is in the last few decades that the Western mind has slipped loose from this absolutist conception of God that has dominated the intelligence of Christendom, at least, for many centuries. Almost unconsciously, the new thought is taking a course that will lead it far away from the moorings of Omnipotence. It is like a ship that has slipped its anchors and drifts, still sleeping, under the pale and vanishing stars, out to the open sea. . . .

§ 2

Convergent Religious Movements

In quite a little while the whole world may be alive with this renascent faith.

For emancipation from the Trinitarian formularies and from a belief in an infinite God means not merely a great revivification of minds trained under the decadence of orthodox Christianity, minds which have hitherto been hopelessly embarrassed by the choice between pseudo-Christian religion or denial, but also it opens the way towards the completest understanding and sympathy and participation with the kindred movements for release and for an intensification of the religious life, that are going on outside the sphere of the Christian tradition and influence altogether. Allusion has already been made to the sympathetic devotional poetry of Rabindranath Tagore ; he stands for a movement in Brahminism parallel with and assimilable to the worship of the True God of mankind.

It is too often supposed that the religious tendency of the East is entirely towards other-worldness, to a treatment of this life as an evil entanglement and of death as a release and a blessing. It is too easily assumed that Eastern teaching is wholly concerned with renunciation, not merely of self but of being, with the escape from all effort of any sort into an exalted vacuity. This is indeed neither the spirit of China nor of Islam nor of the everyday life of any people in the world. It is not the spirit of the Sikh nor of these newer developments of Hindu thought. It has never been the spirit of Japan. To-day less than ever does Asia seem disposed to give up life and the effort of life. Just as readily as Europeans, do the Asiatics reach out their arms to that fuller life we can live, that greater intensity of existence to which we can attain by escaping from ourselves. All mankind is seeking God. There is not a nation nor a city on the globe where men are not being urged at this moment by the spirit of God in them towards the discovery of God. This is not an age of despair but an age of hope in Asia as in all the world besides.

Islam is undergoing a process of revision closely parallel to that which ransacks Christianity. Tradition and mediæval doctrines are being thrust aside in a similar way. There is much probing into the spirit and intention of the Founder. The time is almost ripe for a heart-searching Dialogue of the Dead, " How we settled our religions for ever and ever," between, let us say, Eusebius of Cæsarea and one of Nizam-al-Mulk's tame theologians. They would be drawn together by the same tribulation ; they would be in the closest sympathy against the temerity of the moderns ; they would have a common courtliness. The Quran is but little read by Europeans ; it is ignorantly supposed to contain many things that it does not contain ; there is much confusion in people's minds between its text and the ancient Semitic traditions and usages retained by its followers ; in places it may seem formless and barbaric ; but what it has chiefly to tell of is the leadership of one individualised militant God who claims the rule of the whole world, who favours neither rank nor race, who would lead men to righteousness. It is much more free from sacramentalism, from vestiges of the ancient blood sacrifice and its associated sacerdotalism, than Christianity. The religion

that will presently sway mankind can be reached more easily
from that starting-point than from the confused mysteries
of Trinitarian theology. Islam was never saddled with a
creed. With the very name " Islam " (submission to God)
there is no quarrel for those who hold the new faith. . . .

All the world over there is this stirring in the dry bones of
the old beliefs. There is scarcely a religion that has not its
Bahaism, its Modernists, its Brahmo Somaj, its " religion
without theology," its attempts to escape from old forms and
hampering associations to that living and world-wide spiritual
reality upon which the human mind almost instinctively
insists. . . .

It is the same God we all seek ; he becomes more and more
plainly the same God.

So that all this religious stir, which seems so multifold and
incidental and disconnected and confused and entirely in-
effective to-day, may be, and most probably will be, in quite
a few years a great flood of religious unanimity pouring over
and changing all human affairs, sweeping away the old priesthoods and tabernacles and symbols and shrines, the last crumb
of the Orphic victim and the last rag of the Serapeum, and
turning all men about into one direction, as the ships and
house-boats swing round together in some great river with the
uprush of the tide. . . .

§ 3

Can there be a True Church ?

Among those who are beginning to realise the differences
and identities of the revived religion that has returned to them,
certain questions of organisation and assembly are being
discussed. Every new religious development is haunted by
the precedents of the religion it replaces, and it was only to
be expected that among those who have recovered their faith
there should be a search for apostles and disciples, an attempt
to determine sources and to form original congregations,
especially among people with European traditions.

These dispositions mark a relapse from understanding.
They are imitative. This time there has been no revelation
here or there ; there is no claim to a revelation but simply
that God has become visible. Men have thought and sought
until insensibly the fog of obsolete theology has cleared away.
There seems no need therefore for special teachers or a special
propaganda, or any ritual or observances that will seem to
insist upon differences. The Christian precedent of a church
is particularly misleading. The church with its sacraments
and its sacerdotalism is the disease of Christianity. Save for
a few doubtful interpolations there is no evidence that Christ

tolerated either blood sacrifices or the mysteries of priesthood. All these antique grossnesses were superadded after his martyrdom. He preached not a cult but a gospel ; he sent out not medicine-men but apostles.

No doubt all who believe owe an apostolic service to God. They become naturally apostolic. As men perceive and realise God, each will be disposed in his own fashion to call his neighbour's attention to what he sees. The necessary elements of religion could be written on a post-card ; this book, small as it is, bulks large not by what it tells positively but because it deals with misconceptions. We may (little doubt have I that we do) need special propagandas and organisations to discuss errors and keep back the jungle of false ideas, to maintain free speech and restrain the enterprise of the persecutor, but we do not want a church to keep our faith for us. We want our faith spread, but for that there is no need for orthodoxies and controlling organisations of statement. It is for each man to follow his own impulse, and to speak to his like in his own fashion.

Whatever religious congregations men may form henceforth in the name of the True God must be for their own sakes and not to take charge of religion.

The history of Christianity, with its incrustation and suffocation in dogmas and usages, its dire persecutions of the faithful by the unfaithful, its desiccation and its unlovely decay, its invasion by robes and rites and all the tricks and vices of the Pharisees whom Christ detested and denounced, is full of warning against the dangers of a church. Organisation is an excellent thing for the material needs of men, for the draining of towns, the marshalling of traffic, the collecting of eggs, and the carrying of letters, the distribution of bread, the notification of measles, for hygiene and economics and such-like affairs. The better we organise such things, the freer and better equipped we leave men's minds for nobler purposes, for those adventures and experiments towards God's purpose which are the reality of life. But all organisations must be watched, for whatever is organised can be " captured " and misused. Repentance, moreover, is the beginning and essential of the religious life, and organisations (acting through their secretaries and officials) never repent. God deals only with the individual for the individual's surrender. He takes no cognisance of committees.

Those who are most alive to the realities of living religion are most mistrustful of this congregating tendency. To gather together is to purchase a benefit at the price of a greater loss, to strengthen one's sense of brotherhood by excluding the majority of mankind. Before you know where you are you will have exchanged the spirit of God for *esprit de corps*. You will have reinvented the *symbol* ; you will have begun to keep anniversaries and establish sacramental ceremonies. The disposition to form cliques and exclude and conspire against unlike people is all too strong in humanity to permit of its formal encouragement. Even such organisation as is implied by a creed is to be avoided, for all living faith coagulates as you phrase it. In this book I have not given so much as a definite name to the faith of the True God. Organisation for worship and collective exaltation also, it may be urged, is of little manifest good. You cannot appoint beforehand a time and place for God to irradiate your soul.

All these are very valid objections to the church-forming disposition.

§ 4

Organisation under God

Yet still this leaves many dissatisfied. They want to shout out about God. They want to share this great thing with all mankind.

Why should they not shout and share ?

Let them express all that they desire to express in their own fashion by themselves or grouped with their friends as they will. Let them shout chorally if they are so disposed. Let them work in a gang if so they can work the better. But let them guard themselves against the idea that they can have God particularly or exclusively with them in any such undertaking. Or that so they can express God rather than themselves.

That, I think, states the attitude of the modern spirit towards the idea of a church. Mankind passes for ever out of the idolatry of altars, away from the obscene rites of circumcision and symbolical cannibalism, beyond the sway of the ceremonial priest. But if the modern spirit holds that religion cannot be organised or any intermediary thrust between God and man, that does not preclude infinite possibilities of organisation and collective action *under* God and within the compass of religion. There is no reason why religious men should not band themselves the better to attain specific ends. To borrow a term from British politics, there is no objection to *ad hoc* organisations. The objection lies not against subsidiary organisation for service but against organisations that may claim to be comprehensive.

For example, there is no reason why one should not—and in many cases there are good reasons why one should—organise or join associations for the criticism of religious ideas, an employment that may pass very readily into propaganda.

Many people feel the need of prayer to resist the evil in themselves and to keep them in mind of divine emotion. And many want not merely prayer but formal prayer and the support of others, praying in unison. The writer does not understand this desire or need for collective prayer very well, but there are people who appear to do so and there is no reason why they should not assemble for that purpose. And there is no doubt that divine poetry, divine maxims, religious thought finely expressed, may be heard, rehearsed, collected, published, and distributed by associations. The desire for expression implies a sort of assembly, a hearer at least as well as a speaker. And expression has many forms. People with a strong artistic impulse will necessarily want to express themselves by art when religion touches them, and many arts, architecture and the drama for example, are collective undertakings. I do not see why there should not be, under God, associations for building cathedrals and such-like great still places urgent with beauty, into which men and women may go to rest from the clamour of the day's confusions ; I do not see why men should not make great shrines and pictures expressing their sense of divine things, and why they should not combine in such enterprises rather than work to fill heterogeneous and chaotic art galleries. A wave of religious revival and religious clarification such as I foresee, will most certainly bring with it a great revival of art, religious art, music, songs, and writings of all sorts, drama, the making of shrines, praying places, temples and retreats, the creation of pictures and sculptures. It is not necessary to have priestcraft and an organised church for such ends. Such enrichments of feeling and thought are part of the service of God.

And again, under God, there may be associations and fraternities for research in pure science ; associations for the teaching and simplification of languages ; associations for promoting and watching education ; associations for the discussion of political problems and the determination of right policies. In all these ways men may multiply their use by union. Only when associations seek to control things of belief, to dictate formulæ, restrict religious activities or the freedom of religious thought and teaching, when they tend to subdivide those who believe and to set up jealousies or exclusions, do they become antagonistic to the spirit of modern religion.

§ 5

The State is God's Instrument

Because religion cannot be organised, because God is everywhere and immediately accessible to every human being, it does not follow that religion cannot organise every other human affair. It is indeed essential to the idea that God is the Invisible King of this round world and all mankind, that we should see in every government, great and small, from the council of the world-state that is presently coming, down to the village assembly, the instrument of God's practical control. Religion which is free, speaking freely through whom it will, subject to a perpetual unlimited criticism, will be the life and driving power of the whole organised world. So that if you prefer not to say that there will be no church, if you choose rather to declare that the world-state is God's church, you may have it so if you will. Provided that you leave conscience and speech and writing and teaching about divine things absolutely free, and that you try to set no nets about God.

The world is God's and he takes it. But he himself remains freedom, and we find our freedom in him.

THE ENVOY

So I end this compact statement of the renascent religion which I believe to be crystallising out of the intellectual, social, and spiritual confusions of this time. It is an account rendered. It is a statement and record ; not a theory. There is nothing in all this that has been invented or constructed by the writer ; I have been but scribe to the spirit of my generation ; I have at most assembled and put together things and thoughts that I have come upon, have transferred the statements of " science " into religious terminology, rejected obsolescent definitions, and re-co-ordinated propositions that had drifted into opposition. Thus, I see, ideas are developing, and thus have I written them down. It is a secondary matter that I am convinced that this trend of intelligent opinion is a discovery of truth. The reader is told of my own belief merely to avoid an affectation of impartiality and aloofness.

The theogony here set forth is ancient ; one can trace it appearing and disappearing and recurring in the mutilated records of many different schools of speculation ; the conception of God as finite is one that has been discussed very illuminatingly in recent years in the work of one I am happy to write of as my friend and master, that very great American, the late William James. It was an idea that became increasingly important to him towards the end of his life. And it is the most releasing idea in the system.

Only in the most general terms can I trace the other origins of these present views. I do not think modern religion owes much to what is called Deism or Theism. The rather abstract and futile Deism of the eighteenth century, of " *votre Être suprême* " who bored the friends of Robespierre, was a sterile thing ; it has little relation to these modern developments, it conceived of God as an infinite Being of no particular character, whereas God is a finite being of a very especial character. On the other hand, men and women who have set themselves, with unavoidable theological preconceptions, it is true, to speculate upon the actual teachings and quality of Christ, have produced interpretations that have interwoven insensibly with thoughts more apparently new. There is a curious modernity about very many of Christ's recorded sayings. Revived religion has also, no doubt, been the receiver of many religious bankruptcies, of Positivism for example, which failed through its bleak abstraction and an unspiritual texture. Religion, thus restated, must, I think, presently incorporate great sections of thought that are still attached to formal Christianity. The time is at hand when many of the organised Christian churches will be forced to define their positions, either in terms that will identify them with this renascence, or that will lead to the release of their more liberal adherents. Its probable obligations to Eastern thought are less readily estimated by a European writer.

Modern religion has no revelation and no founder ; it is the privilege and possession of no coterie of disciples or exponents ; it is appearing simultaneously round and about the world exactly as a crystallising substance appears here and there in a supersaturated solution. It is a process of truth, guided by the divinity in men. It needs no other guidance and no protection. It needs nothing but freedom, free speech and honest statement. Out of the most mixed and impure solutions a growing crystal is infallibly able to select its substance. The diamond arises bright, definite, and pure out of a dark matrix of structureless confusion.

This metaphor of crystallisation is, perhaps, the best symbol of the advent and growth of the new understanding. It has no church, no authorities, no teachers, no orthodoxy. It does not even thrust and struggle among the other things ; simply it grows clear. There will be no putting an end to it. It arrives inevitably, and it will continue to separate itself out from confusing ideas. It becomes, as it were, the Koh-i-noor ; it is a Mountain of Light, growing and increasing. It is an all-pervading lucidity, a brightness and clearness. It has no head to smite, no body you can destroy ; it overleaps all barriers ; it breaks out in despite of every enclosure. It will compel all things to orient themselves to it.

It comes as the dawn comes, through whatever clouds and mists may be here or whatever smoke and curtains may be there. It comes as the day comes to the ships that put to sea.

It is the Kingdom of God at hand.